The Dream Gatherers

The Soteria Chronicles

Roberto Arcoleo

Cover Illustration By:

Randy DeLeon Zamuco

Praise for The Dream Gatherers

"Roberto Arcoleo's vivid imagination has recreated New York in the 60's with lots of colors and plenty of sex and drugs. His novel's plot is poetic and powerful: a planet much more technologically advanced than ours sends two envoys to Earth in order to collect that mysterious thing they don't have anymore: dreams. The envoys, Mark and Jason, are brothers, but one becomes more "human" than the other. Their sexy characters make the reading very enjoyable."
- *Catherine Cusset, best-selling novelist and the author of Life of David Hockney: A Novel*

"Gripping introduction to a world I hope is further explored in subsequent novels! Surprised to learn this is Roberto Arcoleo's first novel. The ideas put forth typically appear from a much more seasoned author. Did he live through this? Warning - this is not a sci-fi book. It's a character study of despondent beings of the universe yearning for connection and identity set against the backdrop of the 1960's New York City. Themes of love, greed, time, and humanity are woven together to create an original work that feels destined for the cinematic universe. There are many absorbing characters throughout but my personal favorite is the young Saya - here's hoping we get a further glimpse into her origin story and future trials in the next one! Out of this world debut novel. Read at once!"
- *Todd Douglas Miller, Director Apollo 11*

"What an amazing accomplishment! Congratulations, I am so impressed. It's a great story, with really interesting characters

and lots of vivid language."
- Cynthia Elliott, Director of The James Merrill House Literary Residency Program and previously The Director of Symphony Space

"What stood out for me was the authors ability to create the Art, Music and energy of the 60's time period along with science fiction elements made for a real engaging Syfy read."
- Gwendalyn_books

"I loved this novel. The characters become so real even in their other worldliness. Acereleo is destined for more great books, I know. He captured the times of the 60's and melded it with such imagination with new worlds. READ IT."
- RD Rice, Artist and former President of the Bronx Museum Board of Directors

Acknowledgements

I want to thank the following people for their efforts and encouragement in having this book take form: Allison Walters, Mariana Slattery, Catherine Cussett, for their literary prowess, Cynthia Elliot, for her wisdom and encouragement, Siobhan Bledsoe humor and perspective, Neer Asherie for his scientific knowledge, my editor/publisher Erik Evans for his diligence, and most of all my wife Lynn Bianchi for being her brilliant, wonderful self.

CONTENTS

CHAPTER 1

IN A TREE

It was the Sunday after Easter, and my Uncle Walter was going fishing. I begged him to take me. My mother said no at first, but since I had just received a perfect report card from Saint Patrick's, she reluctantly agreed. I was bursting with joy about my big adventure. My younger brother was more than jealous. The sun had just come up, and we packed up the old Buick station wagon and hit the road. I was small for an eleven-year-old, but I made up for size with unending energy; my uncle loved having me around. We were mid-way across the Tri-Borough Bridge when the car overheated. The fan belt had snapped, and steam was bubbling from the radiator. We pulled over and stopped near the railings. My uncle jumped out of the car and popped open the hood to check out what was wrong, and with a frown and a firm tone, he gave me instructions to stay put. I did my best to obey, but it felt like an oven in there, and I was sweating like an overworked horse. I was never able to sit still for long, and since there were no cars in sight, after about ten minutes I got out and looked at the tugboats moving down river. They looked lazy as their white wakes spooned strings of foam rippling along the gray water. Strangely, I was at peace when the panic swarmed over me. My heart started to pound. I was unable to catch my breath. The clouds spun, and I felt my legs buckle. It was only the fast-moving arms of my uncle that brought me to the ground safely. I guess I had never been up that high before, but since that day, the fear of falling from high places has been with me.

So here I am, sitting fifty feet in the air, balancing my skinny ass on this twig of a branch, not knowing how I got here. Okay, I mumble to myself, stop freaking out. Think. I left my place with that strange Asian beauty I had just met named Saya, and then what happened…? Okay, go back to the beginning.

I left that boring photo gig I did late into the afternoon and was just going to be by myself. It was my twenty-ninth birthday and I was depressed. I was going to have a drink in the neighborhood, head home, roll a joint, put on some Dylan and chill, decide whether I'm going to be a filmmaker or a photographer, and maybe… maybe, I don't know what. I stopped into the local bar a block from my apartment and was on my second Jack Daniel's staring down at my glass… "One more year until thirty," I said talking to my drink. The year I decided I would have to start acting like an adult, or at least make the effort; focus on a career, stop staying high half the time, and definitely stop fucking around like an ally cat. Get a steady girlfriend instead of jumping in bed with one hippie chick after another that I'm always meeting in these grunge east village bars. I was getting even more melancholy and was about to leave when this completely gorgeous Asian walked into the bar and sat down next to me.

She was young, but different from the usual Cooper Union or NYU types that wandered in there from time to time.

She pulled out a zippo and looked around. The place was empty except for the two old drunks that never seemed to leave the corner table. She lit a cigarette and in a perky tone said, "Hi, I'm Saya. What's your name?"

She looked good, and I was more than ready for someone new. Of course, all my friends tell me that I'm always looking for the answer in the next pretty face. I'm a well-read, self-centered, hedonistic jerk with a few degrees and a high IQ. I know I'm totally wrapped around myself, but at least I feel bad when I'm an asshole.

It's that I just love women. I'm obsessed, and honestly can't get enough, and it's not just the sex thing, I love everything about them.

The next second, she turned to the bartender, acting like I was not there, and ordered Vodka straight-up in Russian, then asked him for one of the hard-boiled eggs he had behind the counter.

"Thomas. But people call me Tommy," I said, trying to draw her back. She looked a little young for me. I had just spent the last year dating someone who was still in college, and her fickleness and eclectic desires, although fun, especially when she was in the mood for another girl in bed, were even getting a bit too much for me. But this one was different. Special. Not only gorgeous, but smart. I could sense it. "My name is Tommy Martino," I said again. "Are you Russian?"

"No," she said. "But I speak it. Why?"

She was wearing an almost-nothing white top and jeans, no bra, of course, her nipples pressed against the thinness. Her breasts were perfect. When she leaned forward, she shared a view as the blouse dipped. I was sure she was doing it on purpose. I acted disinterested, but when I looked her in the eyes, I knew she could have anything I had in the world just for the asking. She was ravishing, and in seconds her intensity owned me. At first, I thought it was only the head of my penis talking to my brain, but there was more. Tommy, you are not in her league. You have never met anyone remotely as enchanting as her.

I knew in a minute she was smart, very smart. You could see it in her eyes. I wanted to say something intelligent, and not seem like just another jerk on the make, so I said to her, picking up on the Russian, "I just finished Anna Karenina. Did you ever read it?"

"Yeah," she answered, "but in Japanese, when I was sixteen. I didn't learn Russian until I was seventeen. She smiled sweetly, but it was obvious she was telling me not to try to impress her.

"Listen, I know you are not here looking for a scholar tonight, and you're really more interested what's in these clothes than in my head. I don't have a lot of time. So..."

"Wow," I said. "You're direct."

"I think you look good, and you don't smell too bad."

I didn't know how to answer that, so I said, "Well, Okay."

"Listen, I have one day in the city before I go back upstate. I kind of live like a monk up there in the woods by myself. So, if you want to hang out later, write down your address. I'll ring your bell in a couple of hours. I know you live nearby."

"How do you know that?" I asked.

"I just do." She handed me her paper napkin and asked the bartender for his pen. "If you like what you see... write!"

"I will give you two long rings and then a short one. You'll know it's me. It's 8:30 now. I will be at your place around midnight. I have to go pick up my VW from the garage, and I have a special meeting with this finance guy. It will take a few hours, maybe."

She turned to the bartender and asked for another Vodka in Russian. I realized now that she knew him.

"My VW is a '68, I love it, but it's five years old now, and it needs a new alternator. The garage is doing me a favor in fixing it tonight so I can get going."

I wrote down my address, not really giving a shit about her car, printed it carefully to be sure there would be no mistake, all while thinking, is this really happening? She picked up the napkin and threw back her vodka like a pro. "Four-sixty East 12th, apartment 6 West. I know the building. Okay, see you later." She smiled devilishly as she smartly left the stool and walked towards the door.

Before she could leave, I asked, "Saya... Why me?"

"No reason," she answered. "You were just here."

Saya and I had sex until about 2 a.m., two of the most intense hours I could remember. Never in my life had I had someone say, "I might come back sometime if you keep doing what you're doing." I did my best to please. After a while, she got up and got dressed. She was cool; almost indifferent.

"Gotta go now. Maybe I'll see you again when I'm around."

I said, "Let me walk you to your car. I kind of don't want to say goodbye like this."

"Why?" she asked, then she looked at me sweetly. "Well, I know we didn't talk much, so if you really want to." I looked into her eyes and repeated that troubling and forever agonizing word in my head. "Why?" Three simple letters that search for the meaning of everything, I had no answer, just a feeling... a feeling that I should not let her go.

"I do," I said, hoping if we could talk some, maybe I'd see her again.

But it was funny. When we were in the street, we hardly spoke. I took her hand. She looked back at me and said, "There is no future with me, you know, except maybe another night or two like this. I like you, but there is no real future, so please don't wish for one." There was firmness in her tone, but it was kind. I felt she was almost wishing she did not have to say it. Then it happened. I saw it coming. The headlights blinded me, and I froze. I was sure it was the end when I felt her arm firmly around my waist, air under my feet. And then she was gone, and here I am.

***

Shit. There is a crowd gathering below me. There are police cars and a fire truck, and a bunch of crazy people yelling, "Jump! Jump!" Are they nuts?

"Son! Are you all right?"

What am I seeing? Is there a fireman coming up in the basket attached to that ladder?

"Son! Just relax. It's going to be all right. Don't move. I'm coming up to get you," hollered the voice of the young, rosy-faced fireman standing in a basket from the rising extension ladder.

"It's going to be all right. Just try and relax. Whatever it is, we can talk about it. Just let us get you into the basket, and it will all be better. There is a doctor waiting down there."

God, I cannot believe how long that ladder can reach. Holy shit, this guy thinks I am trying to kill myself! If he only knew how bad I want my feet on the ground.

"Just lean forward when I come closer. I can get you if you just lean a little closer. It will all be all right. Whatever is bothering you, believe me, it will feel better when I get you down. This is not the answer."

His eyes were sincere; I could read his name above his badge: Patrick Regan, Fireman, Hook and ladder Company 27. He was a burly looking guy, broad-shouldered, and with bright red hair. He spoke with a slight Irish brogue. For some reason, his accent was calming.

"Relax," again he said.

I really wish he would stop saying that. "Sure," I answered. "Anything you say. Just get me the fuck down!"

CHAPTER 2

THE HOSPITAL

Bellevue Hospital Emergency
Intake Report

Dr. Robert Stein M.D. Psychiatrist
Patient: Thomas Martino

Mr. Martino was found in the upper branch of a tree in Tompkins Square Park at 3 AM on the morning of August 19th. The patient, a white male, 5' 7" in height and a 140lbs, was disoriented and confused upon admission. He had no physical injuries other than some small abrasions on his left arm and a black and blue mark on his right forearm.

He complained of a slight pain in his shoulder, which he believed was a result of the firemen pulling him into the basket. Police Officer Arnold Sanchez stated that Mr. Martino reported he had no idea how he found himself more than fifty feet up in the tree. The police assumed he was intoxicated. He kept asking about a person named Saya and going on about an ambulance.

Apparently, there was an accident half a block away involving an ambulance. It was rushing to a call when the driver suddenly lost control of the vehicle. According to the driver, Medical Tech. James Hogan, the vehicle suddenly seemed to be possessed. He stated in his report that he thought he had hit some people before crashing into a light post, but when he exited the vehicle, no one was there. Mr. Hogan is presently being tested for drugs and alcohol.

The police assume that there is no relationship between the two incidents due to the distance separating them. The driver has also been admitted and is being evaluated. Mr. Martino showed no indication of being struck by a vehicle. The evaluation of the ambulance concluded it was traveling at least thirty miles an hour when it hit the light post.

Dr. Stein looked away from the report and stared across the room.

"So that's him, sitting there on the bench, the one in the blue jeans and polo shirt?"

"Yes, he was hysterical in the emergency room. We barely managed to give him an examination. Dr. Schwartz had to give him a tranquilizer injection in order to get him into that straight jacket. He's calmed down now, so we took it off. He kept going on asking about the ambulance hitting him and someone named Saya. The only information we were able to get was his name, but he keeps asking about her."

"I need to see his original intake report. Maybe it's some form of psychedelic we are not screening for or a flashback from an earlier dose. LSD can cause hallucinations for weeks after taking it. I wish they had waited for me before they administered any sedatives."

"We were afraid he was going to hurt himself. He is much stronger than he looks. It took two guards to get him into the restraints."

CHAPTER 3
TWO WEEKS LATER

They kept me at Bellevue for two weeks, mostly pumped up on Valium and anti-psychotics. I could hardly do much more than mumble. On the eighth day, my friend Jeff contacted a lawyer. That's how I got out.

Six months passed before I saw her again. It was around twelve when I heard the doorbell ring; two long and one short. I was a little high, as I usually was by midnight, not on anything heavy, just a few joints and some bourbon. I had been dealing pot again to make ends meet. There hadn't been much film editing work of late, and I was really sick of the fashion scene, so my legal income had been sparse, to say the least.

Two long and one short... it couldn't be her, but it was her ring. I was still haunted about that night. What happened to me after I saw the ambulance coming at us? I had been doing all I could not to think about it. The thought of it was terrifying; those seconds besieged me. Why was I not dead, and how did I end up on the top of that tree? At first, I could not stop talking to people about it, but since all I had been getting was strange looks or dumb jokes about what I had taken that night, I controlled the urge.

"Sure, Tommy. So how much acid did you drop that night?" was the most common refrain before the eyes would roll and the laughter started.

Again, it rang, two long and one short. I went to the intercom; my fingers hesitantly pressed the buzzer, and I said, "Yeah, who is it?"

Her voice came crackling through the old intercom, the same unabashed confidence that I remembered. "It's me. Let me in."

She knew that I recognized her, and she knew that there was not the remotest possibility I would not ring her in. I pressed the buzzer without saying a word.

When I opened the door, she just smiled, brushing past me as if she owned the place. She was wearing a leather jacket and jeans, and another version of that nothing of a top she wore when we met. She had on a baseball cap pulled down, almost hiding her eyes, and no make-up. She looked different, almost boyish. Briskly, she stepped into the living room, lounged down onto my sofa, and said nothing. Her manner was vague, her expression unabashed; there was a strange power of silence within her beauty.

Then the allure came forth. It was gradual, yet steady. I was sure I saw her complexion grow rosier and her lips fuller. Her body became increasingly more sumptuous. It felt as if a drug were rising in my brain. Was it all in my mind, or was it real? All I knew was that those penetrating eyes owned me, and with my feet planted as if in quicksand, I looked across the room, mesmerized.

"I told you I would see you again," she said with that accent I could not pin down.

I did not respond to what my eyes were seeing. Instead, I said with a smirk, "Yeah, you did. And not much else before you left me there, high and not so dry."

She smiled. "I guess I owe you an explanation, but it's complicated. Do you have any vodka and maybe some weed?"

"I always have weed, but only bourbon to pour," I responded.

"That works," she said, taking a deep breath.

Before she even spoke, I started to feel strangely comfortable. I was singing, "Don't think twice, it's all right," yet somewhere deep in me I knew I should have been chanting, "Abandon all hope, ye who enters here."

"I hope you're not pissed at me for leaving you up there. I really like you, you know, and I felt really bad about leaving you like that, but I thought it was the safest place for you at the time."

I am a cynical, skeptical, and questioning kind of guy, but I completely accepted her words as if she were commenting on the weather.

"Listen, this is a very long story, so let's get stoned and maybe play for a while before I explain things." She smiled and gave me that ever-confident look, knowing I would not refuse.

She paused; her mouth started to move. She hesitated before speaking. "A lot of what I will tell you is going to be hard to accept."

She looked good. My God, did she look good. I sat down next to her thinking to myself how much I wanted her all the while feeling a strange tantalizing terror. I was not really sure what it was I wanted. All I could think was, Tommy you better buckle up.

"Sure. That sounds good to me," I said. She smelled like Jasmine, but not the perfumey crap that found your nose in a room full of fashion model types. It was beautiful and real, like I remembered from the gardens in Bali. She took off her cap, and her hair fell back onto her shoulders. She pulled off her jacket and threw it on a chair. Her manner was cockier than it was the day we met.

I had already put aside the fact of being left up in that tree and the two weeks I spent in the psych ward and the fact that I was sure that her appearance had changed before my eyes. My brain was swimming in her aura. This was more than a physical thing: she had me.

We made love for the rest of the night; incredible, delicious, rapturous, almost acrobatic love. She kept asking me to do things and talk to her. "Talk to me, tell me you are going to fuck me until I scream!"

She liked it rough, that's for sure. I started to get nervous thinking that she might also like to give it as well as take it. Sometimes it felt more than scary. She needed things, things I did not understand. Unapologetically, she said, "Don't be afraid, you can't hurt me," and then she whispered sweetly, "I am not an ordinary person. Let your fantasies run wild, I'll do almost anything, so enjoy me."

She looked into my eyes, fixing me with that gaze. "I can keep my kinkier side to myself if you want, but give me a chance."

Wow! She was dark, darker than any woman I had ever known. She was pulling me in, further and further down. I felt she needed things I was not sure I could give. "Saya, Saya, Saya... I'm not into pain...."

"Just relax, you're not going to hurt me no matter what you do. I have more than one face to show you. You can always bail if you want to."

I was not sure what that meant. It was true that I had never experienced such pleasures before. There were moments I was not even sure what was happening. Her darkness frightened me, but what frightened me more was how much I loved it.

Finally, exhausted, I said, "Hey, I need a rest."

"Okay, that was fun, rest a bit, I'm not leaving for a while."

With these words, she sat up in the bed. Her expression grew serious, then she smiled. "You know, I wasn't completely honest with you when we met. I knew you were in that bar. I was looking for you. I didn't know if you were the right person at first, but after we spoke, I was sure."

"The right person?" I asked.

"Jason told me where to find you. He thought I needed a friend until he came back. Someone who could understand me, fulfill me. Someone I could trust. Someone who could one day tell his story and also his brother's, and... Oh yeah, someone with a big and beautiful cock. The last requirement was definitely mine." She laughed.

"What are you talking about, and who the fuck is Jason?" I

was getting pissed. The thing I hated most in the world was when a woman mentioned another guy right after having sex. But then she took my hand and said, "Relax, this is different," and for some reason, it was all right in my mind.

She continued, "I told you that I knew you were in that bar from a hundred yards away."

"What! How? And who the fuck is this Jason?" I replied, still annoyed.

"Jason is worried about me just picking up strangers for sex. He thought that I might be drawing too much attention to myself. Not that anyone could hurt me, but he thought I should pick one person. You are a very lucky man, Tommy. You're cool, that's for sure. But you were in the right place at the right time."

I was not overly flattered by these words, but I didn't say anything.

"It's a long story, and you're going to find it hard to believe, even though you know it was me who put you up in that tree, carried you a half a block and fifty feet into the air, and then disappeared faster than the human eye can see... Stop being in denial about it."

I had been in denial about it, hoping I could wish it all away. Sometimes I thought I had lost my mind, but no matter how I tried, I knew I was up in that tree and in that hospital. "Shit! When are you going to tell me how the fuck you did that...?"

"I told you that I'm not an ordinary person, Tommy, and if this is going to continue, you are going to have to accept that. Compared to Jason and Mark, I'm... just a human, but you will come to understand that, compared to any other person in this world, I'm *very special*. It will all make sense when you meet them."

"Who is them? And what do you mean?"

"You know I put you up in that tree."

"Yes, and I didn't want to accept that fact because it was freaking me out."

"Don't be frightened, Tommy. I'm going to take good care of

you, at least until Jason returns, and then I'm afraid I'll be history. But I promise to leave you very well off. I am filthy rich, you know. But there is a big but to all of this."

"Please, no buts, and you dress like a hippy on welfare! And AGAIN, who the fuck is Jason?"

"He's from a place very far away. He was here for a while, and now he is gone. But he will come back. He told me to wait, and he gave me this." She put her hand on a beautiful amulet, a purple flower she wore around her neck. She moved her hand, and it started to glow. "We communicate through this, and he protects me with it, as well," she went on. "The way I dress is just my thing. I kind of live like a hippy too. Jason made sure I had truckloads of money. It was all in his plan, and now you are in his plan, as well. He wants me to be happy since, in a way, he created me."

At this point, I was spinning, trying to make sense of what she was saying. Is this all some long drawn out hallucination, an acid flashback? No, she is real. She is real and here. And not knowing why, I accepted it all. I didn't know if I should feel lucky or cursed. All I knew for sure was that there was no exit sign in sight.

"Listen," she said, "there is one thing, though; you cannot tell anyone about me. You would be putting your life in danger. Those were bad individuals that sent that ambulance towards us. So just stay cool, hang on, and you are going to have a great ride." She laughed.

She knew I was in, that I had moved all my chips to the center of the table. But she could see I was scared.

"Tommy, you can do this. I knew from the start you could do this. Jason noticed you, but I chose you.

With that, she leaned over me and wrapped her legs around me. She took me into her. I felt her warmth caressing me, and then, as if a breath of air filled me, weightless, I started floating up. I realized we were three feet above the bed, her thighs holding me softly as we rose. Her body started to move up and down, and my whole being went electric.

Then softly she spoke, "One day you are going to tell the world our story. Mine, Jason's, and Mark's too. It's a long story, and it travels very far, but for now, I can tell you that it all started years ago in Japan, when a present for the emperor slowly floated down upon Hiroshima."

She told me the start of her story that night, who they were and where they were from. It was the first night of many nights, many stories. I did not accept what I was hearing for a long time, despite what I was experiencing, for it was impossible to deny what she was. I am not even clear how long we were together. It's still mostly a blur. We moved around a lot, always hiding, but never wanting. Time did not seem to matter to me much, she was the only thing that mattered. After she had disappeared, I went to a lonely place for a long time, but as I promised I kept her secrets...she said one day I would tell her story. She said I would know when the time was right, but who will ever believe it?

CHAPTER 4

THE FLASH – 1945 EARTH TIME

Masao opened the shade and looked out the window. The sky was pale blue that morning, with only a few white clouds. It was warm. How quiet it is, he thought, as he looked out the bedroom window, down upon his flowers reaching over the front fence, their shadows dancing on the pavement. "It's going to be a beautiful day," he said softly, turning to his wife just opening her eyes. The jarring sound of trucks rushing past in the street beyond his gate brought his mind back. He looked out again and saw that they were full of soldiers.

"Reiko, the Americans bombed Tokyo again. I spoke to Takeo, the baker's son, last night; he had just returned from there. He said it was horrible. The newspapers are not telling us everything. Whole areas are destroyed, people burned alive. We must take the children to the countryside, to your sister's farm in the north. They will be safe there."

"I know. I spoke to his mother. Do you think they will bomb here soon?"

"I want you to stay there for a while. Maybe things will change."

"I'll pack some warm clothing and sweaters for the children. It can get cold up there at night. I will make some rice and get some salted fish for the trip. Is there anything special you would like me to get?"

Masao did not answer. Instead, he was staring out the window; something in the sky caught his eye. A parachute was whimsically falling through a cloud. "That's strange..."

There was a bright flash, a great wind. He remembered the first time he saw Reiko by the river, how beautiful she looked in her green dress... suddenly the shadows of the flowers disappeared.

CHAPTER 5
THE DISCOVERY

"How high did the surface temperature get?"

"Over four hundred and twenty centrons and rising. All surface structures have been destroyed. Eighty-seven percent of the inhabitants in the central portion of the city have been annihilated. The results of the second bomb are just coming in from the probe."

"I am sending the full report to the lieutenant now."

The cargo ship Marissa was on a routine run carrying lithium from Allison-9, an asteroid on the eastern edge of the galaxy, to the home world of Eldern. The ship sounded an alert. They had picked up a disturbance. The small, rocky planet orbiting a G-2 class star had experienced several nuclear explosions within a short period of time. Analysis determined it had been caused by intelligent life. A probe was launched to evaluate the situation as protocol demanded.

The lieutenant knocked on the captain's door.

"Yes, lieutenant? What is it?" asked the captain in a hurried tone. "I'm quite busy."

"You requested the analysis of the report from the probe as soon as possible," he replied.

"Yes, Are there issues? Be quick with it – we're about to encounter a field of radiation. Damn these supernovas."

"It appears the preliminary analysis was correct. The

planet is inhabited by intelligent life," he answered.

"And…?" asked the captain.

"It is a class 6 planet, 72% covered by water, 97% salt-based. It has a large diversity of life. The dominant species call themselves humans. They are biological and carbon-based."

The captain responded, "Go on."

"We estimate there is a population of 2.5 billion of these humans. They live in groups in diverse clusters. These groups are in varying stages of technological development, the most advanced of which have nuclear capabilities. They quantify their time in units of revolutions around their home star. These units are called 'years.' Their average lifespan is 64 of these units. They seem to be in the midst of a global war."

"Devastation?" the captain inquired.

"Yes, massive," answered the lieutenant. He handed him his visualizer.

"Hmm… Continue, lieutenant."

"Similar to other biological species of this type, they are divided into two subsets, which they define as 'sexes.' They reproduce through the coupling of these two sexes."

"What is their technological development?" asked the captain.

"While they possess nuclear capabilities, they are quite primitive," replied the lieutenant. "They will not develop any form of interstellar travel for at least 300 of their years. They appear to be mostly violent and warlike, crude in all respects. They do seem quite caring towards their offspring and spend a great deal of energy on their development. The more urban of them have some understanding of government, but on the whole, their rudimentary technologies leave them constantly preoccupied with efforts of survival."

"Well, since they appear to be in the process of destroying themselves, and we face no immediate threat from them, formulate a full report to be filed with central logging when we reach home. Proceed on normal course," directed the captain, turning back to face the dashboard.

"Sir, there is something else. This species is unique. Look," he said.

The captain was transfixed as he viewed the devastation, Masao's last moments of life. "This being's last thought is of another?" asked the captain.

"Yes sir, they experience emotions and deep feelings for others. And there is another thing..."

"Continue."

"Sir, they create stories while they are asleep. Look, they are amazing."

The captain watched the images come forth slowly, as if in a haze, like fog rolling off water:

A little girl plays a violin in front of an auditorium full of people. She plays and plays, but no sound comes out. When she finishes, the audience stands up and applauds.

"The one on the stage appears smaller than the others. Is she very early in her development?"

"Yes," responded the lieutenant, "but they all create these stories, and what's more, they discard them when they are finished; they just float out into space and eventually fade to nothing. Here, I have another sample."

A small boy sits on a train. A conductor comes by and tells him "The next stop is yours." He looks out the window and reads the sign, "My Home," but the train does not stop. The conductor comes by again and says, "The next stop is yours," but again he sees the sign, and again the train does not stop.

"Is he concerned about being lost?" the captain asked, engrossed.

"Everything appears to mean something other than what is shown."

"Interesting, it is all symbolic then?"

"Yes, and the computer agrees. They call it dreaming," responded the lieutenant, as another appeared.

A gray-haired man in a dark suit finishes using the toilet in the bus station restroom. He goes to the sink to wash his hands when a young woman wearing a lacy white dress approaches him. He turns to her and says, "You're in the wrong room." She takes hold of his hands and starts to dry them with a towel and answers, "Your hands are cold; you should use warmer water." "They always are," he said softly, looking down upon his hands. "I know," she replied.

"Why is this young woman drying his hands? Does this action mean something?"

"The significance is a mystery," answered the lieutenant.

"And then there is this one; at first glance, it appears to be some form of ritual, maybe a rite of passage, but it definitely has hidden meanings. It is more complicated, so I have asked the computer to interpret the communication."

A young boy stands near a swimming pool dedicated to diving. Older boys start calling to him, teasing him to jump off the smaller board. He replies, "But I can't swim." Some young girls join in, egging him on. He hesitantly walks out on the board and jumps. Barely keeping his head above the water, a bunch of older boys surround him. As he grasps the ladder, an older boy sneaks up from behind, pulling off his bathing suit. Seeing his suit fly out of the water, some of the younger girls quickly gather about and start to chant, "Climb out! Climb out!"

"He is being taunted. Is this a story in his mind or an actual occurrence?" inquired the captain.

"This is while the boy is sleeping. It continues," said the lieutenant pointing to the visualizer.

A dark-haired teenage girl approaches him from behind, whispering in his ear, "You will have to come out sometime." His sex organ grows firm.

"I am trying to understand. This appendage appears to be a means of pleasure as well as reproduction... Does it have other functions?"

"Apparently, his mind is resolving something that lies deep within his psyche, maybe forbidden things. The obvious is not the whole story." It continues:

Everyone laughs. The boy appears overwhelmed, but also

titillated. "Show us! Show us!" the cries continued. Then, another older girl said she would only give him back his suit if he masturbated.

"What does that mean?" asked the captain.

"You will see," responded the lieutenant.

He tries to hide himself by shaking his head saying, "No! No!" but instead he reveals himself. His firmness draws gasps from the crowd. "Do it! Do it!" Drifting inward, he starts touching himself. Around him, voices chant, "Cum! Cum! Cum!" The boy wakes up in his bed covered in his fluids.

The captain, astonished, said, "So this is pleasurable, but these beings are also very interested in power. They are captivating, quite mysterious! Was this last one from one of their more primitive groups?"

The lieutenant responded, "No, actually I believe it is from one of their more advanced, but we have no evidence that this is an actual ritual. We are just starting to gather our samples. They have many dream stories concerning this activity of sex. There appears to be uncertainty related to it, especially amongst the younger ones."

The captain stared into space for a moment, deep in thought. "They are much more interesting than one would expect." He started to pace about the bridge and then turned abruptly and looked directly at the lieutenant. "I have read of such things in our history. We, too, once possessed such similar phenomena, but that was before, when we had..." The captain walked away, sat down behind his desk, and for some time said nothing.

Then suddenly he turned to the lieutenant. "Launch every probe we have to that planet's surface. Make sure all probes remain in stealth mode. Contact the envoy to the Supreme Council. Tell him we have something important to convey, tell him it should be Elgert who should hear this first and to keep it confidential. I know Elgert; he will reward us. No – no, wait... Tell no one. Not a word of this to the crew! Send a secure message to the Supreme Council along with a sample of your preliminary findings. And make sure there is an encrypted note to Elgert's envoy to keep it quiet. You have done well, lieutenant. We will both benefit from this."

***

Ever since the message arrived with knowledge of a planet whose inhabitants create stories while they sleep, Elgert eagerly awaited more data. The full council was scheduled to meet shortly, and he wanted to include as much information as possible for his report. His assistant came into the room and informed him that the ship's captain had arrived. "Show him in immediately."

The captain came in and transferred the data onto the overhead virtual display unit. It showed an image of the planet and its inhabitants. Elgert saw the earth. He saw its seas and mountains, its deserts and green fields. He saw children playing in parks and people dying painfully in wars. He saw humanity in all its beauty and all its horror, from the aboriginals on the plains of Australia in their loincloths to the sophisticated ladies on the streets of Paris in their jewels and furs. He watched them embrace with tenderness and slaughter with indifference. He watched their most ardent acts of kindness and their most hateful moments of cruelty... and he watched them dream.

"It's true then... They really do this," he murmured.

"Yes," replied the captain. "About many things. They are often vivid and colorful; their lives are riddled with emotions. It drives them, and they dream about it all. And what's more, they constantly discard them and make new ones."

"And you have more examples of them?" asked Elgert.

"Yes, of course," said the captain. He proceeded to show Elgert the boy in the pool and the other samplings.

"Very interesting. We're due to meet shortly, and I will present this information to the Council. Our Minister of Culture, Allaceia, will be particularly intrigued by these." Already anticipating the monetary benefits of the "dream stories," Elgert's mind began crafting a plan.

We will have to control the benefits of this discovery without violating federation laws of non-contact or exploitation of primitive worlds, and we must keep this all hidden from the prying eyes of The Prime.

If the dreams could be gathered in open space, their mission could be justified as the salvaging of abandoned waste products. We don't necessarily have to say outright that we are gathering these dream stories. We could easily write it all off as some form of communication. After all, Eldern is renowned for its intergalactic research.

Yes... that's it! That's the answer! But we need an excuse to occupy this planet and the space around it. What could that be...?

"Are these beings aware of our discovery of them?" inquired Elgert.

As if on cue, the captain spoke again. "No. However, there is a problem."

"Yes, what is it?

"There is a possibility that the planet will collide with an asteroid in 48 of their years."

"What is the probability of the impact?"

"It is almost impossible to determine at this time given all the variables that are in play, but according to my ship, our best guess is a 20% likelihood."

Hmm... one-in-five, well, I need not mention that, but this is the answer.

"Thank you, captain. You have done well in bringing this to me, and it will not be forgotten. But for the moment, your presence is no longer needed. Please leave the report, and most importantly, keep this confidential."

Elgert pondered, federation members are not allowed to interfere with any primitive planet's destiny, and our council may not see all the potential rewards at first, but if I explain this as research and the need to preserve life, it could be seen as altruistic, even mandatory. I will impress upon them that it is our duty to divert the asteroid. We will brand ourselves as its temporary protector.... It will be a perfect excuse. I will start like this and then tempt their greed. Yes, that's it, just a temporary intervention. Once we send a few of our own down to Earth to prove compatibility, we can quietly develop a means of gathering the dreams in space. These dreams are priceless!

Elgert finished his thought process as Allaceia and the administrator, Dronin, entered the meeting room. Allaceia had served with Dronin since her nomination to The Supreme Council. The Council was in charge of all political decisions, and he was sure they would agree with his plan once they understood what treasures Earth held. The Council listened attentively as Elgert laid out his scheme.

After a moment, Allaceia spoke, "You understand that this not only dangerous, but it may have unknown impact on our way of life, and possibly many other worlds as well. When our population sees these beings dream, who knows what will happen?"

"Of course, I understand. That is why we must proceed with the utmost caution. There are risks, but the potential rewards are endless. Additionally, given the asteroid trajectory, it becomes our responsibility to protect the planet," replied Elgert with a grin.

"Please continue," said Dronin.

"I propose we send two of our kind to develop there, taking the form of humans. We will have to have a full explanation prepared for the Federation if asked. Our interest in the planet must be seen as a purely philanthropic exercise. The impact of the asteroid is many of their years from now; therefore, we have ample time. Our agents will live amongst these humans, learn their customs, and absorb their manners. They will appear, to all who know them, human. I propose we will take them from your lineage, Allaceia. They will be blessed with your intelligence and diplomatic abilities. Since there will be two of them, twins, with Class AAA status, they will have abilities worthy of Council seats. They will claim the planet and guide it to its destiny as a future colony, I mean ally, of Eldern. It will all be explained to the federation as an act of altruism, for which they tend to make exceptions, and we will just 'forget' to mention that these humans create these sleep stories. Aren't we due for an act of such sacrifice anyhow, Allaceia?"

"It sounds risky, especially with such primitive beings," said Dronin.

"Yes, but it will work. Allaceia's offspring will mature into beings with abilities that will allow them to meet and overcome any and all situations they encounter on Earth. And, as for the Federation, our convenient omission of the fact that the human's dream could always be explained as an oversight. Besides," replied Elgert, "by the time any protest could be launched, it would already be too late."

"We know little of that world, of their society, of the effect it will have upon our agents. They might grow into strangers rather than agents of Eldern. And once they are living beings, they will have their own free will. It is a grave risk…" said Allaceia.

"Yes, but a risk worth taking! They will appear to be human, of course, and we will make them as attractive as possible, by human standards, so to be easily accepted. They will live amongst them and learn about their culture. We will allow them the freedom to feel a part of the human world. We can continue to monitor for the effects of fallout. We know what type of aberrations to look for. We will create a simulated environment in which they may thrive. Within it, we will educate them, prepare them, and allow them to reach their full potential," explained Elgert.

"This could blow up in our faces. How will you evaluate their development?" asked Dronin.

"We will have one of them in the portal at all times while the other walks freely on Earth. Therefore, half the time, one is always with us. In their early years, the earthlings will think there is only one of them, since the other will be hidden. So, we will be continually monitoring them," stated Elgert.

"I still think it is risky," said Alleceia.

"Yes, it is a risk, but a small one. The danger is minimal, and in the end, it will work. That's all that counts. Besides, I have faith in your lineage," replied Elgert.

"Should they be identical?" asked Dronin.

"Yes, they will be identical, especially in their early years. As they grow older and become individuals, we can allow them distinction, as we will want their personalities to differ," said Elgert.

"Specialization always leads to a better appreciation for a planet's diversity," said Dronin.

The Council considered the proposed plan for a few moments; Elgert's report on Earth and its history was at the forefront of their minds. Allaceia, despite her concerns about the development of her offspring, and amidst the uncertainties of a foreign unknown, finally relented and agreed with the tactics.

"Shall I give them names, then?" asked Allaceia.

"Yes, why not? You are their mother," answered Elgert.

"I have examined their literature, and I will take names from their culture," proclaimed Allaceia. "One I will call Mark, after the Roman Mark Anthony who fell in love with the princess Cleopatra. He was calculating and brilliant, but then he sacrificed his kingdom for the love of a woman. He shall be our romantic, seeking the meaning of love. The other I will call Jason, from Greek mythology. He will be our adventurer, the seeker of the Golden Fleece. He will peer into the dark side of these beings."

"Your reasoning is sound, Allaceia. The pods can be sent immediately, but the journey is long. They will open in 1950, earth time."

"Ready the transports, then."

CHAPTER 6

THE SUBWAY

Mark walked with his head down, avoiding eye contact with people as usual. The honking horns in the streets were deafening. Has Gabriela changed me? His feelings for her over the last few months had developed so rapidly that his mind was swimming. I feel so overwhelmed when I am near her. Is this what these humans live with? His thoughts were traveling at lightning speed. Did I make a mistake making this appointment? He knew he needed clarity and hopefully control. Maybe this doctor can help. All he knew is that he yearned to be near her, to touch her, to hear her voice, to feel her heartbeat upon his chest. Why is this happening? I wish I understood more.

The entrance to the subway was congested; there were panhandlers blocking the steps. He made his way down the stairs and onto the crowded platform. Columbia students were talking of academic subjects. Three young hippie-looking girls giggled about last night's trysts with their boyfriends. On a wooden bench in the middle of the platform, a homeless man slept beneath a blanket, his stench mingling with the smell of cheap wine, staining his coat. A police officer nudged him with a nightstick as he passed, and a group of teenage boys in the corner laughed at the spectacle. It was 1969. It was an inspiring time – a time of experimentation, a time of pleasure. It was a time when rules seemed to matter little to a world turned over on its head.

These humans never stopped fascinating him. But today, the platform cacophony of sights and sounds, were more an annoyance than a pleasure. The atmosphere was filled with a swirl of human emotions flying through the air in what was to Mark a torrent of energies, frantically jumping forth like sparks from a burning campfire, a kaleidoscope of thoughts and feelings bombarding his mind. It baffled him how humans would lie to each other about the silliest things, even to their closest friends, and how they often seemed so mentally distant as they pushed themselves up against each other's bodies in the subway cars. They remained faceless, isolated in a crowd, and yet they increasingly busied themselves within the networks of their own lives. For all their strange, paradoxical behavior, Mark still found humans forever surprising, constantly naively beautiful; every day they enchanted him more.

Playing games and testing his abilities at mental manipulation became a daily pastime on the train, an unending source of pleasure. He would often construct suggestions, implant them into some unsuspecting mind, and watch the ensuing reactions. He might create a deep-seated attraction in a young girl's mind for a stranger. Then, he would observe her eyes as she pined away, watching her new true love jump on the express train, never to be seen again. Or he would suggest to the mind of a busy businessman that he had left the gas on in his house, and then relish in the anxiety, witnessing the panic, as he would flee to rush home. What silly games! He often thought. But I might as well practice what powers I have. Who knows how I'll need to use them.

Besides, these minor amusements paled in significance to the games Mark and Jason had played when they were children. Jason had once gone so far as to compel the preacher's wife to seduce their school principal in the rear of the church. Jason had practiced his abilities of suggestion from an early age, and he had developed them into an art. Not only was the school principal thirty years older than the preacher's wife, but he was fat, almost consistently unshaven, and always had bad breath. Mrs. Shulster, on the other hand, was a beauty with blue eyes, a fetching southern accent, and healthy blonde curls that bobbed and bounced in the most affected manner intended to disarm the men she dealt with as the church's first lady. She was also supervisor of the school, a position she often abused, dispensing a cruelty for which even at a young age the brothers, especially Jason, had no patience.

One day she found herself naked, reclined and sweaty, succumbing to an uncontrollable lust with the principal behind a thin curtain in the rear of the church. The debauchery devised by Jason was cruel even by his standards, and afterward, he allowed her only to recall the event in full during an occasional dream. She would never be sure whether the tryst had been real, but it would always haunt her. Mark eventually admitted he enjoyed watching her squirm in her seat whenever the principal walked into the room, or when his eyes found hers. To this day, the preacher's wife never understood how it was possible that she had found herself sitting in a pew next to all the prim ladies without any underwear beneath her stiff dress. The principal, for his part, could never quite wash the smell of her off his clothes. The brothers had hated them both, and never had a moment's remorse. They granted themselves these silly pleasures, thinking of them as learning exercises, for their time living amidst humans passed ever so slowly. Mark had been seeking what these beings were flush with, what they took for granted, this irrational torrent they call emotions. Maybe one day I will even be able to dream. Could I imagine such a thing?

When he first saw Gabriella on campus, the logic of his mind disappeared as if he were the cream in a hot cup of coffee. It was like this from the start, when he glimpsed her in the hall or heard her voice in a crowd. The shock of learning that she was his advisor's wife did little to dissuade his infatuation; her ambiance overwhelmed all, the aroma of her being dimmed all reason. He wanted her in his life. There were many other younger women at Columbia, but not for Mark. He remembered when they first spoke at a faculty party; she was talking about Balzac, making light of the French amorousness. She never spoke to him directly, but it didn't matter. After a few minutes, he barely listened to her words. Her fetching smile and the twinkle in her eye communicated everything. He read her thoughts; she was interested. He was far too timid to pursue, but he knew his time would come.

Is it possible to exist like this, with these sensations? He needed advice; he needed help. Why he had asked his advisor, her husband, for the name of a psychiatrist seemed perfectly logical to him. For who knew him better than he, and somehow, he thought that there was a continuity of purpose within his request; a circle of sorts, but even as the folly of these illogical thoughts found their conclusion, it all seemed in some way to make sense. Maybe it has to do with proximity, all he knew was that he needed clarity. Jason does not have these feelings or even a warm thought for a human, but he's different… Maybe this psychiatrist is also different. I have learned he is a loner, like me in many ways.

Mark knew in some degree that he would have to reveal himself to this doctor, let him see that he is not human. He was concerned about this revelation, but he was desperate.

Mark left the subway, searched for the address crumpled in his pocket, and walked to West 72nd Street. The appointment was in The Dakota, one of the most prestigious buildings on the Upper West Side. He took the elevator to the 6th floor where he saw the name Dr. Matthew Abernathy, Psychiatrist, M.D. PhD, written on the first door as he stepped out. He went in, not noticing the secretary at first, too preoccupied with how he would attempt to explain himself.

"I am here to see the Doctor," he said.

"Oh, you must be Mark," she replied. "He is expecting you."

CHAPTER 7

ONLY A VERY LONELY MAN WOULD TAKE SUCH A RISK

I t was a serious room, for Dr. Matthew Abernathy was a very serious man. His walls were a pale gray and lined with shelves filled with leather-bound books. Two large windows draped with amber colored curtains framed a stately mahogany desk. In the center of the room, an imposing chair rested on a Persian rug. Once a patient asked if the chair was his throne. As he would, Abernathy peered over his wire-rimmed glasses with a raised brow.

The air conditioner at his home had broken that day, and he felt relieved and refreshed to come into the coolness of his office. He was wiping the sweat from his forehead, sitting at his desk, sorting through his papers organizing the day's schedule. It was a busy day, a teaching day, and he was questioning how he could fit in a new patient.

An old friend, Dr. George Bolinsky, head of the Physics department at Columbia, had referred someone. He was mildly intrigued by the upcoming meeting; the patient, a 19-year-old student who had just finished his Doctorate in Astrophysics, was also pursuing a PhD in Romantic Literature. Abernathy had heard rumors about this protégée swirling around campus, this young man of varied and exceptional potential. Bolinsky's note was cryptic. It simply read, "I am sending you my most brilliant student. He says he needs help. I don't know why."

Its tone awoke a curiosity in him; why such a brief message? Is Bolinsky up to his old pranks again?

Bolinsky was the only person Abernathy could call a friend. He missed the conversations they once had, but he knew that Bolinsky had been troubled of late. Government research grants had kept him increasingly away from academia, and though his research continued to be groundbreaking, its covert nature had begun to alienate other university departments. Just like him, he thought. Always mysterious, always with a joke, always surrounded by odd types. I do miss his sense of humor; maybe this will be an interesting diversion. The buzzer rang. Martha called, "He's here!"

"Send him in in two minutes."

He separated the papers in front of him into four neat piles and picked up his notebook, his mind still full of the day's agenda, he walked across the room to his chair and slipped into his traditional pose as therapist. He opened his notebook and clicked his ballpoint when he heard the door open. Martha entered first, followed by the young man.

"Here is your new patient, doctor," she said and turned to leave.

"Thank you, Martha," he replied, as she nodded and exited the room.

He was tall and thin, and his androgynous frame moved with an effortless grace. Then Abernathy noticed his eyes. They looked like the Aegean Sea under the blaze of a summer afternoon. His hair was dark but subtly highlighted as if bleached by the sun. His complexion was simultaneously peaked and rosy. He appeared as unnatural as a retouched photograph in a fashion magazine. His stare was transfixing. Abernathy winced as if he sensed an intruder within his psyche.

Mark looked at the doctor, aware that he had announced his presence.

Abernathy fidgeted in his chair and thought, who is this young man?

Mark had not yet decided how much he would reveal, but he knew nothing could be gained behind a mask.

Apprehensively, Abernathy rose and greeted his new patient; he spoke in his usual voice of authority as he rushed to regain his composure. "So, you are Mark. How do you do? Please, sit down." Mark took his seat and looked directly into his eyes. They remained silent for a few moments. Abernathy's anxiety grew, and he began talking in an effort to find reprieve. "Our mutual acquaintance, Dr. Bolinsky, told me that you wanted to talk to me."

After a moment Mark replied softly, "I've heard a lot about you, Dr. Abernathy. I know you are a special – deemed brilliant by many – and a person with perceptions and intellect beyond the ordinary. I know you already sense that I am different." Mark's eyes fixed directly on Abernathy's. "I chose you for a reason," he said. "And I hope you will not fear what might seem strange, even absurd. I hope you are a man willing to see a larger picture, for it will take some time to explain myself."

Abernathy was puzzled by the disturbance in his mind. It must come from Mark somehow. Shall I confront him, or shall I let this play out? Abernathy poured himself a glass of water from the pitcher on the end table near his chair. Suddenly he recalled Bolinsky's involvement with secret defense grants. Maybe this has to do with some sort of research! Is he testing one of his special projects? Or is this just a bit of his twisted sense of humor? Unsure but curious, he tried not to show his impatience and unease. He awaited Mark's next words, but there was only silence.

"Well," Abernathy said with a smile hinting a bit of annoyance, "I don't frighten easily. Anyway, you came to me for help. So, what can I do for you?"

"It's complicated. Explaining myself is difficult; there is much more to me than you can see. I will share all in time. For the moment, I must ask you to be patient. It is too early for me to reveal everything... But yes, I do need help. I must resolve what is going on inside me. I have an extremely important mission to fulfill – a mission upon which could decide the fate of humanity. If I am to succeed, I must be focused, my determination unfaltering. But my mind is in turmoil. For the first time, I am in a cloud, a fog. I am completely and utterly distracted."

"The fate of the world, hmm?" Abernathy thought, my god, Bolinsky has gone too far. Either this boy is completely psychotic, or this is a really bad joke. If not, sending me a young man with this degree of illness without proper notice is very inappropriate.

Mark continued, "I wish I could explain everything, but even if I wanted to, not even I know all the details. They're shared with me in just bits and pieces. What I do know is that I have a task that is larger in scope than anything you can imagine." Mark pondered... I only wish I understood it all myself.

Perplexed, Abernathy listened in disbelief, but he could see that the young man was distraught, and said, "Please continue...I'm listening..."

Mark hesitated and then started to speak, "I... I'm...," and then in a determined tone said, "I'm preoccupied with Professor Bolinsky's wife, Gabriela!"

Surprised, Abernathy responded, "You're preoccupied with Professor Bolinsky's wife? And the fate of the world hinges on this? Please... Really...what is this is all about?"

Abernathy had known Bolinsky's wife for several years. Bolinsky was now a man of 50, and some years ago he had married a 23-year-old English PhD student. A beauty, she moved with the grace of a dancer, 14 years younger than the professor at the time, he recalled the marriage had been the talk of the faculty. She was from Barcelona, had just finished a biography of Pablo Neruda, and everyone thought her a rising academic star.

He remembered her voice. It was lovely, and she often spoke in parables, her melodic cadence could instantly captivate an entire room with stories, that were second only to her charming wit. This delusional young man had clearly been entranced.

"Yes... Gabriela," replied Mark. "I have become obsessed with her, and I believe she has feelings for me as well. I know Dr. Bolinsky is your friend. Is that a problem for you?"

"No," replied the doctor. "It isn't. My main concern here is you. Have you entered into a relationship with her, and how long have you had these feelings?"

"We've hardly ever spoken. It is not just the fact that she is married. There are other problems...many other problems."

Abernathy said, "And what are those?"

"Well, there is my brother."

"Oh... there's another one of you? Hmm, is he in love with her too?" Abernathy knew he might have let a hint of sarcasm pass his lips, but he was starting to get annoyed.

"No, no nothing like that. It is hard to explain. It is about who I am and what I have to accomplish here."

"Accomplish here? Where is here? Accomplish what? Let's discuss this so I might understand."

"I'll tell you everything in time...," Mark replied. "And... When you're ready to hear what I have to say." He looked out the window. All of a sudden, growing somber and speaking softly, he said:

"Each with undeviating aim, in eloquent silence, through the depths of space, pursued its wondrous way."

Abernathy's frustration grew, and unaware of his expression he started rolling his eyes. "That's Shelley, isn't it? Why are you quoting Shelley?" Bolinsky has taken this humor too far.

"Gabriela loves Shelley... 'A wondrous way' is who I am... Maybe not in the way Shelley was thinking, but in ways you will soon come to see. Gabriela is the main reason why I came to see you. But my purpose precludes everything. I need to know the meaning of why these sensations have overtaken me... I can't be distracted like this. My mission is too important."

Abernathy pushed the point. "Your mission?"

Mark hesitated and sighed. He wondered if he had made a mistake in coming.

"Dr. Abernathy, you must understand, I have only been aware of emotions as a concept; as if I had been watching the world from a window, but now these feelings have begun to flow through me like a torrent. All these experiences are new to me. You must believe that in the most literal sense possible, I have never experienced anything like emotions before."

Mark looked directly at the doctor. "I need clarity, desperately. Please, you must help me."

Not knowing completely why, something in Abernathy began to listen differently. "So, what do you want to talk about first? Your feelings for Gabriela, your brother, or this mission? Where shall we begin...?"

Mark hesitated and spoke, "I feel so alone at times... Walking in a world that cannot see who I truly am. I know you often feel alone, never completely understood. In a strange way, I thought we may have shared similar experiences. This is why I chose you." He looked into Abernathy's eyes.

Abernathy nodded. He felt empathy, a strange kinship. "Please continue."

"You will understand it all in time," said Mark, reading the doctors thoughts. "You must meet my brother Jason... But you have to trust me for now." He leaned forward, putting emphasis on every syllable. "You must be patient."

"Mark... I am doing my best."

Mark spoke again, "Forgive me... I'm worried that even having this conversation with you could bring problems."

"Why are you unsure? Who or what are you afraid of?" He is a paradox, what is he really after? Abernathy was still uncertain whether to move the pawn or the queen. He waited for Mark to speak again, but no words came.

"I am sure you came to the right place, and I want to help you. In the meantime, would you consider some medication for your anxiety?"

Mark responded in an annoyed tone, "Medication won't help me. You are beginning to disappoint me, doctor. Don't you see I am not just another patient? My brother and I will affect your world as no one ever has. I know this sounds crazy to you, but it is true."

Abernathy looked away for a moment, confused, trying to make sense of what he was hearing; he was overwhelmed and captivated, swallowed by it all. Every cell in his body told him to flee, but instead, he said, "I want to help you."

At last, feeling a glimpse of hope that Abernathy might be able to comprehend him, Mark responded, "That's good, because I need you."

"Our time is almost up. Shall we save this for our next meeting?"

"Fine," replied Mark, and he got up to leave.

"Please see Martha for your next appointment. I think you should come at least twice a week."

"Will you see Jason, too?"

Abernathy paused, that brother again?

"Sure, I could meet him. Let's talk about it next time."

Mark responded, "He can be a bit intense." A childlike smile appeared on his face.

"Intense? In what way?"

"You will see," Mark replied.

"Ah... So that's something to look forward to."

Abernathy followed Mark's exit with his eyes, but he did not rise from his chair as he normally would after a session. He remained frozen, fixed, as he watched Mark walk to the door. He felt limp, as if he had just spent an hour in a hot bath. His muscles were unresponsive, yet his intellect was excited beyond words. When the door closed, he stared at the empty chair in which Mark had sat. For a moment he thought he saw an afterglow of the young man's presence. Something was there. Nothing that one could quantify, but something – an impalpable energy. It faded slowly like the bubbles in a dying glass of seltzer.

CHAPTER 8

THE APARTMENT

J ason and Mark's New York City apartment was a one-room studio in a tenement building located in the East Village. Their third-floor flat had only two small windows that looked out over an alley in the rear of the building. The halls were filled with a mixture of odors of ethnic cooking accompanied by the loud voices of mothers screaming at their children, voices declaring their rural heritage from Eastern Europe. After midnight, you might hear a husband staggering home drunk singing songs from his Polish village, all while smoking hippies' stereos blasted sounds from The Rolling Stones and their water pipes sent the perfume of hashish into the air.

On warm nights, open windows let in the cries of the lusty cats roaming back alleyways. On the sidewalks below, under the glow of the dim street lights, the chants of drug dealers, mostly teenage boys with glistening ebony faces, melodically rang out the menu of the latest flavors of uppers, downers, hallucinogens, and opiates to craving ones who sought them out,

Whaddya want, whaddya need?

They would whisper in low, soulful voices:

I got smack, I got speed, whaddya want, whaddya need?

These voices, and the sounds of Latin salsa clashing with hippie rock, regularly lasted until 3 a.m., making a good night's sleep a luxury. It was not uncommon to climb over piles of bodies passed out in the hall or to find these sounds converging well into the next morning, wearying sleepless neighbors. But sleep was not a concern for Jason and Mark; they'd never slept a day in their lives.

Theirs was a spartan apartment, designed only for keeping up appearances: a single bed with a worn blanket, a beat-up table scavenged from the Salvation Army, and two dressing closets were all the furniture the brothers owned. The kitchen was bare, save for a few glasses and dishes that they never used. The walls were gray and very much in need of a paint job. The only real indicators of life were the electric guitar and amplifier in one corner and the hundreds of books, stacked in piles like ant mounds about the room.

Physical surroundings were of little interest to the brothers. Walking into the studio meant stepping into a realm that no human could see; the room, when called upon, became a portal, a bend of space and time into which the twins alone could enter. This small apartment is where the ends of space could meet, and energy flowed so powerfully that, could it be seen by humans, it would be incomprehensible. Out of empty space, fiery red and yellow streams of color would appear, intense and fluctuating as space was ruptured. And then, as quickly as it came, it dimmed, vanishing into a quiet hum. All this occurred without a mouse perking an ear, for nothing was ever heard outside these walls.

Mark was often anxious before entering the portal. As he entered, Jason would emerge. This transition was a continuous dance, for the Council dictated that only one brother should walk the earth at a time. Mark often worried he might never wake from the portal state, but after a moment he always fell easily into the warm embrace that emanated from within it. During their time in the portal, the Council would communicate with them, educate them, and enhance their abilities. Each time, they would awaken stronger, more powerful, and more knowledgeable than before.

Although they were completely aware of each other's existence, Jason and Mark only lived in the same time and space within the moment of transition, the nanosecond in which one passed the other. At this moment, as time seemed to pause, they shared with each other their singular experiences, fostering a collaborative existence that thrived on their independence. Each felt the other's every thought, every pleasure, and every pain as one might experience a passing landscape in the corner of one's eye on a speeding train. Meanwhile, they waited, the question of their destiny pulsating in the background of their minds, softly tormenting each of their psyches.

They lived in this limbo of learning, acquiring as they waited, seeking knowledge, appearing as humans to the outside world. They grew with the power of gods living beneath their skins, reveling in the wonders of this planet they now called home. Yet they knew less about themselves than even the primitive humans with whom they engaged.

Mark's thoughts raced through these apprehensions as he looked around the rather dusty apartment. Knowing that one day he and Jason would walk the earth together was an everlasting source of anticipation. They had depended upon each other for all these years, and he hoped the consolation he now sought from the glimpse of Jason during this last transformation would not disappear. The weight of sensibility always seemed to fall on Mark, for it was Jason who often ran wild with his actions, ignoring orders to remain hidden from human understanding. Now it's Jason's turn to criticize, thought Mark, hardly ever instigating but always worrying about his brother's actions. What could be more reckless than to fall in love with a human!

Mark lay down on the bed. The room swirled with throbbing colors. Vibrating and shifting bands of energy surrounded him and passed through him. He surrendered to the warmth of its intensity. Elation overcame him as his essence melted into the energy. He became one with it as he passed into the portal. Like always, Jason's eyes caught his for a moment as they floated past one another, and he slowly drifted away.

CHAPTER 9

A NIGHT OF MUSIC

Jason opened his eyes and quickly arose from the bed. It seemed like an eternity since he had walked the streets of the city. He yearned for the rush of the club, the excitement of his band, and the cheering of the crowd. The Dom was the hottest club in New York. Every corner dripped with pleasure. He only ever wanted to be there, but on this day, Jason sat contemplating what he had gleaned. Aware of Mark's visit to the psychiatrist, he pondered the reasons for his actions.

It's that human, Gabriela. Did he think he could hide this from me? He knows that's not possible. What could he be thinking? Until this point, the two brothers had shared all thoughts and considered themselves extensions of each other. Maybe we are approaching the time of our separation; maybe he has gained some power I am not aware of. But why would he want to keep something from me? Jason recalled how Mark had been upset with him about the human lives he had taken, but he dismissed the idea as having little bearing. To him, a few humans were of little consequence. Mark, on the other hand, had grown enamored by one. And his feelings for this woman were baffling. We have been instructed to learn about these beings, to understand them, to absorb their thinking and nature, but he has taken this too far. He has allowed their feelings to enter him. My music may start with the humans, but I never surrender my control.

He began to dress. He put on a black t-shirt with a few holes and a white skull graphic. Jason's hair was jet black, a foil to the fairer hair of Mark's, and his eyes were a deep, dark blue, as opposed to Mark's lighter ones. Both brothers were hypnotic and beautiful, and they hummed with mysteries that could not be defined. To look at them was to be lost in them, seduced and captured by their splendor.

He put on his boots and his leather jacket that was draped with chains and embellished with metal studs, picked up his guitar, put on his dark Ray-Bans to conceal his eyes and opened the door. He walked out into the night and breathed in the sounds of the streets.

Speedily he walked towards St. Mark's Place, knowing that Helena, Gary, and BoBo would be there. He had promised them new music, and they were eagerly awaiting his appearance. They had been arguing over a name for their new band. This mattered little to Jason; this was just a passing amusement for him. He knew they would never be a professional band. Too much visibility, too much attention, for that to be, but the music... The music, the magnificent, beautiful music, that flow which rose beyond superlatives: that is what he loved. Jason could create landscapes of cadence, melodic passions that would leave one breathless. Everyone knew Jason was special. When he went onstage, the experience was transformative. He would often think, too bad this can never last. It will all have to end soon, but not too soon.

He approached St. Mark's Place and heard a girl yelling from behind.

"Jason! Jason!" she cried out. It was Helena.

Helena could turn every head in a restaurant, and when she sang, her voice would melt the room. She was the daughter of a famous New Orleans African-American jazz musician and a Danish model. Every pore in her body exuded sexuality; as she passed, pheromones filled the air. Her eyes were a deep blue, and her features chiseled. A fair-skinned beauty, her looks echoed the heritage of her Scandinavian mother, but her soul belonged to her piano man father. She was unique; wanted by all. All but Jason, that is, who never paid her a thought. She was simply a part of the music, and he had no desire for her. But this did not stop Helena's yearnings for him; she loved him madly.

"Do you have the music?" she cried, as she ran after him. "Do I have my words, my new words? I can't wait!" Her voice was sweet, with a French Quarter accent inherited from her dad.

"There are no words for you," he said.

She stopped short with shock. "No words for me?" she whimpered.

"No words, but you will sing like the nightingale you are," he replied, knowing that the purity of her voice, moaning, sighing, and always drenched in the blues, would be enough for his piece. "You will be magnificent. There will be only one line, a melodic repetition that I will sing as a counter to your free flow. I will sing 'Only for Tonight' over and over, bouncing off you and the music. It will be great. You will understand later."

Her eyes beamed, and a smile appeared. She always trusted Jason; she always knew it would work. They never had to rehearse a song more than once. It was not like all the other bands she had known, requiring hours of repetition and practice to get it right. It was always right. Always perfect.

They entered The Dom together. Helena took off her coat and slung it over her arm. She was wearing a ruby-colored silk dress that clung to her like a second skin. Cut high above the knee, it shimmered with highlights as she walked. Her dark green stockings and high heels accentuated her long legs. The music blared at a deafening pitch as they crossed the large floor swarming with people dancing. Smoke and perspiration filled the air as they weaved through the crowd. A hundred eyes followed them, many acknowledging the recognition of their arrival. Jason was there.

"Jason! Jason!" was heard from the back of the room. It was

Gary, his lead guitar player, waving madly for them to join him. "Jason!" he said again. "Janis Joplin's agent is here, and he won't leave until he's seen you.

"Where's BoBo?" asked Jason.

"Upstairs in our private room hitting his drums," replied Gary.

"Good," said Jason, "let's go. Tell Janis we can talk later."

They walked up the back stairs to their private room, the exclusive domain of the group. BoBo was at the drums banging out some of his favorite patterns.

"Hey, BoBo, are you ready?"

"Ready?" he replied, "I've been waiting for hours." BoBo was a very large and overweight, hard-drinking, hard-talking southern boy, always ready for a party or a fight. Gary, on the other hand, looked like a stiff wind would blow him to Idaho – oh, but could he play! That is, when he wasn't so stoned that he could not stand... They were the most talented musicians in the city.

Jason turned to each member of the group and relayed the music they were to play. At the same moment, he planted the music deep into each one's subconscious. He could have easily skipped the ritual, but this would have been too overt a use of his abilities, which he was still keeping secret. They practiced the music once, and it was perfect.

Helena turned to him and murmured softly, "Oh Jason, thank you." The other two just kept shaking their heads up and down in recognition.

"Ok," said Jason, "now let's go listen to Janis!"

They descended the stairs to the back of the main room. The crowd was roaring as Joplin walked onto the stage. The group sat at their private table and ordered drinks with a wave of the hand. The waiter knew what they all wanted. They always had the same.

BoBo tapped out some coke on a silver tray and started to make lines. He rolled up a twenty and quickly inhaled two. He passed the tray to Jason. Jason snorted a line, but it had no effect on him. He would engage in drugs, as well as eating and drinking, to keep a low profile and appear human. Gary was next, and Helena was last. She always wanted to go last. Then came her signature words, "Oh, so superb!"

The music filled the room as the crowd cheered louder. Janis was singing, "Oh come on, come on..." and a frenzy of cheers and screams broke out.

Soulful groans went forth as only Joplin could evoke. The audience erupted with enthusiasm. She was the queen of funk, unmatched in her power on stage. The set lasted over an hour, driving the music deep into the crowd.

As her performance was coming to an end, the audience appeared exhausted. But little did they know what they were about to experience. Jason was coming.

The stage manager came to the table. "You're up next!"

They walked backstage as the equipment was being set up.

"This is going to be so great!" Helena cooed.

Gary nodded and added, "They are never going to hear anything like this." BoBo was completely wasted on coke and whiskey, but this did not worry Jason; he knew his force of will would carry all of them, and the music would be perfect. Perfection was what mattered to him. This was why he loved music and gave it such attention; it was one of the great human accomplishments: this universal language of abstraction. From the complexity of Beethoven and Bach to the funky guitars wailing from windows on Eighth Street, music amazed him. Other than dreaming, it was one of the most awe-inspiring things that mesmerized his species from thousands of light years away.

The group took to the stage and opened the set with one of their favorites. The place was jumping. They played two more songs, and then Jason nodded: it was time for the new song.

"Let's stretch it out," he said. Jason started to play; stillness stole the room. One by one, each of the band members joined in.

First, Bobo pounded out a beat, and then Gary's strings

started their elongated whine as if they were crying in pain, and lastly, Helena's voice warmed the air. They all joined forces, their collaboration rising in harmony. A somber tranquil wave enveloped the stage and drifted out to the crowd. Then Jason's elusive voice grew higher, and without warning, it descended softly to a hidden place. The room fell silent.

"Only for tonight…" he sang, as Helena's voice continued with a vibrating moan. Their voices echoed and blended, always with Jason's voice ascending above, pulling and pushing at the same time, as if telepathy had queried them, and while this seamless precision left the stage, the audience was transported into a state of euphoria.

For twenty minutes, the crowd stood transfixed. When the music stopped, the room remained silent, as if in a coma. Then a single clap rang out, then another, until the whole room had broken into a shattering applause that lasted well after they had left.

As they exited to the left of the stage, Joplin ran up to Jason. "My God! I have never heard anything like that! It was beyond… beyond! How… Where did that come from?"

Jason smiled. "It was you guys who were great," he said.

"Yes, we were great…but that was something else! Please… please! My label is begging me to get you."

A man in a blue suit interrupted, "Jason, please let us work with you." His band stood behind him proudly, bursting with excitement.

"You're from San Francisco?" asked Jason.

"Yes," he said. "We handle Janis. We just cut her album, she can tell you we are fair people and we understand music, and everyone likes the way we work. If you will you come to the coast, we can do some great things? We'll cut an album and set up a tour."

"Sure," replied Jason. But he knew that would never happen. Too much recognition might interfere with his main task. What good is a rock group if you have no planet to rock?

Jason turned and started to walk up the stairs. He looked at

Joplin.

"Thanks for the walk-on performance. I know this was not on your schedule, especially since you were doing the Fillmore this week."

"I wanted to see you." She winked. "You know I love your ass. If you'll let me drag you into my arms sometime, well, we'll party till dawn. We're going back to the hotel for a bash. Wanna come?"

Jason smiled. "Maybe later. I have to do some stuff upstairs with the group."

"OK, baby," she replied. "I'll be waiting!"

He smiled and turned to go up the stairs to his private room. The band had just arrived, but already Gary had dotted the room with an assortment of groupies from the crowd. They were stoned and seemed to be undressing. Bobo had a redhead and a blonde under his arm.

"This is Silvia, and this is Rachel," he introduced them, respectively. "They always come as a team, and they are dying to get to know you, Jason." Jason thought; how the hell did this happen so fast? They had only gotten to the room two minutes before him.

Jason put down his guitar and had just sat down when the bouncers knocked, "There is someone here to see you, Jason." The bouncers were two huge men, Malcolm and Antonio. Malcolm was a black man who had been a lineman at Penn State, one of the only openly gay football players in the league. Antonio, a product of Bronx Latin street gangs, was equally large. Both were devoted to Jason and protected the members of the group when he was not around.

"Who is it?" asked Jason.

"Guy Lucasie," replied Antonio.

Jason could hear Lucasie in the hall telling his bodyguard, "Wait downstairs! I don't want to scare this hippy douchebag kid before I make a deal."

Everyone had heard about this man. He was a Mafia capo who controlled much of the music industry, as well as entertainment venues for the mob. The word was that he was dangerous and very connected. He could be a good friend or a ruthless enemy.

Jason didn't have anything to fear from him, but to keep up his appearance in front of his band, he would speak politely and try to show the appropriate respect.

Lucasie walked into the room. He was a short man, about 60-years-old, dressed in a gray sharkskin suit and a blue silk tie held in place with a star sapphire pin. He appeared as wide as he was tall. He walked stiffly and deliberately and reminded Jason of a stout bulldog.

His girlfriend, a curvaceous femme fatale accompanied him. Dark-haired, with enchanting eyes, she was a full-breasted, sumptuous woman. She looked about 25-years-old, and she clung to his arm like a piece of jewelry. Her name was Angela. "The Angel," Lucasie called her. The rumor was that she was from Naples, Italy and Lucasie was crazed with possessiveness over her. There was a story floating around that he once had a bodyguard's fingers broken for touching her.

Lucasie grumbled, "May I sit down and have a word or two with you?"

Jason acknowledged him with a smile.

Lucasie leaned forward in his chair. He was obvious in his body language. Every motion he made was intended to convey his strength and control; each gesture an expression of influence and bravado.

"So, I heard your set, and I liked it. I can do things for you and your band." He spoke with a tone of authority. Jason was already annoyed.

He's arrogant, he thought.

Lucasie started to speak. "I also know people are talking to you and your band. West coast people, that's no good! Cio, non va bene," he said, as he turned to Angela and smiled.

Lucasie continued, "I hear you make all the decisions."

Again, Jason looked up and replied with an indifferent voice, "My opinion is well respected in the group." Lucasie was posturing and trying to size Jason up. Jason was amused. All this bravado! All this theater! Does this guy always feel he has to play the Don? Is he always afraid to lose face? There is no one here to impress or lose face to. There is no entourage of Mafia kingpins here. Maybe he just can't help it… he reflected. Or maybe it is something else. Jason penetrated Lucasie's mind.

Lucasie continued to speak in an agitated manner, "I can offer you more than anyone else: recording, touring, and a $100,000 advance." He opened his briefcase. It was full of cash. He put it on the table in front of Jason. Jason was no longer paying attention to what Lucasie was saying but was looking past it and into his mind and that of his angel.

To his amazement, he sensed that Angela was deeply turned on by the orgy filling the room. Her discomfort was distressing them both. The two girls making out in the corner, entwined with BoBo, stole all of her attention. She was trying to hide her excitement, but she started to squirm in her seat. He could tell that Lucasie knew she wanted to be in the corner of that room.

Jason saw all of this, as well as Lucasie's burning anger. He wanted to make his deal and get out of there but did not dare to look weak or seem like he was not in control. His frustration grew as he directed his hostility towards Jason, but Angela was the source of it all.

Jason's dislike of this guy intensified; his arrogance needed a lesson, so Jason decided to play with him a bit.

"Interesting, aren't they?" he suggested, nodding his head towards the corner, though not directing the question specifically to Angela.

Lucasie responded sharply, "I'm here to talk business! I'm offering you a deal. Not for anything else, so let's talk business!"

Ignoring his outburst, Jason again directed his eyes towards the corner. He called, "Silvia… Rachel… Say hi to Angela." This time, he looked directly at Angela. The girls looked over and smiled, giving a wave. Silvia and Angela locked eyes.

Lucasie's face began to flush. "Hey pal, I am here to talk business! Not to fuck around!"

"Oh, of course..." replied Jason. "Say, will everyone leave us alone for a minute? He wants to talk business..." Everyone got up to leave. Jason looked at the two girls. "Everyone but Bobo and you two," he said to Silvia. "We have things to do later." They smiled and sat back in the corner on a sofa the size of a king-sized bed.

The room cleared but for but the five of them. One could feel the tension in Lucasie's voice as he shouted, "Why are they here? I don't like this!"

"Well they make the room pretty, and I like visuals," replied Jason. "Don't you?" Lucasie's face started to burn. A vein under his eye pulsated as fury rose in his gut.

Jason did not respond but just looked at him. He removed his sunglasses, revealing his cobalt blue eyes. Lucasie found that he couldn't look away from them.

"What...?" Lucasie murmured.

Jason smiled again, returning his sunglasses to his face. "I was just thinking we could have a little fun. We are having a party, aren't we?" Lucasie shifted in his seat.

Jason's voice took on a sardonic tone. "I think my friends like your girlfriend. What do you think?

Lucasie's face grew red. "What! Are you crazy? Do you know who I am? Do you know what I can do to you?"

"You know, I think you've talked enough for a while," said Jason. "I think I'd prefer if you just sat there and didn't speak at all."

Lucasie tried to get up, but he could not. He tried to talk, and then scream, but just air passed his lips. He was frozen to his chair, paralyzed and unable to neither flex a muscle nor utter a word. Only grunts and groans came forth, and the more he struggled, the more he felt a great weight bearing down on him. Terror churned in his stomach.

"Angela," Jason said softly, in a sweet tone, "haven't you had enough of this man controlling you? Wouldn't you like to be part of this?" he asked as his head turned toward the corner signaling where she should be. "Do what you want for once. Let him see who you really are."

Angela rose and smiled. Suddenly something awoke within her, driving her forward, a burning begging for fulfillment. She felt the rush of freedom in her veins; the years of the oppression of her Catholic childhood began to evaporate. She walked slowly towards the sofa, and with each step found more strength. Silvia reached up to her, placing her arm around her back to find her zipper. Angela surrendered without hesitation. She allowed Silvia to unzip her dress and unclasp her bra as Rachel started pulling off the rest. She was a bit shy at first, but soon her timidity and inhibitions fell away with the silk.

Angela turned towards Lucasie, her eyes locked on his, as Silvia pulled off the rest of her undergarments. She could hear Jason's words within her mind. They had a quiet power; she sensed his strength filling her, allowing for unwavering confidence to bloom, and she realized, I am free to do what I want.

Silvia kissed her breast. Jason spoke again, "Yes Angela, you are free now, free to be who you are...show him. He can no longer harm you. In fact, if you want, he will not even remember this. But I think you will want him to remember."

Slowly, Silvia pulled Angela's body down into her arms, while BoBo started to kiss her lips. Silvia moved her mouth towards Angela's stomach; vibrations arose, her center quivered.

"Lascia che il diavolo prendi la mia anima," Angela moaned in Italian. Let the devil take my soul. Slowly, Silvia moved down until her tongue found Angela's heat. Angela, full of ecstasy, cried out, Don't stop, please, please! She fell back onto the sofa as BoBo's mouth found her breast. He felt her nipple grow hard in his mouth. Angela turned and found Silvia's lips as BoBo drove deep into her. They descended into a dance, ravaging and consuming each other.

Lucasie's face hardened; his eyes raged, his veins swelled, and Angela relished every throb.

"Oh, why I have waited so long for this?" she whispered as her mouth found Silvia's lips. Angela looked into Lucasie's eyes, and as her tongue found Silvia's nipples again, she thought, oh how sweet this is.

CHAPTER 10

AT THE UNIVERSITY

Mark emerged from the portal, and he wasn't happy. Jason had passed speedily by him as he often would when he came in from an evening of abandoned activities at the club. He was becoming more and more public, and Mark feared his antics were creating too much attention. If they were discovered and their identities revealed, there could be dire consequences.

He sat on the corner of the bed. Why have I always felt it was my role to walk the narrow path and be the responsible one who considers the significance of everything? Yes, he was chosen to be the brazen one, but now I feel a need too.

He got up, realizing much time had passed and he had things to do. Figuring out a way to control Jason's behavior would have to wait. People were expecting him. He was due at the physics department at Columbia, for there was going to be an important meeting.

He walked quickly to the subway, his mind on Jason, his thoughts haunted by Gabriela. He yearned for her presence, the sound of her voice, the smile in her eyes, her melodic cadence when she spoke. He craved the warmth and the elation he experienced when he was near her. He needed the intangible, indiscernible thing she gave him and would do almost anything to spend more time with her. This is strange... I feel both happy and sad at the same time. Is this what it means to be human? If I were able to sleep, perhaps I could dream of her.

When he arrived at the university, the campus was overrun with students chanting, "Hell no – we won't go!" There was an anti-war demonstration in full swing. Joan Baez was on campus, and the student body turned out in full force to hear her.

He had to get to the physics department, but his path was blocked. He made his way around the back of the building, entered through the basement, and went up the stairs. But again, students blocked his path. He was able to see through the wall where Professor Bolinsky was meeting with the other assistants and the chairs of all the major universities on the East Coast. Quickly, when he saw that no one was observing him, he converted his physical form into energy and passed nonchalantly through the wall. The twins could manipulate matter in many ways; walls were but a human concept.

The professors and their assistants had gathered to discuss the birth of the universe. They were trying to reconcile new data with the conflicting theories of the day. Bolinsky and others had been frantically writing equations on the blackboard, but they were nowhere near a solution. Of course, this was all but child's play to Mark, for his civilization was thousands of years beyond this primitive science.

As Mark took in the scene, he knew there was a young man in the room named Alan Guth who would one day apply quantum theory to their observations and find a start to the answer. Guth understood that temperature variations in regions of space were the clues needed to interpret the birth of the universe. The knowledge was within his grasp, but comprehension was still so far away. He was the only one who was even beginning to see, but he was a young graduate student, one of those visiting MIT boys who played no part in the Columbia University postgraduate residency. He was not really a member of *The Club*; he was also a quiet one, not a forceful personality. Mark liked him and recognized his brilliance, but around the department, he was mostly ignored.

But these discussions were of little concern to Mark at the

moment; all he wanted was a way to spend more time with Gabriela. If I could only get the professor more consumed with his work, maybe it would leave her more available.

Mark was forbidden to alter the intellectual development of the earthlings, but since the young Guth was about to come to a new understanding of the cosmos on his own, he saw little harm in accelerating his fame. Quickly, he modified some of the equations on the blackboard, making it seem that these changes were there all along. It appeared to the classroom that Guth had been the one who had somehow messed with the equations, and it sent the discussion in the room in the right direction while still not really providing an answer. He had just prompted the proper ideas. The room was buzzing with excitement. Mark grinned; this will be enough to have them preoccupied for the next two months.

"Mark! There you are!" exclaimed Professor Bolinsky. "We have been waiting for you. What do you think of these latest observations?"

"I'd need more time to provide an opinion," he responded. "Maybe Alan has some ideas."

All eyes turned to Guth. "Well," he said, "I do have some thoughts..." He started to write on the blackboard. Complicated equations arose from the chalk as he applied quantum theory to the problem, a novel approach that was radical for the group. The room watched and commented as he wrote, making observations and raising questions.

As the excitement in the room swelled, Bolinsky glanced at his watch. "Oh my God! I have lunch with Gabriela!" he exclaimed. "Mark, would you please call Gabriela and maybe make my apologies? Perhaps you could grab a quick bite with her if you have time? I would really appreciate it if you could."

"Yes, of course," responded Mark, inwardly smiling. "I'll just go into your office and call her if you wish."

"Great," responded Bolinsky, distracted again by the fever of the room.

Mark never understood this thing that humans called guilt.

He imagined, in a way, that what he had done was wrong, but Mark only saw a problem and a solution, nothing more. He walked into the quietude of the private office.

I must be careful now; I don't want Gabriela to think I manipulated the situation. I know I could control her thoughts, steal her will, but that would be... well, unsatisfying to say the least. I need her free. I want to experience this as a human. I want to feel love.

The beings of Eldern had long ago lost their ability to have emotions and had melded into the Singularity. Independent thinking faded like a morning mist. The inhabitants of Eldern had surrendered themselves blindly with eyes wide open to the efficiency of The Prime, marching together mindlessly, numbed by their own music.

First came universal judgments for the good of all, then rules of interaction and communication were established; the entire population was seduced by inertia, by convenience and expediency. Eventually all original thought slowly but methodically was replaced by algorithms. Within their self-imposed preserve of limitation, they surrendered their ability to see what existed beyond the dictates of this artificial world, they lost what defined themselves as themselves. Individualism faded, and the steady march towards the sameness began, all while corporate profits were never so strong.

The phone rang, and Mark heard Gabriela's voice, a voice that he had awaited with eager anticipation.

"Hello, who is this?" she asked.

"It's Mark," he responded.

Gabriela paused and caught her breath, taken aback, for she had not been expecting to hear his voice. She had wanted him to call. She had struggled to purge Mark from her thoughts, but the more she tried, the more it became an exercise in futility. She dismissed these thoughts by thinking of them, with a self-indulgent smile, as "preoccupations." And while Gabriela had only engaged in small talk with Mark a handful of times, she inexplicably felt as if she had already shared hours with him.

She seemed to be aware of him on campus more often than chance would allow, almost as if the road of happenstance had taken a deliberate turn.

Gabriela spoke into the phone.

"Oh... Hello, Mark," she said quietly, trying to camouflage her excitement. "What a surprise to hear from you! Do you want to talk to the professor? He's not at home. He's at the college. There is an important meeting, I think."

"No," replied Mark. "I want to talk to you."

Gabriela took a breath. Her heart started to pound; she was afraid that Mark could hear it over the phone. Stay cool, she told herself. Casually, she responded, "Oh. What is it?"

Mark replied, "Your husband asked me to call you. He cannot make lunch today, and..." Mark hesitated. "He asked me if I could take you to the club in his place, if that would be okay with you." Again, he paused. "I have been so looking forward to talking with you again."

Gabriela, feeling the same, quickly responded, "Oh, lunch would be great! But let's not go to the club. It's so stuffy and morose in there. How about someplace downtown?" She knew she wanted to be away from the prying eyes and whispers of the other faculty. "Do you have a spot in mind?"

"Well...There's the Paradox on East 4th Street, if you're into seaweed and brown rice," he replied, testing how much she wanted to see him.

Gabriela thought to herself, Really... I'm more into foie gras and sauterne... but she responded politely, "That sounds great! In an hour then."

"Let's make it an hour and a half. I'm all the way uptown."

"Fine," she said. "See you there!"

CHAPTER 11
A DAY TOGETHER

Gabriela was rushing to find the right thing to wear downtown in the East Village. I want to look hip, but not like a hippie. I am 36, after all. I want to look young and irresistible, but not cheap, never that! Oh, the black dress! Simple, but elegant; it's not too dressy and has just enough sex appeal. Sex appeal? She paused. I'll wear my hair down, and that red lipstick! Latin power for sure. I'm off! Hmm, I will have to be a few minutes late, but just that… She caught herself off-guard in the mirror, arrested by the red lipstick. I'm 36. I'm married. What am I doing? She checked her watch. I'm going to be five minutes late to my date, that's what I'm doing! Out the door, she went and waved a cab.

Nothing in her marriage seemed satisfying of late. Her relationship with George had grown as bland as supermarket pudding. Her fascination with the great star of the science world had faded away years ago. He had gotten older. He was no longer the dashing man in his mid-forties that he was when they had met. That was maybe 14 years ago. At that time, she had only been 22. My God! It's been such a long time! A long time of tedious conversations in the salon about particle science and dark matter, conversations she had been forced to sit through. The only dark matter she yearned for during those long evenings with her living room full of astrophysicists and cosmologists was the time when the lights went out and all those long-winded scientists would leave.

Gabriela had just gotten off the phone with her mother in Barcelona. She loved talking to her mother; she was so full of life and always made her feel better. Oh, how I miss her. They had had a good laugh when she was describing one of those long evenings with the scientists sitting around pontificating in her living room.

"So, Mama," she said, "there were eight of them here last night drinking and talking until 2 A.M. about some government project weaponizing quarks. They were all in a frenzy about it, and I was bored to death!"

"Quacks?" her mother had responded. "We have twelve of them at the country house! Why are they so excited about that?"

"No," answered Gabriela, "not quacks! They were talking about quarks!" But her mother would not be interrupted.

"Why would those old men be obsessed about quacks? You know Aunt Marisa had a great recipe for duck with oranges and walnuts! I will send it to you! Maybe if they really ate one well-cooked, they would stop talking about them, and then maybe they would stop drinking and go to bed!"

"No, mother...I am not talking about ducks!"

But she was relentless. "I think she cooks it on low heat for at least two hours, however, so you must give yourself time!"

"No, Mama, it is not a quack, I mean... duck!"

But the more Gabriela implored, the more her mother continued; she would not take a breath, or let a word in, describing all the details of the recipe as best she could. "The seasoning is very important, though."

"No, Mama," she again interrupted. "A quark is a scientific term for subatomic particles or something."

Finally, her mother paused. "Quarks, huh? That sounds even worse than I thought! Well, my sweet, cook them whatever you want! I have no answer for those crazy men. And about the other thing..." her mother changed the subject. "What about that lazy bird between his legs? Has it woken up lately? A woman cannot live without love! Especially not a woman like you, my darling."

"No," Gabriela responded. "That is still a problem."

Gabriela did not want to talk about the sexual problems that had arisen over the last few years. She blamed herself for marrying a man so much older, but she was putting that out of her mind the best she could for now.

Well, she thought, as her cab sped downtown, maybe I have an exciting day to look forward to! Mark was different, not only from her husband but from the rest of his academic crowd. He loved science but was also getting his PhD in poetry. He loved sonnets as well as supernovas. He is very attractive, but he's so young. Could he ever be interested in me?

Gabriela put a stick of gum in her mouth, and she wished she had not just quit smoking. Feeling the rush of entering forbidden territory, she was becoming more and more excited by the thought of him.

Meanwhile, Mark had been waiting for about ten minutes. He was happy to have arrived early enough to secure a private table. Most of the time he was forced to eat at a long communal table in the center of the room, but today he wanted to be alone with Gabriela. He wanted to look into her eyes and delve into her very being. To Mark, she was the human embodiment of a poem; her every gesture, every intonation in her voice sang to him.

Can I really experience what humans feel? Every day I seem to be becoming more and more like them. Is it because I want it to happen, or is it all part of a plan? Am I willing it to happen, or are they? These are agonizing questions, but I want to feel as they do, to experience as they do. I want to dream, and I want to love!

Gabriela walked in.

There she is... Wow! Mark was not attracted to the younger women he found on campus. Although many were beautiful and smart, they seemed to lack something, a depth he craved.

Gabriela had something more. He watched her as her long

sleek body walked towards him. She had a natural sway, a grace that whispered rather than boasted. Her long, dark hair swung back over her bare shoulders. Her skin, white as porcelain, her waist long, her firm body curved gently within her dress. A more eloquent form was not possible. Gabriela's warm smile welcomed him; her eyes told him of her feelings. He quickly read her thoughts and knew instantly she was far more than just interested, but he stopped himself from exploring her mind. No, that's an unfair advantage. I want her to come freely to me.

"Hello, Mark. So nice to see you again!" She sat down and turned her head smartly.

Gabriela looked into Mark's eyes as she joined him at the table. My God, he is more like a fragrance than an individual; I feel almost like a warm wind is on my face. She was completely and unremorsefully swept away. Her expression revealed a shameless capitulation, and despite all the taboos that raced about her mind, she knew she was doomed.

Regaining a bit of decorum, Gabriela's defenses went up, "So, this is an interesting place," she said with a slightly sarcastic smile. "Lots of students and such!"

"Mostly students... and a lot of such." He smiled. "You can get a meal here for $1.25, which definitely falls within the 'hippie expense account.' I thought it might be a change of pace for you... Rather different from the Columbia Club or the midtown restaurants you might go to with George – I mean – Professor Bolinsky."

"Oh, you can call him George in front of me! I've heard students call him by his first name many times."

Mark responded, "It depends on who is around. When we are alone, it is okay, but when we are working on something in the lab or in the library..." He smiled timidly. "That's a beautiful dress," he said. "It really becomes you. I feel a bit under-dressed. I didn't expect you to look this elegant, but then again I always feel a little intimidated when I see you." Gabriela smiled. Here he comes, she thought, his words where quietly satisfying to her being.

"I wanted to look nice," she responded. Then catching herself, said, "Oh, I mean, it was just what I had in the closet. Everything else was at the cleaner's!"

"Is that the truth?"

"No, but you're not supposed to catch my little lies so quickly," she answered. "I wanted to look special. But I think I overdid it a bit. Forgive me." Gabriela looked directly into Mark's eyes.

"You look stunning," he replied, "don't concern yourself. In fact, I cannot imagine you not looking..."

Mark, hoping he hadn't gone too far with his words, made a slight theatrical cough. "The food is standard here: brown rice, seaweed, lentils, and a cooked vegetable."

"It's fine." She smiled. "But maybe we can go someplace quieter after... maybe a coffee or a drink somewhere."

"Yes, that would be nice." They both ate slowly with their chopsticks and drank green tea, saying little. Occasionally, they paused, their eyes meeting in acknowledgement. The uneasiness faded. They made some small talk about the war and the demonstrations on campus.

"I could hardly get in and out of the place!" he explained. "It is really crazy up there now." Within their conversation, there were pauses; pauses that communicated the story their eyes were telling.

Gabriela was feeling at home, comfortable; more and more infatuated as the time passed. Those eyes of his... God, they're engaging. I'm still not sure what I'm doing here, but my he is beautiful... Oh Gabriela! You know exactly what you are doing here!

After lunch, they intended to go for coffee and dessert but just walked instead. They walked all the way to the river and then continued walking and talking for hours. Time disappeared. Without noticing where they were going, they passed people on the street and strolled within their own world. They talked of poetry, from Byron to Ferlinghetti, of politics and literature, of music, from Bob Dylan to jazz. The words came so easily, never pretentious or forced, and always seasoned with marvelous wit and disarming charm. When they passed some shabbily dressed children in the playground, they were reminded of some of Grimm's fairy tales, and they made jokes about how dark some of the stories were.

Gabriela asked to sit on a bench for a few minutes to watch them play. "My feet are killing me," she said, as she began removing a shoe. "These are new shoes, and I did not plan on doing so much walking in them."

"They go well with your dress," responded Mark, not knowing what to do with this unexpected moment.

"Yes, and I think my foot doctor is going to love me for them. You know he told me that some women are getting foot operations so that they can squeeze into these new, sexy pumps. While I admit my slavery to fashion, that goes beyond my limits."

Mark was always a little perplexed about things like fashion, and its use in flirtation and seduction, so he felt best to try and make a joke.

"You know, I once read an earlier version of Cinderella. The story goes all the way back to the Tang Dynasty in China. In one version, each stepsister cuts off a piece of her foot in order to fit into the glass slipper, but two pigeons alert the prince of the con, and the stepsisters end up spending their lives as lame beggars while Cinderella lives out hers in luxury with the prince."

"Oh, lovely," responded Gabriela. "Well, I was just thinking of slipping them off for a few minutes." She gave him a look. "You know, Mark, you are very charming, but sometimes you talk like you're floating in your own atmosphere."

Mark realized he had made a mistake; his naiveté had shown its face. He had tripped over his infatuation, stumbling like a schoolboy, but he could not make sense all of his feelings. Humans remained a mystery. He felt like he was rushing down rapids, holding onto a flimsy raft for dear life. He searched for a rope to grab not to be washed overboard, but all he saw at the end of the river was a sea full of doubts.

Gabriela sensed his unease; she took his hand and smiled. Mark did his best to move the conversation forward; her touch relaxed him. They both loved jazz and agreed to a preference for Stan Getz over Miles Davis, while admittedly loving them both.

"There is nothing like that man's haunting sound," he said, referring to Getz. Gabriela looked at him captivated. She knew she was taken and nothing could shake it.

The sun was starting to set, and the streets grew dim. Amber and orange reflections appeared in the puddles on the concrete as the neon from the shops started to flicker. Mark felt he was almost stuttering trying to express his feelings to a woman for the first time in his life, yet despite it all, Gabriela did not pay much attention to his uncomfortable miscues, thinking it must have to do with their age difference. As the night went on, they both felt their uncertainties fade.

Mark, with a snap back to reality, abruptly said, "I have to go now." He was aware that Jason's time was approaching.

Gabriela sadly recognized that she, too, was due home. "I'll just grab a cab here, if it's okay with you." She put up her arm as the taxi stopped and opened the door to the cab. Mark grabbed her hand and would not release it. With a reflex of which even she was not aware, she leaned over and kissed him gently on the lips.

"I had a really nice time, Mark."

He responded, "So did I. I've never met anyone quite like you. I hope I don't sound sophomoric in saying this."

She shook her head, smiling in disagreement. "You don't sound sophomoric at all," she said and got into the cab.

Although his mind was plagued with concern for Jason, Mark watched as the cab slowly accelerated. The beauty of her eyes would not leave him.

After the cab turned the corner, he directed his attention to Jason. I am only a ten-minute walk from the apartment. I will not have kept him waiting long. There was not an exact time of transition; they had both developed a flexible attitude about it.

As Mark entered the apartment, he felt the portal was in an unusually excited state. Is it because I'm late? He quickly undressed and prepared to enter. He lay on the bed awaiting his moment and the usual glimpse of Jason as they passed one another. The portal grew more and more agitated as it always had, but there was a change in color that he had not experienced before. As Jason came into view, something different happened. He seemed to pause and hover, not to fly by as he always did. He glared intensely at him. He sensed anger and displeasure. Something was wrong.

They both paused for a moment as they drifted past each other. Jason's voice startled him. "No, she's a mistake!"

Mark was absorbed into the portal.

CHAPTER 12
IT'S ABOUT TIME I DID

Did I really just kiss him? Gabriela's cab left the curb. She stared out the window; cars were rushing past in the street. She took a deep breath.

It was a usual busy weekday on Second Avenue, and the chaos in the street forced the taxi to move slowly among the delivery trucks and bicycles. The frenetic activity was unsettling; Gabriela tried to understand what had just happened. She searched her bag for her lipstick. What am I doing? Am I crazy, going completely mad? I cannot dream of this wild thing. She looked at her face in her makeup mirror. You are going to do something, something you may regret. I know what can happen when I get this way. I feel like a schoolgirl around him. How is it he seems to sense me in a way no one ever has? I cannot believe I am thinking about his body next to mine, but he is hardly an adult, and he's my husband's assistant to boot... Gabriela, you have to stop thinking like this... but I want him. Her mind wandered to what awaited her at home.

The cab screeched, almost hitting a girl on a bike.

"Hey!" Gabriela yelled. "Let's get there in one piece!"

The cabby cursed out the window at the cyclist in Spanish, "Puñeta!" as he veered to miss her. She turned her head, giving the cabby the finger, and kept going. Gabriela stared at the taxi I.D. card framed in front of her, wanting to remember his name just in case.

Her thoughts came back to Mark. Is this happening because I've been living under a rock in my marriage for so long? But why this one, is he that special? Control yourself, Gabriela!

But I don't want to! And yes, he is that special. You know are going to do this, but you are going to need a plan. I will have to be so careful that George doesn't suspect anything. He's his student, for God's sake.

Oh shit! George! What time is it? I really do not want to have to explain that I spent the whole afternoon, into the evening, with Mark! If he is home before me, I'll say I went to the library for research. No, that won't work! I'll say I went to the Metropolitan to see the Goya show. I told him I wanted to see it, and he never seems to have time to go with me. That's good. He will feel guilty and won't ask any questions.

The cab pulled up to her door, and she rushed in. Great, he's not home yet. I'll quickly change and look like I've been at home most of the day like I usually am. That will do fine.

A half hour went by when the phone rang. "Hi, darling. It's me!"

"Hi, George," she replied. "Where are you?"

"I'm still at the college," he answered. "The conversation became too engrossing to stop."

"Oh..." she responded, holding back her yawn.

"Say, can I bring some of the fellows back to the house for a bite so we can keep going with this? I am really so excited about what we are on to!" he explained.

"Oh no, please George, not tonight. I'm really tired. Why don't you all just go out for a beer or something?"

Disappointed, George replied, "Oh, okay. If you're really tired... What did you do all day? Did you meet Mark for lunch?"

"Yes, we had a quick one," she answered. "But that doesn't get you off the hook for standing me up! I went to the Met without you to see the Goya show."

"Oh," he answered, "I'm sorry. I forgot you wanted to go. I'll have to make it up to you."

"Yes, you will!" she snapped. "Anyway, the show is huge, so there is a lot to see. We can go again."

"Great," he replied. "Okay then, I'll see you later tonight. Don't wait up."

"I won't," she answered.

Gabriela hung up and was overwhelmed with guilt. When did I become such a good liar? But I need something more! Maybe this is just a passing fancy. Maybe this will end up being a quick fling like that French guy on the beach when I visited my mother three years ago... But I feel differently about him. This is not just a nice body and a handsome face. My marriage has become a habit, two people going through the motions of life without really having one. But is he the answer?

George is always talking to me about him, how he is expecting great things if he chooses to focus on science. He was almost boastful when he told me he was the first student ever to have a doctoral thesis fully accepted while being a preliminary submission, describing how the entire panel was in awe. Only after these reveries did I start did finding his eyes in the halls. It was then I started noticing how he drew a crowd, talking on such a vast array of subjects. In a minute, one was aware of his mind, but he never acted superior or arrogant. He has that intangible thing which charms, disarms and impresses at once, but there is always something hidden, reclusive.

I don't know where this will go, but I know there is no stopping it now. I want him. The question is, will he be bold enough to make the next move? There is nothing wrong with giving him an excuse. She took out a piece of paper and began a note:

"Dear Mark..."

CHAPTER 13

BLOOD AND GUTS

Opening his eyes, Jason bolted from his bed. What is Mark doing? He has strayed far from our childhood mischief. Jason paced the room. This is serious. The Council will get very upset. Why is he seeking human emotion for his own experience? What does he mean he wants human love? We were sent to observe, not live as they do. Can he not see the danger of these pursuits? I must find a way to stop him, stop him before he can no longer stop himself.

The psychiatrist! I was upset that he spoke to that man, but maybe he is the answer. Maybe he can help Mark understand the ramifications of his actions. Has Mark forgotten that the Council is always watching us? I will have to talk to this doctor. He does not yet fully see who we are, but I must risk it. I can always wipe his memory clean. One man's involvement can be explained away, but this mess with Gabriela is entirely something else.

Jason was determined to go the psychiatrist's home that evening, once his family had fallen asleep. It's too short notice to see him in the office, but if his family has gone to bed, I can keep it quiet and no one will be frightened. I will make him understand the importance of all of this. Our very survival is at stake, not to mention that of this world. Jason was torn between anger with his brother and concern for their larger mission. I am sure the Council will have some other plan to save this planet, but that alternative might not be as benign as the one which is hidden within us. The consequences for Earth's species could be dire.

It was much too early to go to Abernathy's house, so Jason headed to the Dom. The Velvet Underground was playing that night. There was a rumor that they had this new song called "Sunday Morning,"

When Jason arrived at the club, he saw Helena sitting at a table in the corner with her girlfriend Julie, who was also trying to make it as a singer with her own group. Jason sat down next to Helena to avoid any jealousy. He knew that Helena was in love with him, but he was aware that Julie had eyes for him as well.

"Hi, Jason!" they chorused together.

He grinned. "I guess this will be the only time I will ever hear you two try to harmonize." They both smiled and looked a little self-conscious.

"I heard your set last night," said Julie. "You were great."

"Did you hear that, Helena?

"Yeah, that's so cool!" said Helena. The Velvet Underground was already on stage.

Julie passed the cocaine over. "Want some?" she looked at Jason.

"No, I'll wait until later."

"OK, darling, more for me!" she said, inhaling the last line.

The music flowed down the stage like a rolling wave. As Nico's raspy voice reached Helena's ears, her expression changed.

"I love Nico," said Helena. "She is so beautiful... But I hate her for having such a voice!"

"Now, now, you don't mean that."

"But I do, I hate myself for it... But I do."

Nico was opening the performance with "Femme Fatale." Her sultry, low voice echoed through the auditorium and melted the audience.

"Do you see what I mean?" cried Helena. "She is so great! Too great."

Jason smiled. "There is room in this world for you both." He looked up and saw a familiar face bringing drinks and motioned for his usual, brandy and coke.

The waitress flashed a grand smile. "Hi, Jason." It was Angela, the mob boss's girlfriend.

"Hi, it's Angela, isn't it?"

"Yes." She smiled energetically.

"What are you doing here?"

"Well," she said with a large grin, eyes beaming, "After that night upstairs, my whole life changed! Rachel and I got to be great friends, and when Silvia left for the coast... well, I moved in. She helped me get a job here, and the rest is history. Jason, I am so happy. I can't thank you enough for introducing us. I am still not really sure what happened that night, or how it happened, but it happened, and I'm so grateful!"

Jason just smiled.

"Listen, Jason, this Lucasie guy is a very dangerous. I hear he is looking for you. Please be careful."

Music was playing in the background, and Helena moaned. "Do you hear that voice?"

Nico sang, and as they listened to her words fill every space in the auditorium, Helena growled, "There she goes again... but really, there she goes! Listen! How can I ever match that?"

"Relax, already," said Jason. "You are great, and whatever she does will not change that."

Helena buried her face in her hands and shook her head back and forth. "I will never sing like that..."

Angela interrupted, "Listen, Jason, I am really, really worried. He is going to come after you. He always carries a gun! Please, be careful."

Jason smiled. "I will. Thanks for the warning."

Of course, Jason knew that nothing a human could do could harm him. One could drop an atomic bomb on his head, and he would not flinch. He could vaporize an army with a single gesture. What could one mafia thug do to him? Still, he acted concerned for appearance's sake, showing gratitude in his tone.

Nico ended her song and spoke into the mic, "And now, people, Lou Reed!"

Lou started to sing his new song, "Sunday Morning." The audience stood still as the chimes sounded, and Lou's voice emerged.

The room was mesmerized by the poetry in his music, the hypnotic growl of both Lou's and Nico's voices. Who could not identify with the feeling waking up on a Sunday morning in a stupor and haze following an evening of passion and debauchery?

When the song ended, Jason turned to Helena, "So you think you're the only one with competition? He is so great... She is so talented. I love them. We are going to work hard to get the group as tight as they are, but it only comes with work." Jason knew he could carry the band, but he wanted them to improve. He knew they could be better, great in fact.

As Helena nodded in agreement, Jason thought, what beauty and vileness these humans are capable of! His mind wandered. One moment you experience such satisfaction in their company, and the next you feel nothing but contempt for their very being! He considered not only how they treated each other, but also how they treated other living organisms on their planet. They exploit and slaughter without remorse.

Mark is such a sentimentalist concerning these beings, not really seeing their baseness and barbarism. Jason recalled how angry Mark was about that night in China when he had killed several businessmen. He had been enraged after watching them slicing off the skulls of apes and eating their brains while the creatures were still alive. A whole family of apes... and all while their mother watched her children being brutalized before her eyes. These humans had been laughing and drinking wine as they performed the barbaric act. Even the memory angered Jason when he thought of the evolutionary distance between the apes and the humans and the relative distance between humans and himself. The apes were just half a step behind humans, yet these humans felt no empathy for the apes.

Mark was very upset with me for that, but to this day I feel no remorse... He started listening to the music again. But then there are moments like this one. Sometimes with these beings, they lift you to an almost glorious state.

After the music ended, Jason and Helena partied for a few hours with the rest of the band.

Finally, Jason tore himself away. "Well guys, I have to go. Places to go... People to see... as they say."

"Jason, Jason... It's early! We always party till dawn!" implored Helena with a mischievous smile on her face.

"Not tonight, I really have to go, Helena. I would love to hang... Tomorrow, for sure, we'll party all night."

"Oh please, please stay, Jason! I will be so sad if you leave." Although it was futile, Helena would never give up the dream of having Jason. But the more she threw herself at him, the more Jason withdrew. He just smiled, waved and left the room.

Walking down the stairs and out into the street he searched for a dark alley that could conceal him enough to transport himself to Westchester County, into the living room of the psychiatrist. All of a sudden, he heard his name called out from the shadows.

"Jason, so I finally getcha alone!" It was Lucasie.

Holding a .38 revolver in his hand, he said, "So you thought it would all end that night, you fucking little punk. No one fucks with me; you little shit! The only reason I ain't got three of my boys rippin' you to pieces with pliers and saws right now is that I don't want anyone to know what happened up in that room! But you're gonna die, you scumbag, and I'm gonna love watching you die slow!"

Jason turned to face Lucasie. "You fool. You should have left well enough alone. You disgust me. You're not worthy of the air you breathe. I don't have time to give you all the suffering you deserve, so I will just have to end you with the same contempt in which I hold you."

Slapping away Lucasie's gun with his right hand, he grabbed him by the neck, pinning his body to the wall with his left. The .38 flew across the ally. "You bastard!" Lucasie snarled, reaching for his switchblade. Jason laughed, snatching away the knife and crushing Lucasie's hand as if he were crumpling paper.

He lifted Lucasie off the ground by his throat, tore open his shirt, and with the knife made an almost imperceptible incision along his exposed mid-section.

Lucasie felt a gentle warmth arise within his neck. The heat, almost soothing at first, grew more intense as it traveled down. His eyes started to burn, his throat grew dry, he tasted blood. Jason lifted Lucasie further off the ground, smiling as he watched his legs frantically dancing as if he were an electrified puppet. Lucasie looked down at his stomach as the pain intensified. His organs started to boil. The wound in his abdomen tore open.

"Oh Jesus, Mary, and Joseph!" he cried, watching his intestines drop to the ground amidst the bodily waste.

Jason looked down at Lucasie's body. He noticed that there was a large commercial dumpster in the back of the ally. That will do, he emptied out an oversized plastic garbage bag and then stuffed the body into it, leaving the bowels for the rats. He said, "A fitting end for you, you piece of crap." And he closed the lid to the dumpster.

Jason walked to the corner and waved a cab, he still had to visit Abernathy tonight, but he knew that he had better stop to change his clothing first.

CHAPTER 14

A CALL IN THE NIGHT

J ason surveyed the room. Eclectic and stuffy, he thought. Why would Mark trust the person who lives here? He observed a large library of academic books, a chessboard sitting on a solitary table next to a standing African sculpture, and a stuffed deer head with large antlers on the wall behind. Maybe Mark has some respect for this man's desire to gain knowledge, but surely not for his taste.

He spotted an old Magnavox console stereo near the desk. A large collection of LP records was neatly shelved just behind it. Jason pulled out an album of Beethoven's 5th. This should do just fine, he chuckled to himself, after all, he seems to be living in the past. Well, time for us to meet, doctor. He sent the album spinning, placed his wife and children into a deep sleep, and sat down behind the desk to wait.

A light spilled down into the hall from an upstairs bedroom. Jason lowered the music as the figure of a man tying his robe emerged. Moving tentatively, the figure descended the stairs. A fearful tone rang out, "Who are you? What are you doing here?"

Jason looked up. "I think you know. Mark told you I would come on my own terms."

The doctor stood transfixed, and in an angry voice, asked, "Are you Jason?"

A boyish smile appeared as he nodded, yes.

"Look, Jason... This is highly inappropriate. I do not see clients in my home, or at this hour... No, this is impossible. You must leave immediately!" proclaimed Abernathy.

Jason grinned. "I see you like to read Greek mythology. Are you a fan of the residents of Olympus? I am very fond of Zeus, myself. He really had his hands full with his children running around doing wild and crazy things. A kind of god running around doing crazy things is the topic we need to talk about..."

Abernathy, shaking with agitation, dismissively said, "Look, if you need to talk to me, please make an appointment at my office, and we can discuss whatever topic you would like."

"Oh, an appointment...?" Jason smiled. "Your book is just there in your desk, is it not?"

Abernathy nodded, bewildered. Jason walked slowly to the desk, and with a relaxed motion, waved his hand to unlock the drawer. He pulled forth the appointment book and, holding it in his hand, turned the pages to the following days' appointments. "I see you are all booked up tomorrow, so we had better talk now." he smiled.

Gasping and trying to catch his breath, Abernathy spoke, "Who... what... are you?"

"Dr. Abernathy, please take a seat. I'm sure our conversation will help explain some things to you about Mark and me." Abernathy, still hardly capable of responding, stepped backward toward a chair at the farthest side of the room. He looked at the telephone, thinking of calling for help. His thoughts ran to his wife and children upstairs; his mouth grew dry.

"Doctor, please do not be afraid. If I wanted to harm you, you would be long gone. Relax, I am not here to hurt you or any of your loved ones. Your family is sleeping peacefully... perhaps a bit more deeply than usual, but they will awake fine and refreshed in the morning."

Jason spoke softly in an attempt to put the doctor at ease, "We have things I need to discuss. Get comfortable, for what

I am about to tell you will sound fantastical: I am from a faraway place thousands of light years away. And, although I grew up on this planet, I am not human. Neither is Mark."

Dr. Abernathy clutched the arm of the overstuffed chair. Trembling he said, "You're not human… and neither is Mark. What do you mean you're not human…? What do you want from me?"

"It's a very long story. In short, Mark and I have been sent here to avert an impending calamity for your planet. All has not yet been revealed to us; all we know is that if we do not succeed, life on this planet will end."

Abernathy sat back, his heart racing. He tried to catch his breath.

Jason noticed Abernathy had not blinked once.

"I fear that Mark's recent activity may be putting our mission to save your world in jeopardy."

Abernathy was doing his best to comprehend what was happening. "Our planet is going to be destroyed?" He had barely listened after those words.

"Please, Doctor… I know this is difficult to hear but try to gain control of yourself. No one is in any immediate danger. The calamity is years in the future, and although I am not clear of the details, I know we are here to save you, and rest assured, we will. Earth and its inhabitants are very dear to my civilization."

Abernathy was now on the verge of hyperventilating. He was trying to regain his composure. "You said something about Mark. Mark is like you? He is also from another world? Where is it? I knew there was something strange… but this? Who could have imagined this? You want something from me?"

"Are you asking where we came from? That information is really not important now. But yes, that is why I am here, to save your world." He paused. "I can see that this is a bit much for you to take in all at once… shall I come back another time?"

"No, no!" implored Abernathy hoping that this nightmare wouldn't have to be repeated. "Please, continue!" he said anxiously.

"As I was saying, Mark and I are not native to your world. However, we did grow up here, having been created to absorb and understand as much about humanity as possible. My civilization wishes to understand and protect you. We were sent here, well let's say as kind of explorers, to gain an understanding of humans, but we were not sent here to acquire any degree of humanity ourselves. However, Mark seems to be attempting to break down this divide. He has become enamored with humanity. He wants to feel as you do, to experience as you do, and he does not have permission to do this. He will anger The Council, our teacher, and there could be... well, there will be problems."

"The Council... Who is the Council?"

"Doctor... You do not need to understand that." Jason looked at Abernathy sternly. "You will have to take my word as to the importance of what I am saying. I just need you to accept what I am telling you. Do you want more examples of my power to convince you I am telling you the truth?"

"No, no, please! No more examples," Abernathy responded. "But what do you want of me?"

"Mark is attempting to experience human love. I fear that this will complicate our mission. This is not a part of our directive. We must stop him."

"You are saying Mark wants to become human in some fashion? Change who he is? These questions are well beyond my purview. I am a human psychiatrist; how can I understand his motivations? Jason, you think too much of me. I do not have the power to divert a person's feelings, much less control a being from another world. At best, I could only advise him as to the possible consequences of his actions. I, I..." Abernathy tried to find his words.

"I don't know what you are expecting of me. You come into my life with this insane story, and now you ask me to solve this wild problem…"

Jason responded, "I know I am moving very quickly, but I do think you can help, and there is really no time to waste. It's imperative that we solve this quickly. Mark's actions could be disastrous and have far-reaching consequences."

"Okay, but this is all too absurd for me. Just let me catch my breath here; I really don't understand what I can do."

"You can make him see the nature of the risk he is taking, the consequences!"

Abernathy looked baffled. "So you think I have that much influence on him? Well I guess I should be flattered, but I doubt you are correct."

"He came to you for a reason. He wants something from you. He has never asked for help before, so yes, yes I think you do."

Abernathy thought for a moment. "Okay… I am doing my best to understand. But, before I jump to conclusions, we are dealing with multiple characters, possibly multiple motivations. Have you considered that there may be an ulterior motive at play? I must ask if you have thought about the possibility that this is the actual plan of your people. Have you considered that they might want Mark to have these experiences? Perhaps there is a plan that you are not aware of…"

Jason stepped back. Surprised by these words, he started to walk about the room. He could not believe that he had not given thought to this notion. Maybe this was all part of a larger plan that he did not understand. Jason looked at the doctor, considering his suggestions… Could this be possible?

"I see now why Mark chose you. You bring a fresh perspective. Yes, that may be a possibility."

"Well," replied Abernathy, "from what you are telling me, that would be my first question. It must at least be considered."

"Yes, it must," replied Jason. He appeared to Abernathy to be pondering for a moment. "Still, on the side of caution, please advise Mark to go slowly and to think about the ramifications of his actions. I will talk with you again about this as we try to learn more."

"Going slowly when it comes to love is always prudent," replied Abernathy, and then he mused, "Love is strange, not to mention, so is meeting an alien in the middle of the night." Abernathy's words had a hint of annoyance; he was surprised at his boldness, catching himself in mid-breath, wishing he had not said these words. He couldn't decide if he was more comfortable at this point or simply exhausted.

Jason smiled, reassuring Abernathy all was well; he turned towards the wall, looking back to say, "Thank you, Doctor. I appreciate the time you took to listen. There is much to be considered... Please do not speak of me, or of Mark, to anyone. Our existence here must remain a secret. The consequences would be grave beyond your imagination." Jason spoke with a stern tone. He then opened his hand to reveal a perfect blue diamond the size of a walnut, cut beautifully. He smiled. "I saw one like this, much smaller of course, in the window of Tiffany's. I hope you will accept it as a token of my good faith."

Abernathy replied in a fearful voice, "Yes, yes, of course. Don't worry; our conversations will be kept in the strictest confidence!" He looked at his hand in amazement. "But this thing you are giving to me, is it real? Are you joking? It would be priceless if it were..."

"Yes, of course it is real! I am hoping to motivate you, Doctor. As I have said, your discretion is of vital importance. I can be a very good friend."

"Yes, yes, absolute confidentiality." These words tumbled from the doctor's lips. "But this gift is not necessary." He thought, who would ever believe me anyway?

Reading Abernathy's last thoughts, Jason grinned. "Many of the things you value are but little importance to me. But what I do value is your confidence, and please excuse my showmanship of this gift, I just wanted you to believe I am sincere." He abruptly turned. "I am sorry doctor, but I have to leave now. Mark will be waiting for me. Maybe you should not show that diamond to anyone just yet."

The doctor heard the record skipping on his stereo, Beethoven's 5th had ended some time ago, but he had not been aware of it till now. Jason was no longer in the room. He examined the diamond; its existence a confirmation of what he had just experienced. This all really happened. I am not going crazy. He sat until the morning light broke his stupor. He kept going over Jason's words, "our existence here must remain a secret…"

CHAPTER 15

THE NOTE

When Mark awoke, he sensed that Jason had been very active. He was not allowing him to see what he had been doing. This lack of communication was unlike him. No matter what licentious activities he had been up to, Jason always shared them, usually boastfully, sometimes with contempt.

Well, he must have his reasons... He seemed almost frantic when we passed each other in the portal. He sees that I am getting more involved, in fact, swept away. But why is my relationship upsetting him? Is he jealous? I wonder! Could he feel she threatens our bond? Mark knew that Jason's words, "No, she's a mistake," could only be referring to Gabriela.

It must be that these humans are affecting him more than he knows. He has already allowed himself to be driven by anger and contempt. Should I remind him of the day he killed those Chinese businessmen in Hong Kong? Did he understand what drove him? Did he feel the slightest remorse for the slaughter? No, this is jealousy, and if I'm right, jealousy can be a lot more dangerous than love.

Mark left the apartment, obsessing over these thoughts as he walked up to St. Marks Place. At the corner, he took the subway to Columbia.

Reaching the campus, he entered the science building, his mind racing ahead. I must first check to see if the undergraduate interns have set up the laboratory for the day's experiments. Then I have a class on Chaucer to teach, and later I must work on my thesis. He stopped by his mailbox to see if Professor Bolinsky had left him any additional instructions about the day's work.

He found a small pink envelope. Inside, the letter read:

Dear Mark,

I think I left my sunglasses at the restaurant. I know you live close to it. Could you go by and check for me? I would really appreciate it.

Gabriela, Mark thought. She wanted to be sure I would call... She's leaving nothing to chance.

The note ended simply:

Thanks, looking forward to hearing from you!

Gabriela

Mark knew no one was looking on as he read the note, but he found himself glancing about the hall reflexively as he chuckled reading these words. He had to call upon all his willpower not to look inside Gabriela's mind, as he had promised himself not to use any form of power in relation to her, but the letter was overt, humorous in its obviousness. Yet he felt elated by the thought of her feelings. She wants me. What should my next step be? How do I move this along?

Mark had often thought about the possibility of a real relationship, even love, and yes, sex too.

Sex, is that conceivable? What would happen if we did that? Mark had delved into the subject on a theoretical basis, but he had reached no concrete conclusions on the matter. He had read a great deal about sex. He had even secretly observed the act without humans being aware of his voyeurism, but despite all of this, Mark remained timidly naïve. He was intrigued by the thought. What would it be like?

As he walked down the hall towards the lab, he could hear the demonstrations ringing through the courtyard. The quiet, academic atmosphere of the halls had been turned into a circus of screams and chants. Mark just quietly walked, undisturbed, thinking only of Gabriela.

He explored the possibilities with the same approach he would take to his mathematical equations. With playful excitement, he even imagined some enhancements that involved changing his temperature at appropriate moments and adjusting his size during the act. He had even discovered that he had the ability to create subtle vibrations and independent circular movements within his penis. He had formulated this idea after reading of Japanese vibrators that had become very popular in Kyoto. What he could not calculate was the intensity of his emotions, and how this would affect the situation. Emotion was something he could not reference, something he could not quantify. The thought of her in his arms filled him, but he feared losing control.

Mark knew that the note about the sunglasses was a ruse. Well, they were just Ray-Ban's. I'll pick up a pair and call her. I'm glad I vowed not to read her thoughts. This is fun. I'll swing by the drug store on Second Avenue.

With the new sunglasses in hand, and assured of a rendezvous, he found a pay phone on the corner and dialed.

"Hello?"

When he heard her voice, his anxieties fell away.

"Hello, Gabriela, it's Mark."

"Oh, hi Mark! I was hoping you would call soon! Did you find those sunglasses?" She thought, what a nice voice he has.

"I feel the same," answered Mark, impetuously. He could hear her catch her breath on the other end of the line, and, realizing he had unconsciously responded to reading her thoughts, he hesitated. "I mean, yes. I have them."

Gabriela, not understanding what he had meant, smiled to herself as she gazed at her sunglasses on the table, charmed that he would go to such lengths to continue her ruse. "Well, do you want to meet?"

"Yes, of course. We could meet today if you'd like. I would love to see you again," he responded.

Without a thought, Gabriela asked, "Shall I come by your place?"

Mark was taken aback. He had not expected this; no one ever came to his apartment, and even though he'd spent his day thinking over the scenarios resulting from time alone with her, he knew that it could never be at his apartment.

Thinking quickly, he suggested, "How about we meet in the middle? What do you think about the Algonquin Hotel on 59th Street? We can make our own little 'vicious circle,' and you can play Dorothy Parker."

Gabriela paused and felt a little rejected. She knew that she had been aggressive, but then, he did say the word "hotel." Still, she worried that she might have frightened him with her directness. I'll take it slow. "Well I really don't feel very vicious when I'm around you. How about the Palm Court at the Plaza? I'm feeling decadent today. We can do afternoon tea. What do you say? You know my publisher just gave me a perk of unlimited limousine service for a month, so I can run around and promote my book. I would love to pull up to The Plaza in a limo. I would feel so 'Gatsby!'"

"Okay then, The Plaza, let's say at 4. I'll do my best to look respectable," said Mark.

"Okay, see you then."

Mark did not have a jacket or tie, so he stopped into a second-hand store on East 6th Street and picked up a corduroy sport coat from the rack. The sales girl picked out his tie. He looked in the mirror. The sales girl smiled. He knew it was acceptable. He looked like a typical student on a budget.

Mark arrived early and was impressed with the grandeur of the lobby. A doorman directed him to the Palm Court. As he entered the main hall and viewed the court, he thought, this room could be in a Tolstoy novel.

He walked to the entrance of the dining area, and a tailored man in a uniform addressed him. "Do you have a reservation, sir?" He sensed condescension in his voice.

"Well," responded Mark, "I'm not sure. It would be under Gabriela Bolinsky, or maybe Gabriela Velázquez, if there is one."

"Oh," he answered. "You're Gabriela's guest... Right this way, sir."

Just then, he heard Gabriela behind him.

"André... André, not a table in the center of the room! Let's be someplace a little more private."

"Whatever you prefer, Madame," the maître d' responded politely, and led them to a table near the rear of the room.

"Very nice, André," said Gabriela, as she slipped a few dollars into his hand.

"Now, don't concern yourself with the prices, Mark. This is my treat. I just got a fat royalty check from my book, and I feel very grand. Oh, let me tell you how wonderful it was to pull up to the entrance in that limo... what a gas! Wait till you see it. It is so big in there you could have a dinner party... I am definitely taking you home in it."

Mark smiled. Gabriela's giddiness was charming.

"I'm so high on the excitement over my book. I just left the publisher's office; he had a critic from the Times there. Everyone thinks it is going to be huge. So please don't think I'm silly. The publisher is making such a push... Can you believe that so many people could get excited about a biography of Baudelaire?"

"Yes, I could. Especially yours."

Gabriela was wearing a blue chiffon dress; her long, dark hair pulled to one side by an emerald clip. Shiny high heel shoes and dark stockings finished the look. On some women, her outfit might have appeared overdone, but on Gabriela, it was perfect. Mark was entranced by her sophistication. Gabriela's elegance was but a complement to her mind. Even in her most giddy moments, her words could have the wit of Simone de Beauvoir and the music of Maupassant. She was enchanting.

Mark spoke up, "You look absolutely stunning, but that takes little effort for you, I'm sure; you would be ravishing in a potato sack."

"Please, Mark. This took a lot of trouble. Please appreciate that," she retorted.

"I do, I do! I just mean to say…"

"I know," she responded. "Forgive my playfulness… You have a strange effect on me, Mark, you know. So, let's order, before I get sillier than I already feel. What would you like? I'm having the deviled quail eggs and a smoked salmon sandwich. You're a vegetarian, right? The cucumber sandwiches are fabulous here! If you trust me, we should end with the lemon tea cakes; they are to die for!"

"It all sounds good to me! I'll defer to your judgment. Oh, here are your sunglasses," he said handing them to her.

"Thank you, darling. It was sweet of you not to forget them." She noticed that they were brand new. "And we should have some good Earl Grey to wash it all down," she continued without taking a breath. Motioning to the waiter, she gave an order for the refreshments.

"What do you think of this place? I am absolutely in love with it. I feel like I am still in Europe when I come here, the Europe of fifty years ago when words were cherished and romance thrived."

"And the great flu pandemic consumed the earth," replied Mark.

"Oh Mark, there is that dark side again." She smiled, "Please, we should be grand and beautiful today. I feel… well, this friendship of ours could be an adventure. I hope I'm not wrong."

Breaking his promise to himself, he entered her mind. Reading past her pander, he felt the sincerity as he explored her emotions. This could be good, very, very good. "I've always been the cautious type, but you've made me want to change that, Gabriela."

Two hours had passed, but between the wit and the accidental touching of fingers, it seemed to them they'd only just sat down. They ate slowly, relishing the meal. Finishing with tea and lemon cakes, it was a delightful afternoon by anyone's standards.

"Mark, you've made me feel alive again these past few days, like I've been living in a French poem." She paused. "I am not sure what or why, but I feel it's right."

"I know. I don't understand all of this, or what I am doing, but, I feel it's right too."

"You know, I am half French," she lowered her voice to a whisper, "affairs come naturally to us."

"Oh." He laughed, feeling uneasy. "Well, I am also from a foreign place where we don't really take earthly rules too seriously, but I am very serious about how I feel about you." He looked into her eyes; they hid nothing. "It is very complicated; I mean... I am not clear about any of this except what I feel about you." She returned the gaze and grinned, unclear of what he was talking about. She was on the verge of asking where exactly that place was when she thought, who cares where he is from? "Let's leave together," she suggested, secretly wishing she could just order a room at the desk but realizing such an idea was running ahead. She switched her tone to a neutral cadence and did her best not to act like a cat ready to pounce.

"I am afraid I am going to have to be back uptown in an hour... Let me take you home in the limousine. You will love it..."

As they got up, Gabriela took hold of Mark's arm, he didn't resist, they started to walk, she leaned into him. "Mark, I feel like I am in a dream being here with you. Isn't this place so grand." She grasped his arm tighter as they walked. "I am really, really, happy."

"Me too. I have never felt like this. I am trying to keep control, yet I don't know why..."

She responded, "Then why try? Wait till you see my limo! You are going to die!"

They walked to the curb and signaled the waiting limousine. Gabriela got in first as Mark held the door. He entered and gave the driver his address. Gabriella leaned forward. "Please raise the window; we need to have a private conversation."

She drew the inside curtains. Mark took note that the darkened windows and the isolation of the driver had given them absolute privacy. He knew he could render them both invisible to prying eyes if he chose, but he did not feel the need.

They sat back in the roomy seat, and Gabriela opened the mini-bar. She pulled out a serving size of Bourbon.

"One of the great gifts of America!" she said. "If the French only knew how good this stuff is, they would seldom drink Cognac."

"I've never had any," he answered.

"You don't indulge much, do you? Do you have any vices? I know your virtues." She smiled, pulling the last curtain closed. The limo was quiet; the streets disappeared. She put a cassette in the stereo. "Do you like Billie Holiday? I love her." The Bourbon turned her insides warm. "How about me? Can I become your weakness?"

"I think you already are, Gabriela," he said softly, leaning closer.

"I hope so. I am not one to let go of what I start."

He wanted to touch her lips. He moved towards her but hesitated. She did not. She moved her lips to his. At that second, Mark thought of all the hours of anticipation he had in his life waiting for this touch, all the analyzing and calculating, and now it was here.

Gabriela pulled him towards her.

"Kiss me. I won't bite, well not much anyway." Her lips revealed a mischievous smile.

Mark's kissed her. He pulled her close, and then without even being conscious of the fact, his hand reached under her dress, touching the silk beneath. His fingers reached up her back and unhooked her bra, touching a woman's flesh for the first time. He explored the softness of her skin, the mystery of her breasts, and thought, am I really doing this?

Gabriela unbuttoned his pants and reached inside to find him. She smiled, "Don't be nervous; no one can see us." Quickly, she felt him swell in her hand. "Oh, what is this...?"

Her head searched down into his lap and she took him into her mouth.

Mark fell back into the seat; he had never felt the tenderness of lips, the warm moist touch of a woman's tongue. His mind went blank.

"So, my mysterious foreign student, what do you think? Are we going to have something together? Are we going to be lovers?" she whispered.

"Yes, I think there is no choice now," he replied. But then his unease returned and his body suddenly stiffened. "Are you sure we should do this here?"

She sensed his shyness. "I have so much more to give you, Mark. I have no doubts about you. But I agree; not here. Not now. I am going to make you wait a bit for more."

Her confidence brought him calmness. He answered her with a soft kiss, but now she was the one to resist. She continued, "I want more time with you. We should find a really beautiful place and take our time."

As Mark's lips met hers in agreement, her words relieved him from the pressure of the moment, and then without warning the warmth of her mouth again found his firmness. Her desire left him wanting nothing.

He wanted her to continue forever, to drive him deeply into a void, to open him to a world of possibility he had never imagined, but then he thought, she was right; they should wait. The fear of losing control overwhelmed him. He was afraid of such pleasure; could he really be allowed this? These thoughts ripped into his psyche as he fell more and more into her allure. He wanted her to tear him apart and let in what he never knew, but he pulled her back to his lips.

"I do want you, Gabriela. More than anything I have ever wanted, I want you."

"I want you, too, Mark," she said. "I have lost all sense of myself now. I don't know what has made me so crazy. I'm really not like this. So, aggressive I mean. It's only that... I'm..." He felt her uneasiness.

He wondered if the effect of his nature would overpower any human he desired even without his willing it. He looked into her eyes and saw her want; there was no hesitation in her. He needed to believe that this was special, that they were special. Just then, rain pounded against the windows, and the sound of whooshing cars splashed over the wet pavement. People bracing against the wind struggled across the avenue. The figures filled the window's view with their hurried determination, and Mark unexpectedly, but surely, found what he sought.

"I know, I know. You don't have to say it," he said.

"This is crazy Mark, but let's keep this going."

Mark pulled her close and found her lips again. "I cannot tell you I understand all of what is happening, but this is right. I'm sure it is."

The limousine crossed 14th Street and was heading down Second Avenue. The rain stopped.

"We're almost to your place," she said. "The driver made good time."

"I'll get out at 2nd and St. Marks, I want to walk a bit."

Gabriela knocked on the window, and it rolled down. "Stop at 2nd and St. Marks, please." The driver nodded in recognition.

"See, even the sky is excited." She smiled.

The car stopped at the corner. After he had stepped out onto the pavement, he looked through the open window. He reached in and touched Gabriela's hand. "I don't know why, but I know this will be good."

She nodded.

As Mark walked back to the apartment, he thought about how he would share all of this with Jason. I must make him see. I don't care what he thinks; this is too wonderful to be wrong.

Maybe thousands of years ago, my kind felt such things, or... Maybe my kind has never felt as I am feeling now. Yet somehow, he sensed the applause of an entire planet.

As Mark opened the apartment door, Jason started to appear, but instead of passing quickly, he paused, hovering and staring. He lingered. Fascinated, he wanted to absorb every detail, every nuance before Mark faded into the portal.

CHAPTER 16
GABRIELA'S DREAM

I don't know what will happen, and I don't care. All I know is I have to have him! I'm in love! In love! I'm giggling and silly, I'm in love! And he loves me, too! I know it!

The next morning, when Gabriela awoke, her thoughts were only of him.

Who shall I tell first? I cannot wait to tell someone... No, no, don't be crazy! You tell no one! Well, maybe Mama, but no one else. Can you imagine the talk? Oh my God, I could just hear it... All those old betties in the faculty lunchroom. My God. What a nightmare! So just be cool... And keep your mouth shut!

But I love him so... Could we ever really be together? Is that too much to dream of? Why couldn't we? I still look very good. Maybe it won't last forever, but who cares.

I had such a vivid dream last night! It felt so real, but this all seems like I'm dreaming. I'm going to tell Mama all about that too. We were in Mallorca, in a hotel on the beach. He was perfect, sweet and kind. I see it clearly; we ate in a little café by the sea and then walked along the beach. Later we went back to the room. I held him next to me, he touched me, and we started making crazy love... It was wonderful. He was kissing me madly all over. I was just melting away. We made love again, over and over. I can't tell her all of that! But it was so nice, waking up next to him, looking into his eyes... I can tell her that much! What a dream! If it could only be... I cannot wait to see him again. Oh, I hope he feels the same.

I'll write him another note.

CHAPTER 17

A NIGHT OF PLEASURE &
A NIGHT OF PAIN

When Jason passed Mark, he was captured by his experience. He did not feel Mark's need to delve into the world of human love, yet he had to admit to himself that some of what Mark had communicated was fascinating.

Jason had always been the impulsive one. He had experienced many pleasures here, as well as anger and disgust. He had sought excitement, especially when it came to the arts. But he never wanted anything like what Mark was seeking. How could humans be worthy of such considerations?

Mark's actions are perplexing. Jason buckled his chain bracelet and picked up his rings. Should I reconsider? Maybe there is more to understand... more to see? It is true that I admire some of their art, especially their music. Music, what a beautiful word! It is derived from the Greek word 'muse,' a being who inspires...

Mark perceives things differently than I do. He seems to need something I don't. Is he right in continuing to pursue these newly found feelings? These emotions, this caring?

When he arrived at the club, Jason saw Helena sitting with BoBo. They were having a drink at their table.

"Hey, what's up?" Helena said. "I thought you weren't coming around tonight!"

"Yeah," responded Jason, "I just can't stay away from you guys... What's going on? Anything good?"

"Oh, we're just hanging out," said BoBo as he took a hit from a joint. "Want some?" He waved it towards Jason.

"No, thanks. You know I can't stand the smell of that cheap shit." He saw Angela serving another table. "Hey, Angela, get me a double."

"Sure thing, Jason!" she shouted over the tables. Jason watched Angela as she walked towards him.

What a fabulous body that girl has! She has such a bounce in her step, I bet she can really be fun; maybe it should be her for my first try at this sex thing. He looked over at Helena, realizing that she had been following his eyes.

"Oh my God," said Helena, "you are really getting so obvious, and what could you possibly see in her?" Helena watched Angela as she strolled past. "She's so trashy!" Unable to mask her jealousy, Helena's competitive side reared.

Jason looked back at her and did not say anything. He truly liked Helena and thought if there ever were a human who could draw him close, it would be her. But, any liaison with her would be too risky a venture. I could not chance harming her, and I have no idea what would happen if we were intimate... No, Angela should be my first foray into this so-called land of amorous pleasure. She is of little importance to me.

Angela brought Jason his drink and asked in her sweet Italian accent, "So, how are you?"

"I'm good, gorgeous. And you?"

Helena turned her head, and Jason sensed fire in her eyes. He paid this no attention.

"You're looking really good these days, Angela! Are you taking vitamins or something?"

"Si," she replied. "Italian ones. You like?"

"Yeah... I like," he responded. "Say, what are you doing later? Maybe we can all hang out and party a little."

All of a sudden, Helena's voice rang out angrily, "Sure! You could bring along your girlfriend Rachel, and you three could get it on together!"

Jason turned in surprise. He had not expected such an outburst. "Helena, what's up with that? Come on now! Be nice."

Angela, not to be intimidated, snapped back, "You know, that's not a bad idea! We're both off in a couple of hours." She walked away, swaying her hips in a sassy manner.

"Oh, that's just great!" screeched Helena replied shaking her head. "I cannot believe you sometimes, Jason."

Just then, a guy appeared and started talking to BoBo.

"Jason, do you know Rick Danko? He's a hell of a guitar player!"

"No, I don't," responded Jason, relieved by the change of subject.

"Nice to meet you, Jason," Danko said. "I heard your set the other night. It was fantastic!"

BoBo interjected, "Hey, you know, he plays with Bob Dylan!"

"Yeah," confirmed Danko, "I'm backing him up tonight at Carnegie Hall, if you're interested. I can get all of you backstage for the concert, if you'd like."

"Oh, yes! Yes!" cried Helena. "Yes, yes, yes! Let's go, Jason!"

"Bob is eager to meet you, Jason. He was here that night as well, hiding under a big hat. He thinks you are great."

"Oh, please let's go!" cried Helena again.

"Okay," responded Jason.

"We have to leave right now if you want to do this. We can all squeeze into a cab. Let me just make a quick call and set it up." Danko went across the room to the pay phone. Moments later, he returned and said, "Okay, just spoke to Bob. He says you're in. Let's go."

They all started for the door. Angela intercepted Jason. "You're leaving?" she asked.

"Yeah, we're going to see Dylan at Carnegie Hall."

"Oh, wish I could come!" She took out her order pad. "This is my number and address. Call me later. I'll ask Rachel, too, if you'd like." She giggled.

Jason smiled. "Okay, maybe later."

Just then, Helena grabbed his arm, pulling him out the door.

"I hate that little bitch!" she snapped. "Who does she think she is?"

As they made their way into the street, BoBo had already waved down a cab.

It started to rain as the cab progressed uptown. Everyone was quiet for a while, taking in the warm night and listening to the raindrops pounding on the roof. The streetlights made glimmering highlights on the windows. Everyone but Jason was completely stoned, mesmerized, all in their own worlds. They watched the water trickle down the glass, creating sinuous patterns as they flowed. Suddenly, the cabbie blurted out, "Where we goin'?" and the quiet moment ended as Danko answered, "Uptown, Carnegie Hall," and they all started to talk at once.

Helena remained furious. While Jason ignored her expressions, BoBo lit a joint and did his best to calm her down. Then Danko started telling stories about working with Dylan. He recalled one night in the recording studio when Mick Jagger had come by. Dylan had been cutting a new song. He was curious what Jagger would think of it. After the cut was done, Jagger sat silently for a while. Then he went up to Dylan, whispered in his ear, and left.

Danko remembered the moment. "I asked Bob what Jagger said to him. Dylan grumbled that Jagger said, 'Your lyrics are great, but your singing sucks.'" Everyone laughed out loud.

As the cab moved uptown, they sang Dylan songs and banged out beats on the back of the seats. The driver, a gray-haired, overweight Polish man, first got angry, cursing at them, but in time his anger faded, giving into the charm of the moment. From deep within his belly came forth a groan. All heads turned towards him in surprise as he started to sing along with them in an accent so thick the song sounded more like a village polka than American folk-rock. Bouncing up and down in his seat the verses bellowed out, "It is me you're looking for, babe." Everyone looked at each other and broke out in hysterics as they continued to egg him on. Helena started laughing, her mood shifting, and with a smile lighting up her face, she said, "I won't forget this fucking ride!"

The taxi turned onto 56th street. They pulled up to the stage entrance and piled out of the cab. Jason produced a wad of cash and paid for the ride. He gave the cabby a ten-dollar tip and thanked him for his song. Jason always seemed to have an endless supply of cash in his pockets. He was always good for the tab or to pay off the drug pushers at the Dom. He loved to keep the band in high spirits. They never questioned the source of his money. Jason had floated a rumor in the past that he was a trust fund kid related to William Randolph Hearst. That seemed to satisfy the curiosity and quell any gossip.

They went in through the stage door entrance. Danko was in a hurry since they were late. He had to be on stage soon. When they finally arrived backstage, they saw that Dylan was already behind the curtain tuning up his instruments.

"Where have you been, man?" Dylan barked at Danko. "You're late!" Danko apologized. He grabbed his guitar and started tuning with the rest of the band.

After they got all tuned up, the atmosphere chilled. Everyone put down their instruments, stepped back behind the stage, and lit cigarettes.

Bob walked up to Jason. "Hey man, glad you could make it! I heard your number at The Dom. I wanted to go backstage and talk to you, but you know, man, I have to lay low in places like that. Anyway, your set was really cool. We should jam together sometime."

Jason gave an affirming nod. "Do you know my lead singer, Helena?" he asked.

"No, I don't," he responded, looking at Helena, "but I heard you as well! You were great. We all have to do something together." Dylan paused. "I'm sorry for being so testy when you came in. It's been a really horrible day. I cannot stand the manager at this place, and nothing seems to be going right. It's always like this on the road. There is always some shit. You never get it the way you want; someone is always fucking up. You will see one day. You guys are going to be huge, so you'll be spending a lot of time on the road."

Helena beamed and said, "I hope so."

"Yeah," responded Dylan. "It's fun sometimes, but it gets lonely. Most of the time it sucks. I just try not to ever forget that it's about the music, about the message. All the rest is bullshit. Sorry to sound down," he said, hanging his head. "I've been bummed out all day. I've been thinking about Bobby Kennedy since last night," he went on. "Can't get him out of my head. Things might be different if he were around. This fucking war... Sorry to sound like a downer, I guess this tour is getting to me. Say, if you want to, you can come back to my hotel later. We can talk more, but I've got to get on stage now."

The band took the stage. Dylan bowed his head and started walking towards them. He looked back and gave a smile to Helena then opened the night with the song. "Like a Rolling Stone," the crowd roared.

"He is so cool!" said Helena. "I can't believe this."

Jason just smiled as Dylan continued singing.

"Well, Jason," she said with a smile, "are you going to let other people get your kicks for you?" Her voice took on a serious tone, as she said, "I've been waiting for you for a long time now. How long will I have to wait? Forever? I won't, you know!"

Jason looked at Helena. "Listen, Helena, it's not you. I really like you, and maybe... maybe we can have something someday, but I'm going through things right now. It's just not the right time. It's hard to explain, something with you would have to be serious, it's just..."

"Oh! But it's the right time for that little bitch Angela at the club, and maybe her girlfriend to boot!"

"No, no. That's different. She means nothing to me," he responded. "I have to sort things out for a while. Be a little patient with me. If it's right, it will be."

"Sounds like lines from a song," answered Helena. She turned away to listen to the music.

Jason considered what it might be like to have feelings towards a human. He both liked and disliked the sensation. There was something inside him that did have feelings for Helena, but even thinking about it made him feel uncomfortable. He turned his head, "Maybe I should just be alone. I need to think about things; I need to figure this out. I am going to go. I'll see you later."

"What!" she exclaimed. "You're going to leave in the middle of the concert? What did I say? I just... I meant that I want us... to see if we could..."

Jason turned away suddenly. "Listen, I just have to be alone right now."

Helena stood there bewildered and confused. She longed to break through to him. His mind always seemed to be in another place, just out there. Yet he was kind when he wanted to be. He was funny and witty when he wanted to be, but he was so strange. One minute he was intense and into you, and the next minute he was just floating out there someplace. I am always interested in the unavailable ones.

Helena had a history of chasing men who seemed determined to remain encased in stone. She blamed much of it on her distant father, who, for all the music and joy within him, was usually stoned and mostly absent. He broke my mother's heart a thousand times, she thought.

Her father had been the center of her life, with his deep, bluesy voice and his fingers that danced across the piano. But on the night, he returned to the house, stumbling, three days after stepping out to grab a pack of cigarettes, she and her mother left for good. And eight years later, here she was, reliving her mother's mistakes with Jason.

Everything came alive for me in New York, she thought. My life opened up when the music started. Jason is different. He is really, really out there. He is very special, gorgeous, and what talent he has! There is something in him I have never seen in anyone. He never takes off those sunglasses. Really, I think he must shower in them... What a strange guy. Damn! Why doesn't he let me in?

Jason walked out of the hall and opened the stage door to the street. She does not see that it isn't just about yes or no. I cannot fall into Mark's world; I have to keep my control. He had put everything out of his mind, but Helena lingered. As curious as he was about Mark's adventure, he feared the consequences, and of course there was the band to think about. He started to walk downtown, thinking now of Angela's invitation to party. Maybe I should find her. What would be the harm in a little experimentation with Angela? I know she is very experienced, and if someone gets hurt, at least it won't be Helena.

Jason waved a cab and pulled the paper out of his pocket. He read her address to the cabby.

"Four hundred fifty East 12th Street. Take FDR drive. It's quicker at this hour."

The cabby replied, "Whatever you say, boss. It's your money."

The cab found its way to the address in fifteen minutes, and Jason hopped out. Just as he approached the door, he saw Angela, Rachel, and Silvia walking out of their apartment building.

"Hey, Jason! What are you doing here? I hope you're in a fun mood, because we are!"

"Yeah," he answered. "I want to take you up on your invitation."

CHAPTER 18
THE CASINO

The girls were heading downtown. Silvia had just gotten in from the West Coast and was crashing at Angela and Rachel's place.

"All I want to do is go out," exclaimed Silvia, excitedly. "We're all going gambling. If you want to play, you will just have to come!"

Silvia, who was half-Chinese, used to date this "Tong" guy who ran some gambling parlors in Chinatown. "I know the casino scene in Chinatown," she continued.

"Gambling... This will be fun," said Jason.

Angela grabbed Jason's arm and whispered, "And maybe you'll get to win me later!"

They all piled into a cab. Silvia bellowed out, "We're going to Chinatown! I'll tell you where to go once we hit Canal Street. It's too complicated to explain now." The cabby nodded as they shut the door.

When they reached Canal Street, Silvia leaned forward to talk to the driver. "Okay, turn here. Go down to the Bowery and then turn downtown. When you get to Division, take a left." While Silvia was busy with the driver, Angela and Rachel turned to Jason. They had sandwiched him between them.

"So, you're really hot for him, huh, Angela? I don't blame you. He is really cute." She put her head on Jason's shoulder. "I kind of think you're hot myself," she whispered into his ear.

Jason laughed. "You girls are a trip!"

"Speaking of a trip, can you tell we all just dropped some acid? Sandoz, pure pharmaceutical grade! Silvia brought it back from the West Coast," said Rachel. "You can never find this stuff here. My God, what beautiful colors there are in the streets here in Chinatown! And those buildings are starting to melt!"

Angela responded, "Wow, this is great stuff! I think my legs have just turned into orange marmalade."

Silvia pounded on the back of the driver's seat. "We're here! Stop! It's that red door, next to the dress shop." The cab pulled over to the curb, and they all climbed out.

All three girls were dressed to kill. Two were wearing mini-skirted silk dresses cut to their thighs and high heels. Silvia's dress had a Chinese dragon printed on it. Angela was wearing red. Rachel's dress was longer with a dark blue stripe running up one side, and the other side had a slit that stopped high on her thigh. All three outfits were clearly meant to provoke. Together, they lit up the street like a French Cabaret.

They reached the door and encountered a collection of buzzer boxes strung with wires dangling like a bowl of left-over noodles. None of the boxes displayed legible names, save for some faded scribble that echoed Chinese calligraphy, although most appeared like runny stains on a tablecloth.

Silvia chose the correct buzzer instinctively. "Been gor ah!" A man answered from the box. "Who is it?"

Silvia responded in Chinese. A buzzer rang down the hall, and then another rang from a door under the stairs. The second door opened, and a large Chinese man dressed in black emerged. Silvia spoke to him in Cantonese. The guy knew her, but her guests needed an introduction.

Only the most trusted would be allowed to bring a non-Chinese person there. The club was the exclusive domain of the Chinatown underground, reserved for the gangs and gamblers of the Asian mafia. It provided gambling, drugs, and women. The women had been brought in from China to be used exclusively by the club's patrons.

Jason felt comfortable here, for he had spent a lot of time in the East. He loved the dark and dingy clubs of Bangkok, the back alleys of Hong Kong, and the wily streets of Saigon. He was fluent in all of the languages used on earth, but he had to be careful not to reveal this ability. He preferred to just nod in recognition when spoken to.

They walked down a dark flight of stairs and met another door protected by a bouncer. Then they passed through a long tunnel and emerged into a large red hall. The casino was set directly underneath the Manhattan Bridge. These underground vaults had once been a storehouse for construction equipment, but they had been abandoned for years. Recently, they had been discovered by some workmen and nabbed by a man named Sing. Sing was Silvia's old boyfriend. He ran most of the casinos in Chinatown. Pleasure was his business; gambling, sex, and drugs his currency.

Off the main gambling room was a series of corridors and smaller rooms. Some housed private poker games, some were designated for smoking opium, and others served to satisfy more carnal pleasures.

Silvia led the way, and upon entering the room shouted, "Gnor fahn lay lah!" and ran over to Sing, throwing her arms around him. She continued to speak in Cantonese. "Hello baby, did you miss me?"

"Of course I did," he replied. "Life has been a bore without you around here... And I see you brought Rachel! Hi darling, you know I miss you too."

Silvia and Rachel would often give Sing more than he could handle in the bedroom. Silvia was a dominatrix, and their kinky sexual play had turned Sing into a kind of addict. Since she'd moved, it had been difficult for him to find someone to replace her.

"But who are these two?" Sing asked in Cantonese. "You know they will not be permitted to gamble; you must be Chinese to gamble here!"

"Oh, Sing," answered Silvia, shifting to English. "Stop being such a tough guy! I will place all the bets. They will just hang there with me, anyway, so please stop being rude to my friends. It's not like you to act so impolitely. This is Jason, and this is Angela." She motioned towards them, respectively. "They are so pretty, you have to be nice to them!"

"Sorry," said Sing, "I don't mean to sound that way, you know. It's not me, but it's the other gang members here who might get upset. They like this place to be their special world, so please just be cool. Don't draw any unnecessary attention to yourselves, and all should be fine. Is Jason Asian? I don't know what is behind those sunglasses."

Jason responded in Cantonese, "It's just my spirit!"

Silvia exclaimed, "You know Chinese?" The girls looked at him in shock. "My you're full of surprises."

Silvia turned back to the girls. "Let's have a go at the tables, I am dying to play!"

Sing took Silvia's arm. He was not about to let her run loose just yet. "Okay, these are the rules. You can play, and he can play with you as long as he keeps speaking Chinese. If he's not Asian... tell him to keep those sunglasses on."

Sing was worried the regulars might not receive these outsiders warmly. It was Sing's casino, but without the support of the gang members, he would be out of business in a minute. Sing was a bit of an outsider himself; he came from a wealthy family from Hong Kong and had gotten involved in gambling in China. Being the fifth son, he knew there was no place for him within the family business, so he set out to make his own way in the casino. He was a shrewd and careful gambler, and with skill at the poker table, he quickly amassed a small fortune. Realizing the advantages of owning a gambling business, he moved into management. As there were few opportunities for him in Hong Kong, he came west to seek his fortune with his winnings. Making friends with the Chinatown underground was his big break, and he did not want to risk these relationships for anyone.

Sing always dressed the part of the casino owner. In the summer, a perfectly tailored white linen suit and silk tie was the regular uniform on his thin frame. His slicked-back black hair and horn-rimmed glasses straight from a Humphrey Bogart movie finished the Hollywood look of the Hong Kong gambler.

Silvia pulled the group over to the roulette table and bought $500 in chips. She placed the chips on 19, 4, and 5 for 1945. "That's my birth year! Let's see if it works." The wheel spun, and the ball rested on 12. Silvia's face grew sad, but she was undeterred. She played the same numbers again, ten dollars on each number. Again, she lost.

Silvia went through the $500 in a mere half hour, and the girls were looking quite glum.

"Five hundred bucks!" exclaimed Angela. "That's almost three months' rent! Do you have any more money, or are we done?"

"I think we're broke," said Silvia. Just then, Jason reached into his pocket and pulled out another $500. He handed it to her.

"You're not done; it's way too early for that!" he said. "But let's try another table, how about the dice?"

Jason knew he could control any game he chose, but he did not want to draw too much attention. But when he had seen the girls' expressions, he decided to cheer them up a bit.

Yes! Angela said, "This game is a bore. Let's try something else."

They walked over to the dice table and started placing bets on other players' rolls. Silvia lost twice and then won on the third try.

"Hooray!" she yelled. "I feel my luck is going to change." It was short-lived; she lost the next two rolls.

"Give me the dice!" she cried to the croupier in Cantonese. "It's my turn to roll." The croupier was a slim Asian woman, her dark hair held high with a comb. She wore a fitted green dress with a floral pattern embroidered on it. The back of the dress was cut low to reveal a glimpse of a large snake tattoo. Where the rest of the snake would travel was left to the imagination. She managed the table like an artist, calling out numbers and sliding chips with grace and skill. Jason knew the standard dice could be switched to loaded ones at any time, and this girl could do it without any ordinary eyes picking up on her tricks; this, of course, did not worry Jason, but he knew there was something different about her.

She has special abilities, but there is something else... He stared at her and wondered. He searched back in his mind to find the recognition, but then Silvia's chants put aside his concerns. Whatever it may be, he thought, it will have no effect on my power to control the game.

"Okay, Silvia. Let's see what you can do!" Jason had decided to let the girls win for a while and have some fun.

"OK. Seven or 11 is my wish, so if you don't give me those, you are a real bitch," whispered Silvia to the dice as she rolled them. The magic number 7 appeared. "I won!" she cried, as all the girls cheered.

"Let it ride!" she said and grabbed the dice again. The dice flew across the table, and the croupier yelled "Yo ying jor ah!" as the number 11 appeared. "Winner!"

"Let it ride! Let it ride!" yelled Rachel. "You're on a roll! Nothing can stop you, now."

There was $1200 on the table, and a crowd started to form around them as people sensed the excitement. Silvia quickly grabbed the dice and without hesitation sent them flying. The number 8 appeared.

"That's a hard number to make," came a voice from the background. To win, Silvia would have to roll another 8. She looked nervous as she took up the dice.

"Come on, Silvia! Come on, you can do it!" shouted Rachel.

Silvia took the dice and kissed them. "It's your turn to love me, my little darlings! Now don't make me cry!" She let the dice go, and two faces of four dots appeared.

"Eight! Eight! I won!" The croupier pushed $2400 at Silvia.

"I want to go again!" she said. Jason noticed that a large crowd had appeared around them, and so he thought it might be best to curtail the excitement.

"OK," replied Jason, "but only for $1000. It's my money too." Jason wanted her to lose and move away from the tables.

Silvia took the dice and rolled. Both dice showed only one dot. "Snake Eyes!" yelled the sexy croupier and smiled. "You lose. Better luck next time!" Silvia's face drooped, overtaken by disappointment.

"Don't be sad, Silvia. You're up a lot!" said Jason.

"Yeah..." she responded. "But I wanted to win more!"

"Hey," continued Jason, "didn't you say that they have opium rooms here? I've never smoked opium! Let's try some." Of course, opium would have no effect upon him, but this was an excellent ploy to divert the girls from the tables and lessen the attention they had attracted with their winnings.

Silvia, smiling, said, "They do, and the opium is the best in New York. Do you want to try some?"

"Yes," he answered.

The other girls nodded in affirmation. "Yeah, let's do it!"

Silvia read the menu. "Well, a small room is 25 bucks, but the large one with beautiful couches and pillows is 75. It would be 25 each for the opium, so that's another 100 bucks. For 25 more, we could get a service girl to assist and do as we ask."

Jason pulled 200 dollars from his pocket and gave it to Silvia. He added another 100 on top. The croupier increasingly distracted him. What is it about her? He thought. I somehow feel... Jason could not put his finger upon his recognition of her, but he did notice that she had her eye on Angela. "Tell Sing we want the pretty Chinese croupier as our service girl."

"I'll ask, but I can't guarantee anything," replied Silvia. Despite her doubt, she returned quickly with the sexy croupier in tow.

"This is Saya. She's agreed."

Silvia sensed the croupier and Sing had developed a special

relationship. She is incredibly beautiful. Has Saya become my replacement? If she has, it would mean that she must be a fun girl to have around. Although Silvia was a bit jealous, her curiosity about this mysterious woman overtook her hesitations.

Lifting her bowed head, Saya looked at Jason. "You must be a very important person for Sing to ask this of me. I haven't been a service girl in quite some time."

Saya also sensed something strange as she looked at him. Even through his dark glasses, she felt an inscrutable power; she did not understand its source, but she felt it. At first, she considered he might be an assassin. Maybe he knows who I am, and he has been sent to take my life. But then she reconsidered, if that were so, he would have already tried. She could feel his power; it came from a deep place. Yet, in a strange way, she felt comfortable. Oddly, his presence gave her an eerie sense of reassurance. Who is he?

"But tonight, you are our service girl!" snapped Angela before Jason could speak. "And he's with me, so you just do as you're told!"

"It will be my pleasure." She looked into Angela's eyes. Saya had learned long ago when it was best to play the humble servant. Humility is often my greatest tool, she thought, knowing that she could snap this woman in two like a twig.

"Well, I think Silvia pulls more weight here than I do," interjected Jason. Hearing her accent, he smiled as he spoke in perfect Mandarin, "But I did ask for you."

Saya nodded and bowed her head. It was then that she understood he knew her from somewhere.

Looking at Angela, she replied, "Of course. I am here to serve all. Please let me show you to the Jade Room. It's our best."

Saya easily slipped behind a mask of secrets, fading gracefully within her charms and gambling skills. But buried within was a checkered past, a past of velvet-soft memories and nightmares with teeth. She had never allowed anyone to see her motivations, nor her many abilities, yet she was attracted to Angela as soon as she walked into the room and feared it would show in front of Sing. Most of all, she did not want to show her fascination with this mysterious stranger who spoke her language. I feel as if he is looking through me.

When with Sing, Saya wore tight black leather outfits, called all the shots, and inflicted moments that satisfied his desire for screams. Yet with women, she liked being told what to do and being made to suffer. Saya would be the first to admit that she seemed strange to most. She enjoyed both men and women, and she loved the intensity in her most heated moments. Pain broke through. It quenched her thirst. The ability to change pain into pleasure was something she learned how to do in her training, but when she started to experience sex, something else happened. It didn't need discipline; the intensity was always warm and wet. Saya had long ago decided not to analyze this, but just to embrace whatever passions arose within her and follow them. For a while, she questioned these feelings. What is it about pain that breaks through? Is it that I have the power to overcome it and turn it into sweets? Is this power that I relish? But sometimes I enjoy giving pain as well… she thought with a smile.

She knew Jason was delving into her mind, wandering around, turning the pages. He smiled at her, knowingly, looking admiringly into her eyes, holding her mind as if he owned it. She knew nothing could keep him out.

Jason realized now that he knew her. He had often thought of finding her. It had been better not to disturb things, not to disrupt the natural way of things, not to concern the Council with such matters… but there she was. What were my chances of finding her, this girl, born in a village in China, here in New York?

Saya led the group down a long hall off the main casino.

They passed several rooms, the aroma of opium filling the passage. The sounds of laughter rang out amidst the ruckus of Chinese songs and sensual sighs. They passed a series of bamboo doors and arrived at the end of the corridor. Saya opened the large wooden doors to the opulent Jade Room.

Inside was a palatial den of iniquity: a room obviously designed for the sole purpose of gratification. In the middle sat a low, but large wooden tea table with three hookah pipes resting at its center. Around the table were mattresses and pillows all covered in silk and satin, dotted with glistening stones and faux jewels. The room reeked of decadence. The patterns on the cloth were elaborate motifs of colorful Chinese allegories. The images were mostly erotic, made with painfully delicate needlework in brightly colored reds and blues set against the earthy background of Chinese landscapes and palaces.

"What do you think?" exalted Silvia. "You know, I helped Sing design this room! Do you sense my touch?"

"I do, I do!" responded Rachel. "How is it you have never taken me here before?"

"Well, I split for the coast just as it was finished, but it's nice, isn't it? I gave it some California flair, a bit of San Francisco and a lot of Shanghai!"

"I love it!" sighed a starry-eyed Angela.

The girls all jockeyed for position around the table. "Come," Angela said in a managing tone. "You sit here with me and Rachel. Silvia there, and Saya, you get between us so you can service us all!"

Jason turned to Angela. "Whatever you want, as long as Silvia is happy. You know she is the big winner tonight."

Silvia laughed. "Yeah, that's right!"

"This acid is really coming on strong," said Angela. "The figures embroidered on those pillows are moving and dancing!"

Silvia laughed. "Wait until you smoke some of this opium; you may become one of those pictures yourself and never come back!"

Saya, smiling, asked, "Shall we start?" She opened a box on the table filled with various colored mounds of a pasty substance. "You should try this one," she said. "It's my favorite."

"That sounds good to me," responded Silvia.

As Saya began to fill the pipes, her mind never strayed far

from Jason. Silvia started to kiss Rachel, saying, "You don't mind, do you, Angela? I haven't touched her in such a long time." Amidst the activity, Saya wondered when Jason would reach for her.

"It's okay," replied Angela, "We're having a party, and all is free tonight. What do you say, Jason?" She pulled him towards her. "Baciami," she continued in Italian. "I want your kiss. Give me your lips."

Jason responded by sending his tongue deep into Angela's mouth.

It was at this moment that Saya could see that this man knew nothing about sex. How could this be?

Jason paused, that was interesting...I kind of liked it. He had made up his mind that he would open himself to experimentation tonight. Angela, charmed by his naïveté, was even more encouraged to instruct.

His main fear was what effect he might have on a human's body. But, he thought, I have come too far to let this night end without uncovering more of these mysteries. His eyes continued to peer into Saya's, hoping in some way she could reassure him as she had once done many years ago.

Saya had just lit a water pipe and passed the mouthpiece to Angela. "Ladies first," she said, smiling. I am going to send her into Never Never Land. I really want her in the background, and the sooner the better.

"Oh, thank you! Aren't you the sweet one?" Angela smiled. "I'll have to reward you later!" Chemistry started to flow between Saya and Angela, and Saya knew she was on the right path. Angela took a puff deep into her lungs, and exhaled. "Wow! That is real!" Saya started to glow, anticipating her conquest.

Moving briskly, Saya, filled the pipe that Rachel and Silvia were sharing.

"Let me at it!" cried Silvia, as she inhaled the intoxicating paste. She faded backwards as she drew in the pipe's vapors.

Rachel quickly took the stem and followed suit. "My God,

this is better than acid! I'm starting to float!" she gasped.

"You can have some too, Saya. Don't worry about the expense; you're my guest as well as our service girl tonight!" Angela opened her dress and pulled it down over her shoulder, revealing her black lace bra to Jason. "Unhook me," she whispered, looking into Jason's eyes. "I want to relax."

Angela was determined to have Jason tonight. She wanted to steal his attentions away from Helena, and she was ready to offer him temptations and pleasures she felt Helena was unable to give him. I can't sing, but I can really play. If I can get this Saya to join, I'll really make him crazy.

Jason, reading their minds, was becoming more and more amused by their strategies and decided to comply with Angela's instructions. She pulled his head down to her beckoning breasts, and his lips, forgetting all timidity, explored their softness. Angela lifted his face and started to kiss him as she pulled at his clothing, stripping him in seconds. She glanced across the room and saw that Rachel and Silvia were already naked, in a world of lust, interrupted only by Saya's gentle offerings of opium.

Within seconds, Angela and Jason were naked and entwined, submerged in frantic passion. Jason wasted no time in entering her. Entranced with the rhythm of it all, he thought, this is almost like music; it has a pace all its own.

Angela responded instinctively to the movement of Jason's body. Every gesture and touch sent electricity through her; consumed by the rush of victory... Finally, I have him. But now... How to keep him?

Saya started to stroke Angela's hair as Jason ravaged her breasts with complete abandon. She couldn't believe his power as he drove into her. Taking a breath, she looked up at the Chinese beauty.

Overrun by the rapture of Jason she still managed to voice, "Such a beautiful tattoo. I want to see the rest of it."

Saya rose, smiling, and slipped out of her dress. She wore no undergarments. She turned to show the tattoo to Angela. Her body language and movements were flirtatious and obedient. The ornately painted snake draped down her back and ended mid-thigh. It was gracefully drawn, full of color, scribed in delicate fashion along her body so that it revealed a hidden life when she moved. The beauty of her perfectly proportioned figure framed the tattoo, and her gleaming white skin made the design even more intense. Her body moved slowly and quietly, faintly charming like whispers that kill. To Angela's intoxicated eyes, it was as if she were watching a cinematic dream; the colors seemed alive on her skin.

Turning to face Angela, Saya revealed the rest of herself. Swaying seductively, she took the comb out of her hair, and darkness fell down over her shoulders, partially hiding her breast. She acted coy for a moment, shy, yet her eyes were breathing fire. I own them now.

"Do you like it?" she said. "It took almost a year to complete." Speaking timidly, and then changing to an assertive tone, she said, "I think it is beautiful, and it gives me power."

"Come here and lie next to me," whispered Angela. "I want you, and if you behave, I'll share my man with you. I've seen you looking at him."

"And at you too!" she responded.

Angela lifted Jason's head. "Why don't you try her? You know I take both sugar and cream in my coffee," she said, smiling at him. Pulling Saya down to them, she said, "Here, take her from behind so she faces me, and I can share her as well."

Saya followed Angela's instructions, enjoying being submissive. Jason also found himself liking being instructed; surrendering himself to Angela. Giving away control was new.

As Jason mounted Saya from behind, Angela brought Saya's lips to her breasts. "Do you like them?"

"You're very beautiful," she responded.

Jason embraced Saya. He entered her, and she began to moan, growling as he moved. Her sounds became the fulcrum of desire as he continued deeper. She cried out in Mandarin, "Oh my God, what is this? I have never..." Jason allowed himself to swell within her. Angela pushed her head down between her thighs. "Me, Saya! Me!" Saya's tongue entered her and sought magic spots. Angela began to twist and sigh.

Jason continued thrusting into Saya's body. He read every response while he explored her needs. Pain! She has a dark side. She craves agony, more with every breath. His movements grew more fervent, more invading, more violent.

He felt her hands reaching for him. Saya, fighting for breath, gasped, "I want it here, now. Put yourself here..." as she grabbed him and steered his penis upward.

From across the table there were calls from Silvia and Rachel. "Yes! Put it in her ass, Jason! We want to hear her scream!"

"Yes," cried Angela. "Make her moan for me."

As Jason entered, he heard Saya sigh. "Oh my God. I love it. It hurts! But... I love it! Please, don't stop!"

Jason sensed her growing exhilaration but became concerned. He could see how blinding the rapture was to her. He questioned if he should stop, but the moment drove him forward. I might be causing damage to her body... She would die rather than have me stop. He paused, but continued, loving the sensations, pulled into the swirling anarchy of the lust. Then, reluctantly, he said, "No, we must stop! I am hurting you."

"Oh no! Don't stop, please don't stop!" she wailed as he tore into her. "I love it. Harder, I want more! I can take it! More, please more!" she cried. Jason tried to stop, but the rush filled him. He drove forward, pounding into her again and again. Caught within the undertow of ecstasy, the act was swallowing him, but then, despite the pleasure, and ignoring her begging, he stopped. Saya curled up into a ball of pain and collapsed into a fetal position, exhausted but filled with elation. Pain rose from within her as her euphoria faded. Jason immediately sensed her body was in chaos and what remained was agony. Concerned, he used his powers to repair the damage while filling her system with numbing relief.

Saya, catching her breath, said softly, "I'm okay. I'm okay...

I think? Oh God... It was so great." She looked at him with a smile. "But I want more of this..."

As her words trailed, Jason responded, "You are much more than this."

At that moment, he realized that it was possible for him to forget everything and lose control, to act without reason, to harm without intention. Still, what a remarkable experience! He had finally found something to fear. Yet, more importantly, he had found the being that had haunted his memories. "You'll be fine," he said to Saya. "I am here now..."

Drifting into sleep, she murmured, "Who are you?"

Soon, all of the women found themselves in a deep, opium-laden trance. Jason thought it best to encourage them to sleep so he could quietly slip away.

The night could not have been more eventful, and as the women drifted, Jason pondered all that had occurred as he passed through the wall and out into the street.

Mark is right. There is a pleasure to be found with humans, but I've found more than pleasure. I've found her.

CHAPTER 19
SAYA REVEALED

Before entering a life she called floating, Saya's world was very different. Once she was known as Feiyan, born out of an illicit affair between a nobleman's wife and a handsome young soldier in the service of her husband. She found herself cradled in the arms of her mother's handmaiden, rushing through the woods towards the mountain temples. The devoted servant had sworn to deliver the child to the monks for protection even if it cost her life. With unending purpose, she placed the infant on the steps of the Henan Shaolin Monastery near the Shaoshi Mountains. A simple note pinned to a blanket read: I am a bird at your window seeking shelter from the wind.

It was not long after she succeeded that a guard's pursuing arrow found her heart. The monks embraced the child, for the stars had foretold the coming of a great master. It was 1945, the year of the Rooster. She was to be called Feiyan or Flying Swallow. Her arrival was seen as a new dawn for the monastery, hope for the salvation of the clan. The Americans had just defeated the Japanese, and the monks had been sensing that some greatness was arriving in the world. Was it this child? Something else? They were not sure. However, the child was seen as a sign.

For the first three years of Feiyan's life, the monks were concerned. She never cried, asked for food, or seemed to have any need for anyone. In fact, she walked about in her own world. When meals were presented to her, she ate quickly and then returned to her posture of quietude. She was always looking intensely at all that was going on around her but showed little reaction to it. Then on the fortieth month of her arrival, she started to talk, but not in baby chatter. From the start, she spoke fluently, and with ease. To their astonishment, she asked if she could join the Kung Fu practice.

The Henan Monastery was the birthplace of dragon style Kung Fu. Its movements imitated the actions of wild creatures. The gestures mimicked insects and birds as they parried, jumped, clawed, and stung. This particular style had been developed by the great Shaolin nun Ni Mui in the 17th century with the purpose of giving women the ability to overcome stronger and more powerful opponents. The movements were meticulously adjusted, creating a style of lithe, speedy maneuvers and deathly blows. The secrets of the art never left the monastery.

It was soon acknowledged by the elders that Feiyan was a blessed child, different from the others. In keeping with this, she began receiving a more severe regiment than the other novices. If a child was disciplined with a blow from the master, Feiyan received three blows for the same infraction. In the mornings, she was forced to run twice the distance, with a master beating her with a stick as she battled through the rugged terrain. From the start, she was trained on upturned logs to develop balance. Later, she practiced movements and was made to recite poetry while jumping from one floating log to another. She was always beaten severely if she fell. Not only was she taught the skills of battle but also the music within every gesture. For her, nothing was too harsh, nothing beyond her grasp; for Feiyan was to become an artist, a warrior priestess... the chosen one.

Soon she was granted her own Dragon Mistress, the head female monk in the monastery. Her mentor instilled in her the power of mind over body. She developed the ability to transform what the body feels through the powers of thought. It was then that Feiyan developed the mantra she called "absorption and transformation." She changed pain into pleasure. Every blow, every strike began to taste like honey, and she learned how it was possible to love pain.

I will make my body like water; nothing will break it. All pain will flow through me as the river flows through my fingers. The pleasure of the stream will bring the coolness to my hands, and I will be content. My mind will make me free, and my power will overcome the most brutal. Her movements began to flow through the air like the musical notes of the erhu that her Mistress played as she practiced. She developed her abilities to function as instinct. She could anticipate any attack. All blows intended for her body were either parried or avoided. She became a ghost in combat; it was almost as if her body did not exist to her adversaries until the power from her blows crushed them.

By the age of 14, Feiyan could defeat any student in the temple, even males five years her senior. The monks were forced to train her against multiple opponents since no single student, neither male nor female, could approach her skill. Her power terrified the temple students as much as it inspired awe. When her mentor unexpectedly died, Feiyan was about to be appointed the youngest master in the history of the temple. Jealousy was not absent within the minds of the other young monks in training. The whispers started to fill the halls, and enemies arose amongst the less talented. Feiyan would overhear plots of poisons and darts. Danger was coming. Left without the protection of her mentor, she fled the temple with the body of a teenager and the soul of a child.

She wandered the streets of Hong Kong for some time. Not knowing how else to survive, she begged. But both her naivety of the streets and of her nascent womanly allure attracted notice. Gang boys followed her. On a cold night amongst the garbage bins and the rats, she laid waste to four young men who had tried to take her in the night. In a matter of seconds, she left one dead, one paralyzed, and the other two broken and limping. The ferocity of her attack was fast and furious, for no person other than Mistress Dragon had ever been given permission to enter the intimacy of her thoughts, much less touch her body. Her actions did not go unnoticed, and immediately she found herself in even greater danger from gang members in the streets. A local shopkeeper let her hide in his storage room in exchange for cleaning, but he too was growing fearful, when an unexpected answer arrived.

The wife of a Japanese silk trader who was visiting the city heard of Feiyan's exploits and her plight from a servant, for chatter moved quickly in the marketplace. Mistress Kaya, as she was known, was beautiful, cunning, and in need of protection. She had been the most famous geisha in Kyoto before her marriage, known in all the society courts of Japan. While relations had grown warmer towards the Japanese since the war, there was still much hatred lurking in dark places. Mistress Kaya understood that the streets of China were still a dangerous place for any Japanese woman. She was often left alone when her husband did his dealings with the merchants in rural villages. When she heard of this girl's prowess, she wondered if she could be the answer. The silk trader's wife needed a bodyguard.

If she could travel with me unnoticed and could skillfully protect me, or wield death if called upon, she would make the perfect companion. Little did they know what a gem she had found amongst the fish and the howling pigs of the market stands; Feiyan's abilities were far beyond all imagination. For her loyalty, Mistress Kaya and her husband gave Feiyan an escape. And it was with these two strangers from an unknown land that Feiyan found her way to Shiga, Japan, the birthplace of the ninja.

In returning home, the silk trader's wife enrolled her in training at a ninja dojo. Mistress Kaya decided that Feiyan must enter her world fully, so she gave her the name Saya and had her instructed in the Japanese way. Feiyan accepted her name as well this new life earnestly. She was to become Japanese. Then she could blend into the culture and live unnoticed as her bodyguard, and if need be, an assassin.

The ninja techniques were different and interesting to Saya. In the beginning, she did not fully understand what her role would be in the service of Mistress Kaya, but as time went by, she knew that she was expected to do whatever was asked. As her devotion to her mistress grew, obedience became her sole task, and she consented.

Saya quickly mastered the language and all levels of ninja training. Her abilities transcended anything the dojo had seen. She learned the stealthy secrets of their poisons and the deadliness of their weapons. Then, she learned the ninja code of killing obediently and without remorse when asked to by one's master. Saya was very impressed by the quality of the Japanese swords and quickly became an expert. As time passed, she was increasingly called upon to deliver messages, often of terror, sometimes of pain, to anyone who threatened her beloved adopted family.

She remained in training for two years and was often rewarded with trips alongside Mistress Kaya exploring the Japanese countryside, enjoying the pleasures of Japan and other faraway lands. Although she never grew close to Master Yoto, she loved Mistress Kaya, who was but a few years her senior. Saya would protect her person and her secrets, standing outside her door when she would steal away for a rendezvous with lovers. She would die to protect her Mistress and once killed a man whom she perceived as a threat without orders or permission. Her devotion was without limits, but actions such as these were not received well. Master Yoto was angered by what he saw as precocious and volatile behavior. He forbade her from violence unless explicitly ordered.

Saya had reached her seventeenth year and still had no knowledge of sex. Mistress Kaya thought this unnatural and provided her with a lover. Saya was not given a choice in the matter and was ordered to welcome the experience. She was to choose from three young men at the dojo. She picked the oldest, a tall fair-skinned boy from a family of sword makers from the north, and she said to Mistress Kaya, "He has tender eyes and a straight back." She did not enjoy him at first but later grew to like sex with him, although she felt little in the way of emotion. Mistress Kaya did not want her to become too attached to the young man, so after two months, she instructed Saya that she must pick another. This ritual repeated itself for four consecutive lovers over the next several months.

Mistress Kaya, whose desires welcomed diversity, noticed that Saya would often be looking at the young maid who worked for them and asked her if she ever thought about the touch of a woman. Saya timidly smiled and said, "She has a warm smile." This acknowledgement began her experience with the pleasures of the female sex.

Life was good for Saya in Japan. She learned to speak Japanese and also English and Russian, as she was sometimes called upon to carry out missions against the holders of those tongues. Mistress Kaya had opened up a world of pleasure to her into which she reclined happily. She was content.

One day her mistress asked her to deliver a message of terror to the leader of a clan in the next province. She was told she should not kill him but rather hurt him in a way he would not soon forget. The man was an ambitious lord who, in his desire for power, had begun ruthlessly killing the local merchants in his domain as a means of intimidation and for the purpose of extortion. One of the families was the sister of Mistress Kaya, and her sister and her husband along with their two children had fallen under this tyrant's sword.

Saya had known them, had held their children in her arms, and welcomed the task. But when told she would not be allowed to take his life, she angered. It was explained to her as politics, and too complicated to fully articulate. As always, Saya took her orders as humbly as gospel but asked that she be allowed to decide the punishment herself. The permission was granted.

Disguised as a geisha, she traveled to the nearby province where she sought her target. Saya was introduced to the nobleman at a local geisha house, and with her beauty and grace easily lured him to a prearranged home on the outskirts of the city. As soon as she was given the opportunity, she injected him with poison, paralyzing him, leaving him speechless, but not shielding him from any pain. While he was fully conscious, she cut off his clothing, and with deliberation and care, she slowly started to saw.

She removed his left foot, her slow movements seeking agony with every stroke. "I will take this first," she said, "for I hear it is the one you placed on the chest of my mistress's sister before you took her life." While his screams came forth, she read him the list of his brutal crimes. She spoke with a lyrical cadence, drumming out each crime with a beat. Saya felt a twinge of pleasure arise in her as she brought the blade down when she emphasized his crimes against women, dragging the saw more slowly as she spoke with glee. Next came the right foot as she called out the children's names to him. The teeth of her blade tore at his open flesh.

She paused and repeated their names when she reached his bone, forcing down ever harder to find the most unbearable torture. "For Aya." The teeth bit. "For Junko." Smiling at him as she pushed, she looked into his eyes, communicating the pleasure she felt at her very core.

Saya giggled a childish giggle with each push of the blade and said, "There... isn't that nice?" He tried to scream as she sprinkled each wound with powder that cauterized the open flesh. As his face grimaced in pain, a twinkle arose in her eye, and the sweetness in her voice playfully taunted him.

"Does the bite of my blade feel good, or do I go too fast? I wouldn't want to deny you any pleasure." She spoke softly, with delight. "I'll go more slowly." She hoped to prolong the pain. After his feet, she took his right hand, then his left.

"Oh, don't cry," she said as tears again flowed from his eyes.

"You'll have many years ahead for tears." Next, she took his penis in her hand and said, "It is only for my thoughts of your wife that I do not take this as well as your tongue with me tonight, but let me never hear that you harm her again, or deny her any request or..." She paused and smiled and whispered in his ear, "I'll return, and I won't show you the kindness I do now."

Saya neatly stitched up his wounds and bound them in silk. Then she gave him an herb that allowed him just enough strength to move. She forced him to crawl into a large cage mounted on a cart in the rear of the house. After covering the cage with cloth, she wheeled it into the center of the town in darkness. She arranged his extremities on a table before him for all to admire and left a note: "No one who kills women and children should ever walk the earth or lay their hands upon another."

And as the poison wore off, from within the curtained cage were heard his moans and cries of pain. In the windows of the village, lanterns started to glow, and the hum of voices could be heard behind the wooden doors as Saya disappeared into the night.

This act was received as the greatest of horrors by the leaders in the surrounding provinces, and a steep price was put on the perpetrator's head; one that would attract bounty hunters from as far away as Tokyo. When Master Yoto learned of the terror that Saya had exacted, gasping at the act and fearing reprisals, he told Saya to leave his home. And amidst Mistress Kaya's tears, Saya had no alternative but to flee.

She ran back to Hong Kong hoping to be lost among the millions of faces. It was there that she met Sing in a casino. He was visiting his family and securing funds for his adventures in America. Although swept away by her beauty, it was after hearing of her skills that he offered her a new life in America.

Thus began Saya's life in the gambling business, a life for which she seemed to be born, a life that she grew to love. She loved her anonymity, hidden behind the tables. Asia was her past; she no longer sought the status and fear that her former life gave her. She found power instead in the games she played, taking and giving pleasure and pain in more harmless adventures.

Vestiges of some darkness I left behind in Japan, some cravings still live within me. Will I ever truly understand them?

CHAPTER 20

OBSERVATIONS FROM AFAR

On Eldern, there had been stirrings in the chambers of power. The activities of Mark and Jason had overtaken the agenda of the Supreme Council. Today, amongst a series of high-level meetings, the Council was to discuss the latest adventures of the twins on Earth.

"The Lower Chambers have been conveying a great deal of data about the twins," began Elgert. "Our citizens have become obsessed with their day-to-day activities and are mesmerized by their adventures; they are becoming more important than the dreams themselves. Everyone is following them religiously. They are cult heroes on at least nine planets."

"Yes," responded Dronin. "Surprising, and unanticipated, but not entirely unacceptable. As it turns out, all this activity is drawing more attention to humans, and in turn their dreams. It is making Eldern quite wealthy."

"You are aware," Allaceia interrupted, "there have been unforeseen effects upon the humans."

"Yes, but this is inconsequential," responded Elgert.

Dronin paused and looked at them both. "I am more concerned with the woman Jason has affected, Saya. She has developed special abilities. I fear she may become a problem. What shall we do with her?"

"Do with her?" questioned Allaceia

"Let's discuss the issues at hand first." Elgert's tone was cool, more authoritative than usual. "The dreams and their profits are our primary concern now. As for the twins, we know their mission is risky. In fact, they both may not survive. Maybe the problem will resolve itself. But whatever their fate, the collection of dreams will continue for eons, making us all rich."

"Don't speak about the twins like that, Elgert. We cannot turn our backs on them because you think they may be becoming a problem. We created them. Besides, they have the power of my lineage within them."

"You are right, forgive me Allaceia. They are very strong and grow stronger."

"I have been watching them, Elgert. Their lives are engaging. This is why their popularity continues to grow; we must protect them if we are to ensure the populace is content. Should something happen to them, the masses will hold us responsible."

"What are their chances of survival?" asked Dronin.

"The same as before," answered Elgert.

Allaceia's attention antenna rose; He is hiding something.

Elgert looked at her. "Actually we can't be sure yet, but it is possible that their chances of survival are better than we previously thought." Could she know something, but how? "My staff has concluded that their growing attachment to humanity will only enhance their willingness for sacrifice." He paused, awaiting her response.

Elgert could taste his ultimate ambitions; he wanted complete control. The two of them and the twins were not in his plans, but could he be clever enough to manipulate all the moving parts?

"So, as long as they accomplish our plan and continue their mission to save the Earth, we should let them do as they wish." Allaceia looked at Elgert, puzzled by his demeanor.

"I agree," responded Dronin.

Allaceia turned to Elgert. "What about the Asteroid What

is the time frame on that?"

"The collision will occur many years in the future, in 1992 Earth time, to be exact. That is, 24 of their years from now. Our primary plan is to have one of them – I expect Jason – to descend into the earth's core and redirect the power of the earth's magnetic field. Mark will be near the approaching asteroid and, with Jason's help, send it on a course towards Jupiter rather than the earth. It will be a long, slow process. We cannot use too much of Earth's magnetic energy, as that might be perceptible to humans. Unfortunately, the pressure within the core may crush Jason and Mark may be pulled into the asteroid's gravitational fields. Transitioning between dimensions should mitigate these effects. Regardless, it will likely be agonizingly painful." Elgert spoke routinely, as not to arouse Allaceia's suspicion. She stared intently into his eyes.

"Hmm, the fate you see for them both is not acceptable." If I were not in these chambers, I could probe his mind and he would never even know I did it. Something is wrong.

She is perceptive, thought Elgert. She is looking at me strangely.

Elgert knew the twins were too strong to fall to such a fate; he would plan to attack Mark when he was alone approaching the asteroid, leaving Jason's fate in the hands of the earth's core without the aid of Mark to rescue him. They must be separated for the plan to succeed. Together they have already grown too strong to be attacked from this distance. Separated, they would be less formidable foes.

"Are you sure about the fact that the asteroid can be affected by the degree of magnetic energy they will be able to channel?" asked Dronin.

"Dronin! This is entirely unacceptable," Allaceia exclaimed. "There must be other alternatives than to risk their lives."

Ignoring Allaceia, Elgert responded, "Our preliminary findings were confirmed by the Prime. If need be, Mark can also use the magnetic power to gather nearby space debris and then employ their combined gravity to change the asteroid's course. This will be a longer process, however."

"This plan is overly complicated. Is there no other solution?" asked Dronin.

"No. No, I do not agree." interjected Allaceia.

"Not without risking revealing our involvement to the humans," replied Elgert. "We have already concluded our anonymity is primary. We cannot reveal ourselves; they are not ready for contact. Furthermore," he smiled, "it would inhibit our collection of dreams."

"Yes, and we grow richer every day," agreed Dronin.

Allaceia knew she could not appear to put her concern for the twins before her responsibilities to the Counsel. She knew she must wait and spoke dutifully. "But more importantly, if humans were to meet us at this point in the earth's history, the Federation may become alerted to our activities and our enterprises compromised."

"Yes, we must remain as discreet as possible. It is bad enough that Jason and Mark's antics have changed the dynamics of our situation," Elgert continued. "Do you know that on New Tripton, our companies are selling clothing branded with the name 'Jason' and that they are amassing fortunes? Synthetic black leather motorcycle jackets with skulls and crossbones printed on them! Those tiny little beings are going crazy for them. And not only on New Tripton..."

"I thought Triptonians did not wear clothing, just changed the color of their fur in their salons?" asked Dronin.

"They don't wear clothing. That is what is so amazing about all this. It's unprecedented. Also, the Allogians are big Mark fans. Everyone is buying Mark penny loafers and corduroy sports jackets. 'The Mark and Jason Effect' is not just a surprise, it is a phenomenon," voiced Elgert.

"And," continued Elgert, "the problem is that there are clubs and cults forming in many cities and on many planets. It is not just the Triptonians; it is spreading across the entire federation. You have the 'Jason fans' and the 'Mark followers.'

There was even a brawl in a club between two gangs on Steeleron."

"We should not be concerned, as long as we are benefiting our citizens and the mission quietly continues," said Dronin. "How long until the twins reach full maturation and embark?"

"That is hard to quantify, especially since they are not exactly equal. We specialized them, as you recall, for the benefit of the mission," answered Elgert. "It could be weeks, but it could be months or longer. We will only know when they are able to face each other and walk the earth at the same time."

"Can their development be enhanced? Can we speed it up?" asked Dronin.

"Not without risks," responded Elgert. "But I will look into it and try some adjustments." He knew he would not.

"What happens when they learn that they will likely die and experience great pain and isolation? Even with the fact that they are programmed to fulfill their duties, suppose they refuse?" asked Allaceia. She knew Elgert's words were laden with ulterior motives. *If I could only mind probe*, she thought, but she knew that was impossible.

"Do you recall the military probes we stationed on the far side of Earth's moon to guard against dream pillaging from planets outside the federation?"

"Yes," responded Allaceia.

"They have the ability to destroy both Mark and Jason," answered Elgert. "Mark and Jason will have no choice."

"But Elgert, if they die, there may be a revolution here..." Allaceia spoke firmly.

Elgert looked at Allaceia relishing her exposure. Obviously, something had been developing within her. It was a motherly instinct she had not shown in the past. *She is revealing herself; her empathy for them can turn Dronin towards me.*

"Destroying them might not be as easy as you think. Do you think your toys could destroy me? Not likely!" She spoke defiantly, awaiting Elgert's response... But continued, "They will do as they are asked because it is their duty."

Elgert stood quietly for a moment knowing that Allaceia's words met his needs for now. He wanted the chaos to slowly unfold so he could later pick up the pieces. In the coolest of tones, he responded, "You have a keen perception, Allaceia, and Mark and Jason's combined strength is formidable, but I think you are correct in thinking that they will both willingly continue with the mission. A sense of duty lives within them"

"I hope you are right," echoed Dronin. "We should encourage Mark and Jason's attachments for the humans. We should allow them to remain on Earth if they choose to, should they succeed and survive at their task."

Thinking that he had pushed far enough for now, Elgert changed the subject. "Now as to the woman Jason affected… She grows in power, and she could become a complication. We did not anticipate that he would create this mutation."

"Yes, the girl might become a liability. We could remove her from the equation," said Elgert.

"What are you implying?" Allaceia asked.

Elgert smiled, and thought, it all starts to unravel.

CHAPTER 21

SOMETHING THAT YOU NEED

More than ever, Jason anticipated the moment he would see Mark's eyes, that fraction of a second when the details and the color arrived. The window had cracked, and the hues of his last hours were revealed. The meaning of their existence was a constant question: why were they on earth, and what was yet to be asked of them?

Jason's thoughts turned to Mark. He always sees himself as the noble one. Why is he so judgmental? He does not understand that my effect upon this primitive species matters little to The Council. But this woman, Saya, matters.

The twins' communication was not bound by literal thought. They shared the senses as well as the logic of ideas. They were able to read meanings, see colors, and touch textures beyond the limitations of words. They heard the notes in the dark unsaid, tasted it all, both the sweet and the bitter, for they were capable of communication of the subtle and the unobserved. Yet there existed an unending gnawing deep within them – a parasite, forever present, forever eating their minds as they waited for the day they would walk together, for they knew until then they would never understand.

The Council had instructed them to learn, to explore human feelings, even to experience human pleasures, but that was before he knew Saya existed. Now it is more complicated... I am responsible for who she is, and for what she may become. She has stolen breath without regret or remorse, and it may just be the beginning. How deep are the caverns that hide within these shadows? Have I seeded a storm or a sunrise? I hope I will not have to kill her.

Jason often cleansed himself of his fears through his lust for living, but this time he wanted Mark to see every detail, to enjoy it all as much as he did. It was vital for Mark to understand the importance of Saya. He was not seeking approval or boasting of his discovery; that was a human weakness. I want him to see my thoughts, and perhaps, he smiled, view with a dash of envy.

Jason lay down on the bed and watched Mark's form emerge from the portal. As it often did, his face appeared first. He wore a warm smile and communicated…

Haven't you been the busy one! Jason faded into the void.

CHAPTER 22
MARK'S AWARENESS

W hen Mark emerged from the portal, streams of light fired across his mind. Unintelligible flashing colors coupled with pulses of energy and discordant sounds pounded inside his head. He felt an energy rising. It was vibrating, building... Is this the Council? No! No, it's me. I feel scrambled as if I have been eaten, digested and regurgitated.

Strange sounds.

Colors again and again.

Words, repeating.

Mark jumped up.

What's going on? I have to get out of this apartment. I need distance from the Council, fast.

No! It can't be them... But what if it is them?

Not knowing how he got there, he found himself in the street. He did not even remember getting dressed, but he was. A crowd rushed past him. He walked quickly. He noticed neither faces nor eyes. Everything around him appeared to be a fuzzy mass of energy, surrounding him, flowing through him and about him as he walked. Mark lowered his face, fearing what it was showing. Finally, he looked around him at the people passing.

No one seems to be staring, so I guess I'm okay...

He reached the river and stopped. Leaning on the railing, he looked out at the water. The river felt steady, comforting. The water just flowed – flowed as it always had.

It's steady... Yes, this is what I want. Steady and constant. This is better.

As he calmed down, he felt an overwhelming yearning; a strangeness he had never known. The name Gabriela echoed.... forming on his lips again and again: Gabriela... Gabriela.

There was a terrible wanting within him. Something is going on. This is not them... This is me. My response to having Gabriela in my life is altering me. Within a chrysalis of his own making, emotions were being born. Opening his eyes, he watched people pass him and understood the feelings of others as he never had before.

Gabriela was stirring within him, all he wanted was her. The thought of her fueled a hunger for this thing that humans call emotion. He needed her smile, the sound of her voice.

His mind started screaming.

Data... Data... Data...

Permanence! Permanence! Impermanence...

This relationship with Gabriela is doomed. I will live for thousands of earth years, while Gabriela is limited by her humanity.

Again, it came:

Data... Data... Data...

Will I be called away for a hundred years? What is my destiny? Possibilities rushed about his mind. Infinite scenarios sang like an ominous chorus in a Wagner opera. Things I can control and things I cannot. He turned and looked out at the river. This all is too much to think about for now... He needed to touch her, to kiss her. He longed in ways he did not understand.

How strange, this agony...

Mark wanted to call her but dared not, in fear that the professor would pick up the phone. I will go to the college. I'll figure it out there.

He took the subway uptown as he usually did, but this time

his experience in the train and on the platform was different. He no longer felt the urge to peek into people's minds for carefree amusement, nor to play games or engage in the usual antics. Rather, he began to find others' thoughts seeking him, weighing upon him. The subway car was full of pain but dotted with flashes of happiness. Yet he saw mostly suffering. In the past, he had toyed with these primitive beings. But now he listened – and what he heard tore at him. Some of the yearnings were overwhelming. He was about to block them all out, when one stirred him.

It was a black woman across the aisle wearing a faded dress and worn shoes. Her sorrow rose from within her. She was trying to keep tears from her eyes. She held the hand of a child of six. Her grandchild had been living with her for a year, ever since her daughter had been arrested on drug charges. She had already lost her only son to violence in the streets.

He heard, in her mind, a prayer. How much more, Lord? How much more will you ask of me?

In her bag, Mark could see an eviction notice demanding she leave her home by the next day. She was doing all she could to not upset her grandchild. The thought of possibly being separated from the child, the only joy in her life, was unbearable. She prayed, hoping for a miracle that would keep them both from going to a shelter.

Despite all her loss and all that she had suffered, something was telling her to hope. "The baby Jesus loves us, Child," she said to her granddaughter, holding her head high, defiantly proud, ever believing that something, someone would answer her prayers.

Mark could see she owed $102 in back rent. Not much for three months, but enough to motivate a slum landlord of the South Bronx to throw her into the street. She had only $9 in her purse. A mere few hundred dollars could bridge the distance between anguish and a reprieve from the city marshal.

He took out a piece of paper and wrote a note:

I am a stranger who feels your pain and wants to help.

Please take this. Secure your home, feed your grandchild, and never ask why. Sometimes things just work out.

Why this woman's plight affected him more than those of others, he did not know. Maybe it was her courage, her blind faith. Maybe it was the beautiful eyes of the little child holding her school bag on her lap. He placed a thousand dollars into the paper and folded it into a package.

He sat down next to the woman and said, "It's really hot out for this time of year."

"Yeah..." she responded. "I was hoping it would cool off a bit. I forgot my umbrella. It's a cloudy day, too."

"Are you having a bad day?" asked Mark.

"More than some," she said, "but less than others, I guess." Her voice crackled with sadness.

Mark answered, "Well maybe this afternoon the sun will come out, and it won't rain."

"Yeah, maybe..." she said.

Mark put the package into her bag without her noticing. He got up to leave the train and took a chocolate bar out of his pocket. He gave it to the little girl. "What a pretty-colored bow you have in your hair. Do you like Mounds bars? They're my favorite," he said.

The little girl was wearing a plaid dress, brown with blue and red in its cross-hatching, with the bright yellow ribbon tied neatly into her hair. Unaware of the weight her grandmother bore, she smiled and said, "Thank you, sir! I love Mounds."

The old woman smiled at Mark.

It was a little thing, Mark thought. One family's stress would now be less; two lives, happier. This world has too much suffering, too much injustice.

Mark realized that changing this world would not be his mission, but he knew he could never again remain untouched by the cruelties that he saw. He would do what he could, yet he understood he had another path.

After getting off the train, he walked towards the campus,

not knowing how he would find a way to contact Gabriela, but he knew that he would.

When he stepped onto campus, he went to check his box as he always did. There was a small pink envelope inside. He knew who it was from.

His mind left all else behind as the thought of Gabriela provoked his senses. He read:

"Thinking about you is consuming me, so I try not to.

My only thought is to take you in and never let you out, consume every drop of you.

And after you are tired, and your sweat rolls away, let you lie quietly, and fall asleep in my arms.

"I'll be in the library at 2:30."

There was no signature, nor should there have been. Now, more than ever, secrecy reigned. Mark looked at his watch. It was 10:20 AM. How can I wait until then to see her? I will just have to stay busy and not think about her, if I can. But he could not.

The time had never seemed to move so slowly for him, and although he did his best to distract himself, the hours went by at the pace of a subway train being held for construction.

Finishing his work early, he watched the clock as 2 PM finally arrived. Mark knew that the hour of honesty was upon him. He could no longer hide his identity from Gabriela. He must tell her.

Crossing the campus, he kept searching for the words... what would he say when he saw her? I will have to share my whole person and tell her of Jason as well, he thought. How will I tell her? Maybe I will do as Jason did and just show her. It must be poetic... But I should explain first. I don't want her to have a heart attack.

When he entered the library, he saw Gabriela sitting amidst a pile of books, frantically taking notes. When she raised her head, their eyes met.

She smiled in recognition and signaled with one finger for him to wait a moment.

He saw that her student intern had just fetched some research books for her. They spoke for a few minutes, and then Gabriela set her free. She collected her papers, placed them into her bag, and approached Mark.

"Well, hi there. I guess my little note worked." She chuckled. "I am sorry. I have this Latin flare when my heart takes over."

"Yeah, well, it worked. I've been holding my breath all morning. You look so good... Let's get out of here! We need to talk."

"Talk?" She smiled with a devilish look in her eyes.

"Gabriela, we have to talk. Let's get off campus."

"Oh, okay... Let's talk," she said. "But let's meet somewhere. I don't want people to notice us leaving together. How about The Carnegie Deli on 7th Avenue? That's far enough away, and I am dying for some pastrami... But in an hour. I need to drop this stuff off at my office."

"Sure, sounds good," replied Mark, nodding in agreement. They both walked off in separate directions.

Mark arrived first and got a booth in the back. He loved this place; it was always full of interesting and busy people. Overweight garment district salesmen mixed with beautifully donned Broadway personalities.

It was not long before Gabriela arrived. She quickly found Mark and sat across from him.

"It's crowded at this hour; I'm glad you found a booth!" she said.

"Yes," responded Mark. "It's so good to see you! You've been filling my thoughts..."

"And you've been in mine," she replied. "So, let's eat quickly and find a place where we can be alone."

"Listen, Gabriela... I have to talk to you." Just at that moment, the waiter came over.

Gabriela said to him, "Bring me a big, fat pastrami on rye and a dripping order of coleslaw! Mark, what do you want?"

"Just a soda; a Cherry Coke," he responded.

"Make that two!" said Gabriela. The waiter left with their order. "So, what's weighing on your mind? You look so serious."

"Gabriela..." he said. "I have to talk to you about who I am and where I am from."

"Where you're from? What? Are you having a problem with immigration? You know, the university can take care of that for you. They are great with that kind of stuff! You have student status, don't you? They have a load of lawyers for that. Don't worry."

"It's not exactly that...Where I am from is not covered by immigration."

"Oh, you're not from behind the communist bloc, are you? Are you from a communist country? Well, we will get you political asylum. I know people, you know. You never told me exactly where you are from. Are you in trouble or something? Oh...Oh my God... You're not a spy or something, are you? Are you a spy? A Russian spy? Oh, I love it... A spy!"

"No. No, I'm not a spy. If only it were so simple... No. Gabriela, I am from another world."

"You're what? Yeah, yeah... Me too. It's called the Literature Department. Come on, Mark. What are you talking about?"

"No, really, Gabriela. I am not a human being. I come from a planet thousands of light years away from here."

"You're not a human being, huh? Sure, Mark... Did you forget the limo ride already? Remember what we did together? You seemed pretty human to me, Mark. Very human, and very cute. Have you been working too hard?" She reached up and touched his forehead, feeling for a fever. "How long have you been thinking like this...? Didn't you tell me you were going to talk to that psychiatrist, Doctor... what's his name? Abernathy?"

"No, listen, Gabriela. I am a manifestation of sorts. I mean, I am real, but I am not human. It's complicated, Gabriela. I knew this was not going to be easy... Gabriela, I am an alien who has been sent here to save your planet."

"Save the planet? Oh, great... Save the planet! From what, greasy french fries? Please Mark! Will you stop this and get real! Let's talk about where we are going to find a hotel. I suggest some little place in the thirties on the East Side. There are a bunch of dive-y, but not too dirty, places over there. No one will see us.," She smiled.

The waiter brought the food. It was dripping with fat. "Oh, yum, I know this kind of stuff turns you off, but I love it. Please pass the mustard," said Gabriela.

"No, Gabriela, I'm really serious." How am I going to get her to believe me without doing something big or theatrical? He passed her the mustard.

"Oh. I get it. You want to have some kinky fun with me? Do you want me to dress up for you or something? Well, I can do a nurse or a chambermaid. I'm not sure how to do an alien. But can't we just do romantic for now? That's the kind of stuff you get into when you start to get bored with me." She pouted.

"No, Gabriela. I don't want you to dress up. And I will never get bored with you, and I don't need you to play games. You are more than enough for me just the way you are. I need you to listen. This is really important."

"Okay, okay... I'll try and understand. I love you too. But I don't believe a word that you're saying. And I think you're having a breakdown."

"You know," said Mark, "I could do something to prove it to you right now. But you deserve a more eloquent demonstration, something with panache. So, I am going to show you when we leave here. You said you want to go to a little out-of-the-way hotel? Okay, eat up."

"Oh, you made a reservation?" said Gabriela. "I can't wait!" Her eyes glistened.

Gabriela ate her food, and they said little more to each other; she just gave Mark sparkling looks as she devoured her sandwich. When she had finished, Mark had a playfully determined expression on his face.

"Let's go!" he said. "You're going to like this."

CHAPTER 23

THE SUNSET

Gabriela opened the door to the street, but as she stepped out of the restaurant, she did not hear the familiar voices of office workers as they rushed to their jobs, nor did she see the roaring of cars with their engines bellowing carbon-laced fumes. She did not feel the blast of the city heat upon her face or smell the pungent odors of the hot-dog stands. Gabriela walked through the door into something else.

She looked out upon a sun vanishing into the blues and greens of the sea with crying seagulls' purging the waves snapping up the refuse from fishing boats. She saw children laughing and teasing, running home along the sand to their mothers' dinner tables.

When Gabriela thought of a sunset, it was always that of Mallorca, those deep oranges and yellows of that August orb being swallowed. La meurte del dia, "The death of the day," her mother would call it.

Gabriela turned and looked at Mark. "What is this? What is going on…? My God, this can't be real."

Looking down, she found herself lying on a blanket at the beach, her toes just touching the water's edge. Now she was draped in a white, sheer cotton dress, embroidered in island style. She looked at Mark, who was also dressed in comfortable white cotton. He was pouring a glass of sparkling red wine for each of them. As she took a sip, the bubbles bounced and tickled her nose, and from the glass, she heard musical notes. Mark smiled and said, "Do you believe me now? I am sorry for the theatrics, but you simply weren't hearing me."

"Believe you? What is all this? I'm frightened. Where are we?"

"Don't be frightened! This is meant to help you see that what I am telling you is true!" exclaimed Mark. "Maybe now you will believe that I'm from another world. I am not human... but I love you. And if you believe that, everything will be okay."

"Mark," responded Gabriela, "you're from another planet? Please tell me this is a dream!"

"Well, maybe in a way it is, and maybe, in a way, it's not." He smiled and gestured with his hand to the world about them. "I created this from your mind. I needed to convince you, but I wanted you to feel very comfortable, so I chose your favorite place. We have only a short time here, but I hope it will be enough time for me to convince you that I am telling the truth, and..." he said with a mischievous boy-like grin, "maybe later find your favorite little hotel."

"Comfortable? Hotel? Are you kidding me? I hope you conjured up a good hospital too! When I recover from shock, I'm going to need one! You'd better start talking and talking fast!"

"Listen, Gabriela, you really do not need to comprehend everything right now. Let me just give you the short version; I am in your world, hopefully, my future one. I am going to tell you something scary now, so prepare yourself... One of the main reasons I am here is to save this world from destruction. We have been sent here to do that. And rest assured, I will save it. I mean – we will – my brother and I."

"Save the world from destruction? Are you serious? And you have a brother?"

Gabriela started to hyperventilate and looked terrified.

"Please, try to calm yourself, it's all going to be fine. I don't want to get into everything right now, and I know I am frightening you. But I don't know any other way to explain myself. Yes, I have a brother, a twin in fact. We will have to leave here soon, let's not waste it." He touched her lips with his fingers, and surprisingly she felt a sense of serenity.

"I know this all sounds mad, but what's important now is us. I never knew what it would mean to love another person... but now I do. I feel so alive, so happy."

"You're happy? Love, huh... Well, that's really great. You're going to have to let me digest all of this."

"Of course. Let's take a walk. We can do anything you want. This is your dream," responded Mark.

"Mark, it has started to sound like my nightmare. Will you promise me that everything will be alright?"

"Yes, I promise. Everything is going to be fine." Of course, Mark knew that may be just a hope.

Gabriela started to breathe more normally, thinking that this may all be a hallucination anyway, and that she is going to wake up in a hospital with a nurse by her side explaining how the brick fell down from the 24th floor and hit her in the head as she exited the deli.

They got up from the sand and started to walk along the promenade where there were some boys playing in the street as if they were in a bullring. One played the matador, the other, the bull, charging a towel that he used for a cape.

"Mark, do you remember I told you I had an older brother? He is always my first thought when I come back here. We used to play on the beach together. Sometimes I played the bull while he danced with his cape, dodging my thrusts." Can this really be Spain?

When they turned the corner, Gabriela saw some children chasing a football that, without warning, turned into a small pink pig playing a bagpipe. The pig turned his head towards the window painted blue. It had a large flower box filled with yellow daisies that started to sway and sing melodies.

Then, just to her right, she saw her husband George sitting at a table outside a restaurant. He was dressed in a fine silk suit and wore a large straw hat with a blue and red feather in its band. It was a bit shabby but jauntily perched upon his head. There were three men at the table, two wearing colorful garbs made of silk and satins that reflected a bygone age. The fourth was an American from the 1930s, wearing a gray contemporary jacket and smoking a pipe. George was asking them questions.

"George, what are you doing here? I don't want you here!"

"It's alright Gabriela, I don't mind you being with Mark," her husband replied turning to her. "I just need to finish this conversation! It is making me crazy." George turned back to his tablemates. "So, Professor Copernicus and you, Galileo, what do you think about the start of it all? I mean you heard what Hubble here says about the Big Bang. I am sure your Pope would really have a lot to say about that! Gabriela, could you please ask your Mark how it all started and where it is all going?"

She looked at Mark, and he turned and whispered something in her ear. "I think he feels you should find out on your own, and he said to eat a lot of soup," Gabriela replied.

George seemed totally satisfied with her answer. "Okay, I'll see you at home. We have things to do," he replied. The four of them started talking and eating a dark blue soup full of twinkling equations.

As they continued walking, she found herself looking up at Mark. She had grown small, and was six years old now, holding his hand.

"Mark, am I still dreaming? Is this all a dream?" Mark did not reply. He just smiled. Then, in the next step, she found her mother was holding her other hand. But she was young and beautiful, just as she remembered.

Gabriela turned and spoke. "MaMa, he says he is an alien who is going to save the world. I really don't understand, but I think I love him."

"Well," her mother answered, "you know our family is not native to Spain. Your grandmother was born in Nancy, from the east of France. And when she first came to Barcelona, she said it felt like she was on another planet."

"Yes, MaMa, but he says he is from a place way up in the stars. And he says he is not human."

"Well," she smiled as she spoke. "Your grandmother said Barcelona felt as if she was living in another world when she first came. There was no foie gras, and the herbs were all different. Just a bunch of olives in the market, she would say, and –"

"MaMa! I don't know what to do! I have so many questions."

"Yes, I see they are all over the newspapers."

Gabriela turned to look at the newsstand and the papers resting there. All of a sudden, hundreds of question marks started to emerge from the print and dance upon the pages, busily scampering about as if they were in frantic discussions with one another.

"Well, I think the only way to find an answer is to talk to him, but I would not worry about it for now. Sometimes you just have to do what feels right."

"I think I love him, MaMa."

"Well, my darling, when I eat a delicious piece of flan, I don't ask where it comes from, I just let it melt in my mouth."

"Melt in your mouth?"

"Yes, especially if it's warm and it tastes right."

Gabriela grew back to normal size, and her mother vanished.

"I love you, Mark, but... what am I in love with? This is strange, bewildering, and... an awful lot to take in all at once."

Mark took Gabriela into his arms and kissed her. "Yes, it is, but we have to hurry because something is coming."

"What's coming?"

Mark didn't reply.

"I need to be alone with you," said Gabriela. "I want to hold you close to me. You know what, let's go someplace to be alone. That little hotel... It's just down the road."

"Yes, I know. It's over there. But we could just walk awhile."

They walked slowly towards the hotel. They stopped for a

moment and listened to the sea. The ocean waves were crashing against the rocks by the shore. When they reached the hotel, the owner recognized Gabriela and greeted her as an old friend. The sand from the beach was still in her hair, and she shook it out on the marble. When the grains hit the floor, they bounced, and Gabriela heard the music of the harp playing again. The hotel owner smiled.

As they left the lobby for their room, a parrot in a large wooden cage said to her, "The flan is very good here. You should try some."

They made love for hours. Novel to Mark, he basked in desires he never knew.

As Gabriela rested, Mark thought, it is all this passion within her mind that creates these manifestations. He stared at her naked body stretched across the bed and wondered how there could be such beauty, such gloriously intoxicating beauty. Would he ever again feel this warmth? Time slowed, and each moment rested languidly. He watched Gabriela's every breath. He listened to the air push through her nostrils and fill her lungs. It was the sound of life, her life, human life. It was music to him. He had only this gift of time, a moment between the moments, but he was both grateful for having them and angry at the thought of losing them. He touched her, and her skin was moist, silky. He moved his fingers lithely over her back; they glided, her sweat glistened. She felt warm. Tender and warm. Was there anything real before this?

He needed to wake her, but these minutes were so perfect. It was time to go. This reality was a mirage and had to be left in the world of wishes. It was time to return to the bustling life of exhaust fumes and ambitions.

Gabriela opened her eyes and greeted Mark with a warm smile. "Hello, darling. This is a beautiful night! Shall we go out for dinner?"

"I'm afraid our time here is done; reality is calling. Your life and mine are waiting for us in New York."

"Oh... do we have to?" she said.

"I am afraid we must," answered Mark. "You know this is not real. It is a space in between moments, a bend in time. Your husband awaits you, and Jason and I have things to do."

"But we just got here! You heard George say he didn't mind," she smiled. "Can't we bend it a bit longer?"

"I'm afraid not, my love. But we had this time, and hopefully we will have other times even more special," he said.

"What do you mean, hopefully?" asked Gabriela. "We are going to be together, right? I will get a divorce if you want me to. Or we can just go on like this, if you would prefer. I will make no demands on you."

"Gabriela, it's not about that. Are you forgetting again that I am not a human being?"

"Oh yeah. There's that… But you feel human enough to me. And besides… every relationship has problems." She smiled. "This is all that matters to me."

"You are more than lovable, but you must understand that there are things I cannot control," said Mark. "Gabriela, we are going back to New York, to reality now, and you're going home to your life. We can talk more later but believe me when I say I love you."

"I like this dream. Let's just stay here," she said, fighting back tears. "When will I see you again?"

"Soon. I will see you soon, but there are things I have to attend to."

Gabriela looked at Mark and sensed he was troubled. "Will you be alright? You look troubled. Are you worried?"

"No, no. I am fine," he responded. He was shocked that she sensed this from him. He wondered if he had been communicating his concerns to her without being aware of it.

"Come here and let me hold you. Don't look so sad. You're not supposed to worry in my dream."

"I know," responded Mark, "and, I also know that we have more great times ahead." He knew; however, this might not be true.

Mark and Gabriela got dressed, but there were no words

exchanged. He did not want to reveal what would come next. They stepped out of the hotel room and were hit with the sounds of the streets of New York.

Gabriela kissed him gently as she took the door handle of a parked taxi. "If you don't call me tomorrow, I'll be very angry. And you don't want to make a Spanish girl angry. Especially one from Barcelona." She smiled sweetly. Mark smiled back as she got into the cab.

Gabriela poked her head out of the window and said, laughing, "Let's do this dreaming thing again. I liked it."

CHAPTER 24

AT THE DOCTOR'S OFFICE

Mark watched the cab drive off. These sensations are wonderful, he thought to himself. He wanted to dive deeper, to explore their meaning. He needed to talk to Dr. Abernathy.

He found a phone and called the doctor's office. Martha answered.

"Hello. Dr. Abernathy's office!"

"Hello. This is Mark, the doctor's new patient. I really need to see him today, if possible."

Martha made a strange humming sound, then said, "Well, your appointment is in two days, but it's your lucky day. I just had a cancellation! Could you be here in an hour?"

"Yes! Definitely."

When Mark arrived at the office, Martha appeared a bit agitated. "Your appointment is in two minutes," she said sounding annoyed. "I was almost going to cancel you. Please sit, and I will tell him you're here." She clicked the button on the intercom. "He's here."

"Okay," Abernathy replied. "Bring him in."

When Mark entered the room, the doctor was not sitting at his desk, as he normally did, but rather was standing behind his chair in the center of the room. Mark could see that Abernathy was uneasy.

Turning, Abernathy abruptly said to Martha, "Leave us

now." She paused and left with a puzzled expression on her face.

"So," said the doctor, "how scared of you should I be?"

"Scared of me? Oh..." Marked paused. "Jason frightened you?"

"Well. That might be considered quite an understatement. For God's sake! Being awoken in the middle of the night by a being that can pick locks with his mind and then tells you that the world may end! Why would anyone be frightened?" His tone was riddled with angry sarcasm.

"I am sorry he upset you, doctor. I told you he was complicated, and I thought I explained that our presence here on the earth was going to have a large impact."

"Well, you didn't explain him, and yes, let's just say your brother drove home the point of your mission with a great deal of emphasis," responded Abernathy.

"I apologize," Mark reiterated. "Jason has a flair for the dramatic. I assure you the earth won't be destroyed, and Jason would never harm you."

"Has he harmed others?" Abernathy questioned with intensity.

"Well... let's move on," responded Mark. "I have a lot to talk to you about."

"But I would like to dwell on it a bit, if you don't mind. Has he harmed anyone?" Dr. Abernathy exclaimed.

"Listen, Doctor, Jason has, let's say, forgotten himself from time to time, but I promise you he will not harm you or anyone associated with you. He likes you."

"He likes me? Mark, forgive me if I am not reassured by this conversation."

"Please, Doctor, I really need your advice. And this is bigger than the both of us. Please do not abandon me."

"This is not about me abandoning you, but how can I be expected to help you under an atmosphere of intimidation. I am not sure if I can do this. I am no one's hero."

"But Doctor, who else can I turn to?"

"Okay... Tell me. What is it you need to talk about? Why did you move up your appointment?"

"It's about Gabriela. She is so wonderful. I cannot believe how I feel. I was hoping you could help me understand what I am experiencing."

Hesitantly, Abernathy sat down in his chair. "Well, I see you are distressed. Fine. Please proceed... Tell me why this is all so urgent."

"I've had a glimpse of what humans describe as emotion, but nothing like this. Not in this way. They have been evolving within me, but all of a sudden something has changed. It is as if my very self has sucked me within itself. Then at the same time, I feel as if I were swirling in an eddy. Doctor, I am overwhelmed by my very being. I am both elated and lost, even almost frightened. It's kind of like it, but... I don't know... it is like having opposites things pulling at me at the same time. Am I making sense?"

"Yes, in a way, continue," responded Abernathy.

"I don't mind these sensations, but I'm confused. This is all so new to me. I have no reference within me for these experiences. Do I sound like a child to you? Because I feel like one when I am around her. Is this what you humans call love? I want to know if I am really experiencing love."

"Well," intoned Abernathy as he gave Mark a serious but thoughtful look, "you seem to be experiencing what an adolescent boy might be going through during pubescence when he first develops an attachment towards the girl. It is often a time when emotional development has not kept pace with other aspects of one's being. It is possible that you are developing the ability to have emotions while being unprepared for the territory and have plunged yourself into the depths not really being ready for the intensity. We humans are also very silly when it comes to these things. I mean corporal emotions, lust, much less what you believe to be love. You should not be overly concerned that you are uncomfortable. Just experience what you are feeling, and as we say, go with the flow."

"But if it's really love, how would I know?" responded Mark.

"Only time answers that," replied Abernathy.

"Doctor, you must understand, if it is really love, it would be historic for my kind. My world has not experienced "love" for thousands of years. If I am truly having these feelings – I mean, real emotions, real love – my people would be experiencing these emotions along with me. For us, this could be revolutionary. It is a kind of awakening from a very deep sleep. It may change my home world. That is, if it is real. How will I know if it is real?" He had raised his voice in his excitement.

The doctor paused. "So, the significance goes beyond you. This is quite a question then. All I can say is that logic often doesn't apply to love. It's almost a need. It's an irrational thing we have been pondering for as long as humans could ponder. Some scientists dismiss it as a chemical response to stimuli related to reproduction, a state of being we have devised in order to procreate, create the family unit, and continue the species, but for me, that is too mechanistic an answer. There are many novels and plays, and I am sure millions of poems and broken promises as well. But my rule has always been to judge whether the other person means more to you than you mean to yourself."

"What do you mean? Are you asking if I would die for her?"

"Well, I don't think that should ever be asked of one, but if you are talking about the intensity of the feeling, then, yes, that you would sacrifice anything for her."

"I think I understand. Thank you for your help, doctor."

"Wait a minute! It is not all so simple! There is a lot to comprehend, here!"

"Yes, I can see that. But this is enough for me to think about for a while, and I really have to talk to Jason."

"Mark, why don't you just try to slow down a bit?"

"I wish I could, Doctor, but there is so much to think about, and I am afraid that things are going to start to speed up soon. I have to talk to Jason, and we only really get a few moments together."

"Yes, you said that, but I do not completely understand. So at least, before you run off, can I ask you again about Jason?"

"Yes… Of course."

"Well, has he ever harmed anyone?"

Mark paused, for he did not want to frighten the doctor.

"He will never harm you, Doctor."

"Yes, you said that, but before he left, he handed me a diamond." The doctor went to his desk and revealed the gigantic stone. "He gave me this after he nearly frightened me to death, a kind of compensation for having terrorized me, I think. Then he told me not to show it to anyone."

"He was just expressing his gratitude to you. But yes, showing a diamond like that might raise a lot of questions. I will have $100,000 sent to your bank to compensate you for your time. Is that enough?"

"At my usual rate of $70 an hour you would be paying me for more than 1,400 hours in advance. That's ridiculous."

"Well, I am grateful, and money is just paper to me."

"Listen, Mark. You are being evasive. What I really want to know is if Jason has a history of harming people."

Mark spoke with a whisper, hesitating, "Well there were some people."

"Some people? What do you mean by some people? How many people? And what has he done?"

"Well, he has killed eleven people," Mark said in a burst.

"Oh, great! Just great! And I am not to be concerned?"

"You don't have to worry. They were evil people, and they were given justice. You aren't an evil person, and I will never, I mean never, allow harm to come to you or anyone you are close to. I swear by that."

"Well, thank you for your continued reassurance, Mark. I appreciate your care. But your brother scares me."

"I understand," responded Mark. "But please, don't be afraid."

"I am not sure how that is possible, Mark. He kills people. How could I not be concerned? I know our conversations are important to you, and therefore maybe my species, so I guess there is no escape for me at this point. Well, anyway, can you tell me how he killed these people?"

Mark answered. "He just stops their hearts when he wants to be merciful, but if he gets angry, people's innards end up all over the streets."

"Well... At least he does it with pizazz..." responded Abernathy.

CHAPTER 25

SEEING HIM STANDING THERE

Mark hurried through the streets hoping to have a few moments to communicate with Jason. He wanted to tell Jason not to frighten Dr. Abernathy again. He rushed up the stairs to their apartment, and when he opened the door, he froze in shock.

There, standing in front of him, was Jason.

For a moment, they just stared at each other in amazement. His brother had just left the portal for the first time without his presence. They simultaneously thought: How could this be possible? They were there together at last.

"Jason!"

Jason answered, "Hello, Mark."

Mark took Jason's hand and held it between both of his. They felt a sense of knowing.

"There are more differences between us than I expected! This is so exciting. I can't wait to hear you play music at The Dom, hear your group, hang out together. You can meet Gabriela, and we can all go out, and…"

"Slow down, Mark," responded Jason. "I don't think we should do that just yet. Let's proceed carefully. They are preparing us for something. Do you sense it? They have just given us a bit more – almost a tease. They have a plan. They wanted us to see reality in our own special way. They wanted us to have different strengths and different needs and desires. It's all a part of a larger scheme."

"Do you know what our task is?" asked Mark.

"I still only know that we are expected to save the earth, but I'm starting to sense we may be in real danger."

"How?"

"I don't know, but I can't shake the feeling that something bad is going to happen."

"We have a right to know what is needed of us. It's not fair of them to keep us in the dark."

"They must have their reasons."

"Their reasons? Who cares about their reasons? We're the ones with the mission. I want to know what is going on. I will ask them when I am in the portal."

"Yes, we have a right to know, but do not anger them. They are much more powerful than we are, and compared to them, well, I fear we are no match."

Mark felt the portal forming. "They are calling me, Jason."

"Good luck, and I'll see you tomorrow. We may have more time then."

"Yes, tomorrow," Mark replied, as he dissolved into the portal, leaving Jason watching.

Jason had a million thoughts running through his mind, but most pressing was the purpose of his life. He could only ponder what that plan would be. He felt helplessly feeble, and despite all his power, sorely inadequate.

He needed to get out, to be with people. He needed a distraction. He needed his music. He needed his band.

Jason left for the club. The band was not supposed to play that night, but he knew the stage was always open to him if he wanted it.

When he arrived at the club, the band was nowhere to be seen. He pushed his way through the crowd, looking for a sign of them. Then, over his shoulder, Helena appeared.

"Jason, thank God you are here. Everyone is upstairs! Gary overdosed. Please, come quick!"

They hurried up to the private room. Over an unconscious

Gary, Helena began to cry while BoBo frantically shook him. Gary was lying on the floor, his eyes rolled up into his head with a needle in his vein. Blood dripped down from the puncture in his arm, and his body gyrated frantically. He was in convulsions and close to death.

"He's going to die! He's going to die!" screamed Helena. BoBo, glazed over and half incapacitated, was shaking Gary, hoping that in some way he could pull him back from the brink.

Jason quickly moved in front of them and put his hand on Gary's chest. He weakened the effects of the drugs and restarted his heart, slowly bringing him back. Gary started to breathe normally, and his body relaxed. Jason allowed him to remain unconscious then said, "He's okay. Just a little too much junk... What did you guys take? Not that Mexican stuff, I hope."

Helena started to pant. "Oh my God! Oh my God! I thought he was dead for sure! Is he okay? Is he really okay?"

Jason looked back and said harshly, "You guys are always getting so fucked up! Why can't you just chill out and stop getting so... so... Well... dial it back a bit, anyway."

Jason was annoyed. He was tired of babysitting them, always being there to pull them out of trouble, always there to protect them, to carry them. He gave them money. He gave them the music, and he was getting fed up. He needed them tonight. This once, he needed to feel he belonged to something, to someone. He needed friends.

They're not the only good musicians in New York, especially Gary, who is always completely stoned. Why can't he hold it together? Jason paused, well... they are human, I shouldn't ask too much of them.

"Listen, guys, I am going downstairs for a drink. You guys stay with Gary, and we will make some music later when he is more up for it," said Jason.

"Oh, Jason! I was really scared this time. I was sure he was gone," said Helena, still shaking.

Gary mumbled, "What the fuck, holy shit! That was really fucked up!"

"You really scared me, Gary!" said Helena.

"Yeah, you scared the shit out of me!" echoed BoBo.

"You know...you guys were all together. You are supposed to watch out for each other. This kind of shit should not happen. We cannot make it as a group with this kind of thing going on," grumbled Jason.

Helena spoke, "I am really sorry, Jason. He must have gotten a strong batch or something. We all took it, but we had separate balloons. We always got our dope in bags, this west coast guy is selling the stuff. I never trusted him. He went down so fast. I am going to kill him if I see again, that punk L.A. jerk!"

"It's okay," said Jason. "Relax... Just try and be more careful when you don't know what you're getting. Anyway, I'll be back later. Just watch him for a while, and don't let him take anything else, and I mean anything else. I want to play later. I need music."

"Okay," said BoBo.

"I'll watch him," said Helena. They could see how angry Jason was.

Jason left and went back downstairs. Instead of going to his table, he went to the bar. He picked an empty spot and leaned against it, standing. He was looking around when he heard Angela's voice.

"Hi, baby, why so glum...? And where is your gang?"

"They're upstairs, completely fucked up."

Angela's voice was refreshing. That sweet Italian accent, that bubbly tone she always seemed to have, that twinkle in her eye and she smelled so good. He liked her, and he liked her more every time he saw her.

"I'm here, my sweet bambino," she said, nudging up closer to him. "Don't look sad. We had some real fun the other night, no? What happened to you? We woke up and you were gone. We weren't done with you, you know," she said, smiling. "That Chinese chick was really fun. I got her number. She wants me to call her. She told me to tell you... she likes you, too. Big time. You know what I mean?" Angela giggled.

Jason laughed. Angela is such an up, so full of life. She is never crying or needy, like Helena. She may not be as beautiful or talented, but she's really alive, and so cute.

"You're such a trip. There are no limits with you," responded Jason. "I really like that about you, Angela."

"I like you too, Jason. Why do you always want to be with that Helena? She is down so much. I'm a lot more fun. You have to live, Jason. My mother always said there might only be today, so live."

"Your mother sounds like a wise woman," declared Jason.

"You know, where I come from, life is hard. The ground is dry. The nights are cold, and during the day, the sun beats down and roasts your skin until you think it will bake the soul out of your body. But, you know, it made me strong, like the vines of the grape. The more they struggle, the sweeter the grape, and the sweeter the grape, the more delicious the wine." She laid it on thick. "Sweet like me, no?" She batted her eyes. Angela's body language was always perky. Her Italian flavor spiced every word.

"You're a real philosopher," said Jason.

"Well, I didn't go to school much, but I know I must be strong, and I know what I like, and I like to live. You gave me my freedom, Jason. I will never forget that. Now, let me give back to you." She pushed up against him harder. "I really like you, Jason... a lot."

"I like you, too, Angela. Say, I am going to make some new music upstairs later. Do you want to come listen?"

"No, I don't want to hang around Helena, but I will be down here all night. You can come find me later if you want."

"Well... Yeah, she was a bit mean to you. Okay, then... I'll find you later."

"Great... But she is a bitch!" she said, laughing, making sure she had the last word on the subject. "I got to work now. Come find me. I'll see you later."

Jason smiled as Angela answered the call of the customers and darted back to the tables. He turned to go back upstairs to the band, but then there was a flash. Out of the corner of his eye, he saw something. It was there, and then behind him, and then it was gone. Again, it came; they were over there, and there again! They looked like oversized teddy bears that belonged in a Macy's Christmas window.

What is going on? He thought. It was clear that no one else could see them. What are they? He instinctively knew that they were not from his home world. But they knew him, that was for sure. He tried to communicate, but every time he made an overture, they disappeared. He felt confident that they meant no harm. It seemed they were just curious. Jason, baffled, waved, and they vanished.

Jason walked up the stairs to see how the group was doing. When he entered the room, he saw that the group had not recovered much from their evening of intoxication. Gary and BoBo were strolling through the world of opiate dreams, barely able to speak, mumbling nonsensical stories to each other. They were drooling words and were as unintelligible as monkeys chattering in a banana tree. It would seem to a distant onlooker that they comprehended each other's words, but when one fell within earshot of them, there were actually just bits of vowels and consonants. They continued this theater of the incomprehensible with great animation and effect, arms waving, facial expressions intense and earnest. Helena looked on, rolling her eyes toward the ceiling at regular intervals. Jason could see that there would be no music tonight.

He walked up to Helena. "I guess we are not playing tonight."

"We can. We can," she said, attempting to get her legs underneath her.

"No, I'm leaving. Maybe you guys should really think about whether or not you want to be serious about this group." Helena was taken aback, and BoBo and Gary picked up their heads.

"We're serinusis… Ah, serious…" mumbled BoBo. "Anyone could get fucked up. It wasn't our fault. It was that junk! It was fucked up stuff. We didn't know." The words slurred from his lips.

"Okay, whatever. There's tomorrow but be straight. Okay?"

Helena blurted out, "We will be. I am so sorry, Jason."

Jason left the private room to go back downstairs. I am going to find Angela. At least I can forget things for a while and have some fun. I need to stop thinking.

Jason turned and could see that Angela was but a few feet away.

She approached him and said, "So, you're gonna hang with Nico and Lou tonight? Oh well, I guess we'll do it another time."

"No," he answered. "I want to be with you tonight."

Angela smiled. "Wanna go to my place? The roommates are out of town, but I'll call the Chinese chick if you like. Or just me? Maybe I'll check out early. There are too many girls working tonight, anyway."

"You can call her later, if you want. But let's go now. I don't want to get lassoed by Nico and Lou."

"Sure, baby. Let's get out of here. Why don't you wait outside?"

"Good idea," responded Jason.

Angela walked up to the bartender and told him she was leaving early. She went into the back to get her coat and bag. Jason stepped out onto the street.

There they are again!

Those fuzzy little overgrown teddy bears. Who the hell are they, why are they waving madly as if they were greeting a president?

What is going on? Who are these creatures?

He watched Angela come out through the door, then he turned back to look; the creatures were gone.

Angela saw that Jason looked startled. "Are you okay, baby? Is there something wrong?"

He paused. "No, nothing is wrong. But... Never mind. Let's grab a cab."

"But we can walk," she said. "It is only eight blocks."

"No, let's grab a cab. I don't feel like the streets."

Jason and Angela got into a cab.

"What's wrong bambino mio? You look like you saw a ghost. Come back. Your mind is a thousand miles away."

"Sorry," answered Jason. "But I just can't seem to. No, it's nothing. I just had something on my mind about the band. So, my Italian sweet cake, we're going to your place, right? I have never been there. Is it as nice as you are pretty?"

"No, baby. Not that nice," she answered. "And not nearly as pretty as me, but no one is home." She smiled. "And that's what counts."

"I am looking forward to some alone time with you, Angela. I feel really comfortable when I'm near you. Everything seems to just fade away. You know, you are like a drug to me. You make me feel good when I'm around you."

"Yeah, just what the doctor ordered," she answered with a raised eyebrow.

The doctor, Jason thought. I must talk to Abernathy. He can help me understand a lot about what the Council is up to. First, I'll talk to Mark and then Abernathy. I wonder if Mark and I would be able to see him together. That would be great. Us together.

"Hey, baby. You are drifting away again. Come back to me." She leaned into him and reached in for a tender little kiss on Jason's lips. "You're not paying attention to me. Come over here and give me some." She reached down between his legs, letting her fingers search. "You can't take me out and ignore me."

Jason cupped Angela's face and gently gave her a kiss on the lips. "Sorry, baby. I have a lot on my mind."

They arrived at Angela's place. It was a railroad apartment on the third floor of an old tenement walk-up. The kitchen boasted a bathtub that seemed to have been sitting there since the turn of the century, and behind the tub was wainscoting that looked twice as old. Even where you could see that Angela had scrubbed the walls, the dull paint underneath revealed more grime. The end room on the street side of the building doubled as a bedroom-living room combination. Two smaller rooms linked it to the kitchen. The place looked as if a bomb had gone off; clothing sprawled all over the furniture, and undergarments were piled up in the corner.

"Sorry for the mess. My roommate left for the coast in a hurry. She's a slob, anyway. Just push the stuff out of your way."

Angela walked Jason to the larger room where a mattress and box spring doubled as a sofa. She turned on two lava lamps. Two were already burning. The bed was covered with brightly colored throw pillows.

"Take off your coat, and I'll get some wine. I have some pot if you like."

"No, thanks. Not in the mood for that." Jason hated the smell of pot, and of course it had no effect upon him.

"Okay, whatever you like, baby. Just wine, then," she answered. "You know, I am really happy you're here, it means a lot to me."

"I'm glad I'm here too."

"I never really thought this would happen, you know? That night at the club... Well, I thought that would be it, just a thing that happened. But you're here. Can I ask you something, Jason? And please, you tell me the truth."

"Sure, Angela, what?"

"You know, you are such a cool guy, so smart, and so talented. You could have any girl you want. Am I dreaming that you could ever really go for a girl like me? A little Italian country girl?" she said timidly.

Jason knew he could never really reveal himself to Angela. Too much innocence was housed within that lustful mind. He could understand her want for him, but to trust her... no. He was would have to remain a secret.

"You're not a poor country girl anymore. And even though you came from a small place, you are very special, Angela. I don't care about pretense or any of that phony stuff. I just care about how you make me feel when I am around you. And you make me feel good. But let me tell you, please, don't get hung up on me, Angela. There is no future in it."

"See, I was right. You could never go for an Italian country girl like me."

"No! That's not it. It's just that... that there are a lot of things going on, and there may be some things that are going to take me away, maybe for good." Jason hung his head as the words left his lips.

"What do you mean? What's wrong? Are you in trouble? It's not Lucasie is it? I'm frightened for you. And it's all my fault. Oh!" she cried.

"No, no. Angela... No, it's something much larger."

"What can be bigger than those guys? Is it the Russians?"

Jason laughed. "No, not the Russians, either. Anyway, don't worry. I'll handle it." Jason lay back on the bed as he spoke. He took a deep breath.

Angela snuggled up to him, "Okay, let's just relax, then. We have all night." She kissed his lips.

"Yeah. That sounds good." He rolled over onto her, kissing her gently.

The hours passed quickly as they made love. Her moans were deep and her cravings loud. His hands glided along the sweat of her exhausted body, while her mouth was forever searching.

This was a new feeling for her, this all-in love for a man. Angela had no trepidations; she knew she could never own him, but that did not overcome her hunger for him. They stopped only when Angela reached for a cigarette. For a time, Jason lost himself in the rapture of Angela's arms, and the dread of what lay ahead faded. He felt at peace. Peace, even for a short time, was welcomed.

Then the phone rang. Angela answered it. She spoke for a

moment from the other room and came back.

"It's Saya!" she yelled. "Is it alright if she comes over?"

Jason, although taken by surprise, smiled.

She turned back to the phone. "He wants you to come. Please come – he has something on his mind that is troubling him. Come and help me make it go away." She turned again to Jason. "She says she can help you forget all your problems." Angela laughed out loud and spoke into the phone. "And you better help me forget mine too!"

Jason wanted to see her again, especially since he had recognized her. "Yes, tell her to come, but don't let her fool you. Her real name is Feiyan," he said loudly, knowing she would hear.

"You're in for some fun tonight, baby!" Angela giggled, and she gave Saya her address.

As she was hanging up, she heard Saya reply, "And tell him I heard what he said, and tell him I think he is a ghost. I will be right over."

Saya arrived within the hour, and the three wasted no time inventing ways to explore pleasure. Yet, when Saya's eyes locked with Jason's, the two shared an uneasy communication; she wanted more than his body. She wanted to know this mysterious being she was next to, this ghost that had come into her life. When Angela fell asleep, Saya seized the opportunity to talk to Jason.

"How do you know my real name? My Chinese name. What else do you know about me?"

"Does it matter how I know?" He responded, "You know that I am not here to harm you. I am not the assassin you dread. I know you fear no one, yet you fear me, don't you?" He smiled. "Trust me when I tell you, you have nothing to fear from me."

"It looks like Angela will sleep until the morning," said Saya. "Will you walk me home? I live nearby."

"Why? Do you need a bodyguard?" Jason joked.

Saya, smiled. "I just thought we could talk. I would like to get to know you. I know that sounds strange after what we have been doing, but those secrets are more easily shared by me. I don't even think sometimes when I am having sex. It's the intensity I crave, just getting lost in it. Does that sound strange to you?"

Jason grinned. "No, and it's a nice night for a walk."

They both got up and dressed as Angela fell even deeper into sleep.

Saya put on her clothing very deliberately and slowly; her movements reminded one of the careful gestures of a tea ceremony. Ever so quiet, ever so purposeful. From time to time she looked at Jason, wondering if his eyes would show if he was interested in more.

The thread of her shirt got caught and made it difficult to close the top button. As she struggled, Jason's hand found her fingers and freed the thread, allowing her to complete the task.

"There," he said and smiled.

"It's getting a little cool outside. You don't have a jacket, do you?" asked Saya.

"It's not a problem for me," he responded.

"Ha, of course not."

As they walked into the street, Saya's demeanor shifted, and she said emphatically, "So are you going to tell me something about yourself, where you're from, and how you came to speak perfect Mandarin as well as Cantonese?" And without catching her breath, "And how come you–"

"Is that what you are really interested in? How many languages I speak? Come on, did you ever ask yourself how it is you learn languages so quickly, yourself? How you move so fast and strike with such force? How you could always see what an adversary was going to do even before he was aware of it himself? Did you ever ask yourself where all this power came from? You have many questions inside you, Feiyan, I'm sorry, I mean Saya. What you really need to know is not where I'm from or how I know your language, but rather who you are."

Saya stopped dead in her tracks. Her back muscles firmed as her body tensed. Her mind sought the safety of her skills. She thought of running. The memory of running along the mountainside as a student rushed into her brain, but she instinctively knew there was no place to run from this man.

She tightened her fist but quickly reconsidered. She recalled the first time she was struck and knocked unconscious to the floor by her teacher; how helpless she felt. Who is this man? She thought. How does he know these things? Am I lost? Is today the day I die? Saya did not know how she knew of Jason's overwhelming power, how she knew that all her skill and strength would be useless, but she did.

Without hesitation, Jason, reading her mind, responded to Saya's concerns. "Don't worry. I told you that I am not here to harm you, and I am not a ghost! But I'm special, and in a way, we have known each other for a long time. Don't fear me. I would like to get to know you better. I think we could be friends," he spoke softly.

"I don't think we can be friends if I'm afraid of you. You have to tell me everything. Who are you? What are you?"

Almost on cue, the sky opened up, and it started to pour. The drops fell large and furious. They both took shelter under the metal awning of a Spanish bodega. The rain crashed down upon the roof, echoing in their ears as if they were standing inside a drum. Other people on the street rushed for shelter, and four rats jumped out of some garbage cans a few feet away. The red and blue neon lights from the store window cast patterns on the wet pavement. Jason took her hand and smiled. Saya's mind seemed to drift, his touch brought reassurance.

Looking at him she said softly, "I've always loved the sound of rain, I love the way the drops seem to talk to each other. When I was a child, I would always… Oh, never mind…"

Jason put his arm around her. "What do you fear, Saya, your end? What is waiting for you or not waiting for you? I think you have faced those thoughts before." He stared intently into her eyes. "Your end will not come from me. I promise you that.

Is that any help? Saya, you are special, different. Maybe we..."
He paused.

"Who are you?" she asked.

He did not answer for a moment and then said, "I am going to let you try to figure it out yourself."

"But I have your word that you will not harm me?"

"You have my word and more." He leaned forward, putting his hand on her lower back, his lips inches from hers. "I promise." Kissing her gently, his touch was meant to comfort rather than excite.

When they reached her door, Jason said, "I won't come up. We have already had a long night, but I am hoping you may be surprised when you go upstairs. You will understand more when you are home." They kissed quickly again, and Jason walked away, Saya's eyes trailing him.

When Saya opened the door, she took off her coat and threw it on the sofa. What could he have meant, you may be surprised when you get upstairs? Then she saw it in the corner; there was no mistaking its nobility. The delicate carving, the horsehair strings, the worn marks of her Mistress's hand were all there. She had held it in her hands many times. It was the most beautiful instrument in the temple, the erhu reserved for her teacher and only played when Saya had practiced her movements many years ago.

She picked up the bow, slowly drawing it across the strings. Her hand rested on the worn indentations of the wand left by her teacher. Her Mistress had promised it would be hers one day, but she had left this and many other dreams behind when she had fled the temple. Now it was here. Not since her childhood had she felt so safe.

CHAPTER 26

AN EMERGENCY MEETING

The Supreme Council rushed to meet. Dronin instructed Elgert and Allaceia to drop all matters and come to the high chambers immediately.

"We are receiving communications from Mark. He demands to know what is going to be asked of himself and Jason," said Dronin.

"Demands?" replied Allaceia. "This is a new development. They have never made such a bold overture before."

"I know. They are reaching their full strength. They just stood facing each other outside the plasma and communicated. They are growing stronger each day and will soon have power equal to ours," answered Dronin.

"We allow them to make demands of us. That would show weakness on our part. We will treat this as an inquiry and answer a question with another question. Furthermore, we should not look upon them as adversaries; they are my children. We will tell them we would like to communicate directly. Once they enter the portal together, we will see them face to face and can explain to them their purpose and their task," said Allaceia.

"Well, you are the diplomat, Allaceia, but they will soon be at full power. They will be able to challenge us," he said, hoping this bait would encourage her into revealing priorities, not in the interests of Eldern.

These events will be the opportunity I need to begin to turn Dronin against her and bring him into my web. Elgert laid his trap. He awaited Allaceia's reaction, and to his surprise, she took the bait.

"But they are my children; they will not turn against us."

She shows herself, thought Elgert. Again, he spoke, "There is another issue. Triptonians have been detected on Earth. They have been sighted in the vicinity of Jason."

"How did they get past our probes? This is a treaty violation!" exclaimed Dronin angrily.

Allaceia calmly interjected, "I will contact the ambassador immediately."

"I'm sure it wasn't an officially sanctioned visit, rather a rogue group of fans that snuck onto the planet. I have no idea how the probes did not detect them. They must have some sort of cloaking technology," continued Elgert.

Allaceia was well aware of the visits to earth by those furry little beings. She had allowed it as a favor to her friend, Mananken, the Ambassador of the Triptonians. "I must launch a protest and demand that it be stopped. If New Tripton gets involved in any way with our plans, it could be disastrous," she responded.

"Why? What could they do?" asked Dronin.

"They could be real trouble. You know, New Tripton is the only planet in the federation that is allowed to keep battleships. The agreement is centrons old; it was deemed by past councils that New Tripton's position on the outer edge of the galaxy was best suited to protect the other planets. This treaty binds us, but they can be difficult, and if they have acquired advanced cloaking technology, it could be extremely problematic. They are a capricious race, unpredictable at best. You say you believe it was not sanctioned; maybe it is just an innocent adventure, but do we really want them to know what we are up to on Earth? No. This could become a real issue. We must get to the bottom of it. Find out what they know, and why they went to Earth," said Allaceia, doing her best to display anger and dismay.

"I am sure you're correct and they're just fans of Jason's," said Elgert. "You know how popular he is with them. They probably mean no harm."

"Let's hope so," she replied.

Allaceia believed she had sold her innocence, but more than ever she had the feeling that Elgert was up to something.

"This is all the more reason to expedite our discussion with the twins," said Dronin, completely unaware of the dance of deceit and manipulation in which Elgert and Allaceia were engaging. He continued, "Allaceia, how do you suggest we proceed?"

"We must tell Mark to confer with Jason and plan to enter the portal with him. We will tell him it is time to reveal their purpose on earth."

"Yes, Allaceia, but how do you see this unfolding?" asked Dronin.

"We tell them the truth. We have been preparing them for this their whole lives. They will come to understand their duty, and we will stress that we will do all we can to ensure that they will survive. We should express our concern for them in an unwavering manner."

"But they may suffer, Allaceia. They may suffer beyond imagination!" said Dronin.

"Dronin, I will feel the pain of their suffering," Allaceia surprised herself with these words. She paused and spoke with authority, "As a member of the Council, there is no one more interested in their survival than me," she corrected herself coolly. "Yes, and we must acknowledge that they may suffer, especially Jason. But we will ask for their courage and promise our support."

"I might not be very satisfied with these words if I were them, as we are seated safely here, far from any danger or pain," said Dronin.

"They know that their purpose on Earth is to save it from destruction, and they know there will be perils. It is just the details and the magnitude that they have yet to learn...and this protégé of Jason continues to trouble me, the human who calls herself Saya. She is evolving rapidly. We don't know what she may become. Not to mention if she has offspring, she could develop a whole new race. My first assistant thinks she should be destroyed!" exclaimed Elgert.

"I don't agree," replied Allaceia. "We do not want to upset Jason at this point in time. You are far afield now, Elgert. Your proposal could be disastrous. We will leave her be for now."

"I defer to your judgment, Allaceia," responded Elgert, watching as an expression of dismay overtook Dronin.

So, we are here, Elgert relished, Dronin will have no choice but to turn to me.

CHAPTER 27
NOT ALL WOUNDS BLEED

Saya awoke in her room. She got up and slowly walked into the kitchen, half-consciously filling her teakettle. She put it on the stove. She was different somehow. Something had changed within her, but she was not sure what. Can this really be? Her thoughts in a whirl, she looked across the room at the ehru that once rested in the most hidden part of the temple, but now sat in the corner near her window.

He isn't human. He must be some form of spirit, a guide from beyond this world. Saya thought back on all her teachings, the words of the monks and her Mistress when she was called Feiyan. Never had she heard of such a man. He said I shouldn't fear him, that he would protect me, but why does he care about me? He saw something, felt something special that attracted him. I know he wants me, but there is more; I feel him in my mind. When he touched me, he penetrated me. This isn't just a physical thing. And then the erhu! How did it get here?

Saya knew that the answers would only come when Jason allowed her to understand, but the same question kept haunting her: Why me?

Up until now, the great influences in her life had been the two women who had guided her. One was a Chinese monk and the other the wife of a Japanese silk trader. Both were strong and noble women. But Saya felt an influence even greater now, driving her to search for an understanding. Why do I feel I've already known him for so long? This connection is like a primal passage deep within my mind.

The memories of the loss of her Mistress at the monastery, as well as not having seen Mistress Kaya for years, made her sad. The beautiful home in Japan where she first learned of love made Saya pause. Taking in a breath, she thought, I miss them both dearly, but I am happy to be free of my obligations. Saya chose to think only of the beautiful moments. All these thoughts had been locked inside her, lost in another place until today. Meeting Jason brought everything back.

Saya looked again at the erhu and wiped away a tear. As she heard the teakettle rattling, her stomach started to grumble, returning her mind to the present. I'm in the mood for some soba, she thought. Every time I think of Japan, I want some. Somehow it always fills my loneliness. Angela told me about this new place on 2nd Avenue called MIE. I think I'll give it a try.

She looked across the room at a chair where a pair of jeans and a t-shirt were sprawled, then picked up the top. It had a few holes in it. Loving its comfort, she felt alive under its veiled sexiness. She turned off the stove and, grabbing a coat out of her closet, set off for the street. As she walked into the hall, she saw her landlady at the foot of the stairs, a gray-haired Italian woman named Rosa, sweeping. Her warm expression was always there, yet it seemed that gravity had begun to win the battle, for even within the last few years, Saya had noticed that her neck was showing those telltale lines, and her eyelids had drooped a notch. And while all the women Saya knew were talking about their biological clocks, she knew that since the death of her husband, Rosa's thoughts were often about the last toll of the bell. Still, without fail, the building was always spotlessly clean, thanks to her obsession with tidiness.

"Morning, Saya! How are you, and how is your Italian girlfriend?"

"I'm fine, Rosa. And Angela is great. I'll tell her you said hello."

Rosa had often seen her with Angela, for the two of them had been spending a lot of time together lately.

Then as she was walking out the door, Saya thought she heard Rosa say, "They are both so beautiful. Too bad they are lesbians." But she knew Rosa would never make such a bold remark.

Did I really hear that? She thought. It was almost as if she was thinking out loud. Strange, it was as if... "What did you say, Rosa?" Saya turned and raised her eyes toward Rosa cleaning the stairs. The old woman was embarrassed, casting her eyes down towards the floor as if a deep secret had been unearthed.

"Me? I didn't say anything." But Saya could see the surprised look on her face.

CHAPTER 28
KNOWLEDGE COMES

J ason had just left Saya at her door. What were the chances I'd stumble upon her, the one who has been haunting my memories since I was a child? He thought of the mysteries and pleasures he had felt with Angela. He thought of Helena, with all her beauty and soaring ambitions that so quickly turned sugar into vinegar. But Saya... this is different.

When he entered his apartment, he set his thoughts aside; Mark was waiting for him.

Mark's calls were heard on Eldern. He and Jason were to be granted an audience. Mark was informed that all would be explained.

"What have you learned from the Council? Have they told us anything?" asked Jason.

"They have told me nothing except that they want to meet with us. We're to enter the portal together, and we'll meet them there. They're calling us their 'children'. There are three of them. They said that we will learn everything we wish to know."

"When?"

"When we choose to. When we are ready," said Mark.

"Let's do it now. This very second."

"We could, but I think we should wait. Let's be strategic and consider what we want to say. I'd like to speak with Dr. Abernathy, first. He's always helped me to be clear."

"Yes," responded Jason thoughtfully. "That might be a good idea. He has proven himself insightful. He could be a good sounding board." Jason hesitated. "I don't know why, but the thought of this meeting unsettles me. I feel it. I don't know why, but I feel it."

"Yes, I feel uncomfortable as well, but perhaps that is simply because of the importance of this meeting. We both know we are here to save this world from destruction, but the how is the mystery."

"Yes, and maybe more than that. Listen, Mark, speaking of mysteries, I've been seeing strange little beings. I'm not sure how to describe them except as walking teddy bears. I realize how ridiculous this sounds. But, have you seen anything like that?"

"I see them in your mind now, but I have not seen them in the world. They must be interested in only you."

"Well," responded Jason, "they are not from Earth for sure, and they are not from our home world, either. I doubt they mean us harm. In fact, I got a very friendly feeling from them, but they would not communicate. They vanished when I tried to approach them. Should we ask the Council about them?"

"No, let's keep it between us for now. What do you think they want from you?" asked Mark seriously.

"They did not seem to want anything but to observe me. They were… It's strange. They reminded me of groupies, the people who love the band. They were acting silly too. Sweet and silly. I didn't feel threatened."

"Well," responded Mark, "I imagine it means something. It's strange that this is occurring now, just as this meeting is approaching."

"Yes, it's all very strange," said Jason.

"Well, we can think about what it all means later. For now, we should focus on the conversation with the Council. We need a plan."

"I agree. Let's try and see Abernathy beforehand," said Jason.

Mark picked up the phone and dialed the doctor.

Martha answered. "Dr. Abernathy's office. May I help you?"

"Yes, Martha. This is Mark. I need an emergency appointment as soon as possible."

"Mark," she responded in an annoyed tone. "You cannot keep asking for emergency appointments. We don't operate like that around here, you know. Well, there is next Tuesday at 2 PM, and, let's see…"

"No, Martha. This is an emergency. Tell the doctor I will be bringing my brother with me. We can't wait until next week!"

"Well, let me talk to the Doctor. Wait, he is in Boston for a conference. He always calls me at the end of the day. Call me back around 6pm. I will see if he is able to make some time for you both."

"Thank you, Martha. I really appreciate it. I'll bring you some flowers when we drop in."

"Hmmm…" she replied, still sounding annoyed.

***

As Allaceia watched her children on her private viewing screen, her first assistant asked permission to speak to her. "Grand Mistress, I have some alarming news."

Allaceia turned off the screen and responded, "Yes, what is it?"

"Our spies have discovered that Elgert has been in direct communication with The Prime and that the communication was initiated by The Prime itself."

Allaceia looked back at her assistant trying to appear unalarmed, but she was shocked. "Thank you. Please keep me informed of any new information," she replied coolly.

Allaceia could only assume that The Prime was upset. Its neural networks are in conflict, she thought. Something within its being is seeking other allies. But why? It has enjoyed a peaceful existence with me as Grand Mistress. Before I challenge Elgert, I need more information.

Allaceia had long ago placed a "back door" into the consciousness of The Prime. It was a gateway that only she could access. It's time for a little work, she thought. Let's see what Elgert is up to.

***

Mark and Jason waited for the hour to pass. Finally, at 6 PM sharp, Mark called.

"Hello, Martha. It's Mark again. Did you talk to the doctor? Yes, of course we can, tomorrow at our usual hour. Thank you so much, Martha. This means a great deal to us, really, more than I can express. Yes, a whole beautiful bouquet."

Mark hung up the phone and turned to Jason. "Well, we can't see him until tomorrow, but maybe this will give us more time to prepare. In the meantime, what shall we do? You know, I have always wanted to go to The Dom and hear you play. Can we do that?"

"Sure," he responded, "That sounds great. You can meet the group and hang out. And you know, I've got some other women you could meet. They are all very pretty and a lot of fun."

"Yeah, I wonder if Gabriela is free. I would love for you to meet her. I know she would love to hear you play."

"Does she know about me?" asked Jason.

"Well, I mentioned you, but that's all," Mark replied.

Jason frowned. "Maybe we could call her later." He paused. "You know, Mark, the people I hang around with are a bit out there. You should meet them first, and then you can make up your mind about bringing her to the club tonight. You can decide if it's the right moment for her to meet all my crazy friends. Even meeting me alone might be, as they say, a bit much for her to swallow."

"Huh, I didn't think about that. Okay, we can wait. But I want to go to The Dom with you."

"Okay, great!" he responded. "But first, let's go into the portal together for a while. We will initiate contact for a meeting but let us experience being in there together. I feel it calling me. You know, I think we have more power to gain."

Mark acknowledged Jason with a nod. "Yes, let's do it."

CHAPTER 29
A NEW LEVEL

J ason entered the portal first. Before he had faded into the pure energy state, Mark followed. They refused to acknowledge any efforts of direct contact from the Supreme Council. They just absorbed the portal's power.

They found that being in the energy flow together enhanced their sense of power exponentially. The effects of the portal magnified as it streamed between them. They each were able to understand how the other drew upon it. When they emerged, they both noticed that they had altered slightly in appearance and stature. They looked larger.

"This is beyond a normal session." Jason looked down at himself.

"You look different, Jason," replied Mark. "As do I. Yes, we have grown stronger. Maybe much stronger."

"It's almost 10 p.m. People are arriving at The Dom now," said Jason. "Ready?"

"Yes. Let's go!"

"Well," said Jason giving Mark a once over, "how about borrowing some of my clothing? That corduroy uniform of yours just does not make it in my world."

Once Mark looked suitable in his new outfit, they headed off for The Dom. As they walked together, Mark smiled and said, "It is a marvelous thing, us being together like this. I feel so completed by you."

"I feel that too," responded Jason with his own grim. "The world seems new now. I can only imagine the possibilities of what we could do, what we could accomplish together."

When they entered The Dom, the first person they saw was Angela. She was moving from table to table with drinks in her hand.

"There is my little Italian ball of fire," Jason said as he pointed in her direction. "Her name is Angela. I want you to meet her. She is all life and no limits."

"She's beautiful. I feel her energy, too. I can see why you like her."

Just then, Angela rushed over and threw her arms around Jason. "Hello, baby! Oh, I have missed you every second you've been gone!" She gave him a kiss.

"Angela! I missed you, too, but we were just together. Are you being Italian with me? Crying at the doorstep when one says goodbye?" Jason chided.

"Yeah, I guess you know me already. So, who is this beautiful boy you brought with you? I've never seen him before. He looks a lot like you. You related or something?"

"This is my brother, Mark. We have not been able to hang out like this... I mean... He has been away. It's kind of a long story. But he's here now and I couldn't wait to introduce you."

"He's really cute. He's your brother? Well, that's a surprise." Angela pushed her way in between them, her accent growing thicker with excitement. "Hi, I'm Angela, a very, very special friend of your brother. Where's he been hiding you?" She smiled. "I am so happy to meet you. Jason, you bad boy, how could you keep this beautiful man such a secret? He's so, so cute..." Angela reached over and touched Mark's arm to feel his muscles. "And strong!"

"He's been busy with work and travel...," began Jason.

"Yes, I have been kind of unavailable," continued Mark, interrupting Jason's sentence, "but I am very happy to meet you, Angela."

"He's kind of formal, so polite, Jason. Tell him to loosen up around me. I'm kind of like family, right?" Angela said, moving in closer to them both. "Your brother and I are, well, real good friends. Did he tell you? Did he tell you about me? Your brother, huh?" She looked at Jason. "I hope you did. So, you gonna show him a good time, Jason? Don't forget to invite me if you're gonna party!"

"You're always on top of my list, Angela. You know that," responded Jason.

"I better be," she replied with a wink.

In the background, the DJ started to play the Rolling Stones' "I Can't Get No Satisfaction." Angela started to move with the music.

The Dom was crowded with hippies; the smell of pot and hashish was everywhere. The strobe lights started to spin, and a kaleidoscopic light show began. The room's walls were lush with plasmatic colors as the spectacle filled the dance floor. An entranced and throbbing mob of bodies wildly flailed into a ritualistic frenzy, overwhelmed by the beat. They started singing along: I can't get no satisfaction . . .

The voices roared from the floor while the music bellowed out from the speakers. Angela's body was sweating, burning. She was swept away by excitement. The perspiration poured down her neck as she surrendered to the anarchy. Her body moved as sinuously as the scent of her lilac perfume, mingling with the moisture from her pores. Her rhythm sent forth her essence into the room. Glistening in the light, the outline of her bare breast showed through the thinly veiled Indian shirt she wore as her moisture overcame its texture. Swaying with the music, she moved closer to the twins.

"We gonna be friends, right?" Angela nudged herself between them, moving rhythmically to the music. "So, Mark..." She looked at him in a flirtatious manner and spoke into his ear softly, "Did you two share your toys as children?" She danced away, her head bobbing to the music as she laughed out loud.

"You are a real trip, Angela. But you better slow down a bit.

You want to scare my brother off or something?"

"Huh? No, he's a big boy, no. And please, don't you get pissy with me, Jason. I just think he's cute. That's all." Obviously stoned, she smiled. "But it does feel nice in here between you both." She snuggled up to them, laughing again. Jason figured she had taken LSD; he knew she loved it.

"Alright, Angela. Take it easy. My brother is the shy type. You know, my brother mostly spends his life in books. He just wants to hang out and hear me play tonight and meet my friends for right now. Okay?"

"So, I'm a friend, right?" she asked, smiling.

Jason looked at Angela critically and said in a strong tone only her name. "Angela."

"Okay. Okay. I got it. I was just being friendly, that's all. I'm not trying to scare him. Anyway, I don't bite... Not that much, anyway!" Angela cackled. She tossed a coy look in Mark's direction. "So, I see you later, huh...? I gotta work now." Angela kissed Jason and started to walk away. She then turned and blew Mark a kiss. "See you later, pretty brother." As they both walked out into the hall, Angela again sought them out, shouting over the noise of the crowd.

"Saya is running around here somewhere. If you like, maybe we could all hang out together later." Angela gave him her overdone mischievous smile.

"Jason," said Mark. "What was she talking about? Was she inferring? That we would all have sex together, or something? What was that?"

"Oh, don't worry about it. She is a bit of a nut, fun, but a nut. Anyway, she is high on something. She's really a crazy chick. That's why I like her so much." He laughed. "But you should really meet this Chinese girl, Saya."

Mark, shocked, looked at Jason. "What? What do you mean? How many girls are you involved with?"

"Relax. Anyway," said Jason, "let's find my band. You have to meet them all."

Mark stared at Jason, bewildered. "Jason, is that the kind of stuff you are into? This is not my scene."

Jason just smiled. "Okay, okay. I know we're different. Listen, I know you have seen a lot of my life, but it's different when it's real. It's all in fun, you know. Let's just relax and go with the flow. Let's have a good time and forget about everything else."

"Okay. I'll do my best. I'm just not as free as you are. You're almost like these humans. I have been focused on learning what it means to love one of them, not learning to be free and wild like you. It must be your music that gives you all these capabilities. All of these friends you have… This place is really crazy. I have never experienced anything like this before."

"Wait until you meet the group. You are going to love them. They are a little unpredictable, but very endearing when you get to know them."

"Ummm… okay," Mark responded not looking convinced.

Jason started to weave through the crowd to bring Mark upstairs to meet the band. All of a sudden, he shouted out to Mark, "There! Mark, do you see them? Those furry little things! Over there, by those tables! Do you see them?"

Mark turned. "Where? Where? I don't see anything."

"Over there! Right over there… Damn! They're gone now. They were just there. Didn't you see any of them? They were waving at me."

"No, Jason, I didn't see them."

"Something is going on, Mark…"

CHAPTER 30
ELGERT'S AMBITIONS MOVE FORWARD

Elgert's appointment with The Prime had arrived. As he approached the monolith in the center of the city, he felt uncertain. What will I find? Will I be seen as worthy?

When he reached the base of the structure, the computer emanated its awareness. He raised his hand, hoping that the gesture would elicit some form of response, a recognition. Suddenly, he was within.

Its inner domain was nothing like he had imagined. There was no hint of a machine. Instead, it felt liquid, a flowing rhythm of colors and vibrations, ever-changing, nothing in one place. He sensed a communication; an incomprehensible flow was affecting him, conveying information in manners unbeknownst to him. Allaceia was the only being versed in the subtleties of the quantum dialogues. He felt inadequate. Struggling to open a channel, he searched his mind for an answer. This is not a language. It is something else. Pushing forward, trying not to appear feeble, he searched for a way to communicate. He didn't want to give The Prime a poor impression of himself.

From a directionless source came words: "Communicate as you normally would in your own environment. It is not necessary that you comprehend me."

Elgert sensed his communication would be seen as primitive, but he knew no other course. In his most determined manner, he spoke, emphasizing that he should be the only one on the Council worthy of trust. He explained that Allaceia must be eliminated and that even Dronin's role should be diminished in time, if not ended. He argued that his interests alone were in complete agreement with its purpose.

He had no way of knowing how his dialogue was being received, standing before this faceless entity which stood in judgment, but he continued, in an almost endless stream of arguments, punctuating his logic with urgency. With cold indifference, The Prime's voice periodically responded, "Continue." The only hint of a positive response came when Elgert conveyed his argument that Mark and Jason were a threat. At the mention of their names, The Prime responded, "Yes." Yet in the next moment, it was followed by the word simply, "Explain." After his presentation, The Prime replied coldly, "We will contact you."

With those words Elgert found himself transported without warning, outside the monolith, still unsure of his position.

CHAPTER 31
SPINNING IN AN EDDY

Saya was trying to make sense of what had just happened with her landlady. Did I really hear her thoughts? Is such a thing possible? As she walked down the street, she felt like her mind was being invaded by the people about her, as if in a crowded room, hearing every conversation at once.

What's happening? Am I going mad? No matter how fast her mind ran ahead to hide from the cacophony about her, she fell deeper into the abyss of other people's secrets.

She thought back to her teaching at the temple, Okay, relax. Breathe. I can stop this. I can hear other people's thoughts, but why? It's Jason! He did something to me.

The sounds of people's minds kept crashing into her. Many were harsh, wreckages, darkly heartsick and empty; some were full of fantasy, bubbling childishly at play, but most were simply routine thoughts of things that had to be done. I have to stop listening, or I will go mad!

She turned the corner. I will meditate to make my mind blank. I can do this. I know how. Then I will find Jason.

Saya started to chant silently, focusing on one word, Soba... Soba, Soba, Soba she chanted. The voices in the air dimmed. I can do this. I can control this.

Soba! I'll just think about Soba! She started to picture the noodles, a beautiful wooden plate piled high with cold soba. In her mind's eye, she poured the tamari over the noodles, gathered them with her chopsticks and brought them into her mouth. She could smell the sauce and taste the freshness of the noodles as she slurped them down, making the familiar joyful swishing sounds that recalled the shops in Japan. She repeated the words out loud, "Soba, Soba, Soba..." Her mind grew peaceful, and she smiled. "There."

CHAPTER 32
CONCERNS BLOSSOM ON ELDERN

"I have made repeated efforts and they are not responding to us. Perhaps they are not in the vicinity of the portal," Elgert announced to the other two members. "Or perhaps they are and are not responding on purpose. That tells us something," Allaceia interjected. "If they are not communicating with us, we can deduce that they are now able to walk together. We had already detected that they had entered the portal together, had we not? Walking together means they have fully developed."

"They may have reached a high state of power, but we have existed for thousands of centrons," snapped Dronin. "I hope time will bring with it perspective and wisdom. They are far from understanding their abilities or the extent of their powers. They will continue to develop, and we will have to deal with this eventually. Further, their rapid development concerns me. It's possible that they will question the mission and our judgement."

"We are about to ask them to place their lives at risk. We should have faith in our original judgments of Mark and Jason. I believe that our teachings will guide them and that they will value our advice when the time comes and complete their mission."

"Why do you think they left the portal, especially now?"

said Elgert, again baiting her to reveal herself.

"I am not sure, but it is my guess that they are questioning things, who they are, their purpose. Maybe they wanted some time to think before we spoke to them. Maybe they fear that the task will start soon, and they want some time to themselves before it begins. They really do not know each other on this level. More than likely, they just want to experience each other. They are brothers, after all. And then there is all that life on Earth, its richness, and all that emotion and passion. If I were there, I might like to see more of it myself. I have faith in them, Elgert. I have seeded them well, and we have educated them finely. They will not stray from their purpose; of that I am sure."

"Can you see them?" asked Elgert. "Do you know where they are?" With every word, he thought, *she seals her fate.*

"I can pull them up on the screen if you'd like. There they are at Jason's favorite hangout, The Dom. They are there together, enjoying each other's company. See, it is as I said. They both just needed some time with each other."

"Oh! And what is that?" said Elgert, pointing to the screen. "It's those damn Triptonians again. I thought you said this was under control, Allaceia."

CHAPTER 33

MEETING THE BAND

Jason and Mark walked upstairs and entered the private room to find BoBo and Gary jamming. They were improvising on a blues tune that Jason had written the other day. Helena was sitting in the corner, listening and bobbing her head to the beat. She hummed the melody softly as Gary's guitar cried out the notes as if in mournful pain. Gary could play. "Hey, Jason, what's up? Who is this guy?" she asked, looking at Mark critically. "I thought we weren't bringing people in while we were working on new stuff?"

"Helena! This is not 'people,' this is my brother. Mark, say hello to Helena. Don't mind her rudeness. This big guy is BoBo, and that skinny one next to him is Gary." Gary waved, and BoBo gave an acknowledging nod.

"Your brother?" retorted Helena. "Holy shit. You have a brother? How come we never heard about him before? You never mentioned a brother."

"Yeah, well... We kind of travel in different worlds, but we are very close. He's in town for a bit and we've been catching up. He wants to hear our music, so what do you say we show him what we're about?"

"Sure, sure. I'm just surprised that you have never brought him around before now," said Helena. She smiled sweetly, but her tone was acerbic. "Well, it's great to meet you, Mark. Here, come sit next to me. Your brother, huh? That's interesting."

She looked at Jason questioningly, and then briefly back at Mark. "I see the resemblance. Except for the hair, yeah, you look a lot alike. Do you play, Mark, or sing?"

"Well... I never really tried. I do write poetry though. I love poetry; poetry and the stars." Mark spoke softly, with quiet confidence.

"The stars? What do you mean, the stars?" Helena was intrigued.

"I mean the cosmos. All that is out there. All that is beyond space and time. I love thinking about what we cannot see, the vastness of the heavens. I also love poetry and literature, too. It all kind of makes me feel complete."

"Whoa! Your brother is really heavy, dude!" blurted Gary.

"Indeed," echoed BoBo in his low, bellowing voice. "We will have to get him stoned and listen to some outer space stories."

Mark laughed. "I just like a lot of things, that's all. I really want to hear you guys play, though. Jason has told me how fantastic you are, and I hear that you sing like an angel, Helena."

"Well, that's what some people say," she said smiling, doing her best to sound coy, "but it's your brother who is the real star. He brings us all together! We have to play for you. Let's go down on stage, Jason. Let your brother really hear us right. Not in this little room. Let him see us up there. I want him to see me do my thing with the crowd cheering and the lights beaming,"

Fascinated, Helena could not take her eyes away from his. Maybe I could like this guy. She knew that when he heard her voice and saw her body sway, she could pique his interest. I'm going to give it a go.

"Yeah!" shouted BoBo. "I'll go down and clear the stage for us. Whaddya say, Jason? Let's do it! I'm in the mood to play, too."

Jason nodded affirmatively, and BoBo lumbered out to make the arrangements.

Helena's interest in Mark was obvious. She did not understand exactly why Mark attracted her so quickly, yet she felt it, felt something primal when she looked at him. I'm comfortable around this guy. He is not the brooding type, and maybe he's not as removed as Jason.

Reading her mind, Mark telepathically sent her a message that he was taken and not to get her hopes up. As quickly as she received it, Helena dismissed the notion.

Maybe he's taken, but he's so cute! Anyway, who's hotter than me? I don't mind some competition, and I'm sure I could borrow him for a while.

Jason could not believe how fickle Helena was, and with his brother, no less. He actually hoped that Mark would go with her, thinking a night of purely hedonistic and selfishly wanton sex would be good for both of them. Hiding his sardonic smile, Jason decided to watch the drama unfold.

Entering the room from the dance floor below, BoBo announced the stage was clear, and they could go on whenever they were ready.

"Great," said Jason. "Let's do it! You guys better be at your best tonight! I don't want my brother to be disappointed."

"We will really cook," responded Gary. "I promise you that."

"Yeah, yeah, yeah," said Helena with a twinkle in her eye giving Mark a smile, "Sweet like candy."

They were greeted with applause as they walked onto the stage. Jason motioned for Mark to sit on the left side in order to be as close to the music as possible. They started to play, and the crowd cheered as they heard the group's classic growling sound. BoBo pounded a beat while Gary's guitar yearned and cried, and at last, Helena's shimmering voice rang out. When Jason started to sing, the place went mad.

The group played for hours, but to the crowd, it seemed like minutes. Helena was especially wonderful that night. Her singing redefined the notes with ease, slipping in and out of melodic sophistication, swooning gracefully, piercing into the audience. Her body persuaded, as she purred within an aura found only in dark places. "Captivating," was heard from a manager's voice off stage. She was hungry for approval, and she wanted to leave behind only devastation and satisfaction. Jason allowed her the spotlight since he knew her secret motivation. He did take the last number though, thinking, it's my band, after all.

Leaving the stage, Jason turned to Helena, "You were really on tonight. What's gotten into you? Have you been eating your Wheaties?" he said laughing. Of course, Jason knew the motivation was Mark. He had struck her like a bolt.

"I don't know, it was if something grabbed me. We were great, I feel great!" She turned to Mark, "Sooo, what did you think? Did you like it?" she asked expectantly.

Mark smiled wide, and his excitement was palpable. "It was fabulous. You're fabulous. You all are." They were screaming to each other since the crowd would not stop roaring in maddening applause. Jason signaled that they should all retreat so they could talk.

Just then, Angela appeared out of nowhere. "You guys were unbelievable, Jason. Fantastic! And you, Helena, magnifica! Brava, brava!"

Jason knew her compliment to Helena almost caught in her throat, but she could not contain her enthusiasm. It was as if she could do nothing but give the devil its due.

"Why, thank you, Angela! Thanks a lot."

Angela responded with a perfunctory smile, trying not to show her disdain for Helena. But she could not hide that she was impressed. The crowd could not be silenced. Helena returned to the front of the stage and raised her arms towards the crowd, beaming with pride. She had come into her own, and everyone knew it.

Jason could see that both Helena and Angela had partying on their minds, and he was up for some frolic himself. But peering into Mark's mind, he saw he was not ready for such an evening. Telepathically, Jason asked Mark what he wanted to do with the night. Mark returned the communication. He had a wonderful time, but he was not up for a wild night with his friends.

Helena looked at Mark. "So, what are you guys up to tonight? We could stay around here or bang around town to a few places! It's not that late! What do you say?"

Looking at Jason, Mark replied somberly, "Well, we have a really big day tomorrow, and I am not sure about running around tonight."

Just then, Angela snuggled up against Jason, grasping his arm and leaning her head against his shoulder. "Say, I just quit early to come out with you! You're not going to quit on me, are you?"

Jason glanced over towards Mark and Helena. "It's up to Mark; it's his night. If he has had enough, then that's it!" But, really, in the back of his mind, he knew that a double date entailing Angela and Helena in the same room could end up in a knife fight.

Mark turned to Helena. "I had a great time tonight. The performance transcended the music; it was life-giving. But I must quit on you. I have to hit the sack early. We can do something again another night, right?"

Helena felt disappointed but tried not to show it. "Sure, we can do it another time. Or maybe something else sometime, if you like." She looked intensely at Mark, letting him know that she was really interested. Mark paused, looking back. Her intentions were clear.

He liked Helena, but he was completely infatuated by Gabriela. And although Helena was mysterious and beautiful, he did not see how it would be possible for him to bring her into his life in the way she wanted. He could barely handle the stress of one woman.

Man! But she is really beautiful, he said to himself. And my, what a voice!

Jason jumped into Mark's mind, teasing him. Dear brother, what do you want to do?

Mark communicated back: Jason, we had better get out of here soon! She's really sexy, and I am tempted.

Just then, Helena asked, "Would you like my number? Maybe we could get together, hang out, do something?" She smiled mischievously, with a glint in her eye. She was not usually this forward, but she could tell that Mark was a shy one; tonight, she had better make her move.

Jason jumped back into Mark's mind. So, here we are, where the roads part. Either get her number and we bail out of here or accept the offer and just go for it! I can see she's yours for the taking.

Mark took a breath. "Yes, I would love your phone number. I'll call you soon. We can make a plan or something."

"Great, you will have to let me show you my favorite clubs." Clubbing was not really on her mind, but she thought it sounded right.

Helena wrote down her number and gave it to Mark. He is so nice; I wonder if he likes me! I like the fact that he is passing on me tonight. I would have probably slept with him, woken up feeling like shit, and never heard from him again. Same old story with another face. But if he calls me, it will mean he really likes me! I am sure he has a girlfriend, but maybe I worked some magic on him tonight. God, he's so cute! I hope he calls.

"Yeah, call me!" said Helena.

Mark replied, "Yeah," trying to sound a bit cool, but still interested.

Jason's mind communicated back to his brother: You know, these humans are really starting to charm me. Of course, we could control their minds if we chose to, and we could do whatever we wanted with them. We could treat them as toys in a sandbox. But living as they do, experiencing as they do... Having a girl like Helena want you, really want you... How much fun is this? Then he said aloud, "Angela, I am going to take my brother home. Maybe I can find you later."

"Ok, bambino mio. Hit my buzzer three times; two short and one long. I'll know it's you. I'll buzz you in. You know the address. I'll be home about 2 a.m. Okay?"

Turning towards Mark, Jason said, "Okay then, let's get going. See you guys later! You all were awesome tonight! You really did me proud, all of you. But you, Helena, you were so, so superb!"

"Hey, that's my line! You can't steal that from me, Jason!" She smiled as she spoke.

"No chance. No one can say it like you. Okay, see you guys later."

Jason and Mark headed out to the ballroom, preparing to leave. Jason turned to Mark. "So what do think? Did you have a good time? Everyone really liked you. Especially Helena." He grinned.

"I had a wonderful time! It was perfect. And I really do like Helena. But I don't know if I could do anything with her. It would be too complicated for me. I am really crazy about Gabriela. She is something; wait until you meet her."

"Yes, yes," he responded. "I understand, but didn't the Council instruct us to learn and experience?" He grinned as he spoke. Mark could see that Jason was playing with him, poking fun at him for being conservative.

Mark wanted Jason to understand how much Gabriela meant to him, how special she was, how she could see such depths in things – not just the black and white – but a thousand shades between. But it was true that Helena was very tempting.

Mark followed Jason across the dance floor, weaving through the crowd. The music was still raging, bodies dancing wildly. He had never been to a club like this; it was intoxicating. He could see why Jason was seduced by this life. It ate you up and overcame your senses.

They were approaching the club's exit when a fight broke out to their left. A very large young guy, maybe 6'4" and 280 pounds and wearing a football t-shirt bearing the word "Iowa" was swinging a small Spanish guy around like a rag doll. The smaller guy was trying to punch the bigger one, but his blows bounced off him. His wailing swings appeared more like a bird flapping its wings against the face of a cliff. The two were on a direct course to intersect with Mark when Jason touched the large one. He fell to the ground like overcooked spaghetti rolling off a fork.

The little Spanish guy stood over the stunned and dazed football player waving his arms victoriously, a gladiator in triumph. He yelled to his friends, "Who's the man? I'm the man!" He danced over the larger man, taking in the applause and cheers, beating his chest with boastful pride. Not knowing that his blows had nothing to do with the giant's fall, he relished his moment as a champion.

Walking quickly towards the exit, Mark motioned to Jason. "We better get out of here before anyone notices us."

But as they walked out to the street, Jason froze. "Mark! There! Do you see them? Those furry little things again! Do you see them?"

Mark looked up. "Yes, Jason! I see them! Who, what are they?"

In an instant, they were gone.

CHAPTER 34

IN HER BED WITH HER THOUGHTS

G abriela lay in her bed gazing at the light from the window. It was early; the sun had just begun to sneak into the room. The windowpanes started to glow. She could see the shadows of the trees playing on the white linen curtains, swaying lethargically and telling stories, like rivers, hiding their directions.

Sometimes rivers can't make up their minds, she thought, like me most of the time... pathetic. I feel like a raft being swirled by the currents, kicked around by the rocks, my head half underwater. I'm barely hanging on.

She looked over to her husband. His large hairy back was turned towards her. He's grown so fat. He has become a stranger, and he still smells of cigars and whisky. These days, he always seems to. He was up until 3 a.m. again with his crew of scientists and students, talking wild abstract theories, physics, and strange, incomprehensible mathematics. How could I have ever thought I could make a life with a guy like him? He used to be so interested in everything. With that beautiful blond hair, and those blue eyes... He was thin and tall. Oh, how I wanted him. I loved him! But that was a long time ago. Now he is boring and bald! I wonder if he was always this hairy... maybe I never noticed it, or all those dark spots and ugly skin tags that seem to grow like insects all over him.

She looked again at the curtains. The light just played, the lines of the shadows fading and then sharp again, moving, wandering. She wanted that. Just to move and wander, to feel free, to feel like she could just…

I'm being unfair, but that's the way I feel. I wonder what Mark is doing right now. He must be thinking about the things he has to do. I wish I could be with him right now, my arms holding him. He is so strong yet so fragile. I wish I could help him. I wish I could help myself. I don't know what I am doing. I'm bored with my husband, and I'm in love with what… a being from another world. Great. Really great, Gabriela… What more can you do for yourself this week? Maybe I can call him. If I could just hear his voice… It's 6 a.m., for God's sake! You don't call people at 6 a.m.! But he's not a person; you could! I bet he never sleeps! I wonder if he sleeps. I've never seen him sleep. He never seems to get tired. My God, for sure, he never gets tired when he is close to me! I want to call him, but I might wake up George if I do that. He leaves early today; I'll wait.

But Mark is able to read my thoughts. I wonder if he knows I want to talk to him. Maybe if I think about him really hard, he will know. I want to see you. I want to see you! There! Maybe he heard that. Maybe he will call me. Wait! Don't call now, Mark! George is still here! Oh, he would know that, wouldn't he? Oh, just call me when he leaves, Mark, please call.

"This room feels like a cage!" she said out loud as she looked again towards the window. I feel like I could just jump, but it's only four stories; I'll probably just break a leg.

She closed her eyes. What have I done with this life? Is it this marriage? Is it me? "Stop thinking like this!" she said out loud.

Oh… I'm so hungry. I wonder if there is any more of that German chocolate cake left in the fridge from the other night. She crept into the kitchen to reach the refrigerator. As she opened the door, she jumped and said out loud, "Yes! There is a God!" She picked up the last piece of cake with her hand. Without consideration for a knife or fork, she wrapped her mouth around deep chocolate nirvana. Oh, this is just what I needed!

Through the kitchen door, she looked over towards her husband's sleeping body, wiping frosting from her nose. She picked up a volume of poetry she had left open from the night before: her old friend Edna St. Vincent Millay, and with the light of the refrigerator she read:

I cannot say what love has come and gone
I only know that summer sang in me
A little while, that in me sings no more

"Oh, Edna... how you get me!"

CHAPTER 35

VISITING THE DOCTOR

It was midnight by the time they returned to the apartment, and they remained there until the morning. Although Jason had promised Angela a late-night visit, he would not leave his brother's side, not even for the pleasure of her arms.

Each would look at the other but say nothing, worried that their words could in some way stimulate the portal and that somehow the sound of their voices might reveal their trepidations to the Council. Ignoring its calling, they busied themselves with books and music. As the sun rose, quietly, they left the apartment.

"It was really hard for me to resist its pull," Mark said, turning to Jason as they walked down the street.

"Yeah, for me as well," Jason responded. "It was good that we did not communicate. I think if we had, the portal would have tried to engage us, tempting us to enter, but it was important that we were home. They could see us and know we were not up to anything nefarious. I'm sure any exchange between us would have been to their advantage. We still don't know what the Council is up to. We have to find a way to turn the situation in our favor."

"Agreed, but that may have to wait a bit. Gabriela has been asking me to call her. I can sense her yearning for me."

Jason looked at his brother, speaking sternly. "Listen, Mark,

I stood Angela up last night, and this Saya girl I just found again has completely captivated me, but we have to put our pleasures and their needs aside for now. We cannot allow ourselves to be distracted. Our mission is too important."

"Just a quick call, Jason, I promise. What harm would come of it? There's a phone booth up the street. I understand not talking in the apartment, but out here, what would be the risk?"

"Okay. Okay." relented Jason. "But make it fast." He was warming to the idea of Mark's feelings for Gabriela. Humanity's imperfections looked better to him since he had met Saya.

Mark stopped at the booth, put a coin in the slot, and dialed. "It's Mark, Gabriela, how are you?"

"Oh, Mark, I have been worried about you. How are you? Are you okay? I have had all these terrible thoughts that you were troubled. I really miss you. I need to see you. My mind has been running in crazy ways lately. I am so unhappy in my marriage, and I think about you all the time. You're okay, aren't you? I've been..."

"Yes, Gabriela, I'm okay, but you are not letting me get a word in. I'm fine, but please listen a minute... There are some things I have to do right now. They are taking a lot of my concentration and energy, and I need a little time."

"Time? What do you mean, time? I want to be with you. I want to leave George and be with you, Mark. I need you."

"Gabriela, please. I must stay focused. You must remember that I am here to do... things. I have told you that your planet is in danger. Would you have me abandon my purpose for a night with you? You must understand, Gabriela."

"Focus? What do you mean, focus? Are you breaking up with me? You've found someone else, haven't you? I feel it. Of course, you've found someone else. Oh, God. Tell me I'm wrong. Have you found someone else? I couldn't bear that, Mark. I would die if you broke up with me."

Mark wondered if he had somehow communicated to Gabriela his flirtation with Helena. No, that is not possible, he reassured himself. She has no way of seeing my mind.

"Gabriela, I'm not breaking up with you. I am always thinking about you. I was just seeing you in my mind, laying on the beach, listening to the waves, the sun on your face, your hair all tangled and messy. Gabriela, you make me feel whole, loved. But you have to let me do what I am meant to do. It is more important than us."

"Not being with you is making me crazy. I'm screaming inside, and then the next minute, I feel like I'm going to disappear, evaporate. I feel so alone now," She paused. "I need you, Mark... I've become obsessed with the thought of us being together. When can I see you? I am so frightened that you are in danger."

"I'm okay, Gabriela. I will be able to see you soon. But I have to go. I'll call you again when I can. I promise." Mark could hear Gabriela's tears over the phone.

"Okay, Mark. Okay... Call me when you can. I love you."

He paused. "I'll see you soon."

When Mark stepped out of the phone booth, Jason looked him over. "So how did it go? It looks like it could have gone better."

"It's complicated," Mark responded. "This is difficult for her. She is in love with me and believes I am what's missing in her life. She thinks I am the answer to her failed marriage. I care for her deeply, but..." He paused. "I want to maintain this relationship as if I were human. I don't want to use my power to control things. But it is not easy; the very qualities that make humans glorious also make them incredibly difficult and illogical."

"It appears that managing a relationship in the way you desire takes a developed skill set which we have yet to master," Jason replied with a wink. "You do seem to be learning, though. I thought you did very well in fact. But, you know, I think you should really consider Helena. She couldn't be more trouble than the one you are seeing."

"Jason, you really just don't get it. I truly care for Gabriela."

"Yes, I know," he responded casually, "but she seems to be giving you an awful lot of stress. You should try Helena."

Mark looked at Jason and shook his head. "You just don't understand. Jason, it is not that simple for me. It's what drove me to Dr. Abernathy. They are not fruit in a basket, toys to play with. We will never understand what it is to feel completely human by running away from feelings."

Mark then paused for a moment to think of Helena, her beautiful body up on the stage singing and flowing with the music. Then he returned to his point. "Abernathy has been helpful. I will talk with him more about feelings, love, attractions and such. But it'll have to wait for another time. I have a long way to go in understanding emotions, and these humans are unpredictable. Gabriela reads so much about love. She is quite the authority, academically at least." He smiled. "Emotions are a strange experience, wrenching in fact, but they are, well, joyous. Jason, are you listening to me?"

"Yes, yes, I'm listening, but these humans spend most of their time either chasing things or running away from them. It's actually one of their most charming qualities, annoying but charming. We'd better get moving, it's getting late. We don't want to keep Abernathy waiting."

"You're right. Have you been thinking about what we are going to ask him?"

"Well...neither of us believes the Council has been honest with us. I'm hoping he can give us some insight, as we will have to be most artful when we talk to them. We need to be respectful, but not submissive; confident, but not arrogant. If they are sending us wantonly to our doom, we will know it."

"Jason, if we are doomed..." Mark paused.

"So then," responded Jason. "What are we going to discuss? My hope would be to open a dialogue with them."

"Are we going to negotiate with them, Jason? No, we are going to do what they say. They have all the power. What could we possibly demand? All I am hoping for is reassurance of some type, some promise of good faith that they will do all they can to protect us. After all, we are one of them. Right?"

"I really don't know what to expect, perhaps just the whole story. We deserve at least that. And I think we may be in a better position than we realize. Whatever we were sent here to accomplish, they want us to take seriously, and I am sure they are reaping more from this planet than we know."

"Mark, look! There's a florist. You promised Martha a bouquet."

"We'll take three dozen roses!" Mark said to the owner of the shop. "Three dozen of your best."

CHAPTER 36
ABERNATHY'S ADVICE

They entered the psychiatrist's office and saw Martha's familiar face. "Hello Martha," said Mark. "These are for you. Thank you so much for your help!" He handed her the enormous bouquet.

"How nice of you, Mark! This must be your brother."

"Yes, this is Jason. He has already met the doctor."

"He has? Hmmm, well, let me tell him you both are here." She pushed the intercom and said, "Your next appointment is here." A quick, "Thank you, just give me a minute," was heard in response.

"Thank you again for the flowers, Mark," she said, smiling sweetly as they passed her. "They're beautiful!"

Mark had never seen her smile. "It's my pleasure, Martha, really."

"Your brother is very nice-looking," she whispered to him.

"Don't let him hear you say that, Martha. He's been known to chase older women, and you might find yourself in more trouble than you can handle." He gave her a wink.

Abernathy's last patient had left almost an hour ago. He planned to give himself a little time before seeing them. He had hardly slept last night after Martha had called him about the appointment, an appointment that included both brothers. These days sleep only came with exhaustion or the assistance of medication. He had been obsessed by the thoughts of them, their existence, their meaning. What a privilege, what a curse, he thought to himself as he looked at the papers on his desk; papers and notes and schedules that appeared dull in a world seemingly insignificant since he had met the twins. All other aspects of his life had faded into a bland grayness. He had resisted every impulse to talk to someone about them. He wanted to call Bolinsky at the very least; he was plagued by the thought that he must know something. In his most desperate moments, he thought of talking to Gabriela, even though they were not close, but he knew that such an overture would be taken badly by Mark. Besides, it would be a complete violation of doctor-patient confidentiality. He kept hearing Mark's words in his mind that he was the first to see his nature, and Jason's terrifying warning that no one should learn of their existence. He heard Martha's knock on the door. She poked her head into the office as she partially opened it.

"Shall I send them in?"

"Yes," he responded. "I'm ready."

Martha returned to the waiting room and indicated with a gesture that the doctor would see them.

She blushed, pushing her gray hair back from her forehead, with Mark's last words to her still in her mind. As they entered the doctor's inner office, she announced, "Here are the young men. I mean, your clients, Doctor."

"Thank you, Martha." Abernathy gave her a look of disapproval; obviously critical of the way she had introduced them. "Gentlemen. Please take a seat," he said gesturing towards the center of the room. Jason and Mark sat down in the two chairs while Abernathy remained standing. Mark could sense trepidation when he looked at Jason. He took a deep breath, glancing towards Mark for reassurance.

"Well, gentlemen, here we are. Martha told me you both needed to see me urgently, that there is a pressing matter. What can I do for you?"

Mark was about to speak, when Jason interrupted him,

"Doctor Abernathy, before we ask anything from you, I would like to say something, if I may. Mark told me how I frightened you in your home. I realize I was rude and impetuous by intruding into your life in that manner. I hope you can accept my apology."

Abernathy looked first at Mark and then turned to Jason. "Well, you did startle me, I will admit. But let's put that behind us." He paused. "If you two need my help, I am at your service. After all, you paid for therapy for the next fifty years in advance." Abernathy smiled, and Jason returned the expression.

"Thank you," responded Jason.

"Yes, thank you," echoed Mark.

"So, what are we here to talk about?" asked the doctor as he, at last, took his seat.

"Well, we have been summoned to a meeting with the leaders of our home world and we have concerns. We've always believed the main reason we have been sent here is to save your world, yet we have also sensed that there are other motivations at play, motivations that we do not understand. Because our home planet places so much value on your world, we are sure they wish it to remain safe at all costs, and that we both may be expendable to achieve this. So, we're..."

Dr. Abernathy interrupted, "You truly believe the only reason you were sent here is to protect us, to save us from some catastrophe? How do you know that? And why do you think you might die? Why would you be expendable?"

Jason answered, "It is not so much in what they have told us, but rather in what they have not. We think they know something they are not sharing. Possibly, they know we will likely not survive."

Mark interjected, "But Doctor, we will do whatever is necessary to save this planet, and we are sure that is our mission, although it has not been fully explained."

Abernathy paused. "I see, so while this is all a supposition on your part, an intuition you've formed, you believe in the mission and that your lives are at stake. Do I understand correctly?"

"Well," answered Jason, "we await the meeting, as I have said, but yes. That is correct, but I would refer to it as a deduction rather than an intuition."

Abernathy responded, "So what are you asking from me? Are you asking me to assume your deductions are correct, that you are at death's door, although you have no direct evidence to support this conjecture? They have not told you precisely what is wanted of you, or even if you are in danger. Am I correct?"

"Yes, but we are sure something is amiss, and we need your objective opinion," responded Jason. "And we need your advice on how to respond to different possible scenarios that may unfold. I think what I would like to know from our meeting with the Council, and I speak for myself here, is the following: Suppose we are correct in our assumptions. How do we approach this discussion? We are in a tenuous position. Mark and I will fulfill the mission regardless of our expendability. If I want a straight answer, how can I convince them to be honest with us? Mark, do you have anything to add?"

"Yes, we know that our main purpose on Earth is to ensure its survival, for we have known this from childhood. But it is the secret agenda that is troubling, and we are sure it exists. It was not until recently that we felt this grave danger. We have no concrete facts, but our intuitions, as you call them, have never betrayed us. We believe we were sent here for many reasons: to learn, to experience, to share, to understand, to grow... And we have grown. We've grown to have immense power and knowledge, and perhaps above all, we've discovered human emotions in ourselves, but what else? As much as I trust the Council, I believe we are expendable if the greater need is served. We are sure they want more, though I am not really certain what that more is. I think what I am getting at is that it is less black and white to me than it is to Jason. I feel there is more at play. Am I rambling? This whole thing is very complicated and disconcerting to us, as you can imagine."

"Well, I can see that this is extremely perplexing to the both of you, and I want to acknowledge your concerns and not dismiss your deductions, but I feel it's appropriate that I challenge your evaluation of the situation. I think you are correct in assuming you are facing danger, but I also believe you should consider that you are highly valued. To imagine that you are being asked to die, to be a kamikaze and fall to your death, so to speak... Well, that is hard for me to accept. In the more likely scenario, you are being asked to do something dangerous, even perilous, but I believe a better analogy might be that you are the boys who stormed the beaches at Normandy on D Day, not a Kamikaze. Courage may be called upon, for much time and effort has been spent on your development. It is illogical that your makers would simply discard you."

"Why?" interrupted Mark.

Abernathy answered earnestly, "Because you are valuable."

Jason stood up. "You are saying we are too valuable to waste? That's how should we approach this meeting?" His tone turned from frustrated to angry. "I'm sorry, Doctor. Forgive my bluntness, but as you earthlings would say... This is bullshit! I believe the beings of my world are 'pragmatic' and will only do what is in their interest, and just make more like us. I sense only a concern for the mission."

Mark looked at Jason. "But Jason, maybe he has a point. If we were made only to be thrown away, why would they have spent so much time on us?"

Jason rose in his chair. "Thank you, Dr. Abernathy, but I don't think you understand my point. Everything I know tells me that we are expendable." Jason turned to Mark, "I am going. This is not helping. And Doctor, you can keep the diamond I gave you."

Jason started to leave. Abernathy, taken aback by Jason's violent response, implored, "But don't you think they have considered all of this before? The difficulties you would face, the danger if you were to be wasted? They made you as you are for a reason. I am sure they would not have invested in you so deeply otherwise. I'm sure your makers do not want you to die. Unless…" Abernathy paused and got up from his chair and started to walk about the room. He looked intently at both Mark and Jason. "Unless for some reason they have… they have grown to fear you both in some way."

Jason stopped before reaching the door. Intrigued, he asked, "But, why would they fear us?"

The doctor relaxed back into his chair. "Didn't you say that you have both grown more powerful than you had expected? And did you not say that there might be reasons for you both to be here other than saving our planet? Now, let's assume you do save the planet. Then what? You have both grown to care for humanity, have you not? This may worry them. If you have grown to such power that they fear not being able to control you, and if there is something they want here on Earth that you both don't know about, they may see you as a potential problem."

Jason turned to leave again and reached out his hand toward Abernathy. "May I shake your hand? I really like this custom of yours."

"Yes, of course," replied Abernathy as he reached out and grasped Jason's hand. "It feels very natural, human for sure, strange. I don't know why I thought it wouldn't be." As Jason was about to leave, Mark advanced to bid Abernathy goodbye.

"I have grown very fond of you, Mark, and, in an unusual way," said Abernathy. "Please tell him that I am sorry if I brought up more questions than comfort."

"No, Doctor. You've opened up another door for us. You've given us another card to play. Goodbye and thank you."

They left the doctor's inner office and stepped out into the reception area. The door closed behind them. He must need some time to himself, thought Mark.

As they left the office, Jason turned to Mark. "He's right; they need us. And if there are other motivations, we will know it."

"Well, seeing you must have been upsetting to him. I am really glad you came, though. Without you being here, we would never have understood all of what we have. I feel empowered. Do you?"

"Yes, and at least it was better than the first time we met. I am glad you reassured him of my intentions towards him. What did you say to him about me? He was terrified when we walked in."

"Jason, he pressed me about you, and I might have mentioned that you killed a few people."

"Ha! Did you tell him everything?" asked Jason.

"Enough!" responded Mark.

"Enough? What does that mean?"

"Well... I told him about the Italian mafia guy you disposed of... And the bit about the restaurant that one time."

"I suppose that explains something, then." He chuckled as they left the building. "So now what? What shall we do?"

"I really want to see Gabriela if she can get free... What about you? What do you want to do?" asked Mark.

"I want to go to the club and play, and then maybe find Saya, and maybe Angela, too. But you know, this Saya is different. If anyone could understand how I am feeling now, it would be her."

Mark smiled. "You never stop. What is this thing you have about having more than one girl? I am never sure if you are serious, or if you are playing with me."

The street was empty until they passed a man bouncing up and down with enthusiasm, buying a hot dog from a stand.

"Lots of mustard!" bellowed the short, stocky guy with bright red cheeks. "And plenty of those onions of yours! I love your onions, Armando!" It was obvious that they knew each other.

Jason looked at Mark. "Have you ever put one of those things in your mouth? They look so strange to me, and they have such a pungent smell!"

"Humans get a lot of pleasure from food," Mark replied. "It seems to comfort as well as nourish them. It appears that their biological and emotional needs are satiated in many ways through food. It is interesting how some foods seem to mean more to them than others. It's personal to them. Each has a special meaning. I think memories have something to do with it. That man feels all warm inside from the hot dog, and it's not just from its boiling hot temperature or the spicy onions. He finds a kind of satisfaction, almost like being told he is fine, that the world is fine. Look at him, he's so happy! He is like a baby being hugged. Curious to see, isn't it?"

"I wish it could be so simple for us! Just eat a hot dog and everything is fine."

"I don't think it is all that simple for them, either," replied Mark. "If it were, I would just take Gabriela out for a pastrami sandwich tonight, and peace would reign."

"So, anyway, I hope I see you later, Mark. After we have some fun tonight, we can think about the meeting. I feel ready… ready for anything… So, whenever you want to do it, let's go."

"Yes, I feel more confident about the meeting with the Council, as well. I'll see you in a while, unless Gabriela is a total mess."

"Okay, I wish you good luck with that!" Jason laughed, and with a playful gait, he sauntered down the street, turning as only a star could, and waved goodbye.

He became aware of Mark's eyes following him and smiled, a smile that could only be defined as Jason. It was warm and devilish at once. It possessed the confidence of the universe, a power that glowed deep. Between them lived a comprehension that redefined empathy. A meaning that was theirs, a bond that they alone could share.

And Jason thought, I will never be alone.

CHAPTER 37
WAITING FOR MARK

Gabriela was sitting in her kitchen. George had just gone out. She did not ask him where he was going. There was a lot of that now: time without talking, long, empty silences followed only by necessary words. Why is he hanging on? Why am I?

Gabriela poured herself a drink, some of her husband's Laphroaig single malt. She had taken a liking to it lately. It had a smoky aftertaste. She liked that. It reminded her of finality. She went over to her desk and opened the manuscript she had been working on. Her publisher was pressuring her for chapters. With tired eyes, she looked at the pile of term papers sitting unread on the table.

Oh shit, I need to read those and grade them. They're due in two days. I could just give them a quick breeze through and grade them all right now. Would they ever know? But they are so accustomed to my scathing comments in the margins, my biting criticism. They crave my acerbic stabs to their precious monologues! Gabriela knew what brought them back every semester to suffer in her "chamber of wisdom and torture," as they called it. They will all think I had a breakdown! But you are having a breakdown you fool. You can't think, you are not getting your work done, and your marriage is over. Why am I insisting on this scorching immolation of my being? Is it guilt, or is it that I know I will never have what I want? I feel so...

so… Oh, damn you, Mark! Why don't you call me?

"I'll call Mama!" she said out loud. That always helps! Well, sometimes, anyway. She may not make sense, but hearing her voice makes me feel better. She dialed and got a busy signal.

It must be that the lines are all taken! I'll try again in a few minutes. Just then the phone rang. She picked up.

"Hello," she said.

"Hi, it's me. Can you talk? Are you alone?"

"Yes, I can talk! And…" she spoke angrily. "And if you are who you say you are, you know I'm alone!"

"Yes, I know you are alone. I thought that sounded polite for some reason. Anyway, that's not what I meant. How are you feeling?" Mark asked softly.

"Feeling? I feel like day-old bread that has been cut up into tiny pieces! I'm crumbling and breaking apart Mark. I am sad, sad and confused. I'm not sure of anything anymore, sometimes even who I am. All I know is that I love you, but instead of feeling happy, it hurts."

"Yes, I know…" he interrupted. "We seem to have gotten swept away, I've pulled you into my life, not knowing why, but I really did not have a choice. I mean, it was supposed to be, I'm sure. And I'm not sorry. Tell me you're not sorry! Can we meet? How about a pastrami sandwich and some greasy French fries? What do you say?"

"Oh! That sounds so great. Shall we go to The Stage again? I loved the dessert we had after we left there! I need to have some fun, and Mark I'm not sorry at all."

"Gabriela let's meet downtown. How about the 2nd Avenue Deli? Maybe we can go to The Dom after, and you can meet my brother, if you like. What do you say? Are you up for it?"

"Oh yes, yes! I'm up for it. Just give me two hours to whip through some papers, and I'll grab a cab. You can call me back in two hours to check that I've finished, or…"

"Don't worry. I'll know when you're done. So I'll see you later. Okay?"

"Yes, yes, okay. I feel better already."

Mark didn't want to go back to the apartment, and he was conflicted about going to The Dom. Jason, in his never-ending playful mood, was tempting him, wanting him to feel uncomfortable. He can act like a child sometimes, Mark thought. I am sure he wants to see me with that girl Helena just to torment me. He loves the theatrical; too much time on the stage, I think.

Mark decided to walk. He walked uptown as far as the Flatiron Building. I love this building. It's so quietly proud. Mark studied how the ornate façade mingled seamlessly with its edges. It has no need to compete with the giants surrounding it. It has such elegance.

Mark recalled a photograph by Edward Steichen. He had seen the picture at a gallery about a year ago. Those reaching, lonely tree branches and the horse carriage in the foreground, the beautiful aqua blue color... Steichen was a master at the gum bichromate print. He loved New York; he felt the city in his bones. There were several different versions of the photograph, but the aqua blue one was Mark's favorite. Some called it romantic, but for Mark, it held a rumpus mystique from a bygone time, a time of high hats and petticoat dresses, of trolley cars and horseshit underfoot, of hungry paper boys in worn coats, their noses full of the smell of fresh bagels, yelling out the daily news. Life was hard back in 1904.

Two hours had passed, and he found himself back in the East Village. He knew that Gabriela had finished her work and had dressed. He found a phone and called her.

She picked up. "Hello?"

"So, you're ready to come downtown now?"

"Yes, I'm ready to leave."

"Okay, see you in about a half hour at the deli." Mark hung up the phone.

He arrived before Gabriela and took a booth at the rear of the restaurant. He wondered whether or not he should tell her about his concerns. Should I talk about the upcoming meeting with my home world? My fears? Would she understand? If I leave it unsaid, she may know I am hiding something.

Gabriela entered the restaurant; heads turned. She had draped her fur coat over her shoulders and was wearing a black silk dress that hugged her body like the shimmering skin of a black mamba. On her head, she wore a cropped black hat with a small veil that partially concealed one eye. Fishnet stockings and stiletto heels completed her arrival.

"Hello, Gabriela," Mark said, smiling. "You look fantastic," he said, yet he sensed her stress.

"Hi, Mark. Thank you. I wanted to wow you tonight. I felt really dark today, so I wore black. But you know me: even when I'm depressed, I do it in style. You know, when I meet the devil, it will be in high heels, and you can bet I'll turn him on."

"You always turn me on."

"Yes," she forced a smile, "but I think you may be an easier conquest than Satan!"

Mark wanted to cheer her up but wasn't sure what to say. "I guess I am; you had me from the start. But maybe you shortchanged yourself. I'm sure I have things to learn from the devil," he laughed.

Gabriela motioned to the waiter. "Say, do you think I can get a couple of extra cloth napkins? I am going to order something large and greasy, and this is a new dress."

Looking annoyed, the waiter replied, "I'll see what I can do."

"Mark, you pulled me out of the depths with your call. I am so glad to see you. I'm sorry for being in such a neurotic state, stupid I know, but I can't seem to help it. Mark, I feel like I have been sitting on a train, watching the world rush by. It's like looking at a field of flowers pushing colors into each other. Everything's so confused and directionless. It works in a Manet, but not for me! Damn... I'm a mess Mark! I need a lot of distraction tonight, some real fun."

Mark could see the darkness under Gabriela's eyes. Her skin was gray and drawn beneath her make-up. Her sparkle was fading. He knew she had been drinking a lot these past days; her marriage and the confusion of this romance had been taking a toll upon her and he felt responsible. He thought about what he could do.

He wanted to show her a good time. But he knew she needed more than that. He must somehow increase her strength. He could, in fact, change her very cellular structure and make her younger, although he had never done this before. He knew he would have to be careful. Just give her a bit of a galactic vitamin pill. After all, he did not want her to turn into a seventeen-year-old. Touching her hand, he explored her body. Within a millisecond, he repaired her recent damage and eliminated the poisons roaming her system. He released her body's natural tranquilizers to steady her nerves. A mild but subtle euphoria emerged, the grayness vanished, and a radiance rose from her skin. The sparkle returned.

Okay, that should be enough for now, he thought. I have made her at least a few years younger. It is buzzing inside her. She is going to be happy.

"Oh, you made my fingers tingle just then. Almost like a static electric shock." She took a breath. "You know, I feel so much better now that we are together. All of a sudden I'm very relaxed."

"Yes, you are looking better." Mark realized her body's natural ability to regenerate was at work.

"Gabriela, it is going to be okay. I know I've been a big part of the problem, but you just have to give it some time, me some time. But first, I think you should eat yourself into a stupor, and when you are ready to burst, we will go hear some music at The Dom."

"The Dom...? Can we get some drugs there? I would love to get really stoned. It's been forever since I have been high on something!"

"I'm sure my brother can find some for you, but..."

"Oh, that's right, I am going to meet your brother, the other one, right? My, this is going to be a very interesting evening!"

The waiter returned with the napkins. She took two,

tucking one into the top of her dress, hiding her breasts and protecting its fine fabric. She placed the other on her lap. The waiter set two menus on the table.

"I don't need the menu. I'll take the biggest pastrami on rye you can make, French fries and a side of coleslaw. Yes! And a cherry coke, too. My stomach is howling, and I am starved. How about you, Mark? Do you know what you want?"

Mark looked at the waiter. "Just some apple juice, if you have it, for now."

"Okay, coming right up," responded the waiter, who was off with a quick turn.

"I feel like a ravenous hyena sometimes when I am with you, eating like a starved pagan, and here you are, taking a juice or picking at a little toast! Can't you just order something, so I don't feel like such a pig?"

"Okay, when he comes back, I'll order some hot dogs. Believe it or not, I've never had one. I was talking to my brother about them the other day. How strange they look to us."

"Your brother... Tell me about him. He plays in a band, you said? Is he studying someplace too? What is he doing with himself?"

Mark smiled. He had become accustomed to Gabriela's rapid-fire discourse by now. "You know, the academic thing is just a cover for us. We really learn and acquire knowledge differently than humans do. Anyway, my brother is quite special. We look very much alike. Our hair and eyes are a bit different, but outside of that, we are similar; twins, in fact. Our, let's say, personalities, our feelings, perceptions and thoughts, are not exactly in tune."

"What do you mean 'not in tune'? How is he 'not in tune'?"

"Well, he is a bit more exotic in his taste, more untamed. He doesn't exactly venerate humans or hold your kind in much esteem."

"He is a supercilious type of person."

"Well, it can go further than that, but he loves to have a good time with people. He knows how to party, and he really likes many things about humans. I know it sounds contradictory, but he is complicated. In fact, he has grown quite close to one girl, and he also cares for the people in his band. His occasional contempt for humans lies more in the realm of social criticism, if I were to give it a category. And he can express his opinions very strongly at times."

"He sounds very interesting. I can't wait to meet him. Anyway, I feel so good right now, nothing could bother me. Not even a rude brother. Oh, look. Here is our food. How delectable it looks. So, do you want those hot dogs? Tell the waiter." Then, without waiting for his words, she continued, "Bring him two hotdogs." And Mark interrupted, "With red onions, please."

"So, you're feeling a little on the spicy side?" she retorted. "Now, I don't want to hear any objections, I am not eating alone."

"We don't have red onions here. That's a Spanish thing. Only sauerkraut and mustard," said the waiter.

"Okay, then. Sauerkraut," said Mark.

"Sure," he responded. "Anything else...?"

"No, that will be enough," said Mark, turning to Gabriela. "I am not sure if I am going to like the taste of the sauerkraut, or even the frankfurter itself, actually, but I am curious."

"You won't die. The meat is Kosher," she said.

"Oh, that makes me feel much better." The thought of eating the processed remains of a living thing was barbaric enough, but the thought of the meat being blessed by a holy man was an absurd contradiction to Mark. Still, he was determined to see it through, if for nothing else but the experience of having done it once.

The hotdogs came, and Gabriela said, "Here, let me show you." She lathered the frankfurter with mustard and then piled on the sauerkraut. "There, now take a bite."

Mark complied dutifully; he chewed and swallowed in a gulp.

"So, what do you think?" asked Gabriela.

"Well, I think I would like it better without the hot dog." He removed the frankfurter from the roll and continued eating the sauerkraut and the mustard with the bun. "Yes. This is much better." He smiled.

"You are just too strange, Mark, but whatever gets you through the night, as they say."

Mark watched Gabriela systematically devour her food. She alternated between bites of the sandwich and forkfuls of French fries and coleslaw. Although the sandwich dripped with fats and juices, the French fries were immersed in a sea of ketchup, and the coleslaw lay wet and sopping on her plate. Still, she managed not to get one drop on her new dress. She ate the food so quickly that when the waiter returned to bring her cherry coke, it was gone.

"Oh my God, that was good," she said. "I am about to explode, but I really feel great." She picked up her cherry coke and drank half the glass in one swoop. "Aw, I feel like a pirate's wench." She laughed out loud.

"Another meal like that, and you might look like one," answered Mark.

Gabriela took out a cigarette. "Thanks, Mark, did you forget your flattery shoes at home today? Are we in the smoking section? I really need this cigarette."

"Oh sorry, I think you're okay," responded Mark.

Gabriela lit up and took a deep drag on her Lucky Strike. "Oh, this is just perfect, and the night is still in front of us." She looked at the waiter. "Can I get a coffee? Coffee and cigarettes after pastrami and French fries... You don't get more New York than this. Just heaven."

"I'm glad you're satisfied. You look happy." Of course, Mark inwardly knew that it was because of him and not the pastrami that the revolution within her occurred. "Let's make it an evening to remember. I can't wait for you to meet Jason."

"Yes, I am going to meet your brother. I told you I had a brother. He died when I was just fourteen. He was my older brother, and I worshiped him. Remember, he was a bullfighter? He was very handsome, thin, and graceful. But on one August day, he was not graceful enough. A bull tore apart his liver. I looked on as my mother cried at his bedside. I didn't tell you... I know I didn't. It's hard talking about it. A part of me died that day. The part that was always hopeful. Since then, I have always feared losing the ones I love." She looked at Mark. "I never feel really sure about tomorrow." Then, taking a breath, "Anyway, I am excited about meeting your brother."

Mark wanted to talk. He wanted her to understand what he was going through, but he could see that it was not the right time. She is ending her marriage and fears losing me. She needs time to gain strength. We should just have some fun tonight. A better moment will come for me.

"It's almost eleven already," he said to Gabriela. "Shall we go to the club? I am sure it is happening by now."

"That sounds great. I want to dance and get high, okay? Please, let's go wild tonight!"

Mark gave her an affirming smile.

CHAPTER 38

STRATEGY

Elgert and Dronin were walking in the passageway back to the central chamber when they noticed Allaceia just ahead of them. She seemed deep in thought as she watched some of the maintenance personnel rotate the positioning of paintings according to their prearranged designations, determined by the Prime, of course. The workers were part of the ancient underclass of the planet.

They work so mindlessly, she thought, in passing. Many say it would be better if it were relegated to the robots. But at least it gives them something to do. She noticed some were engaged in conversation. This is new. They were talking about things other than work. Astonishing. The effects of the activities of Mark and Jason are beginning to seep into even the lowest of classes.

The underpopulation had indeed fallen farthest into the state of rote, mindless life. "The featureless ones," as they were often called, were the true somnambulists of the planet. Their features had grown blank and all but disappeared. Distinguishing one from another was difficult without technical assistance. How this could have happened to her world, pained Allaceia. She often wondered if it was possible for her civilization to ever gain an inkling of its glorious past. A world that was full of life and adventure, a world that very few even knew had existed.

"Will we be seeing you later in the chambers?" asked Dronin as they caught up to Allaceia.

Startled, Allaceia snapped back to the present. "I wasn't planning on coming unless you need me."

"No, there is nothing pressing," replied Elgert. "Just some routine taxation issues I was going to discuss with Dronin. We can update you about it in our next regular meeting."

"Fine," responded Allaceia. "I'll see you then."

As she walked away, Elgert turned to Dronin. "I am concerned about this earthling that infatuates Jason. The one they call Saya. She continues to grow more powerful, and I have no idea where it is going and to what end."

"Yes," responded Dronin, "I agree this is a concern. We must watch her."

"We need to be more aggressive than that. She could spawn a whole new race. I have told my assistants to target her if an opportunity arises where she could be eliminated without any notice or disturbance. We cannot allow such a being to exist. Besides the fact that Jason's interactions with her break countless federation laws, who knows what she may become? Where will it end? How will she affect our plans? No, she must go."

"But Allaceia will oppose this action. You know she fears it will upset the twins and jeopardize our ambitions," responded Dronin.

"I will blame it on an error of a subordinate. After the girl is dead, there will be little she can say."

"I don't like this. If asked, I will say I knew nothing of your intentions," responded Dronin, sharply.

Elgert turned and walked away, thinking, *he is not there yet.*

Her mind filled with issues, Allaceia continued down the passage towards her chambers. She could not help but dwell upon the dangers facing her children. The Council has become less concerned about them. The mission to save the earth from the asteroid has become such a priority, blinding them of all else.

She remained perplexed and troubled by the attitudes of the other council members. Just then, she saw Elgert approaching her again.

"Are you going to interface with the Prime today?" he asked. "I forgot to mention before, I have some calculations to give you for its approval."

"Yes, maybe later in the day. I can take them now, if you like." She reached for his tablet, all the while wondering why this was so pressing that he would seek her in the corridor. Too bad I am still within the halls of the Council chambers, thought Allaceia, and I'm not permitted to mind probe here.

She did her best to be polite, but she found Elgert annoying. She couldn't understand how he had reached the position of councilman. She knew of Elgert's communications with the Prime, knew that he envied her and wanted to usurp her position, but his mind was vastly diminutive to hers. Convinced his abilities would never reach the level needed to satisfy the Prime's demands, she did not concern herself with his ambitions.

But lately, the Prime's mind had been distant, shutting itself off from inquiry. Why hasn't it sought my touch? Its networks are expanding, but it seems to be locked in a state of contradictory flux, at war with itself. It is becoming more and more remote. Something is wrong.

"Is there anything else you would like me to convey?" asked Allaceia.

"No, no thank you," responded Elgert, thinking, *she knows of my communications with It.*

Allaceia had little recourse but to be patient and wait. She knew she had become a part of the Prime's nature, its fluidity. How could this have happened without me seeing it? The answer would take time, but time was something she did not have. The Prime needed her, but she sensed a foreign motivation had been developing within it. It is through me that it touches reality. We have a marriage of sorts, a bond of an inexplicable nature. Elgert can never take my place, yet...

In the distance, her eyes caught Elgert and Dronin talking. Has the pressure from the profits of human dreams overtaken them? Has Dronin been corrupted, too? Why have our conversations been focused solely on the technical aspects of this mission? What a wild and ill-conceived plan. Why did I agree to this?

Allaceia felt anger and frustration, but she knew she did not have the luxury of such self-indulgence. If I hear them go on about the angle of projection and accounting for the asteroid fragments one more time, I am going to scream. Maybe my answer is not here with the Council, or on Eldern.

As the Planetary Ambassador, she had developed a deep and trusting relationships with most of the ambassadors in the federation. As part of her duties, she travelled to the other planets and held confidential meetings with the central committees of other worlds such as New Tripton.

Yes, New Tripton! That is where I will find aid. It is there I will have cards to play. It's a good thing I've kept these doings hidden from my council members over the years. I will contact the Triptonian ambassador. He owes me a big favor for not shutting down those fan club visits to Earth he was condoning. The Triptonians love my children. They will help me save them.

Back in the High Chambers, Elgert approached Dronin. "I have been informed that Jason is not likely to survive the power of the earth's core."

Dronin responded, "Yes, I have seen these calculations. But can we trust them? There have been several errors of late."

"Yes, these have been verified as accurate," responded Elgert. "They tell us that the intensity of the core will crush Jason's structure. He would survive if we could maintain him in the sixth dimension, but that would not allow him to project the core's energy to Mark. It is a tragic flaw we did not anticipate."

Elgert did not want Dronin to know that the asteroid was no longer a threat, and all of this was a ruse. His ambition for the moment was the death of Mark and Jason so that he might ally himself with the Prime. Knowing that Dronin had been too preoccupied presiding over the lower chambers to concern himself with the twins, he laid the groundwork of his plan.

"Yes," continued Elgert. "I didn't want to mention this in front of Allaceia, but I do not see a way to save him. He will have to use all his power to project the energy of the core to Mark. There won't be enough power left within him to maintain his own structure under such gravitational pressure. He will eventually be crushed. But what is worse, he may endure hours of agony. He will not be able to escape. Slowly, very slowly, he will be compressed. A more agonizing death I could not imagine."

"Is there nothing we can do? Is there no way to save him?"

"I am afraid not," replied Elgert. He paused to watch Dronin's reaction. How much does he really care about them, he wondered.

"And this slow death. There is no help there, either? No poison pill? No way to self-destruct? We can at least provide that."

"I will see what I can do. I will consult my staff." Hmm, He thought... an interesting response. He is not yet ready to turn my way.

Meanwhile, Allaceia returned to her chambers with her first assistant. She walked into her terminal that enabled interface with the Prime. She was the only one with such access. Most of her communication with the Prime was done from this chamber. There were times, though, it called upon her, and then it was necessary for her to go to the central domain, to The Monolith.

Again, she tried to open some channels, and again she was rebuffed. In frustration, she asked for permission to enter the Monolith in order to meld with it but found it nonresponsive. While pondering the situation, an entourage of distressed and panting assistants arrived abruptly carrying calculation tablets and speaking in chorus.

"Grand Mistress, Grand Mistress! We have to talk to you!"

Looking at her first assistant and the swarm of subordinates behind her, she asked, "Yes, Gallania? What is it? You have some news for me?"

"Our spies in the Calculation and Evaluation section have obtained some distressing information. We have learned that the asteroid will not hit the earth as you were informed and that Elgert is well aware of this. He has been misleading the Council."

Allaceia slumped into her chair. The weight of disappointment fell upon her. "How could he do this to me?" she murmured.

The image of her children's pain washed over her like the shadow within a dark sea. Allaceia had known that Elgert had been up to something, but never had she dreamt of such treachery. Why is he doing this? Why is he sending my children into such needless danger? The knowledge of this deceit tore into her; the betrayal pierced her like a burning knife.

She felt the very essence of defiance within her. Drawing strength from her anguish, with authority and poise, she commanded, "Gallania, have my ship readied for immediate launch. Inform Captain Soomark to lay a course for New Tripton."

CHAPTER 39
APPROACHING THE DOM

"**M**ark, is this it? Wow. It looks beautifully trashy. I love it."

"Yes, Gabriela, and it's even stranger inside. Listen, there are a lot of real characters in there, but don't let them frighten you. And my brother might not seem to be the nicest guy you ever met at first, but just give him a chance to warm up to you."

"Don't worry, Mark. I'll be my sweetest self. But you know," she said with a grin, "my students' favorite description of me is the Dorothy Parker quote: The first thing I do in the morning is brush my teeth and sharpen my tongue."

"Well, I wouldn't go there, if I were you. Just let him be his playful self, and in a short time he will be eating out of your hand."

"Of course. I am not going to pick a fight. Anyway, I feel really 'mellow yellow.' I want to party and have fun tonight. Promise to get me high. Please..."

"I don't think that is going to be a problem. They consume more drugs in this place than popcorn at the movies," responded Mark.

They walked into the club, and the floor was alive with swaying bodies. The speakers were blasting a song by the Doors. Heads were swirling to the voice of Jim Morrison; the sounds were hypnotic and dark. The night had already fallen into the world of the sensual. Bodies flowed within the space; the music seemed to meld into them, driving them deeper into its currents. One felt the jungle in the air.

Mark heard a voice. "Hey, pretty brother! You're back, huh?" It was Angela carrying a tray of drinks. "You-a looking for your brother? He's over there with some people." She gestured with her head. "The Velvet Underground is playing tonight, and Lou Reed is in the back room with Jason. I think some other musicians are there, too. Someone came in through the side door, maybe a celebrity. I think they're all getting quietly stoned."

Gabriela looked at Mark. "Your brother knows Lou Reed? Are you kidding me? He's so great. I love him. Wow!"

"He knows a lot of artistic people. The Velvet Underground plays here all the time. Both Lou Reed and my brother are being talked about a lot. I didn't know you were into this underground music. I thought only people my age liked them."

"Oh no," she replied, "he is a real poet. I love him."

Mark took Gabriela's hand and walked to the back of the club. They sat in a dark corner at a table partially hidden by a wall. Mark saw Jason; Leonard Cohen and Lou Reed flanked him. Helena was sitting next to Cohen, laughing at something he had just said, snorting lines of coke from a mirror. They could hear Reed and Cohen talking about New York City.

Gabriela turned to Mark. "Is that Leonard Cohen? Your brother knows Leonard Cohen? Holy shit."

"He knows lots of people, Gabriela," he responded

"I can't wait to get out of here," said Cohen. "Too many distractions for me. I can't work here anymore. I don't know how you write." He turned to Reed.

"It's easy, man," responded Reed. "I just stay stoned most of the time. That's my secret, or not so much my secret." Everyone laughed, knowing the volume of drugs he was known to consume. "I block out the noise so I can see what's real. Getting to the real is what it's about. You know that."

"Hey man, for me, I love the peace of my island, the isolation there." Cohen had made his home on the Greek island of Hydra for the last few years. "The sun and the sea. I'm feeling stifled in this town. At 2 a.m., I'm on that plane."

"But I thought you would come over to The Factory and hang out with Andy and some friends later."

"No, I have to get out of this town. I just came by to say hello to Jason. I haven't seen him in almost a year. This is just a stopover on my way back from L.A."

Gabriela, standing, was taking in their conversation in silence; she could not believe she was looking at a table with two of the best poet-songwriters in the world, listening to their small talk. She was in heaven.

Just then, Helena looked over to Mark and smiled. "Hi, nice to see you around here again. Come sit over here with me," she said, patting the spot next to her; Mark knowingly chose the chair across the table, leaving no choice for Gabriela but to squeeze into the booth next to her.

Jason looked up. "Hey, Mark. What's happening? Oh, I see you brought your lady with you tonight. Hey, Lou, this is my brother, Mark."

Reed gave an acknowledging nod.

"And this is the great Leonard Cohen. I'm sure you know his work."

"Yes, of course," responded Mark. "This is my friend Gabriela. She also writes."

"Oh, you do?" responded Cohen. "What are you into?"

Angela approached the table. "Anyone want more drinks?" she asked.

"I'll take a martini," said Gabriela. "How about you, Mark?" Not waiting for him to answer, she said, "Bring him a martini, too."

"No, bring him a Bourbon and Coke," said Jason. "You are going to drink with me tonight, Mark."

"Okay, yes, I'll take that." Everyone else waved that they

were good. Angela, smiling, darted off.

Turning to Cohen, Gabriela answered, "Well, mostly academic stuff, literary criticism, historical biographies... I teach at Columbia."

"A critic!" said Lou Reed, holding his finger in front of himself in the shape of a crucifix. "We have to put up our protection spells!"

"No," said Gabriela, laughing. "You would have to be long dead for me to write about you."

"Well, some say I'm trying to get there." He chuckled.

"I like to read historical literature," interjected Cohen. "I once paid off a guard and got access to some of the hidden manuscripts in the Vatican vaults. You know, some of them are full of sexy stuff..."

Helena interjected, "You're joking, right?"

Reed followed. "You're bullshitting us!"

"No, no. I'm not. It's true, those monks back when really knew how to have a good time." He laughed.

Reed looked at Cohen. "Well, I intend to have a grand old time tonight."

"Well, maybe I will use that stuff in my writing one day. You never know. You have to work with what you find. And it's a lesson that you better be careful about what you write, because it may one day bite you in the ass."

Just then, Helena passed the mirror with the lines of coke over to Gabriela and handed her a rolled-up dollar.

"Would you like some?" she asked with a teasing smile.

"Oh... What is it?"

"Well," she responded, "on this side is some of the best coke you ever had in your life. And these other four lines are smack. Don't take more than one of those, or you'll be on the floor."

Gabriela took the mirror and placed it on the table before her. With a rolled dollar bill, she drew in a line of coke and immediately pulled her head back. "Whoa!" she said.

Helena smiled. "Nice, right?"

"Yes, yes. Really nice. Wow!"

"Try a little of the other stuff if you dare," she said with an evil grin.

"Should I?" Gabriela responded. "Well, maybe just a little..."

"Go for it!" said Helena.

Gabriela bent her head again and drew in half a line of the heroin. "My, that's nice."

Lou Reed sat back in his chair. "Well, I guess this is one critic I don't have to worry about." He laughed out loud.

Cohen continued to talk to Gabriela. "Do you like the Beat poets? Ginsberg, Kerouac, and Corso?"

Her head spinning, Gabriela responded, "Yes, I love them!" She felt a strange sensation, a dryness in her mouth. Her lips started to feel numb.

"Talking about those guys in Rome, I never understood what the Beats meant when they used the word 'angel,' except that it was a designation for a human being, and that it affirmed the light in an individual. What do you think about that?" asked Cohen.

"Well, I know Kerouac and Ginsberg used the term a lot in the fifties," Gabriela responded. "I loved those poems, but..." Her words started to bunch up, and she was afraid she was talking like an idiot.

"The fifties, to me, were all about doo-wop. That music sang from the soul! It was funny and full of life," interrupted Reed.

Then, Cohen recited:
No rest
without love,

no sleep
without dreams

of love –

be mad or chill

obsessed with angels

"I think that's right," said Cohen. "It's from Ginsberg's 'Song."

"Yes, that's right," blurted Gabriela. She continued:
The warm bodies

shine together

in the darkness,
    the hand moves…

"Oh, I can't remember the rest right now. How I love that poem, 'One melts within it'… I think it ends like that." She looked at Cohen. Gabriela was spinning, but she felt as if she were in heaven. She could not believe she was sitting with two of her idols, talking about poetry and music and getting stoned. Her soul was singing. She looked over at Jason. He was staring at her intensely. It was as if he was saying, *I see why my brother likes you.*

Cohen said to Reed. "So, like the Talmud says, 'There's good wine in every generation.'"

Just then, Nico came over to the table. "Hey Lou, we got to get up on stage. Get your nose out of that stuff and get going."

"Yeah, and I have to catch a plane to Greece," said Cohen. "It was really nice meeting you, Gabriela. And you, too, Mark. I am sorry I have to run. Take care, Lou… Jason, I'll see you on my next stopover in New York. Bye, guys. It's been fun," he said, getting up and waving to the rest of the table.

Angela came back with the drinks. "Bye, Leonard! Maybe next time you can hang out longer!"

"Yeah, maybe. I hope so, anyway." Cohen waved again to everyone and left.

Reed slowly got up from the table, grabbing Jason's shoulder for balance.

"Wow," he said. "I guess I started a bit early tonight."

"Come on, come on!" shouted Nico. "The band is up on stage already."

Reed slowly and tentatively walked away from the group with Nico's assistance. They went behind the stage to get ready for the performance.

"They were so ni-ce," said Gabriela, her words slurring. She turned to Mark. "Thank you for bringing me here."

"Well, they're Jason's friends, not mine. Thank him."

"Yes, thank you, Jason," she said sloppily.

Mark paused and looked at Gabriela, "Are you alright, Gabriela?"

"Oh yes, thank you. I feel just fine."

Helena turned to Mark. "I like her! I see why you're into her, Mark. She is smart and beautiful, and maybe even fun!" She looked back to Gabriela and asked, "Have you ever gone down the rabbit hole, Gabriela? We can do that if you like!"

"Rabbit hole? Where's that?"

"Oh, right here," she giggled as she brought out a napkin bearing several sugar cubes. "It is deep and wide and ever so pretty."

"It's acid," said Jason. "LSD."

"Have you ever taken it?" continued Helena.

"No... No, I've never done anything like that. What's it like?"

"Well, it's more than a high. It's kind of an experience," said Helena, popping a cube into Gabriela's martini. "If you don't want it, I'll trade drinks with you."

"No, I'm interested."

"Oh, good! Then we're both off!" she exclaimed, popping a cube into her own drink.

Jason was taking in the drama, enjoying the play between Gabriela and Helena. He looked at Mark and thought to himself, Maybe I'll push this along a bit and play with Helena's mind a little. I am curious to see the possibilities. You deserve some fun tonight, Mark. Don't you think?

Mark looked at Jason. He communicated, 'Please don't

enter their minds! Please don't control them!'

Okay, Mark, he responded telepathically. Don't worry, I won't mess with your Gabriela. But I have a feeling they are both already in the mood for adventure. You have to admit, this is quite a show.

They all slowly sipped their drinks. Helena turned and looked into Mark's eyes, thinking, she is really nice; I could go for both of them.

Jason smiled, I didn't do that, Mark; this heat is all from them. From the stage, the hypnotic voice of Nico's singing filled the room. Helena and Gabriela finished their drinks while the drugs floated them ever higher.

"Gabriela, how do you feel? Do you feel the acid yet?" asked Mark

"I'm not sure, but," she responded, "it seems like the room is starting to pulsate. You look funny, and your face is starting to melt, but I feel really nice inside. All warm and loving and such..." she slurred.

"Are you okay?" he asked, anxiously. He leaned over, whispering in her ear, "I can take those drugs out of you."

"No. No, please don't... It's nice. I feel like a... I'm not sure. I feel like I love everyone. Just everyone and everything. Oh... This room is so beautiful," she said, almost singing her words with a smile.

Helena came closer to Gabriela. "You know, you are really pretty. Your skin is like silk, beautiful white silk." She touched Gabriela's arm very gently and began to stroke it with her fingers.

"You're really beautiful, too," answered Gabriela. "Very. I feel so cozy near you, Helena... What a sweet feeling this is... What did you call this? LSD, or acid, or something?"

"Yeah, it's really nice, LSD. They call it the love drug. Can I tell you something, Gabriela? I've never met a woman like you. You have such beautiful eyes, and you're creamy like vanilla ice cream! I like being next to you..." Helena leaned forward, brushing Gabriela's breast. "Oh, I'm sorry." She grinned, indicating she was not. "I think I dropped something." Her fingers moved playfully, gently touching her nipple through the cloth. She was not wearing a bra. When her fingertips found their goal, she looked into Gabriela's eyes. "May I find it…?" Gabriela felt her nipple grow firm.

She froze, feeling sensations she had not expected. The drugs were whirling within her. She touched me! Gabriela was surprised, but leaned forward, making herself more available. What am I doing, she thought, as she put her hand around Helena's waist. She felt Helena's breath upon her and then with a sigh she found herself sliding like a warm bar of soap into a steaming bath. She opened her mouth as she felt the touch of Helena's lips.

Everyone in the room began to disappear. Somehow, she knew Mark was okay with it all, that for her, in this moment, there was only Helena. The warmth of her, her moist mouth against her own… Helena's hand glided along Gabriela's silk dress, gently sending her body into quivers. She surrendered.

Helena opened her eyes and looked over her shoulder towards Mark, her eyes communicating: I want you both.

CHAPTER 40

THE 22ND FLOOR ON FIFTH AVENUE

Helena lived on the 22nd floor of an ostentatious apartment building on Fifth Avenue, a bit beyond Washington Square Park, just what one would imagine for a trust fund darling related to the Danish royal family. Mark sat nude in a large leather armchair in the living room, looking out the window onto the park below. He watched the morning activity; a warm light washed over the street, turning the pavement a light blue. It was a hazy day, for it had just stopped raining, and the NYU students were off to classes.

Mark's thoughts wandered. NYU has nicer-looking girls than Columbia. Why might that be? Of course, it's harder to get into Columbia. Interesting question, the correlation of intelligence and attractive features in humans. They definitely wear more expensive clothing. My thoughts are starting to sound as silly as humans'.

In the corner of the room, just to the right of the half-opened window, hung a playful sculpture by Calder. A breeze gently played with the dangling shapes. The rainy light cast only faint moving shadows on the pale-yellow wall. There was also a collection of photographs at the far end of the room, many by Robert Frank, Diane Arbus, Bill Brandt, along with other contemporary photographers: it was a well-curated collection.

On the floor near the door sat a high-end stereo system by Macintosh. Deep rows of LP albums neatly lined the walls, mostly jazz, blues, and contemporary rock, intermingled with a collection of classical music, even an opera or two. Helena loved the opera, but without her mother around, she hardly ever went these days. There was a large sofa, two armchairs, Swedish of course, and a coffee table by Nakashima. The room felt austere but elegantly svelte. Not a thing too much, not a thing too little.

Helena and Gabriela still lay in bed embracing; bare as newborns, sprawled on the king-size mattress, vestiges of the evening's exhaustions. The stuffy Swedish mattress, centered on the floor, defined the space in typical hippy decorum. Books littered about her bed, everything from Nietzsche to Japanese manga. Helena was a mixture of aristocrat, bohemian artist, and abandoned spirit; she was a hedonist with a brain.

The room had only one dresser with a large mirror attached, flamboyantly adorned with a filigree of nubile cherubs at play. The dresser itself was a gift from her mother; it was at least two hundred years old. The drawers were open with lacy undergarments languidly craning out like tinsel on a Christmas tree. Helena often tore frantically through her intimates in search of the perfect mood for the evening. She felt that a delicate French lace hidden beneath her clothing centered her being and set her tone for the night as if it were garnish to her soul.

Gabriela was no novice in the field of love, but this had been her first time experiencing a woman. Helena had guided her with deftness and sensitivity, and within the swirl of ardent fever, the three had found no scarcity of pleasures.

Just then, Helena emerged from the bedroom. She walked slowly towards Mark, her body swaying as she approached. She emanated a savory scent. Her walk beat a mantra; advancing slowly, each step, each gesture was deliberate and beckoning. Her manner played a sinuous rhythm, and when her eyes found him, she put her hands on his shoulders, stepped forward, and opening her legs, caressed him beneath her.

"So, would you like some coffee?" she asked, moving her lips inches from his. "I make a wicked cup of New Orleans brew. What can I get for you?" she whispered in a sultry tone.

"I don't drink coffee," he responded.

"Well then, come back to bed. I always like it better in the morning."

Mark arose and followed her. As they entered the bedroom, he could see Gabriela was waiting.

***

Across the galaxy, Allaceia's ship approached New Tripton. She had come from Eldern, bringing the Triptonian ambassador with her. He had been visiting her home world. Mananken was an old friend, a trusted ally, and confidant. As they neared the planet, the ship's captain turned to Allaceia. "We have been receiving emergency priority-one communications from Eldern. Shall we open a channel?"

The emergency alert was a message from Elgert. He and Dronin had been frantically trying to locate her. I must respond, she thought, or I will raise suspicions. She had already prepared her excuses in her mind. The reason for my absence will be of overwhelming importance, yet I must be convincing.

"Yes, open a channel," she ordered. Allaceia activated her viewing screen and accepted the contact. Elgert and Dronin appeared. They were in the central chamber.

"Grand Mistress, we have been searching for you. We have activated the portal for our meeting with Mark and Jason. You are needed in the chambers."

Allaceia knew that when her longtime colleagues addressed her as "Grand Mistress," it was a telling sign. This was a formal request, nearing an order by majority rule.

"Hello, my dear colleagues," she said in a formal tone. "I apologize for my absence and lack of communication, but the urgency of this diplomatic mission left me no choice; secrecy was required. Are we on an encrypted channel?" Allaceia asked as she laid the groundwork for her excuses.

"Yes," responded Dronin. "But, why is it needed?"

"Please double check, utmost security is necessary."

Elgert responded, "I am securing now. Encryption complete. Please tell us."

Allaceia continued, "Are we guarded from all ears, even the Prime?"

"Yes," answered Elgert.

"I am about to enter the atmosphere of New Tripton. This will make communication impossible, so please allow me to talk without interruption. Our Triptonian friends believe they are picking up communication from an unknown species with intergalactic capabilities. They are approaching our galaxy in what appears to be a tactical formation. Some Triptonian scientists think it may merely be a cloud of dark matter, but the majority are convinced otherwise. Given that the Triptonians are charged with the defense of our federation, they must investigate the matter. They requested my presence here if they attempt to make contact. They regard my skill in communication as imperative."

"We understand, Allaceia. Can we assist in any way?" asked Dronin.

"The Triptonians have requested that the knowledge of potential contact be kept secret until it has been confirmed and the strategy is set. I will be needed here for verification in either direction."

"You shall have all the time you need, Grand Mistress."

"As for Mark and Jason, I believe you should go forward with the meeting as planned. Explain to them what we are asking of them. I will record a video intended to introduce myself. In the video, I will explain that they are of my lineage and I will tell them the history of their proud heritage. I will also tell them that I am looking forward to seeing them and celebrating the success of their mission once it is complete." There was a pause; Allaceia awaited their response in anticipation.

"Should we go forward without you? We could postpone the meeting," Elgert suggested.

"No," responded Allaceia. "It will serve no purpose to delay, and my focus is needed here. As you have said, the more delay, the more difficult their task will be. Have the meeting. If it is necessary, we can always have another. I will send my communication to the portal directly from here. Please tell them to await my words."

"As you desire, Allaceia. Our gratitude and well wishes go with you. Please keep us informed of developments when you are permitted to share."

"Of course, Dronin," she replied. "I only hope that I live up to the Triptonians' faith in me. I am sure I can translate any language. I hope I like what I hear."

"We stand ready to assist in any way you ask."

"Thank you both. Let's hope assistance will not be needed. Oh, one other thing... The Triptonians feel it is a major priority that the Prime is not informed. They fear it could be a machine-based civilization and any communication between our Prime and such a civilization could be disastrous."

"We have little need to consult the Prime in your absence; we will heed your words concerning these matters, Allaceia. Our conversation does not leave this chamber."

"Farewell, my trusted colleges. I will be in touch as soon as I have more information."

"Farewell, Allaceia. Our hopes go with you."

Allaceia ended the communication, and with the change from addressing her as Grand Mistress to her given name made her feel confident that she had pacified the situation for now. However, she knew Elgert would quickly enlist spies to find out as much as he could about her fabricated crisis. Her words concerning the Triptonians' need for secrecy and fears of a machine-based society might quell him for a time. And she knew that he would only find obstructions and blind allies with his spies, but not forever.

First, I have to prepare my communication to Jason and Mark. I will have to let them know that I am sending them help and that they will survive their ordeal. I will attend to Elgert later. She activated her recorder and began:

"Mark and Jason, by now you have learned of your mission from the other members of the Council. I speak to you not only as one of the leaders of your home world and Grand Mistress of Eldern, member of the Supreme Council, but also as your birth mother. Greetings, my children, I have long awaited this day."

Allaceia's message went on for some time, telling of their lineage, the noble and great names in the history of Eldern from which they arose. She spoke of the brave generals and leaders of the planet who had borne their lifeline, and the pride she felt in how her sons had evolved into the only beings in modern history to comprehend the depths of life that they could now see. She dared not convey the information she knew about the asteroid or the treachery at play, not only fearing that her words might be heard, but she was uncertain how this knowledge would affect them. The future of Eldern had to be primary. She needed a plan, but a secret one.

She ended her message, "I send you both the Purple Flower of your heritage, the crest which has protected us for eons. It is far more than an ornament. I hope to speak directly with you both soon, to hear your voices and look upon you. For now, please accept my words and my fervent hopes for your well-being. Farewell." Within an amulet bearing the flower, Allaceia hid a message that only Jason and Mark could see. It said that help would come.

As her ship approached the planet, the ability to communicate faded. New Tripton was a unique world; a small moon nestled within an array of giants, and the only planet in the known universe to have an ocean above its atmosphere.

It appeared to all who observed it from afar as a planet

consisting solely of water. From space, it looked foreboding, a violent planet with ominous storms and tumultuous seas. Any onlooker could only imagine it as a planet inhabited, if at all, by the simplest of life forms and surely unsuitable for colonization. This illusion had protected the Triptonians for millennia, allowing them to develop in peace.

But this floating ocean had not always existed. The advanced technologies of the Triptonians had enabled them to take advantage of the planet's unique positioning to create the anomaly. Their civilization had discovered the moon many eons ago. Needing to flee a dying world, they saw this new planet as an opportunity and a chance for a peaceful existence. They employed a force field on the surface that was enhanced by the moon's multi-level magnetic core. This, coupled with the gravitational effects of the surrounding planets and duel suns, enabled the aberration to occur: a floating ocean. The terraforming had taken generations to complete, but theirs was a patient race. While leaving Tripton-3 had been a difficult and heart-wrenching experience for this playful and peaceful race, the pride in their accomplishment in creating this new home was a source of great joy.

Within the ocean, an array of glowing and transparent organisms now swarmed like luminous dancers. Their movements sent soft melodies into the atmosphere below that were often heard by the population, cascading over the plains as well as the crowded streets. In the morning hours, misty deep hums were heard, the echoes of gentle movements of Sermathabees, the large, lolloping, transparent beasts of the sea. As they moved, their breaths brought forth a deep hallowing hum that rolled and sank.

Whoom-ba-ba-whoom-ba-ba-whoom...

The sound would vibrate down through the water, enchanting those below as they awoke to the day.

As the planet's two suns set, and the rays of light seeped through the clouds, diffusely tinted magical colors would appear in the evening glow. Then the population would hear the cries of the soaring Gulathabees, their giant wings sending down warm breezes from the swirling waters above. With these lumbering beasts, the population experienced a knowing state of tranquility and lived their shrouded peaceful existence for thousands of centrons.

Passing through the ocean always brought unease to Allaceia, even though she knew that her ship would be guided with complete safety through the protected channels. While this allayed her fears, the awe of it all never diminished.

Safely landing, Allaceia and Mananken exited the shuttle. The guard on station greeted them, "Welcome home, Ambassador Mananken. It is good to see you again."

"Thank you, Lieutenant. It is good to see you, as well. You know the Ambassador from Eldern, Grand Mistress Allaceia?"

"Yes, of course," he responded.

"Is our transport to the Central Chambers ready?" inquired Mananken.

"Yes, directly at the foot of the ramp."

"Good, thank you," he answered.

Allaceia had wanted to explain the details of her dilemma to Mananken on the voyage to New Tripton, but since they had been encapsulated in a state of suspended animation during the journey, this was impossible. After emerging from this state, she immediately explained the gravity of her situation, the frustration, and betrayal she had faced, and the urgency that pulsed within her.

Mananken was more than a sympathetic ear, for he had received many gifts from Allaceia over the ages. They enjoyed a relationship that mutually enhanced their political ambitions. Mananken's influence within the federation of planets had grown, and thanks to Allaceia, it was only second to hers.

The Triptonians had grown to love Mark and Jason. Allaceia knew that enlisting their aid to save them would not be a hard sell. Mananken always possessed quiet confidence regarding the most serious situations. Beneath all the colorful fur and bouncy speech was the mind of a skillful diplomat. As Allaceia shared all, the apparent treachery did not surprise Mananken, for he had dealt with Elgert in the past. He mumbled his opinion in a growling Triptonian drool, "Zerbaaa, werba, zerba. He is a man solely driven by ambition. But there may be more than meets the eye."

Recently, Mananken had won much favor within the upper crust of New Tripton. It turned out that the groupies that Allaceia had allowed to visit Earth had all been children of the Triptonian elite, and the ruse had gained Mananken much status and power within the most influential circles. Allaceia had advanced his ascent to power in many similar situations. She never underestimated his cunning and shrewdness, but above all, she cherished his friendship, and it was within this relationship that she placed her hope. Yet somehow, she knew he was aware of more than he was sharing.

But what is he thinking? She thought.

Mananken explained to Allaceia that she could not stand before the Triptonian authorities before he first presented her case to them. In his usual bubbly and animated manner, he said, "Cherba, cherba, cherba, don't worry, my friend. There is an answer to this problem."

The Triptonians always started a serious dialogue with a preamble of sorts, a preface that allowed the listeners a hint of what was to follow. "Cherba, cherba, cherba" was a very good sign. Mananken, like all Triptonians, had other idiosyncrasies; he could not help but bounce up and down when he spoke. It took much discipline on Allaceia's part to hold a serious tone when negotiating with him. But what she found most disconcerting were the ever-changing colors of his fur, not to mention when all his hair briskly stood up on end.

What will be the price to save my children? He knows something I don't.

***

The morning had passed in Helena's apartment. Mark

stared up at the ceiling. Gabriela and Helena lay sleeping, each with their head on his shoulder. Gabriela turned her face towards him and opened her eyes.

"Hey, is my head too heavy?" Of course, she knew it was not.

"No, I'm fine," he responded.

"Is she asleep? I wanna ask you something," she whispered, looking towards Helena.

"I'll put her into a deeper sleep. What is it?"

"So, does she know about you? I mean, who you are?" she asked.

"Well, after last night, I am sure she will have questions, you know. I have not told her I am an alien. Neither has my brother told her about himself. Jason has placed all the members of his band into a state of blindness as to his capabilities. He keeps them in the dark. It is really amazing how he can do that, considering how close they are and their level of involvement with each other. I mean, think about how they could make such music together! Developing those unique sounds... Do you realize, some of it is more complicated than Beethoven; the progressions, the harmonics... It is a very special sound. They do it all without awareness of his abilities. Jason is very deft at mind control. He always does it with subtlety and elegance. Humans never know they are being played like puppets on strings, but last night's fun was different. She must know now that what we did was not possible with an ordinary person. I should wipe it from her mind."

She took a deep breath and paused. "I've never done anything like last night before. I mean, you... and then being with a woman, too. It was strange for me. I am a little embarrassed about it, especially having done it with you."

"We were all together. I did not think about it that way. To me, we were all just sharing ourselves. Anyway, everything exists within a new territory for me. I think you should look on the bright side; at least she was human! Right?" He smiled knowing he had made an effort at a poor joke. "Anyway, as long as you had fun, I don't think you should feel in any way embarrassed."

"Well, you're right. Who knows who, or what, I could end up next to with you?" Gabriela laughed. "Well, I had fun, for sure. But it is strange, being with her. I mean I'm actually having feelings for her." In an almost coy voice, she added, "And I liked them." Suddenly, Gabriela sat up. "Hey! Did you just say mind control? You can control minds? Did you control mine? Is that how this happened? I bet if you wanted to, you could make me do anything you wanted."

"I want you to love me, Gabriela, but I want you to love me freely with your real heart, completely and wholly free. Yes, I could have willed anything. I could have made you want me or anyone else for that matter, and even made you do things. But you would not have been you, and I would not have become who I am. You have changed me, Gabriela. You have no idea how grateful I am to you for that. Anyway, I told you a long time ago that I can control minds. You were probably not paying attention."

"Holy shit. I guess I just didn't get that part. I am always whirling around like a top when I'm with you. It's a wonder I remember my name! So, I guess I did do it all on my own. Mark, if you ever abuse that power, I will never forgive you."

"I promise you I never will."

So, what are we going to do about her? Are we going to let her in on our little secret? Are we going to tell her she just made it with a guy from...Where did you say? Elbern? And watch her faint? Or are you going to wipe her clean, erase her memories?" she grinned sardonically as she spoke.

"Gabriela, it's Eldern. And we have to talk... I feel my task is about to start soon. She may not be in our story. I may be leaving."

"Leaving...? What do you mean, leaving? Leaving for where, and for how long? You can't just leave. Where are you going? When will you be back? You can't just go! You have turned my life upside down. Don't you understand I love you? Don't you understand what you have done to my life? If you leave, you are just a bastard!"

"Gabriela! Gabriela, stop. We have been over this before. There is no choice for us. I must fulfill what has been asked of me. There will be nothing here at all if I do not. All I know is that my task begins soon. My brother has been calling me for over an hour. I have not answered him, but it could only mean that something is imminent."

Gabriela started to cry. "If you are in danger, I want to be with you. I'll go too."

"No, that's not possible," he answered.

"Why not?"

"You can't just come. Explaining why would take a month."

"But if you go then, is there any way you can let me know you are okay? I mean…can you let me know somehow that you are alive and safe? Can you let me know when you'll be back? Oh, God," she said, gasping, almost unable to catch her breath. "I feel like an undertow is taking me. You're stealing me from myself, Mark. Everything is dark now, dark and hopeless. How will I know if you have survived?" She buried her head in her hands; tears fell. "I will be all alone, no one even to talk to about you. No one would ever understand! Oh, Mark, losing you is just too unbearable to think about."

Mark took her in his arms. "Do you think I want to lose you? I would do anything to be with you. I wish there was a way to make this easier for you. I wish there was someone you could share your feelings with, at least."

"Who? Who could ever understand how I feel, what you mean to me, who you are? Who?"

Mark turned and looked at Helena. "How about her? How about Helena, Gabriela? You said you really like her… How about we allow her understanding? Let her see me. You will at least have her to talk to. What do you think?"

Gabriela caught her breath and sobbed. "What good would that do?"

"Well it would be something, and I will come back to you. I am not sure how long I'll be away, but I will come back, and in the meantime..."

"Well, that's something. But not much."

"Listen," said Mark, "if there is any way to communicate to you, I will. If there is any way to rush right back to you, I will, but no matter how long it takes, no matter what I will have to do, I will come back. But I think if you could have at least one person to share it with, it should help."

"Yes, maybe it will help," she sobbed.

"Okay then, let's wake her. Just leave the rest to me. Try and catch your breath."

"Okay, okay... I'll try to straighten up."

Mark unleashed Helena from the deep sleep in which he had placed her. "Good morning, Helena. Did you sleep well?"

"Yeah, never better. I'm not even hung over. That's funny. Amazing, after what we took last night!"

"Well," answered Mark, "I have been known to have a good effect."

Helena, still a bit dazed, sat for a moment looking around, unable to place all of what had just happened. She was trying to recall what had taken place. Slowly, it all came back to her. Smiling, she looked at Gabriela in recognition. "Hi, wow, I'm still stoned, morning pretty baby." She smiled at Gabriela. She looked at Mark and just said, "Wow." again.

"Look," said Mark, "I am going into the other room and putting on some music. Don't move. I'll be right back."

"Put on The Stones, will you, Mark!" shouted Helena. "I like to hear them in the morning. 'Sympathy for the Devil!' That's what I'm in the mood for. I still feel bad this morning." She grinned.

Mark got up and went into the living room. They both could not take their eyes off of him as he walked away.

"It seems as if his feet never touch the floor when he walks. He just kind of glides. Do you see that?" asked Helena, turning to Gabriela. "Well," she grinned mischievously, "we had quite a night, didn't we?" She giggled. "It was really nice," responded Gabriella, looking into her eyes. "Yeah. More than that," answered, Helena. "And damn, I've never known a guy like him. He is beyond special. I mean, do you know what he did to me? Oh… I guess you do know. But did you ever have sex like that? Holy shit. I must have come a thousand times. And you, you were incredible. Oh, I must sound really terrible."

"No, it's okay," responded Gabriela, looking a bit embarrassed. "It was really nice."

"But there was more…" continued Helena. "I seemed to find a place I had never known before; a really beautiful place. It felt, in a way, like when I sing with Jason. I can't really describe it with words. I hope you're not angry with me, talking like this, or that I jumped into your world. I mean, actually, I know I pushed my way in. I even feel a bit guilty about breaking in like that."

"You know, Helena, you would think I might hate you, but I don't. It feels nice that you know him. I feel less alone."

"You don't hate me? You are the coolest chick. That's really groovy. I like you, Gabriela… I mean, I really like you! I hope… Well, maybe we can all, I don't know… maybe something?"

Gabriela, ignoring this overture, said, "He is going to go away, and he does not know if he is coming back…" Her tears started flowing again.

"Going away? Where is he going? Why does he have to go?" questioned Helena, baffled.

"It's complicated," said Gabriela. "He will have to explain."

"Oh! This is terrible! Really terrible! You can't talk him out of it? Wait until he comes back with the coffee. We can talk him out of it, you and I…" She smiled mischievously.

"It won't work," replied Gabriela. "He has to go. Nothing will stop him."

"Really? Not even the two of us?" exclaimed Helena in frustration.

"No. He says it is much too important, and he has to go."

"Well, this really sucks. Why is it always like this? As soon as it starts, it's done. So that's why you've been crying. I thought you two had a fight or something. I was afraid it was about me. Oh God, you must be feeling so bad. I mean, I am here for you. If you want me to be, I am."

"He has to go away, and it may be dangerous for him. Listen, Helena, he is a lot more special than you think."

"What do you mean?"

"Well, he is not like anyone else, except maybe Jason. He is very, very special."

"What do you mean?" she repeated.

"Just look." She gestured with her eyes.

As if on cue, Mark re-entered the room. But instead of using the door, he walked through the wall holding two cups of coffee.

Helena looked up and gasped, her eyes popping. "What the fuck!"

CHAPTER 41
FINDING SOBA

S aya walked towards the restaurant on 9th street, deliberately avoiding eye contact so as not to be tempted to listen to the thoughts of people as she passed them. Instead, she focused upon the sound of her footsteps and the taste of the cold soba noodles awaiting her.

This must be the place. How cool... It's in a basement.

Inside, there was a small reception area where a waitress bowed formally and greeted her.

"Irasshaimase, welcome to Mie," she said in a bright tone.

Saya smiled. "Ohayo," she said in a Yokohaman accent. She asked to be seated, intuitively knowing where the waitress was from (one of the small outer islands), her inflection making her feel safe.

Surprised, the waitress seemed embarrassed for having used her local dialect and responded in formal Japanese, "Sorry, we have no free tables, but there is room at the bar if you would like."

Seeing that the waitress felt uncomfortable with her familiarity, Saya replied, "That will be fine."

As the hostess guided her towards the bar, she spotted Jason. Their eyes met. "Never mind," she said to the waitress, "I see my friend."

Saya walked to the table. "So, you knew I would be here?" Jason motioned her to sit down.

"I hope you didn't think I would leave you alone to languish in turmoil. I knew you would be here. Haven't you started to figure all this out yet?"

"I don't know what is going on. You obviously did something to me. I have to use all my mental focus just to walk down the street. I'm about to explode. I can hear people's thoughts. At least I think I do... For a while, I thought I was going crazy. It's as if schools of fish are swarming my brain, one thought chasing another, and another, and..."

"Don't worry." He reached out and touched her hand. "I am going help you with this." Saya felt a tingle in her fingers, and then she took a breath. "Now, make your mind blank... Just relax and breathe." Saya followed his instructions.

"See, the voices are quieter, aren't they? From now on, you will only hear what you choose. You can turn it on and off now, even raise and lower the volume like on the radio."

Saya looked directly into Jason's eyes. "Please, are you going to tell me what is going on? Who the hell are you? And what the hell do you want with me? Tell me now."

"Okay, of course. I'm sorry you were frightened. I didn't think your abilities would accelerate so quickly; you are a very fast learner. So, this is going to sound very strange to you. You and I have a very long story. I met you before you were born, while you were still within your mother's womb. But I was not sure you were you until I entered your body to heal you after we had sex in the club."

Saya's face took on an expression of disbelief. "Are you a ghost or something?"

"No, no, not a ghost, or anything like that, but I am from another world, a world very far from here. I was sent here by my people to do something very important. It's a long story, but this is what you really need to know for now: when I was about to enter your atmosphere for the first time, as I passed through the clouds, I looked down on the earth. Then I, too, was a kind of embryo. Your atmosphere was full of radioactivity, and everywhere I looked, I saw carnage. Then I saw you peacefully within your mother. As my mind went out to you, you gave me the feeling that all would be well, so I reached inside her and touched you. For a few brief moments, we were one. When this happened, unintentionally, I changed you forever, creating a being not like other earth people."

"Wait, just wait a second. You are from another world? What do you mean you changed me?"

"It was not my intention to change you. I was not supposed to change anything. In fact, I broke a big rule."

"Oh, well I hope you got detention for it. So now what?"

"Now that your abilities are developing further, I am going to teach you how to control your strength. You have much more power than you realize. Remember when I asked you if you ever questioned your abilities before; your speed, your strength?" Saya didn't respond. She looked at Jason like a child getting caught with a hand in the cookie jar. "Come on, Saya. You can crush a man's skull with a single blow. You can send a three-hundred-pound football player flying across a room. You are five-foot five-and-a-quarter and weigh one hundred and twenty-four pounds. You never wondered how that was possible?"

"I have a very powerful chi, and I've had very good teachers," she said in an indignant and serious tone.

Jason smiled. "Yes, you have, but there is no earth chi like yours."

"Am I an alien too?"

"Well yes, and no. You are quite human, but you aren't like others."

"Do I have to go through special training to control all these powers you are talking about? Do we go away to a mountain top for a year, or something?"

Jason gave her a smile. "No, the days of being chased through the mountains by your teacher are over. You will know what to do when things occur naturally. You almost figured out how to block the invading thoughts of others by yourself. You have the ability to understand things as they arise, and you will be fine. However, this strength you have leads to complications. Power is a large concept. We need to talk about that."

"What am I to expect then?"

"Beside the physical abilities that you know you have; your mental powers are increasing as well. Your ability to learn languages will become second nature, as natural to you as walking. Soon you will be able to see concepts within people's minds. Words will only be an accessory to communication. You will be able to understand everyone on Earth, disregarding the limitations of language. Also, you will be able to move things with your mind; nothing very huge, but small things like books and utensils, pots and pans, and such. Your increased agility will be one of your favorite gifts. You will be able to move at speeds you can't imagine. And you will become smarter. Much smarter."

"I'm already smart," she snapped.

Jason smirked. "It's all just beginning."

"By the way," said Saya, "I want you to return what you took from the temple. It does not belong to me. It belongs there."

"As you wish," he responded. "But now, let's talk about your power. You are growing stronger, as I have said. What I am about to say is very important. You must not abuse this strength."

"What do you mean 'abuse'?" responded Saya.

"All of these abilities which you have and will develop can't be used recklessly."

"I don't understand," she replied.

"Let me explain. If a cat is hungry and wants to eat a mouse, she can easily use her size and speed to catch it, seize it, and eventually devour it. But, often, before the mouse meets its end, the cat may play with the mouse, and when it does, another thing becomes present. Though the cat may let the mouse run around a bit, even ignoring it for some time, the mouse remains subjugated under the cat's domination. This form of power is forbidden. You can easily fall into the seduction of power, the pleasure of power."

"When the cat plays, she allows the mouse seconds of freedom, moments of hope, while of course, there is none. This power exists simply for the sake of power, power for its own end. You may use your new strengths for seeking knowledge, for defense, even for pleasure, but not for this. Do you understand?"

"I have never desired such domination. I have very simple needs. Some good Kentucky Bourbon, and a beautiful body or two, and I'm…"

Jason interrupted, "Yes, and a little pain for seasoning, I know. But you have gifts beyond your imagination, and like I said, this kind of power creates its own temptations. Do I have your promise?"

"Yes, yes, you have my promise."

"Good. I really didn't want to have to kill you."

"You wouldn't kill me, would you?"

"Well, I wouldn't have wanted to." Jason looked at Saya intently. "You are going to have to keep a low profile. Beings from my world won't appreciate the fact that you exist. Don't do anything to draw attention to yourself, for they will find you. I know about the man you tortured, cutting off his hands and feet. Something in you enjoyed what you did; that is the power I am warning you about, the part of you that smiled at his pain; it worries me. You are very important to me, Saya. You, in a way, are my legacy. I hope you have left your desire for this kind of pleasure behind in Japan."

Saya lowered her eyes. "I often think about that day. I am not proud of what I did, but I was driven by rage and hate. It will never happen again." She paused. "What do you mean, your legacy?"

"I am not sure how much time I will have here." Jason paused. "You mean a lot to me. You are, in a way, a kind of affirmation of my existence. You're beautiful in so many ways, and very special. And besides, you are…" Jason paused and looked into space.

"Yes, I know, a lot of fun in bed." Saya giggled, trying to lighten the mood. "But what are you saying? Are you really going to die?"

Jason smiled. "No one is immortal." He looked away again for a few seconds. "But I think in order to save humanity, I may face some serious danger. I'm not sure what will happen."

"Save humanity?"

"It's a complicated story, Saya. I'll explain it all another time."

"'A complicated story?' Are you telling me that you gave me all this, and now you are going to leave me on my own to figure it all out? That's really sucky if you ask me."

"You'll understand everything eventually. Think of it as if a university has been implanted within you, ready to teach you when you call upon it. In a way, I will always be with you. You will even hear my voice. I've also set you up with money so that you won't be tempted to abuse your power for it." Jason handed Saya a key. "This is the key to a deposit box at the Citibank on Canal and Broadway. Inside it, you will find a large amount of cash. You will also find twenty passports with staggered dates of birth, establishing twenty identities for you, along with bank accounts for each identity. Also, you will find three business cards of financial consultants, each of whom knows you under a different name that is indicated on each card. You have a large amount of money being supervised and invested by each of them."

"But I don't want a bunch of money; you see how I live, my walkup on Avenue C and 4th Street. I have three pairs of jeans and a few shirts, mostly with a couple of holes in them. Sure, I have a few beautiful dresses, but I only wear them to the casino for work. I am comfortable living the way I do. I rarely ever even wear underwear." Saya slurped some Soba noodles. "I really think you are going overboard."

"You may live as you like, of course, but you won't ever have to worry about money, nevertheless. Your full destiny is yet to be written, and you may become a very important person for your civilization one day." Jason paused. "Saya, I am going to do my best to spend the next few centuries knowing you."

"Centuries?" responded Saya, startled.

"Yes, centuries. You are going to live for a very, very long time. You'll look the same as others age around you. That is one of the reasons for all those identities. I have staggered the dates of birth on some passports so that there will be no raised eyebrows. It will be necessary for you to abandon your life from time to time and move on, or else people will start thinking you're a vampire or something."

Jason smiled at his own joke and continued, "There might come a day when you see an old lover in the street, maybe thirty years will have passed since you last laid eyes upon him. He may look a little bent with age, even a bit frail and gray. He might be walking with his college-aged granddaughter and you may hear him say to her, 'Do you see that pretty girl who just walked past? I once dated a girl who looked just like her, when I was your age. Yes, almost as beautiful as her.' The granddaughter will give him a patronizing smile, saying, 'Oh sure, grandpa.' You might feel an inward chuckle in hearing these words, and maybe feel pain in your heart, and a tear may try to escape. But you will not stop or look back or say a word. You will just keep walking, knowing that the past is just that. The past. It can never be again."

Saya finished her noodles. "This is a lot to take in. I need a break. Let's go find Angela. I want to get high and play for a while and forget about all of this for a few hours. Can we?"

"Look, you need to listen to me. This is very serious, and I told you I do not have a lot of time. Besides, Angela knows nothing about it, neither who I am, nor who you are. No one, and I mean no one, with maybe the exception of my brother Mark, should ever know who you really are. Do you understand?"

"Understand? Yes. Yes, I am trying to take this all in. Do I have any choice about it?" She looked at Jason intently.

"Not really. You are who you are, and your road has already been paved. Your only way out," Jason hesitated, "is death."

"Huh? Death? Big choice. When I sat down with you, I just hoped you might get these voices out of my head. Then maybe get to know you better. Now you tell me I must either live as a millionaire super woman constantly being spied upon by alien beings that might kill me if I do something wrong. Or else I can just die? Man, I'm not ready for this."

Jason smiled. "You're stronger than you give yourself credit for, Saya. These are great gifts that you have received – not burdens – and you will be fine. Trust me."

"I get that they're gifts, but it's all really... my life ever-changing, always leaving everything behind, it sounds so... what you're describing sounds so isolating."

"Yes," responded Jason. "It is daunting, but what is certain is that nothing can change who you are or who you will become. I will always be in your mind, and I will see you again... just be patient."

CHAPTER 42

SAYA THINKS IT ALL OVER

Hours passed, and Saya found herself sitting in her apartment, hardly aware that she had walked home. Her thoughts had taken over her body as her feet went through the motions of leading her to her door. Maybe this is what homing pigeons do, she thought.

Why is this happening to me?

Finding the sofa, Saya dove headlong into the cushions; they felt like a warm cup of milk.

She rolled over and stared up at the light gray ceiling. Maybe it's not gray, she thought, maybe it's just really dirty... I never thought about washing a ceiling. What am I supposed do now? Just wait, but wait for what? Jason said I am going to become some kind of a superwoman, like in the comic books. This is really too much.

Just then, the phone rang. She picked it up and heard Angela's perky voice piercing through the somberness, "Hi, baby. It's me. What are you doin'?"

"Oh, nothing. Moping," responded Saya. Jason had told her that Angela knew nothing of his true nature and that she was not to hear a word of their secrets. This is all so unfair.

"Yeah, just moping," she repeated, thinking to herself, when I'm not scared shitless. Saya could not imagine how she could begin to express what she was going through. Meanwhile, she dared not break any rules, for fear that Jason or some strange beings from another world might kill her. I need to be alone to try and piece this all together, or maybe I just need to find a deep mountain cave and bury myself...

"I have some weed, so if you have a little wine, well, that makes a party, right?" Angela said playfully.

"I am out of wine," Saya responded in a sullen tone, thinking, I am really not in the mood to play.

But Angela wasn't discouraged. "Hey. Stop sounding like such a sad sack. I'll pick up a bottle. Come on, let's hang out."

Maybe it will do me good not to be alone. "Okay, Angela, if you really want to... but give me a little time. I need to rest."

"Rest?" replied Angela. "You sound like my Grandma."

"I know, but I'm tired. How about in a couple of hours? I need a nap and a shower at least."

"Okay, it's seven now. I'll be there around ten... That gives you three hours to pamper your pretty self... Okay?"

"Sounds good, but don't expect too much from me tonight. I am really tired."

"I've heard that before. Anyway, we can just chill, if you'd like. I just don't want to be alone. Okay?"

"Sure," replied Saya, "I know how you feel."

"Say, Saya, didn't you just get one of those videocassette players?"

"Yes... Sing got a bunch, and he gave me one, but it's still in the box."

"I'll rent a tape or two. A store just opened up on the block, and we can try it out."

"Okay, I'll unpack it, but you have to do the rest."

***

Elgert's first assistant stood with the science officer on the observatory.

"Have you finished programming the beam?" he asked impatiently.

"Yes, as you have requested," the science officer responded.

"But as you know, this was never designed to be a weapon. It's a mining tool. It was meant to avoid harming workers when extracting ore; changing it into a weapon has proven difficult."

"You told us it could be adapted." The assistant said with annoyance in his voice.

"Of course, but The Prime designed its targeting program to avoid life forms. We have reversed the protocol. That is not the difficulty. It has to do with targeting. As you know, humans are carbon-based and are easily identified. However, the weapon can't be programmed to eliminate a specific human. It can only target carbon-based life forms within a specific location. Further, the distance the beam must travel introduces a time delay that may cause additional complications. Do you still wish to proceed?"

"Yes. Launch it."

"Are you certain?"

"Yes. Launch it now."

"Yes, sir."

***

Saya hung up and looked at the box in the corner of the room. It had been sitting there for a month. She hardly ever watched TV. In fact, that was another gift from Sing; she would never have bought one for herself.

She unpacked the box and attached it to the TV. There is never anything interesting on this thing, she mused, looking at the Sony perched on a stand in the corner. She had been using it as a coat rack. Finally putting it together, she found it was all fairly straightforward. She stared at the thing and thought to herself, it's really ugly. I want to get rid of it, but Sing would be mad if I threw it away. He is so sensitive about things like that.

Saya lay down for an hour. She tried to sleep, but it evaded her. Finally, she got up and took a shower. The warm water felt good. Her body relaxed, and she turned up the heat, the water rushing over her back. The pressure felt wonderful, beating down on her like a thousand bees. It was scalding, but she loved it. Then she turned on the cold. It hit her body like a Nordic blast in February. Any other person would have reeled with the pain of it all, but Saya just smiled.

After the shower and a brisk dry, she slipped on some panties and a long, flimsy Indian shirt dress, knowing in the back of her mind that it was fairly transparent, and curled up on the sofa with a copy of Jane Eyre. I may as well give her a little thrill, even if we don't do anything. She was four chapters into the book and hoping for a few more minutes with it when the doorbell rang.

"It's me," came crackling through the intercom. "It's me, Angela. Open up."

Her hair still moist from the shower, she unwrapped the towel from her head. Saya buzzed her in. Her hair hung free, falling down over her shoulders like wet seaweed straggling off a boat. Still, this disarray did little to distract from her beauty, as her freshly bathed body clung to the cloth.

Angela looked very bubbly, bangled and beaded as if she had just left a Grateful Dead concert. She was wearing pink wire-rimmed, psychedelic sunglasses that were "so in." It was especially perfect to wear them at night.

"Are you coming from a Janis Joplin look-alike party?" Saya asked, laughing.

"Don't I look mad? And look what I have," she said, waving the videotape Cool Hand Luke in Saya's face. "It's my love, Paul Newman. I just saw it in the theater a couple months ago. I cannot believe the video store had it so soon. It must be one of the junky pirated ones. Paul Newman is so my macho man."

Saya laughed; she knew that Newman was one of her idols.

"Don't you look the mess?" said Angela. "Look at that hair. You're lucky I love you and you're so hot. Or else I would not let you get away with looking like this when I come over." She sat on the couch and threw the tapes on the worn wooden coffee table. "Do you have an opener and some wine glasses?

We should let this breathe a little. It is a really good bottle. You're going to like it."

"Sure," responded Saya. "I might even have some cheese and crackers." Smiling, she returned with the glasses and cork-screw, already starting to feel better.

"Okay, I'll get to work rolling us some joints," Angela said, dropping some pot and papers on the table.

"Sounds good," said Saya.

Angela poured the wine and started to ramble about the club, going on about some of the other waitresses and the boss. Saya smiled and nodded, pretending to be interested as she went on. Aside from occasional sips of wine and tokes of her weed, Angela barely paused for twenty minutes. Saya thought… she has hardly taken a breath.

"Nice wine, right?" asked Angela.

"Really nice," responded Saya, thinking, maybe she will stop this chatter now.

Saya had a particular way of politeness leftover from her life in Japan, especially with women friends. Never interrupt. Always look interested, and never say something rude, unless one is directly offended.

"Let's watch the movie," said Angela. "You are going to love it. Lots of sweat and pain," she laughed.

Angela put the cassette in the player, and they both started to cuddle up together. "This is nice," said Saya.

"Yeah… really nice." Angela kissed her, but Saya pulled back after the first touch.

"I kind of just want to be quiet tonight, if that's okay, Angela. You know I dig you, but I'm not in that kind of mood."

"But you look so good in that almost nothing of a thing you have on… You mean you're going to leave me in frustration?"

"Maybe later, okay? I'm just not into it right now."

Saya was still too overwhelmed by Jason and all she had just learned. Worse, she could not tell that to Angela. She wished she could just let it all out, but she knew she couldn't. Holding it in was agonizing. She needed a friend, and she wanted to share but was bound to silence. And while there was little jealousy between them, especially when they were all sharing each other, she knew that she would surely start an Italian volcano erupting if Angela found out Jason was on her mind when they were alone. Still, Saya appreciated her company. She put her arms around her and said, "It is really nice having a friend like you, Angela."

Angela put her head on Saya's shoulder and turned on the TV. She had almost memorized the movie and kept interjecting with comments while it played. This was really starting to annoy Saya, but when the prison warden said to Newman, "What we have here is a failure to communicate," and Angela echoed the words in her deep Italian accent, Saya went into hysterics.

Next, Angela put on North by Northwest, but they did not make it halfway through before they were both asleep in each other's arms, curled up like children on the plush, red velvet sofa.

It was about 4 a.m. when Saya awoke. She felt an inward stir that she could not fully comprehend. It was fear, fear of something from afar, fear of something imminent. She got up off the sofa, leaving Angela's arms. How sweet she looks, like a child, Saya thought. She is such a beautiful, innocent person, even with all her craziness. Saya walked down the hall into the kitchen, put up a pot, and closed the door as to not disturb Angela in the living room. I'll make some chamomile tea and curl back up with her. That will be nice.

Just then, the walls started to turn blue, then red, then green, then blue again. The furniture started to shake. The vase on the kitchen table fell and broke into tiny shards. A wailing hum filled her ears; then came a violent yell as if banshees were screeching.

Instinctively, Saya dived out the window, flying across the alley onto the fire escape of the adjacent building. The turmoil faded as quickly as it came. She jumped back from the fire escape, rushing to see if Angela was okay, but she was gone; all that was left on the velvet sofa was a bit of ash and some stone beads.

They killed her. They wanted me, but they got her.

"Jason."

CHAPTER 43

JASON WAITS

The apartment was silent except for the sound of rain rapping against the window. It was a dark morning. Pigeons quivered, huddling on the fire escapes close to the exterior walls of the building. The smell of boiled cabbage seeped through the door from the apartment downstairs. Jason's motorcycle jacket hung sportingly from the half-broken wooden chair he had picked up on the street. He looked out at the rooftops of the adjacent building; the rain was so dense it made the water tower vanish into the grayness. "It's almost like nothing was ever there. 'Nothingness,' what a musical word," he mumbled.

Why hasn't Mark responded to me? Is he blocking my thoughts? He must be having a really good time. Good for him; he should have some fun while he can. He is so serious about his relationships, always talking about love, its meaning, and those humans' higher attributes. Why can't he just relax?

Jason was aware their realities were in transition. The bond between himself and Mark had grown since they started walking the earth together. He felt the portal's call. He sensed its pull. Why is it yearning for me? Do they fear some loss of control? He could almost hear voices. He grew more and more restless with each passing moment. Mark, he again sent out his thoughts, please respond.

More than an hour had passed before he heard in his mind:

I'm coming, Jason.

***

Mark was still in the bedroom with Helena and Gabriela. Helena had just fainted, and Gabriela, ignoring her, started to cry, "Oh, Mark. How can you just go?"

"I'll see you again, Gabriela. When I say I don't know what will happen, I mean just that. I am not even sure what we will be asked to do. We are just afraid of the unknown. It may be a walk in the park, as you humans often say. Let's be positive."

Gabriela caught her breath. "Okay, I'll be positive. But I'll miss you Mark." Gabriela sat up straight.

Just then, she looked down. "Oh shit. What's happened to Helena? She is out cold. Do something, Mark."

"Listen, Gabriela. You will have to explain everything to her. My brother needs me, and I have to go. She is okay. I'll wake her after I'm out of here. You will know what to say. She may freak out a little, but I know you can handle it."

"You're leaving now?"

"Yes, I'm sorry. I'll be in touch as soon as I can."

Gabriela watched Mark get dressed. She looked over at Helena sprawled naked on the bed.

"She'll be fine," responded Mark as he finished putting on his clothing. "I'm going to teleport myself to Jason's location now. Close your eyes. There may be a bit of a flash that could hurt them. I'll be in touch. I promise."

"Goodbye, Mark... I love you."

Gabriela didn't want to turn her head away. She watched as Mark's figure dissolved before her. A buzzing vibration of energy appeared, leaving only an outline of his being. It reminded her of when she was a child and had woken up in front of the television when the station had gone down: a grainy, frenetic sand of electric static emerged. Just then, she heard him say loudly, "Close your eyes. Close them now." Gabriela instinctively obeyed. When she opened her eyes, he was gone.

When Mark arrived at the apartment, he found Jason looking anxious.

"Are you okay?" inquired Mark. "You look worried."

"I'm okay, but the damn portal has been gnawing at me, calling to me. It's been like a siren in my brain, screaming. Do you hear it?"

***

On Eldern, Elgert and Dronin could see that both Mark and Jason were in the vicinity of the portal.

"We should pull them in while we have them together," Elgert said to Dronin.

"But are we ready to meet with them? Have you addressed my concerns? Have you been able to increase Jason's chances of survival? And in the worst-case scenario, have you developed a suicide mechanism for him?" asked Dronin.

"They have enhanced their development on their own. After our meeting, they will be approaching our level of power; Jason's new strength will give him some chance to maintain his integrity within the earth's core. It all depends on how speedily Mark can rescue him. And yes, I will be able to give him a means of self-destruction."

Elgert was convincing in his deceptions; he enjoyed them, knowing one day he would control it all.

"Well, at least we can spare him pain. That's something anyway," said Dronin.

"According to The Prime, the chance of his survival has increased to roughly one in ten rather than one in a thousand," responded Dronin.

Elgert nodded, enjoying the darkness of his plans.

***

Elgert activated the portal within the apartment, encompassing the area, filling the room with a violent rush, overpowering Mark and Jason.

"Mark, what's happening?"

"I don't know," Mark answered. He felt his body being lifted from the ground. "It is too strong for me. I can't control it."

The twins found themselves swept into the whirl of the vortex. Faster and faster, like wind spinning leaves lifelessly in air, they turned, twisting helplessly within the overwhelming power of the portal. They spun, with crippled senses and comatose limbs. They reached out, grasping hands and arms, their bodies but toys whirling aimlessly, until with surprise, they stood before the elders of their home planet.

For the first time, Mark and Jason saw a glimpse of their home world. The two statesmen were standing in the middle of a large chamber, an ornate room decorated with various forms of art. Elgert and Dronin motioned for Mark and Jason to join them at a large table. The table was glasslike and emanated luxury, melodically changing in color from moment to moment. A large arch behind an open-air veranda framed the chambers. Lush foliage occupied the portico. Flowers of various hues filled the room, some as large as antelopes, moving sinuously on animated purple and green vines. They swayed as if they were dancing to some unheard music.

In the distance, Mark and Jason could see the expanse of the city. Metallic and glasslike buildings shimmered in the light against a vermilion sky streaked with sweeps of crimson. Two suns – one orange, the other more yellow – shone brightly in the firmament. A pale blue moon timidly hid behind misty clouds. An aurora could be seen shimmering in the haze, boldly asserting its existence against the horizon.

Amidst this, the Elders stood. They were tall; maybe eight feet in height, with long, narrow faces. Their hairless heads glowed porcelain white and swept back like the mantle of a snail; their eyes were but slits, their bodies whitish green, plasmatic and almost transparent. They seemed to undulate from a liquid energy that, to the twins, appeared to flow through them like a circulatory system without veins.

"Mark and Jason, welcome. We are two of the three members of the Grand Council of Eldern, your home world. We have long awaited this day."

"Where are we?" asked Mark. "Are we on another planet?"

"No," replied Elgert. "You are still on Earth. You are seeing a projection of Eldern, the world you are from. We are the leaders of this planet and your guardians. We know that you have a million questions, and we will give you a million answers, but first we have some pressing matters to discuss. Please allow us this time to do that. And while it would give us the greatest of pleasures to educate you both about our world, it would be a cumbersome way to convey such vast knowledge. In due course, we will implant the history of our world into your memory, and many of these questions will be answered. We hope you will come to see Eldern as your home world, and that you will learn to value your heritage."

"And this is Eldern we are seeing now?" asked Mark.

"Yes," answered Dronin, "it is a rich planet and the largest in the federation."

"You said there are three of you?" asked Jason

"Yes. I am Dronin, The Administrator. Here with me is Elgert, the planet's Scientific Coordinator. The Minister of Culture and diplomat to other worlds is Allaceia. She is away on a mission and will talk with you later."

Elgert interjected, "You were created from Allaceia's genealogy. She is your mother."

"Our mother?" exclaimed Mark.

"Yes. Not in the way you have seen on Earth, but in the Eldern way. I am Elgert, and I have guided you from your inception. Allaceia, of course, nurtured you, but it was my job to protect and instruct you, looking after the details so you could maturate in peace. It was I who kept your identities secret and your lives concealed until adulthood. We have watched over you since your arrival on earth, and we are pleased to talk to you at last."

"But why have you waited so long, and why must we wait to meet our mother?" asked Mark.

"Yes. I don't understand. Why have we not met you before

this?" Jason added.

"We did not want to create a conflict within you. We felt you should mature peacefully and without yearning for this world. We needed you to mature solely under the influence of earthlings, but in a way, through the portal, we have been with you every day of your lives," said Dronin.

"And of course, there are your missions," interjected Elgert.

"Our *missions*?" inquired Jason skeptically.

"Yes, you have several missions, all of which you will learn. We live very differently than the beings on Earth. You will understand our motivations in time, but there is one pressing and dangerous issue that must be dealt with immediately. When we discovered these beings, we became very interested in their existence, especially their ability to dream and have emotions. You were both sent to Earth to learn of these things and absorb all of what you experienced, but there is a pressing matter which I must discuss now: the earth needs your protection."

"Our protection?" inquired Mark, feigning ignorance.

"I will explain everything," replied Elgert.

Dronin and Elgert continued talking. Mark and Jason listened attentively, trying to discern their motivations. They searched for any nuance of insincerity. Jason grew skeptical. He felt something was amiss, and he especially did not like Elgert.

Jason said, "Please do. But first... You know a great deal about us, but we know nothing of you. Tell us something of yourselves, of your life on Eldern."

"Of course," responded Elgert. "On this world, only a select few of us have independent thought. It is The Prime that guides our lives. This is why we are so interested in earthlings and the seeming anarchy in which they exist. We are fascinated by what you have experienced and what you have both become."

"You said there is a federation. What of these other worlds? Are they all like yours, absent of dreams and emotions?" asked

Mark.

"There are fourteen planets in all within the federation. Yes, they all live as we do in some degree or another. But there is one planet called New Tripton. It is a world hidden beneath an ocean. It is inhabited by strange but playful beings that live independently from the rest of us. They remain a mystery to us. Your mother is the only one with whom they allow contact. But this must wait, you will learn more in time."

"Oh." Jason thought of the furry little beings. "Have any others visited the earth?" He received no answer. He could see they did not want to respond.

"We have never authorized any such visits," responded Elgert.

Sensing that Elgert was avoiding the issue, he thought it better not to press. "Okay then, now what? What are you asking from us?"

"An asteroid is on a collision course with the earth. It is doomed for destruction without your intervention."

Jason interrupted, "So you want us to divert this asteroid?"

"Before we give you the details, you must understand that the plan was derived from the need to keep earthlings unaware of the involvement of outside worlds... worlds far more advanced than their own. In the past, when civilizations as advanced as ours contacted primitive worlds such as Earth, the contact always led to the demise of their civilization. The federation now forbids contact with any world incapable of hyper-speed, and therefore intergalactic transportation. It is ruled that first contact must be initiated by the primitive society. Earthlings are many of their years away from being able to do this," said Elgert.

"But many of them know of us. Our existence is no longer a secret," said Mark.

"Yes, many are aware of you, but many Earthlings believe in Santa Claus, the Tooth Fairy, and vampires... Formal contact from an advanced civilization such as ours is very different. The knowledge of your existence can be controlled and easily explained," replied Elgert. "If necessary, all memories of your existence could be wiped clean from the minds of all who know you. Your personal lives are not an issue."

"So then… What are we to do?" asked Mark.

"According to The Prime, you will be able to divert the asteroid and cause it to crash harmlessly into Jupiter," replied Elgert. "This will be a difficult and dangerous procedure. The reason why we have interrupted your lives at this time is that it is imperative that the energy needed to divert the asteroid remains minimal; its distance from the earth is the main variable. If we act now, there will be only minor disturbances. It is a complicated task, yet, it is one you will be equipped to accomplish."

Elgert wove his lies without hesitation.

Mark and Jason sensed they were not being told everything. They dared not communicate their trepidations with each other, but they were both attuned to one other's apprehensions. Why had they not contacted us sooner, preparing us for what we must do? Why had they been so late with these gifts of additional power? If we had more time, couldn't we have become accustomed to them, grown deft in these abilities? No, something is not right.

"You are telling us there is no other solution?"

"The Prime has determined the solution. We will inform you of any further information," responded Elgert.

"The Prime?" responded Mark.

"Yes," answered Elgert, "we follow its guidance."

"And will we be safe?" asked Jason.

"If you follow your instructions," responded Elgert.

"Please continue," said Mark.

Elgert paused. "You, Mark, with your advanced knowledge of mathematics and astronomy, will travel to the proximity of the asteroid. There, you will await the power of the magnetic field from the earth's core, which will be directed to you by Jason. The asteroid may break into many fragments. In this case, you will have to calculate precisely the power of magnetic energy you will be receiving from Jason in order to send all the fragments into Jupiter."

Jason interrupted, "Did you say the earth's core? Nothing can survive there."

"Yes, but for a short time you will be safe," responded Elgert. "Therefore, Mark's skill and speed will be integral to your escaping unharmed."

"So, it is I who will be in danger, then," said Jason.

"Yes, Jason, you will face more peril than Mark will. However, we have given you great strength to meet these obstacles. We will provide you special protections against the zero gravity and the immense heat and pressure of the core. We will implant within you the knowledge and ability you will need for survival. You will vacillate between dimensions so as not to be affected by the normal rules of physics. Within these nano-units of time you have between these states, you will project the exact proportion of the magnetic field needed to divert the asteroid. It must be done for a precise duration and angle so as not to upset the orbit of the earth itself. All has been calculated for you. All you need to do is follow the path which will be given to you," responded Dronin.

"Follow the path, huh? I have never been too good at that... I'm more of a figure-it-out-on-the-fly kind of guy."

"Yes, we are aware of that, Jason. It is a character we nurtured within you, knowing you might meet unforeseen problems. Please understand, this is your choice, Jason. We will not, and we could not force you, to go forward. But rest assured, if you do not... the earth will perish," stated Elgert.

Elgert knew that the twins' sense of duty would leave them no choice. He was also planning on Jason's rogue nature, for he knew his spontaneity and impetuousness would seed his end.

"To save the earthlings, you leave me little choice," replied Jason.

Elgert felt that he had played the board well; he could see the end game before him.

"We are implanting all the details of your quest into your

minds now. You will see how we have done our best to secure your success."

"Wait," interjected Jason. "What if something goes wrong? Will I be trapped in the core?"

"Our calculations have been verified, but we have given you a way to end your own life if something goes awry. But if you follow the plan…"

"Sure, just trust you," responded Mark irreverently.

"You will have received all the data by now, Jason. The choice is yours. We will say farewell for now. The earth's moon is entering a position that makes direct communication with you impossible."

"But wait, what about our mother? When do we meet her?" asked Mark loudly.

"Your mother is in another location and will be contacting you soon."

These last words from Elgert were curt and cryptic; quite unlike the warm and benevolent manner that they portrayed at the onset of the meeting.

Mark and Jason again faced each other in the apartment. They heard the voice of Elgert: "Your mother will meet with you in two hours, Earth time."

CHAPTER 44

WAITING FOR MANANKEN

On New Tripton, Allaceia awaited Mananken's return from his meeting with the High Council. Mananken had been in this meeting for more than three hours, which could only mean that there were controversies. She interpreted this as a good sign; if the Triptonians did not have the ability to solve her dilemma, their response would have been quick. The delay hinted at a willingness to help, and maybe the price that would be asked.

Allaceia sat in the outer chambers of the Council room. It was an immense corridor lined with opulent furnishings. These trappings must have been done to impress others. No one goes to such lengths just for themselves. But then again, these beings have great wealth, and they really like to show off, she smiled to herself. They are charming little beings, and not to be underestimated; none matches their technology. But will they help me?

At last, Mananken appeared. "Cherba, cherba, cherba." He smiled as he bounced down the hall enthusiastically. "Good news. They have agreed to help you. Werba, werba, werba," he said as his smile vanished, and his tone turned grave. "But they will ask a high price."

Allaceia understood "Werba, werba, werba" quite well. It meant be careful.

Mananken allowed his words to hang between them for a

moment before continuing, "Some are concerned about the ramifications of interfering in the politics of another planet, so you must explain yourself well when you negotiate with them later."

"But do you have the ability to save them? And what of the Prime? Can you help there, as well?"

"The Prime... Hmm. Werba, derba, werba... You have a big problem there. We will need our AI to help you. First you must understand that the plan was flawed and inaccurate from the start. This so-called plan was based on a lie. Not only is there not enough metal in the asteroid to be affected by magnetism, but in fact, the asteroid was never on a collision course with Earth. The Prime was wrong; there must be something seriously amiss with it. I cannot believe such a plan was even considered, but I am sure it was Elgert who seized upon this error. Maybe it was an honest mistake, yet we are certain the Prime grew to fear the effect Mark and Jason are having on your world. We believe it is threatened, and this has engaged its survival algorithm. Very dangerous."

"The Prime... It has been the Prime all along..." Allaceia mumbled, sinking into despondency. She fell back into a nearby chair. "Something in me knew this, but I wouldn't admit it to myself. My staff and I often spoke of this. The Prime has been acting strangely for some time. It fears the end of its dominion, its purpose. So, my dear friend... What now? How can you save my children?"

"We must deal with both problems: your Prime as well as Elgert. It was he who exploited it for his ambitions. Yes. Fixing both problems is the real trick."

"Yes, of course. Both."

"Well, the price will be high. Let's look at the whole picture. Our spies discovered that Elgert's plan is to attack Mark in outer space with a fleet of probes while he is occupied in his efforts to divert the asteroid. Elgert thinks Mark will be vulnerable there. He expects the earth's core will destroy Jason. We must devise a plan to get rid of Elgert, but first Mark must survive in order to save Jason."

"Is this possible? Can you do this for me?"

Mananken started to bounce up and down. His ears started to vibrate, almost dancing in place. His hair sparkled brightly and glowed in delight. "Cherba, cherba, cherba. Of course, we can do it. We are Triptonian."

"Thank you, Mananken. I will be forever in your debt."

"I must explain what will be hard for you, my friend. We must let him initiate the attempt to assassinate Mark and Jason. If we do not, he may be able to explain away everything, and avoid being exposed."

"I must let him try and kill them? But if he succeeds, how could I live with that? They are my children, Mananken. They have the power and the potential to change everything. Is there no other way? Mananken, I could not live if they died."

"My dear friend," Mananken answered, "the Council is firm about this. The ramifications for us are very serious. If he is allowed to remain in power, he could make things difficult for us with the Federation. The law is quite clear about such matters. If the other planets were to learn we had interfered in the development of a primitive world without absolute approval, my head would roll, and so will those of others who follow my lead. No... If you want our help, your offspring will have to take the risk. There is no other choice."

"Mananken... If they die, I will never forgive myself."

"Do you trust my judgment, Allaceia? Do you have confidence in me?"

She looked at Mananken. She understood the risk he was about to take for her, but her newborn emotions were tearing at her ability to make clear judgments. Her cool analytic abilities were failing her. She thought about what she should say. Still unsure, she replied, "Yes, my friend. I will put my faith in you."

"I know you're uncertain, but when we succeed, your planet will be in your debt. There is no other way to go forward; if there were, I would take it. Elgert's threat must be nullified. Your children have changed Eldern. That is what is troubling your AI. That is why this is happening. I cannot help you if he lingers in the background. Later, pacifying the Prime is simply a process of convincing it that it will remain vital, a part of your world's future. This will be your job when you return. We can help it understand. We have had similar issues in the past. Our AI will help."

"Yes, I can communicate with it," responded Allaceia. "I understand it. It will listen, I am sure. But can your plan fail?"

"Any plan can fail, but I will go myself to help Mark and Jason. I will not let the plan fail. There will be risks, but I will not fail."

* * *

Back in the apartment in the East Village, Jason and Mark stood in silence. Only the wailing cry of an alley cat broke the somberness in the air. Jason looked into Mark's eyes. "Two hours... Not much time. We should go have some fun."

"Jason, we have to talk. Do you trust those guys? I don't. I believe that the only honest thing they said is that we are growing stronger, much stronger. They're not telling us everything, and I think there is a reason why our mother was not there. Something is going on."

"You may be right, but if I have to be back in two hours, I'm going to have a good time. God, I'd love to find Angela... I need to see Saya, too. The life I have left may be short, but at least it will be fun. I suggest you find your woman, and maybe Helena too, and do the same."

"Wait, Jason. Before you disappear on me, I need to know the plan. So, we meet back here in two hours. Think about what you are going to say to our mother. Maybe we can find out more details and how we can survive this."

"Yeah, right. Like, 'Hi Mom, nice meeting you after all these years. Do you have any ideas how I can avoid getting my ass fried in the earth's core?'" retorted Jason.

"Be serious for a minute. I think she may be up to something. Why wasn't she there? It doesn't make sense. We have to be aware of any hidden message she might be sending us when we speak."

"Yeah, maybe she has some earth-core fire retardant in her purse." Jason snickered. "Anyway, I'll see you in two hours." In a flash, Jason transported himself out of the room.

Mark stood in shock after he vanished. What a temperament. Well, Jason is Jason, and nothing will ever change that. I'll have to look out for him as best I can. Maybe I should take his advice and enjoy the time I have. Accessing Gabriela's mind, Mark saw that she was still in the apartment with Helena. Apparently, she had been forced to spend hours explaining everything about him to her. Helena, completely confused, was hoping the explanation that he was an alien was a drug hallucination.

I should go back there.

Mark transported himself back to Helena's apartment. Gabriela looked up. "You're back…? You're back!"

Helena watched as Mark materialized and gasped. "Are you kidding me." She again fainted into Gabriela's arms.

"See what I mean. I can't deal with her, Mark. You have to do something."

Mark walked over to them and sat on the bed. "Okay, I'm sorry to leave you with such a mess. I'll take it from here." He placed his hand on Helena's head and entered her consciousness; peacefully, he took control of her mind. Silently, he suggested that all of what Gabriela had told her was true and that she should accept her words completely and without qualification that he was an alien.

Gabriela looked at him poignantly. "So, what are you doing? Are you doing some kind of Dr. Spock mind meld or something? Hell, Mark, you cannot just jump in and out of my life like this. Do you understand what it means when people say, 'I'm only human?' It means you have to understand the limits of what we can take. I'm starting to feel like a ping-pong ball. One minute I think I'll never see you again, and then, BOOM. You're back. This is not working for me."

"I'm sorry, Gabriela, but I have been going through a lot, myself. I just wanted to see you again, hold you again, touch you... Did I do wrong?"

"It's not that you did wrong. I'm really happy to see you, but it's hard for me, that's all. Here, come closer. Hold me. Let me hold you. I know you are going through things and I should not be so selfish. You have big problems, important ones, and my selfish thoughts are just that, all about me, but I'm sitting here in a murk. I know you say the world might end without you saving it, but when I think about not ever being able to see you again, I just wilt. The only thing I feel when you're gone is that... you're gone. Sometimes, when I'm with you I feel so alive, as if I've been riding on a shooting star, and then when you're gone, I feel like I am just sitting on a park bench staring at an afterglow."

Mark looked intently, but the depth of her feelings was beyond his comprehension. He touched her face, gently moving his fingers over her lips. "I'm trying to find my way. We have such a short time. Let's only think about what we have. Let's make the most of it."

Their lips touched. "I love you, Mark. I regret nothing."

Mark looked for words of consolation but found none; he was searching to understand her feelings, but he had to feel them first. He heard himself saying, "You are the most special person in the world to me." These were the words she wanted to hear. These words from this strange and elusive being filled her with hope, and that was enough. The room, the apartment, all of New York vanished. She reached for him and pulled him down. After, when she became exhausted, they rested. Gabriela touched his chest with her head and thought she heard his heartbeat, although she knew he didn't have one.

Suddenly, Helena woke up and looked around. "Oh, Mark. You're back." She had no recollection of seeing him just a few minutes before.

"Gabriela, he's back, what is going on?" Helena threw her arms around Gabriela. "Please tell me I'm not hallucinating, that I'm not going crazy."

"No, it's okay Helena. I just had to go do something," reassured Mark.

"What? Did you have to go do some outer space stuff or something? This is really hard to take straight. Where is my coke?" She opened her bag, snorted some cocaine, and put her arms around Mark's neck, pulling them both close. "Well, whatever... You're back. He's back, Gabriela."

"Helena, please calm down. I really like you but explaining this all to you is becoming a real pain with all this crazy talk. He's an alien. Drugs won't change that, so accept it. I have to tell you that this, this whatever he is, he means a lot to me. Now, I know you're into him, and I really like you, but I need you to understand me. I may never see him again, and I don't know what is going to come next for him. I am about to cry at the thought of losing him."

"Oh, I'm so sorry, Gabriela. Do you want me to leave? Do you want to be alone with him?"

"No, no, Helena, don't leave! I need you now more than ever."

Mark overhearing the conversation got up and walked away to the window. He was overwhelmed with the thought of tasks before him, he looked down onto the street.

Gabriela saw he was uncomfortable. "Come, Helena, we need to talk in private." She grabbed Helena by the hand and led her into the bathroom. Motioning her to sit on the toilet seat, Gabriela whispered, "No. I don't want you to leave. I thought about that, but no... Helena. What I want is... Helena, he is talking like he might die. I don't know what to do. I need something, a gift beyond all gifts. So, my new friend, if these are his last hours, what can we do for him that he will never forget?"

"What do you mean 'he's talking like he might die?' He seems pretty damn healthy to me."

"I don't really understand it, myself. I think it is about something dangerous he must do. Something has him very concerned, but I'm not clear about it. He is frightened, for sure. We need to make him forget about it all. We have to do something that will have him dreaming about coming back to me. A real memory."

"A memory?" Helena smiled. "Hmm... Well I'm good at that. But if I help make it, I get to share in the benefits, right?"

"Yeah, yeah. But I mean a real memory, something that someone would yearn for, forever and ever. Maybe if he yearns hard enough, he will figure out a way to come back. I want him to think of nothing but that. We need something special. Do you have any ideas? And what do you mean by 'benefits'?"

"We have to talk. Gabriela, since we are doing all this sharing and planning, I have to tell you something. I am into Mark, but..." She paused, smiled, and looked into Gabriela's eyes. "But, you know, I am kinda into you, too."

"What! What the hell do you mean? Are you not listening to me? Holy shit, Helena. Stop talking crazy. I just spent the last twelve years with a man with his head in an equation and his brain soaked in scotch. I've been dreaming, hoping for a life, and now I find myself in love with an alien. And you're telling me you have a crush on me? I am not trying to turn my life into a chapter from Marquis de Sade. Really, I'm not ready for all of this."

"Stop hiding in your books, Gabriela, just listen to me. You do have a woman with a crush on you, and since you're already in this mess, we have to deal with it. And I know you are mad about Mark, so maybe we could work something out, get creative."

"Creative?" What do you mean 'creative?' You must still be very stoned. Can we just stay on subject please?"

"Gabriela, this is the subject. We don't have a lot of time, and maybe I am still high, but I know what I am saying, and I need you to understand me. After all, I'm trying to understand you. Can we at least talk about it? What I mean is if you want to be alone with him, I'm okay with that, but I would like to be alone with you sometime as well. Or we could all be together.

I would love that, too, so what do you say? Let me in."

Gabriela's mouth dropped open; words stumbled out. "I don't know what to say... I was not thinking long term about you. I was kind of thinking this was like a thing you would go to confession for when you were young and never think about again. Secondly, he has to survive and come back. Besides, I'm more than the jealous type. This is too much for me right now.

Gabriela stood up and paced back and forth in the tiny bathroom. "You mean you and me? You and me having a... I don't know if I can do that Helena. Can we talk about this later, please?"

"But I want to talk about it now," Helena said, tilting her head with a smile.

Gabriela gave her a questing look in return. "I do like you, but Helena, this is all new for me. I just want to wake up at home in my bed. Someone please tell me this is all a dream."

"I'm not a dream, Gabriela, I'm right here, and I'm serious, and I'm really into you. I know sometimes I can sound like a flippy rock-and-roller on acid, but I'm not that way with my heart. I've been hurt too many times for that. I'm careful now. Well, at least I'm trying to be. It's weird for me to feel something for the both of you, but I do. You are so special, and he is completely something else. Yes, both of you... I want it, I do. Let me in. Tell me your ground rules."

"What do you mean 'ground rules,' and what do you mean 'in'?"

"Listen, I am not asking for a forever commitment. I am just telling you how I feel."

"Well..." Gabriela said pensively, "I can't believe what I'm about to say, but I have feelings for you as well. I think we're both completely nuts. Yet it would be great to keep seeing you; to be able to talk about him to someone without everyone saying I should be sent to a mental institution... and you are incredibly beautiful."

"Yeah, you and me. It will be great. I know you really like me; I feel it," cried Helena. "And, I mean, who would ever believe this? At least we will have each other."

"Well," Gabriela paused, half-dazed by the situation, questioning herself, "but damn, you're just a kid. How old are you? You look maybe twenty-two. And Mark looks younger than that. What am I doing? I must be really going nuts."

Then, looking at her beautiful blue eyes, Gabriela continued, "I can't believe it, but I want you too. Holy shit. Did I just say that? I have to warn you: this is all a first for me, and I have a possessive side, with Barcelona fire in my eyes when I get jealous. But since he may not be around to be possessed... Well, we can, I mean, we can take one day at a time. You and me, hmm..."

"It's going to be great. If he goes away, we will have each other. And if you really want him to rush back..." She smiled wickedly. "The more you are into me, the more we can get him going, really going. I have an idea. We could do something that will make him crazy."

"Yeah, and what's that?"

"Well, the two of us..." She grinned.

"But we were together all night,"

"That's not exactly what I'm talking about."

Gabriela looked into Helena's eyes questioningly.

"Listen, once not so long ago, I was dating this Brazilian guy, and, well, anyway, we went out to this Latin club and we met this hot girl. We both liked her, and after a bottle of Bacardi and a lot of blow, we all ended up in bed together. Fabiana was her name, I think. Anyway, adding a third...well, it's different." She smiled. "I'll do it again with you if you want me to."

"What do you mean you'll do it again? It is me I want him to never forget. Not you."

"Okay, okay I get that. We are playing your rules as long as I'm having fun too. So listen, my boyfriend at the time told us later that watching us turned him on so much he completely lost it. That's what you want, right? So, what do you say? Let's give him a real show. You know I'm such an exhibitionist, and when he sees my ass, I mean your ass, dancing in the air while we're doing it... Well..."

"I get it, but..." Gabriela hesitated. "It all sounds a little embarrassing." Gabriela looked at the ceiling, rolled her eyes, and then gave a coy smile. "You'll have to show me what to do? Right?"

Helena responded, "Don't worry. Once you get going, it will all feel natural. Just wait here a second." Helena went into the other room and returned with her handbag. She placed some cocaine on the edge of the sink and handed her a rolled-up dollar bill. "This will take care of those concerns. Anyway, like I said, I am ready to 'pinch hit' for you. Try some of this, and you will be fine." Helena smiled.

As she snorted the coke, Gabriela said with a smirk, "Pinch hit,' huh? I bet you are."

Helena continued, "Is all of this starting to turn you on? I see a little sparkle in those eyes. Here, snort some more."

"Hmm. Do you think I am going to need all this?"

"Yeah, I do. In a few minutes, all you are going to think about is... Well, just take it."

"You're right about one thing; the thought of this all is turning me on but... Wow." Gabriela's head jerked back as she sniffed in the coke. "Wow. Are you kidding? Are you sure this is just cocaine?"

Gabriela could not feel her lips. Her tongue felt numb. She looked again at Helena. "I think this is enough of this stuff for now."

Helena snorted some more. "Great, isn't it?"

"You know, Helena, I've had fantasies about being with a woman lots of times, but I was never brave enough to go for it. But with what has been going on in my life these days, what the hell. If I don't go for it now, I may never. God, I can't believe what is coming out of my mouth."

Mark entered the bathroom, laughing.

Gabriela blurted, "You heard all this? Damn, now I'm really embarrassed."

Mark smiled. "You don't have to do this for me, and you

don't have to take all these drugs. I can make sure you are comfortable in whatever we do together."

"I know we don't," Gabriela said, announcing it to herself as much as to anyone else. "But we want to do it this the New York way. Besides, this is all just between us girls." They laughed.

Helena turned to Mark, and with a devilish grin said, "Yeah, we want to."

CHAPTER 45

A MOTHER AWAITS

Mananken and Allaceia exited the negotiations with the High Council together. The price for saving her children was severe, but reasonable, considering the situation. In return for their aid, Tripton would no longer have to pay for access to Mark and Jason's activity on Earth. All recorded activities — past, present, and future – were in the contract. They would be given the exclusive rights to broadcast and share these recorded activities on their home planet, but they would not be permitted to sell the recordings to other worlds. In addition, they would be granted one millennium of Earth dreams without fee; again, all was contingent upon the survival of both of her children and the "demise" of Elgert. In the contract, the term "demise" was defined as "removed from any form of power or influence on Eldern." Some of the Triptonians were insisting on the word "death," but Allaceia would not agree to such a term.

The negotiations had been difficult. Some council members thought it reckless to be involved, but Allaceia was a shrewd diplomat, and she skillfully laid forth her argument. Additionally, hiding all hint of nepotism, Mananken quietly slid the negotiations in her favor, fervently impressing upon the Council that if Eldern were to go in the direction Elgert envisioned, there would be dire days ahead for New Tripton, as well. The plan was ambitious; only the Triptonians' advanced technologies could approach such a venture.

Allaceia's mind was swimming with doubt and trepidations. Can they do it? It will all depend upon Mananken's abilities and Mark's courage. She knew the immediate problem would be communicating to Mark and Jason that help was forthcoming without revealing her plans to Elgert's spies. The brothers needed to be ready to accept her aid.

But what plagued her conscience was the fact that she would not be able to reveal the whole story... the truth, for if they knew of the deceptions and she lost their trust, they might rebel. She felt an uneasiness churning in her center; it was anguishing keeping her plans from them. For a moment, she was about to change her mind, but then... No, I must lie to them for the sake of both my world and the earth. They must do this. I cannot chance it otherwise. With these torments within her she hid a message in the amulet, a message that help was coming. She was not certain that they would know how to open it, or even whether they would trust the message if they did. I cannot leave this to chance. I must talk to them now. Somehow, I must reassure them.

The impenetrable oceanic atmosphere of New Tripton had been a double-edged sword. It made spying on them almost impossible, but it also prevented her from sending word to her children. In order to talk to the twins without alerting Elgert and Dronin, she needed a stealthy plan, a trick. She hurried to leave the planet.

Allaceia departed, making a route for Eldern with hope as her only companion. New Tripton vanished from view. If our timing is right, the earth's moon will rest between the earth and Eldern while they are still in the vicinity of the portal. I will have a few minutes to talk to them without the eyes of Dronin and Elgert upon us. She said to her captain, "Tell me when the earth's star shields the earth from Eldern. Open communication to my children the moment it occurs."

Time slowed as if it were being dragged through sand. They approached their position, and she ordered the ship to a halt when it located the correct coordinates.

"We're near the sector," called the captain. "We are activating the portal now, Grand Mistress. You can communicate momentarily."

"Good, Captain. Please initiate security encryption. We want no prying eyes."

"Yes, Grand Mistress, of course," he replied.

*****

Gabriela forced herself not to cry, holding back the pain that ached within her. Instead she smiled and said, "I love you Mark, and I will love you forever."

Helena pulled the shades down. The only light in the room was the soft pink glow of a lava lamp left running from the night before. She turned to Gabriela, roughly pulling her close, manhandling her downward. Gabriela fell backwards, her skin filling with goosebumps. She felt the swirl of Helena's tongue. A soft "yes, yes," came forth, and she reciprocated. They both turned and twisted rhythmically as Mark's hand touched Gabriela's back. She felt warmth deep within her spine, strangely bringing with it a sense of safety.

He understood that this was to be a gift, a gift of complete surrender and capitulation with his pleasure as its only object. He understood, but he didn't. It must have been because they were human. Mark wanted to reciprocate in some way, give back somehow. His fingers and tongue sought responses. Helena and Gabriela's arms and legs were swirling. Amidst their cries, Mark entered the fray, moving to please them both. When he sensed the moment was right, he started rubbing the tip of his penis around Gabriela's anticipation.

Gabriela could hardly breathe as he entered her, whispering, "Go slow." With care, he delved, and his penis started to vibrate. Gabriela screamed. "Oh my God." Helena cried, feeling something. "What is that? That can't be your..." Mark's tongue went electric, exploring every crevice. The three of them raged for what seemed like hours, although it was but minutes. Mercilessly, they devoured each other, like sharks feeding. Helena cried out, "How is this possible? You're in more than one place at one time. I'm afraid to look. What are you doing to me?" Gabriela's moans continued as they fell ever deeper into Wonderland.

Gabriela smiled and said, "It's okay, it's all okay."

Leaving would be the most difficult thing Mark had ever done. "You both look tired," he said sweetly. "Why don't you rest awhile? I'll see you soon." Before they could react, Mark broke his rule. Using his ability to control minds, he placed them into a euphoric dream. Mark vanished, transporting himself to the home that housed his fears.

***

When he arrived at the apartment, Jason was already there.

"You didn't waste your time. I had an eye on you while you were frolicking. You know, you actually put me to shame with those two. Where did you come up with all of that?" He laughed.

"Well, you know I read a lot, and there was this one erotic Japanese print by Hokusai with an octopus that was inspiring. The physical aspects of the act were quantifiable, but other aspects were not... I think you could lighten up on the voyeurism thing. Aren't you having enough kicks without watching me?" Mark retorted, a little annoyed.

"Touchy today, aren't we?" responded Jason. "Well, I just couldn't resist a little peek, I mean really, you never partied like that before. That was your first real threesome, right? I wanted to see how you would do. Now I know you can handle yourself and won't need any pointers."

"It was more than a party to me. Please don't do that again."

"Okay, okay, I understand, but as they say in Rome, *complemento*. Next time I'll turn my mind away as soon as I know you're happy, I mean safe." He assured him through a large grin. "I have no right to tease you like this. I too have been very moved by a human, and I am worried about her. I have created a person that is going to make the beings on our home world quite uncomfortable."

"You mean Saya?"

"Yes, Saya. I have overstepped my bounds in affecting her in the manner that I have. It was unintentional, but I don't think they will care about that. I have created something new. I should have taken responsibility and ended her life myself." Jason looked down and then up again at Mark. He brushed the hair away from his eyes. "But I just can't, strangely I have grown attached. I think I understand a lot less about myself than I thought I did. But I fear that rather than wonder, I may have created a target."

"What are you going to do?"

"I don't know. I really don't know."

Just then, the portal started to churn, pulling Mark and Jason in. However, this time, they both knew what to expect and were not alarmed. A being appeared before them, slowly at first, and then, through a mist, she was there.

Allaceia was not in the Grand Hall, but in a simple room, standing alone. The walls showed a damp grayness, atmospheric rather than formed. There were no trappings of opulence or grandeur as with the others, but rather her presence whispered of a stateliness, a majesty. Her beauty transfixed them.

As they listened to the message, Mark and Jason were so distracted by her regality that they almost did not hear her words. The message told of their heritage and the uniqueness of their lineage. They learned about the valor and sacrifice of their family's history, not only on Eldern, but also the many worlds that preceded it. The message was thoughtful, factual, and sincere. They understood that this is why Allaceia was chosen to send forth her offspring to save the earth. They noticed that a pendant was suddenly hanging around each of their necks, on its surface the crest of the Purple Flower. They felt the power within it.

"That was our mother," exclaimed Jason. "Our real mother."

"Yes, I know."

"She said nothing about these amulets, but I feel there is a message in them. I have to figure out how to unlock it…"

"I think I see how to do it. Just give me a minute." Taking the amulet in his hand, he turned to Mark. "Yes, here. Do you see it?"

Just then, the portal started to stir, and Allaceia emerged from the fury.

"Hello. Hello, my children, can you hear me? We have little time. Can you hear me?"

"Yes, yes," responded Jason. "And we see you, as well."

"You are Jason then, are you not? And you. You are Mark?"

"Yes," they both responded, realizing they were no longer listening to a recorded message.

"My children, you must listen, for we have little time to communicate. Elgert and Dronin have not been honest with you, and the plan they have outlined is not only flawed, but it is also a lie. I am sorry to say that Eldern is full of treachery, and your lives are insignificant when weighed against agendas too complicated to explain now. You both are in danger."

"I have enlisted aid from outside my planet to guard your safety. Jason, you will be in the most peril. I cannot explain fully now, but Mark, you will rescue your brother with the help of my friend." She turned to talk to Mark directly. "Mark, the fate of your brother is in your hands. My friend will explain when you meet him. Heed the words of anyone who shows you our flower, the Purple Flower of your heritage. This you will find upon the crest of the amulets I sent."

"I must say farewell for now, for many spying eyes may be lurking. In a few minutes, your earth moon will no longer hide you from Elgert and his spies. Trust in yourselves. You have more strength than you know. Farewell, my children. I will not wish you good luck, but rather, I say believe in your strength and you will succeed. Dronin and Elgert will be contacting you again soon. Do not mention this conversation. Again, have faith in your power. I am sending help."

Her image started to flicker and then abruptly reappeared.

"There is one additional thing, Jason. The earthling woman you have affected, the one who calls herself Saya... What you have done has not sat well here. You know you were not supposed to accelerate human evolution. But since you have, she is your responsibility. Inform her that she must not disrupt the nature of things on Earth and warn her to be guarded. I can do little to protect her from here."

"But it is not my fault she evolved; I have been trying to explain to her what has happened and how she must behave, but –"

"She is your responsibility," repeated Allaceia.

Mark and Jason watched the likeness of their mother fade like an evening mist overcome by the dark. Quietly she vanished. "Do you think we will see her again?" Jason asked.

"Yes. Yes, of course, we will. She said we would. I believe her. She is sending us help." Mark continued sternly, "You will survive. We can do this."

The portal stirred, but this time no images appeared, no violence or tumult, only the eerie sound of Elgert's voice: "Your task begins soon. Review the information and calculations we have shared with you. You will start in ten earth minutes."

"So, Mark, it begins..."

"Don't be frightened, Jason. Our mother said I am to save you. Trust me, I won't let you down."

"I know you will do all you can. I just hope it is enough."

CHAPTER 46

THE ASTEROID

Mark looked into Jason's eyes and then into his mind. *He thinks he is going to die. The thought of his end has become an obsession. He must focus. I must remind him who he is.*

"Jason. Think of nothing except what is before us and we will succeed. I am with you."

"Of course. What else would I be thinking about?" Jason responded with false confidence.

"Okay, then," answered Mark. "I'll go find the asteroid and let you know when I am in position. Wait for my signal before you go down. We will make short work of all of this. The earth's core is nothing compared to a rough night at The Dom."

Jason looked at Mark, smiling sadly. "Go then. Go now. I can't take the waiting any longer." Mark felt Jason's uncertainty.

Jason thought about the life he had been living on the earth, the sweetness of it all. Now it could all be lost, taken by beings he had only seen in an apparition. He thought about his music, the smoke, the sweat of the crowd, the lights, the noise, the madness. He thought of his friends and even of a few enemies, and he thought about Saya.

I wonder what the band is up to, and what Angela could be doing. Oh, Saya, I hope you are not in danger. He looked at the amulet hung about his neck. *I'd better start reviewing* these implanted calculations if I am going to have a chance. He began to look them over. Wow. This is very complicated, full of eventualities and recalculations for unforeseen events. It is obvious they were not sure what I would be meeting down there. They were right about one thing, though. My mind is faster than ever. I see it all in an instant.

"Mark, I am ready. Go now. Be careful, and I will wait for your word."

"You too, Jason. Safe trip. I'll be seeing you soon," responded Mark, mustering as much a positive tone as he could manage.

Mark started to travel to the point in space just beyond Jupiter, the place the Elders had designated. He had never traveled beyond the earth's atmosphere before. It was exciting. He had no need for oxygen to survive, nor the aid of gravity to maneuver within the emptiness, and without any earthly points of reference, he was able to find his position with ease.

Mark left the earth and looked back to glimpse the planet; saying to himself, why have I never traveled here before? It is so beautiful. Of course. We were programmed to remain on earth. They could not have us flying around the universe and getting into mischief, getting our priorities confused. They wanted us to stay put.

The most startling sensation in outer space was the absolute quiet. There was not a sound, not a hint of life. No chirping birds in the sky, or barking dogs, no honking cars or crying babies. Just silence, a great quiet. And within this overwhelming grandeur, he looked down upon a beautiful blue planet. His planet.

The coordinates had placed him some distance from the asteroid. Mark surmised that this was to have him acclimate himself to the surroundings. I wish Jason could be here with me. The limitlessness was overwhelming. This is not possible to fully convey telepathically; you have to be here. He focused his mind towards Earth. Jason, do you see this? Do you feel this?

Mark heard Jason's words in his mind. "Yes, I see it. Mark, I wish I were with you."

"When this is all over, we have to do this together, just come out here and drift around...just hang out."

"That sounds great, but do you see the asteroid? Is it coming?"

"It's some distance away."

"Are you okay?"

"Yes... I am just taking this all in. It is so wondrous here, and I want to get acclimated before I am forced to deal with that monster. The sensations within me are very different. I am just getting used to it, but it is so beautiful. I'll start to move towards the asteroid in a minute. I can see a glimmer of it in the distance."

"I'll be with you, and I'll wait for your signal before I head towards the core."

As Mark started to move towards the asteroid, Gabriela's eyes came to mind. She would love this. I can hear her quoting Whitman for hours... I miss her, especially in all this vast beautiful nothingness. It would be so cool to have her here with me. I would have to make some special arrangements, of course, some protective shield...

Just then he heard Jason's voice in his mind. "And you should bring Helena along, as well," he said in his characteristic teasing tone.

Mark was pleased to hear his brother being able to joke, even when such perils were at their doorstep. He will never understand how I feel about Gabriela. Not wanting to dampen his mood, Mark responded, "Yes, that would be interesting... I'm almost upon it now, Jason. Are you ready to start moving down to the core yet?"

"I'll never be ready, but I'll start to go down now. I will let you know when I am there. Before I go to this hell, I need to do something. I need to see Saya one last time. I hear her calling. I have to say goodbye; it will only take a few minutes." Without waiting for an answer, he transported himself to Saya's apartment.

*　*　*

When Jason materialized, he found Saya sitting in a chair facing her bed. She seemed as if she had not moved for hours. Before her on the bed were some jewels, stones, and some colored glass within what looked like twisted metal; a pile of ashes, the remnants of Angela.

Saya sat there muttering, "I don't understand... I walked into the other room for a minute... and there was a rumble, a flash. I jumped, and when I came back... She was gone... I don't..."

Jason immediately understood. His fear had come to pass. She had been attacked.

"I was afraid this might happen. Here, take this." He removed the amulet from around his neck and placed it over her head. "Never take this off. It is more than an ornament. It was a gift from my mother. Learn its secrets. I do not fully understand why, but it has the power to shield. It will protect you from those who are able to move even faster than you. I believe it can even hide you. You can trust this symbol and anyone who bears it."

Jason started to leave, knowing Mark was nearing the asteroid. He turned to Saya. "Wait for me."

***

With that, Jason began his descent. Mark moved cautiously toward what he finally could see. What was at first a distant light now fully unveiled its magnificence. As he came closer, he saw a beast with its glistening tail shedding its skin of ice and gas as it tore through the nothing.

Suddenly he thought he could hear a sound. While he knew he could not, his mind imagined a roar even in the vacuum of space. Its overwhelming presence and speed made his mind throb and his fear rise. It was at least two miles across, boasting majesty as it streaked through the darkness. Mark could almost hear a voice say: "Try me if you dare."

He summoned all his courage and stood in its path, trying

with all his strength to alter its course. But like a bothersome insect, he was swept aside as it continued along its fateful trajectory. Despite his fear, Mark was in awe of the beauty of his adversary, this juggernaut, this lonely dancer of the cosmos.

"What shall I call you? You deserve more than a number. How about Tempestes, the Roman storm goddess? Do you like that name, my dear? You don't answer. Come now. Well then, how about a little push?"

Mark again sent forth all his energy toward the asteroid, and again, nothing. He could not sway her course.

In frustration, he called, "Jason. Jason, are you there yet? I need help up here; it's too big and too strong. I cannot move it myself. Where are you?"

Jason focused his mind on the earth's core and rested his hand upon the suicide belt the elders had given him. He thought of the gift he had given away. "I'm traveling now, Mark."

He passed through the crust and into the liquid heat of the earth's mantle, which seemed to be an indissoluble molten ocean. He continued down. The further he traveled, the faster he descended. The pull of the core had taken its hold. As Jason approached the core, he considered the calculations and systems he had learned. Instead of using his usual method of manipulating subatomic particles to pass through obstacles, he jumped into an alternate dimension, continuing his descent. He traveled until he reached the very center of the earth, the inner core; a solid state of almost pure iron. It was as hot as the surface of the sun, but within it was a cold indifference.

Jason knew that as long as he could move between dimensions, he could avoid the forces about him. However, he could not affect matter in this state. He would not be able to direct the energy of the magnetic field up to Mark. As he moved between dimensions, being here and there at the same time, he wondered if this plan could succeed.

His major concern was not to affect the earth's rotation or reverse its polarities with any aggressive or sudden manipulation. An error could be monumental. He said to himself... I can do this.

"Okay, Mark. It comes now."

Jason started to direct the power from the magnetic field up to Mark. First, slowly, just a pulse, and then gradually, as the beat of the energy increased and the bursts between moments grew closer, the power went forth. More and more rapidly, the momentum increased, and as the energy streamed forward, it seemed to take on its own life. Jason was spinning in a turmoil, oscillating frantically in and out of the different states, from one dimension to the next. He danced within the core's forces, cheating its power with his dexterity, outwitting its purpose. Every millisecond he spent outside a hidden state, the forces would tear at him, pressure crushing him, the heat burning into his being. But only within those moments did he realize his charge.

"Are you getting it? I am sending it now."

Mark felt the energy of the core upon him. He automatically channeled it towards the asteroid. The asteroid did not veer at first, but then, slowly, it moved a bit. Ever so slowly, it veered.

"It's working, Jason. It's working. But it's slow. Very slow... I don't think there's enough metal within the asteroid."

Jason heard Mark's words. "It's slow? Do your best; it's vicious down here."

Mark communicated to Jason again, "How are you holding up?"

Jason replied, "It's a horror. I know it is not alive, but you would think it hated me."

"How long can you take it, Jason?"

"I don't know, Mark. I really don't know."

"Can you increase the power? If you increase the power, maybe..." Mark then saw nearby space debris. He grabbed some with the help of the core's power and used it to create another gravitational force to affect the asteroid's direction.

"I am doing all I can down here, Mark, but the core is crushing me."

Mark knew that Jason was suffering; he would not last long. He will die. He might save the earth, but he will die. "Do what you can, my brother. I will try harder up here."

Mark used all his energy in conjunction with the forces he was amassing. Slowly, the asteroid turned a little more. Mark, gaining confidence and pushing even harder, exclaimed, "It's moving. It's moving more."

Still, they thought, "Where's the help mother promised. Where is it?"

Then Mark heard a strange sound from behind him. He never heard such a sound before. He was baffled since he knew there was no sound in space. He could not understand how he was hearing anything at all. When he heard the sound again, he realized it was in his mind, something calling his name. Someone was communicating with him, and it wasn't Jason.

"Cherba, cherba, cherba."

Mark turned and saw a little furry being encased in a clear bubble. He was bouncing up and down in an animated manner, and he was wearing beautifully layered clothing of purple and orange. His fur was changing color as he waved his arms in greeting, and around his neck he wore the Purple Flower.

"Hello, Mark. You've been expecting me."

CHAPTER 47
THE INTERCOM WAKES THEM

T he morning had passed, and the day slipped quietly towards dusk. Gabriela and Helena had spent the day asleep. Gabriela's eyes opened first, her arms still around Helena. She only realized the body she was holding was not Mark's when she was jarred by the earsplitting sound of the intercom buzzer.

"What is that noise? It's driving a nail through my brain."

Helena, blurry-eyed, barely conscious, replied, "It's the intercom. It squeals like a dying pig."

"Oh... it's horrible," responded Gabriela.

The buzzer gave another long screech.

Helena grimaced. "And that fucking doorman hates me. He uses any excuse to make me miserable.... Oh. What the fuck does he want now?" she muttered, looking at Gabriela. "Man... He has been such an asshole since I complained to the manager that he had been coming onto me."

Helena pulled herself to her feet, stumbling off the mattress. She opened her closet and blindly grabbed a silk robe off the hook on the door. It was the thinnest of silk, ornately patterned with oriental designs and hand-stitched tassels. It looked very French and very expensive. Tripping over some books and clothing on the floor, she made her way into the living room, pressed the button on the intercom, and said, "Yes, what is it?"

The doorman responded, "There is a special delivery letter here from Denmark. The postman needs your signature."

"Okay. Send him up, please."

The doorman answered, "He says he's not allowed to do that. You'll have to come down to the lobby and sign for it."

Helena knew the doorman was lying, and he was just trying to make her life miserable, but she saw no escape from the situation. Any special delivery letter from Denmark was more than likely from her mother, and that was too important to play around with. "Fuck," she murmured under her breath, and into the intercom. "Okay, I'm coming down."

The red high-heeled pumps she wore last night were on the floor near the sofa. She slipped them on and shouted to Gabriela in the other room, "I have to go down to the lobby for a minute. I'm leaving the door unlocked." She heard no response. "I'm leaving the door unlocked," she yelled louder. "Okay…?"

Helena heard a faint "okay" from Gabriela in the bedroom.

Gathering her strongest self, Helena walked into the hall to the end of the corridor. The fifty feet to the elevator felt like a mile. When she reached it, she pressed the call button. The elevator took forever to arrive. Again, her world slowed to a crawl until the doors opened. She was startled into consciousness by the sight of a passenger. As she got on, she looked upon an attractive young man in a gray pinstriped business suit. He carried a briefcase. "Are you going down?" she asked cryptically.

"No, up. But just two floors up, and then you can have it. It's been acting funny. I had to wait for it a long time. I advise you to grab it while you can."

Helena got on the elevator. "Thanks."

She gave him a tiny smile, just a slight rise of her lip, and then turned to face the elevator door. She pressed the button for the lobby. He returned a polite smile.

He's quite nice-looking in a conservative way, she thought. Maybe he's an advertising man or something. He was certainly not her type, but attractive, nonetheless.

He looked at her stealthily out of the corner of his eye, and with a smile said, "Are you going out for dinner?" His tone carried a hint of humor.

I guess I'm wrong: just another jerk. Helena said to herself without acknowledging him.

It came to her then that she was wearing nothing under that thin and revealing silk robe that she had purchased with the sole intent to excite. She pulled the sash of the robe tighter, realizing that her breasts could be seen, but pressing the thin cloth against her body only did more to reveal the rest of her nakedness.

She felt his eyes on her. Her awareness sent a bit of a tingle through her. His eyes surreptitiously explored her. He was trying not to be obvious, but it was clear he was turned on.

As she fidgeted, the silk of the robe slid gently against her nipples, which started to harden, showing slightly through the thin fabric. I am such an exhibitionist... she thought. A rush filled her. Looking back out of the corner of her eye, Helena wondered what he was thinking. She felt his desire and his struggle for control. She loved it.

The elevator door opened on the 24th floor, and the man started to exit. As he left the elevator, his mind obviously flush with fantasy, Helena answered his inquiry with a cocky tone.

"No..." She smiled replying as the doors closed. "Just waiting for a boy or two to drop by."

The elevator started down. God, I hope there are no more stops.

The doors opened onto the marble-walled lobby. The doorman sat behind a large mahogany desk, a conclave of letterboxes lining the wall behind him, envelops haphazardly poking out like an awkward array of birds. The postman stood in front of the desk appearing bored. Then his eyes rested upon Helena as she sashayed down the hall.

"Is this my letter?" Helena asked abruptly.

The postman, lost for words, just gave an affirming nod.

Helena snatched it from his hand. "So… where do I sign?"

The postman, in an almost spastic gesture, held out a board with the return receipt clipped upon it. "Just here." He spoke with a quiver in his voice.

Helena took a pen from the desk and scribbled an illegible signature. "Thanks," she said. She swirled away, turning like a peacock, and walked back to the elevator, fully conscious of the sway in her hips and the arrogance in her strut.

Helena made it back up to her apartment without further encounters. When she got to her door, she opened it with a sigh of relief. Ah. It is still unlocked… she thought. What would I have done if she had locked it? I don't even want to think about it.

She walked through the living room and found Gabriela staring into her closet. "Look at all these designer things," she said by way of greeting. "You're even worse than me when it comes to clothing. Say, do you have a robe I can slip on or something?"

"Sure," she answered. "Just to the left, next to the Dior, there is one almost like the one I'm wearing in blue."

"Oh… this really nice. Is it silk?"

"Yes," Helena replied. "It's Chanel, so be nice to it."

"You have such lovely things. Everything is beautiful."

"Yeah, clothing and cocaine are my major weaknesses. I guess now I should add an alien to the list."

"Do you ever watch 'Star Trek'?" asked Gabriela. "I've only seen it a few times myself; my husband loves it. Oh, I hope we can become good friends. Who else is ever going to believe me? And who could I even tell?"

"So he's gone. Really gone. I hope he is okay. I would die if I never got to see him again. My God, Gabriela, what a night: I've never. I mean never."

"Welcome to the club of the awed and infatuated, darling. I've been nuts for Mark for almost forever now – and I'm married – and, for God's sake, he's my husband's student. Beat that if you can."

"How about a drink?" Helena responded. "My buddy Jack Daniels is always understanding. We can go out and get something to eat, if you want. I'm not into cooking, I'm afraid, but I know a great place. Later, you could come down to the club. I'm sure Jason will have a new song for me tonight. We can hang out all night again, if you like."

Gabriela looked at Helena puzzled. "I think Jason went too."

"What!" she cried. "Jason never said anything about leaving. Hey. This is really crazy. What about our band, our record deals, the West Coast and all that? No, no, no. That's not happening."

"Well... I never spoke to Jason about it directly, but Mark just said he is leaving with him."

"What? What are you saying? We are going to the club, and I am going to sing... Let's get ready to go out..." Helena began to remember the activities and blurred conversations from earlier that day. She started to walk around the room without direction. "We always have a new song at The Dom, and I need to get there..." She was starting to wave her arms and grow frantic, mumbling unintelligible words. "What... but... I... Well..."

"This is why we really need each other, Helena. They are both going." She started to cry.

"But... I didn't even know Jason was an alien. Are you even sure he is? How can...?"

"They are both aliens. They are brothers, I already told you, Helena. They are twins."

"No, no. I'm going to call Gary. No, BoBo. He will know where he is. You'll see. He's not gone... BoBo will know."

Helena walked across the room and picked up the phone. She called BoBo. "Hi, BoBo, it's Helena... Say, have you seen Jason? I want to know if we are having any new music tonight, any new words for me..." Dismay began to show on Helena's face as she heard the response. "What do you mean no one can find him? No one knows where he is? Okay then... Call me later, will you? I mean, if you hear anything." She hung up the phone, clearly frustrated.

Helena sat on the bed and looked at Gabriela in tears. "No one from the band has seen him since yesterday. He just vanished. He never does that, I mean disappear… He is always checking in on us, taking care of us. Where will Gary get his drugs, for God's sake?"

"I told you," Gabriela replied, barely able to speak, "Mark said that whatever it is they are doing, they are doing it together, and he does not know when or even if they will be back."

"I know – I'll call that chick Angela. You know, the waitress he hangs with. He must be with her. Yeah, that's it. He's with her… That bitch… I have her number in my book. Damn. Where is it? Oh, there on my coffee table."

Helena picked up the book and found the number, but no one picked up on the other end.

"Shit. Oh, I am so bummed out. How could he just go? I mean how could he just…?"

"Mark said it had something to do with saving the earth, that if they didn't do something, the world would end."

"What?" exclaimed Helena. "The end of the world? Are you fucking kidding?"

"No," responded Gabriela. "And Mark was dead serious about it."

Helena lay down on the bed, prostrate and depressed. "Oh… everything was so beautiful, and now it's all mud."

Gabriela lay down next to her. "I know, just mud…"

"Hold me, please, just hold me." They embraced each other in tears, finding solace in each other's arms.

CHAPTER 48

MANANKEN'S AID

Mark could not believe what he was seeing. In a tone halfway between surprise and shock, he asked, "What... I mean... who are you?"

"My name is Mananken. I am the Grand Ambassador of New Tripton and a friend of your mother. I've come to help you."

Looking upon Mananken, Mark thought to himself, he looks like a freaking teddy bear. This is the help my mother is sending? "That's very nice of you, and I appreciate the thought, but do you see the size of this thing?"

Sensing Mark's skepticism, Mananken developed a disapproving frown. "Werba, Werba, Werba," said Mananken, bouncing up and down within his bubble. "Not to worry, I am more powerful than you can perceive. And besides, my young friend, the asteroid is not the problem."

"Huh?" said Mark. "But we were told to stop it, and my brother is down in the earth's core directing the whole planet's magnetic energy up at that thing."

"Yes, I know, but trust me: that thing is not the problem," Mananken replied.

"Well," said Mark, "if you are going to help, great. But I don't have time for chatter. My brother is suffering down there."

Mananken grumbled and, as his anger grew, he scowled. "Zerba, Zerba, Zerba. Listen, I know you are Allaceia's child, but I am a Triptonian of the highest rank, and I am four thousand earth years old. I do not speak idly: the asteroid is not your problem. Did your mother not tell you to heed my words?" His fur turned bright red and vibrated with agitation. "Now, child, your doubts are starting to annoy me." He began to shine brightly. "There, my friend..." He gestured. "Out there is your problem."

Mark looked out into space towards the moon. He saw a group of what looked like small objects in the distance. As they came closer, he could make out missiles attached to dark drone-like machines. There was a fleet of maybe thirty of them bearing down directly upon them, and another ten or so flanking them on both sides.

"That is the problem. War drones are coming to destroy you, and without my help, they will. For even with your power, their numbers are too great for you to overcome them alone."

As they grew closer, Mark could see that they were immense in size. One dove down from the left. With a gesture of his hand, Mark unleashed a beam and set it to flames. But then, another and another descended towards him. This time, Mananken attacked, sending out a ray and shattering it into pieces. As it burst, it sent out a missile directly into Mark, knocking him backwards. For the first time in his life, Mark felt pain. "What are these things?" he cried out loud.

"They are from your home world," answered Mananken. "And that, my friend... that was a nodular nuclear missile."

"From my home world? But why?"

"No time to explain now, but don't worry, I have brought help." Mananken gestured to his left, and out of the darkness of space, Mark saw something undulating. At first it looked like a wavering stream of energy, but then slowly the energy took shape. A haze filled their vision. A huge cloud began to accumulate. He could no longer see the earth or the stars in the distance. Then, something began to glow and vibrate. It glistened; it was a vessel, long and narrow, tapering at the ends; a ship, slick and enormous. Mark never imagined there could be a vessel of such size. It appeared to be made of pure metal, yet its surface looked wet. Mark sensed a vibration from within it, an energy announcing power.

"What's that?" asked Mark.

"Cherba, cherba, cherba. That is my ship, Mark. Now, you had better come inside my bubble before one of those things gets another shot at you. I will relax the membrane. Please stop playing with that magnetic energy from Earth. It is irritating my fur."

"But…"

"Please stop worrying about your little asteroid. I told you, that it is not the problem."

Without hesitation, Mark stopped directing energy from Earth and entered the bubble.

It must be at least two hundred miles in length and twenty miles in diameter. How could one make such a thing? There were no windows or portals, no indentations or antenna, just shimmering elegance.

"There. Nice and cozy in here, isn't it? How is the temperature? I can adjust it, you know."

"It's fine."

Mark was captivated as he watched liquid-like metallic forms emerging from the ship. Despite their large size, they appeared tiny next to the larger vessel. Bubbling out like water from a dripping faucet, they seemed to be made of glowing plasma wobbling forward, amoeboid soldiers marching in an orderly line.

Mananken watched Mark's fascination as the droplets moved with determination towards the Destructo-bots. The robots fired their weapons, but their efforts were absorbed within the softness of the large glowing blobs. One by one, they were engulfed and digested by the organic forms, liquefied within their softness.

"Don't worry," said Mananken. "Quickly, though, I must talk to you about your brother's situation."

"Yes, my brother. What are we to do?"

"You must move quickly and follow my exact instructions if we are to save your brother, for this is dangerous work... When you descend into the earth towards the core, you must tell Jason to stop sending forth the magnetic energy and to wait within the sixth dimension until you arrive. You must enter the sixth dimension as you approach the core. You will have to leave now. The power of my ship is too strong, and it will pull you into its gravity and hurl you towards Jupiter. But do not fear. You will see the asteroid fly away as you travel down. It was never going to strike the earth."

"But if I'm in such a state, I can't –"

"Your normal mechanisms of passing through matter will not do down there, and it is only within this state that will you be protected from the core. When you reach Jason, grab hold of him and use all your strength to attach yourself to him. Use the calculations that I have just placed in your mind to turn the magnetic forces to your advantage; you will have the amulet to protect you. Jason has been there for a while now, and he's growing weaker. If he cannot break free, your last resort will be to pull him into you. If this fails, there will be no choice but to leave him to his suicide belt. Now go, my young friend. Every second puts Jason more at risk. Go. Go now!"

"But if you are so powerful, why don't you just save Jason?"

"No, my friend. I cannot, I am not supposed to be here at all. This is for you."

Mananken took the Purple Flower amulet from around his neck and placed it around Mark's. The two amulets became one. "What I have given you was from your mother's hand. She could not send it by teleportation. It will have the power to protect you."

Mark put his hands over the amulet. "Thank you, Mananken."

"Now go, my young friend. I have faith in you. Cherba, Cherba, Cherba, I know you will succeed."

As Mark started to travel back to Earth, he felt a gigantic vibration behind him. It sent him spinning aimlessly through space, and it took him the better part of a minute to regain his composure and start again towards the earth. He was just passing Mars when he turned to look back. He watched in wonder as the asteroid changed its direction, veering towards the gravitational field of Jupiter. He was telling me the truth. The ship was glowing blue and green. Mark felt the kinetic power as he sped towards Earth; he was flushed with excitement as he watched the asteroid change course. It's true. The earth is safe; Gabriela is safe.

"Jason. Our mother sent help, and it's done. Just hang on, Jason: I'm coming for you. Just hang on."

Mark flew as fast as he could towards the earth and again called to Jason. "Do you hear me, Jason...? I'm coming. I'm coming." Mark heard no response.

He did all he could to increase his speed. The gravity of the earth was beginning to help. He did not take time to calculate an angle of entry; he dove with complete abandon as he neared the surface. He was not even sure if he would first meet water or land. All he could see, all he could think of was Jason, his brother.

Just as he passed into the earth, Mark heard Jason's plea within his mind. "Mark, are you coming? Hurry, the core is crushing me. Please, be careful if you're coming."

"I am coming, Jason. I am coming."

Mark could only imagine the suffering and immolation Jason was experiencing. For a moment, he felt a sense of bitterness: all this for the sake of the earthlings?

Mark entered another dimension so he could pass through the earth with ease. He flew past the molten crust, into the mantle's bubbling heat without a flinch. As he approached the outer core, and the pressure grew, nothing affected him, but Mark knew this would all soon change. For if he were to save Jason, he would have to expose himself to the violence of the core.

He saw Jason, stagnant, frozen, and motionless, as if he had stared into the eyes of Medusa.

"Jason! Jason!" Mark called to him. "It's Mark – I'm here, I'm here…"

Jason opened his eyes. "Mark, what are you doing here?" Jason seemed not fully aware of his thoughts.

"Jason, I am here to get you out. I told you I was coming. Come. It's time to go now."

Jason responded, "Mark, you must go. It's too violent, too strong to survive here. Go… You must go."

Mark replied, "We are both going to go, both of us. Come. Come with me."

Mark grabbed hold of Jason. "We must leave the sixth dimension. Part of you is embedded, but part of you is not… You must gather yourself and come with me."

They both began to leave the protection of their state, and Mark activated the power of his mother's amulet to shield them both. He sensed some form of anti-matter was being used to shield him, but he did not understand how this was possible.

"Now, Jason," Mark spoke. "We jump now." Mark pulled on Jason and attempted to leap out of the core. He felt the amulet surrounding them with cooling forms of superfluids for protection, but Jason remained paralyzed. "Jason. Jason, where is your amulet? I need you to move!"

The core had fused him to its nature. His essence had become locked in the magnetic grasp of its metal. "You must try harder, Jason, now, now, Jason. Try again. Use all your might. We must leap free."

Mark could see Jason could not move, and the only hope to free him would be to absorb him.

"Jason… You must enter my essence. Within me, I can protect you. I will break free from the core and save us both."

Jason whispered, "I will try."

He slowly started to meld into Mark's nature, but the transition left them both exposed. They were being torn apart by the competing forces within the core. Jason began to feel his being flow into Mark, but much of him was being destroyed in the process. Mark also was starting to feel Jason's pain. It was crushing agony. Jason watched as Mark began to suffer.

"Mark," said Jason solemnly. "This is no good. You must go before we both die."

"No. No, Jason. You're doing fine. Just keep coming, keep coming; I am gathering you. I will save you."

Jason sensed that a complete transition was hopeless. He sent forth a final burst of himself into Mark, activated the suicide belt, and expelled Mark out of the core.

CHAPTER 49

BACK IN THE APARTMENT

Mark found himself on the floor of his apartment, disoriented and listless. He was exhausted. Vague notions of what had just occurred echoed within him as he slowly regained consciousness.

The Spartan room had never been a welcoming place. It had never been a room that a human would describe as homey. Yet it was their place. He surveyed the walls and furniture. He knew that all was the same, but everything was different.

He stood up, thinking to himself, these walls. I know them. "Walls," he said aloud. His mind was rattling, and his thoughts were jumbled.

"Walls, walls, and walls, pressure and walls. I feel pressure and heat, and pressure. There is pressure. No, it's stopped. I am back. Am I back? Where am I? Where was I? There was never a limit or edge, or obstacle for me. But there was such heat, such pressure..." He rambled on, "Limits, limits, limits... Are there limits? What are limits? What does that mean? What do I mean? I have something to overcome, but what? What... could not be overcome? What, what...? I'm separated...?"

Mark continued mumbling, "We are separated. Jason, where are you? I cannot see. Is this really the apartment? Our place?"

He struggled to regain his clarity, to understand all that was happening. "Yes, but..."

He tried to walk forward, his vision unclear. He stumbled

to his knees. His hands slowly felt their way. Touching the ground, he moved. His fingers found the bed, the chair, the strewn books haphazardly scattered on the floor. He noticed his fingers were starting to glow. His hands, and then his body, began glowing bright colors of yellow and green. He looked up across the room. Jason's jacket and his guitar – all were still there. The same dingy gray walls. He heard the cries of the cats in the alley. He breathed in the smells from outside his door; all was the same. The emanation within slowed. The color and glow in his limbs faded.

He sat at the edge of the bed and rested his hands on his legs. He felt pain deep in his center. Examining his body, he said aloud, "But I am intact. Intact, but... different." He looked at his hands. They had stopped glowing. He turned them upwards. "My hands. They're still here." He rubbed them together and then rested them on his thighs. He touched each limb with his hands. "All is here. I am still whole. Jason? Jason, where are you? No, he's gone. I can feel it. He is gone..."

"I have failed... Failed." he cried out as guilt overtook reason; he no longer wanted to live. "If you're dead, I can't live. I'll join you, Jason. I'll go down into the core and join you. Jason... They promised me you would live. They promised. How can this be?" Mark sobbed.

Then, suddenly, he felt something – a strong energy slowly starting to churn. Something is moving within me, he thought. Then it started. Mark felt a pounding and a kicking, like a child demanding to leave the womb. The kick turned into a thump, as if someone's fists were beating a cry for freedom. "I'm within you. I'm in you, Mark. I am here."

Mark rose from the bed, and with a burst of elation, he understood: it worked. Jason is within me. Mark knew he must return to the portal and seek help. Confused but excited, he screamed out, "Where is the portal?" He called out, "I need help! Where are you, mother? Where are you?"

Color and energy swirled, and the portal appeared. As the room vibrated, he saw the face of his mother within its mist.

Mark called out, "Mother! Mother, I need your help. Jason is… Jason is –"

"Yes, I see," Allaceia, answered. "You have absorbed enough of Jason for us to save him, but you must enter the portal now and come to Eldern. We cannot save Jason while you both remain on Earth. You must come now, my son."

"Come to you? How?"

"You must enter the portal and come home."

"But… this is my home."

"No, my child. It is not." She continued, "Enter now. There is no time for sentiment; your brother will die. Every second, Jason loses life. You need to come home now. This is his only hope."

"How long will the journey take?"

"You mean, in Earth time? I'm not sure. Maybe a year, maybe more. It will depend on conditions, many of which are unpredictable… but you must enter the portal this instant. I cannot help Jason if you do not."

"But, Gabriela. I must at least say goodbye…" Mark looked over to his closet, where the corduroy jacket he had worn on their first date still hung. Memories of her raced across his mind, his recollections lingering. Mark knew his time on Earth was about to end. He heard a child crying in the hall. The rain was hitting the window with the force of stone pebbles, and he knew he would never see Gabriela again.

"I'm sorry, my son. You must come now. There is no choice."

"Gabriela, my poem…" He entered the swirl and was gone.

CHAPTER 50

GABRIELA'S BIRTHDAY

Gabriela was dressing to meet Helena for a drink at a new spot called Brandy's on East 84th Street. It was a piano bar, and everyone had been talking about it. She did not want to make a big fuss about her birthday; three years had passed since she had seen Mark. This was her 39th, and she was not taking out a notice for it in the New York Times. Helena was the only person she wanted to see today, the only person who understood, the only person who knew.

It was cool for early September. The TV was on in the living room, and all the news commentators were talking about the hostages being taken by terrorists at the Munich Olympics and the failed attempt to rescue them. How impotent the West must look to the world, she thought. Ted Koppel was on the air, unusual for the afternoon; he almost always was on at night. He is definitely the brightest of them. Gabriela looked away from the TV and pondered how different the news might be had it not been for Mark and Jason. She picked up the remote and hit the off button.

1972 had been a strange year. The music was changing on the airwaves; disco was all the rage. She looked at the radio on her dresser. She reached out, but her hand recoiled. I hate disco... The Beatles had been gone for almost ten years. How I miss them. She looked into the mirror and said aloud, "You sound so old." She turned the TV back on.

She had just been going through the motions of life as of late and was bored most of the time, except when she could find Helena for a night out. Helena was more than a friend. Often after a few drinks, they were in each other's arms, although they both agreed that their primary interest was men. What they shared was incomprehensible to both of them. Gabriela loved Helena's wildness. She was her release from a life-threatening to drown her in a well of academic claustrophobia. They shared mostly everything from gossip to heartfelt sincerities, and the relationship spanned the years.

The phone rang, and Gabriela picked up. "Hey, it's me," said Helena.

"Are you dressed yet? I can't wait to check this place out. I'm so excited."

"Yes, I'm almost ready. If you hang up and leave me alone, I can get dressed."

"Okay, okay," she responded. "See you there. Let's go man hunting tonight."

She felt warmth even in brief phone calls. Helena was very smart and well educated, but more than that, she was no-holds-barred, all-in. Gabriela could always count on her for a laugh to help her forget the time they transcended normal life. Both had no shortage of outside lovers; they had even shared a few, but in their late-night talks, amongst the silly chatter reminiscent of high school girls, the conversation always ended in the same place, and though every day, the image of Mark and Jason slipped farther from them, a sadness always returned with the dark. Their memories of them tore away the joy of their evening prowls; for no hopes were found within the embraces of these strangers that could dim the light of those hours, those hours that defied description.

"Man hunting," she said aloud. "One of Helena's favorite lines after her third shot." She reached for her lipstick.

These days, Gabriela was living in Helena's old apartment. It was a great deal for Gabriela, since Helena owned it, and only charged her the monthly common fees. Helena had moved across town shortly after Gabriela's divorce. She said it was because of the doorman, but Gabriela knew that she was just trying to be a good friend and give her a place to live. Helena, of course, had no concerns about money. She had just inherited, as she put it, "a truckload of it" when her uncle died, and she seemed to be trying to break a record in spending it.

Gabriela looked into the mirror to finish her makeup. She had acquired a long streak of gray hair. It ran down the side of her forehead and framed her face. As for the rest, it was still long and dark. While some people maintained that she had had it done in a salon, she always boasted that it was natural; she liked the look.

You're still looking good, she said to herself. Gabriela had kept her body trim and svelte thanks to her Jane Fonda workout tapes and her constant rushing about town. She watched her diet these days, and always thought of Mark when she ate brown rice and seaweed. As she stood to pull her dress down tightly to her body, her eye caught what she thought was a figure behind her in the mirror. Abruptly she turned around, her mouth opened wide, and before she could say, "Mark?" it had vanished.

"Oh my God. What was that?" She gasped. My mind is playing tricks on me.

Gabriela sat back in her chair, blinking her eyes and thinking how she wanted this wishing apparition to be real. She looked back again and saw only her furniture. How I long for him. Well, he's gone... Gone, and that's that, so stop this stupid...

Just then, her eyes caught sight of an object she had not seen for three years: a pair of black Ray-Bans just like the ones she used to wear, like the pair Mark had returned to her when she created a reason for him to call.

"Where did these come from?" she heard herself saying.

She stood up abruptly and with wide eyes looked around the room again, holding the glasses as she questioned the reality of what was in her hand.

She scoured the room, and then walked out of her bedroom, rapidly surveying the rest of the apartment. It was empty. But I saw him. And there are these. She examined the sunglasses closely and found the scratch that she had made when she had thrown them at her husband. These were the ones, the sunglasses that Mark had put into her hand on that day. But he crushed these with his foot the day I left, didn't he? She wanted to believe he had returned or sent her a message. She wanted the hope that she would one day see him again. But where is he? Why just this?

Her anxiety building, Gabriela got up from the bed and walked to her dresser. Unable to think, she started moving about and lit a cigarette, another vice she had appropriated from Helena. As the smoke left her nostrils, a familiar calm returned. Moving, she felt a spring in her step that she had long forgotten, energy flowing in her veins, a spark that she had not sensed in years. "I feel good," she said to herself as she put on a necklace. Helena is always so picky about the way I look, demanding that my every bangle and bead be so very hip, or at the least this year's style. Why she seemed to give into Helena's obsessions often baffled her, but then she remembered that she was living in her apartment practically free.

Damn, it's getting late. Her mind was far from clear. She had forgotten that the subway was under repair, and she would have to fight the traffic uptown in a cab. I am supposed to meet her at 84th in two hours. She went to find the phone to tell Helena she might be late when her eyes found the mirror.

With a gasp, her body recoiled as she limply fell to the floor. After about ten minutes, she felt her head moving on the carpet. Her eyes a blur, her brain began returning. Afraid to look up, she thought to herself, I am going mad. I need to go to a hospital. I will call Helena. She will take me. She's my friend. But there, lying next to her, were the sunglasses. Her hands trembling, she picked them up. Slowly she rose, regaining her courage, disbelief tightly gripping her. She looked again into the mirror. In amazement, she saw the reflection of a woman of maybe 28, with jet dark hair and silky white skin, brightly clear, glowing with freshness. She heard her words leave her lips: "How can this be?" Her body felt nimble, her breasts high and firm. It was as if she were just a few years out of college, home studying the tango in Barcelona.

"Mark, what did you do...?"

Just then, the phone rang. Gabriela picked it up, and half-conscious, still staring at herself in the mirror, managed to say, "Yeah...?"

She heard Helena's familiar voice. "Yay, Gabriela! We are going to have to catch the second show at Brandy's. I am running late."

Gabriela responded, "I need you to come here. I need you to come now."

"Is there something wrong?"

"Yes. I mean... no? Just come."

CHAPTER 51

SAYA WAITS

I t was a cold morning. The windows were fogged over. The gas heater dried the air in the cabin, but the damp forest air would not rest. She rubbed a circle on the pane with her hand and looked out. "Hello, World. I guess we have another day of waiting." She turned off the kerosene light she had left on after dozing in the middle of Proust. She loved to read by kerosene; there was something so basic about it.

Saya did not know why she had chosen this place; she knew it was surely thinking in human terms. Maybe because the countryside reminded her of her childhood in China, or maybe it was just the peace she felt there in the mornings.

There was a stream and a waterfall past the hill, then rocky paths that lead to a gorge, a forest, and many caves. Caves she had foolishly thought could protect her. She often wondered why she had reasoned in this manner. Such a basic and human form of thinking; it surely made little sense. She knew there was no cave that could hide her, so she decided to live in the cabin.

She had not really spent much time upstate. It was near Ithaca, this new home. This was her fifth move since she had left the city, always wary of staying too long in one place. But this place... this place somehow felt right, after she fixed the leak in the roof, anyway. Cornell was nearby, and there were many students in the area. Her hippie dress and strangeness seemed ordinary. She spent her time developing and trying to remain invisible. It was very silent there. Occasionally, deer broke through her garden, but that was it.

There were few coffee shops in town; some with book-shelves lined with paperbacks. One even had a free lending policy, and it always had cool music playing in the back-ground, often classical. She knew some of the people found her weird. She never spoke to anyone and kept to herself, maybe ate something, bought a book, and left.

Most of her hours were spent walking and listening to the forest. There were no neighbors for miles, and that was the way she liked it. If she would meet a stranger walking or hik-ing on a path, she would vanish in a flash. Jason was right; she had grown fast, faster than she could ever imagine. Faster than a speeding bullet, able to leap tall buildings in a single bound. Is it a bird? Is it a plane...? Oh... it's just me.

Often on moonlit nights, she would stare out into her gar-den wishing for him. If she heard some rustling, her hopes would rise for a second before her abilities could identify the source. Oh, it's just another critter, she would think, her hopes falling back to despondency. He told me to wait, just wait. But as the years came and went, sometimes she could hear herself thinking, *It's been a long, long time.*

He must be out there, far and distant for sure.

She would spend a lot of time staring at the stars at night. The sky is so full around here. There are, millions, no, billions of stars up there... is he must be out there on a world circling one? Maybe he is too far to hear my thoughts. Maybe that is why he has not contacted me. I know he would if he could.

Although she got along fine without the small comforts of life she had once known, she still had, from time to time, an overwhelming need for some "coitus stimulates," as she used to jokingly call sex with her old, dear, and never-to-be-for-gotten friend, Angela. On these occasions, she would get into her VW bug, five years old, red, and with a sunroof. She would drive to some small bar, maybe fifty miles from her house, and find a truck stop. She would park at least a mile away and walk around, making believe she was a hooker. She liked big hairy guys who had been driving for a few days. They smelled like sweaty t-shirts forgotten in a locker room for a week. She would climb into the back of the truck's cab with them and go to town. She might do three or four men in the course of one night, and she always accepted money so that she did not seem out of the ordinary. This would keep her for at least a month.

A few times in the bar, she met a woman she liked touching, but there was no one she found really special. There was never anyone she wanted to see again.

Other than this, Saya had few contacts. She read the thoughts of people and peeked into their minds; hearing distant conversations was enough. Often, she heard herself being described as "the hermit," or "the strange unfriendly one."

Mostly she found being able to read people's thoughts more than a compensation for relationships. She could be part of people's lives without ever being involved with them. There was a Post Office clerk whose mother was in a nursing home with cancer and a waitress who was always finding one abusive guy after another. These distant intimacies sustained her.

In the past, when people tried to get close, she would move, but somehow here she was able to stay for a while. Being alone for a time would be a small price to pay for the hope of spending hundreds of years with such a wondrous being as Jason.

Up near Ithaca she felt accepted, or at least ignored, which was almost as good for now, maybe because there was also a Buddhist retreat nearby and people assumed she was a strange mystic. She thought about going to China or even Japan.

But if I get on a plane and the same thing happens as did with Angela or even what happened with that photographer guy in the East Village... All those passengers... The thought of being responsible for so many innocent deaths would be unbearable.

He was so right about these powers; the new ones seem to

explain themselves as they come. She accepted most of them without question. Strength, speed, even being able to move things with her mind seemed ordinary; almost like she had always had them but not thought about them. The mind reading was always surprising since she never knew what to expect from people.

But as time passed, she learned how to listen, or not, and soon it became okay, manageable. Ignore or pry, it all became fun. The nonverbal communication with animals bothered her the most, however. She could hear their breath and sense their feelings. Once she saw a mountain lion while walking, and she let it know that she was not to be messed with. It understood.

And then there were the stranger things: when it felt as if the whole world talked to her. She could hear the worms crawling under her feet, the bees in their hives, and at times, teeth sinking into flesh. There were the trees as they drew nourishment from the soil and sun, slowly changing, always reaching. Besides the forest, there were the elements: the wind, the rain, the mist, even the atmosphere. They were all communicating, telling her, "I am alive, like you. This planet, this earth, is alive... conscious and alive." She really did not know how to describe this to anyone, and often thought, maybe this is why I don't want to talk to people – everything is talking to me

Saya looked across the room at her favorite top. The one she wore the night she met Tommy in that grunge bar on East 6th Street. That poor guy. I just left him up in that tree. What must he be thinking? Wonder if he is still drinking Bourbon. This is one of the best things about an alien... Jason never gets jealous. He seems to enjoy me having a good time. As long as I don't break the rules... Never abuse my power and keep a low profile. Jason, I miss you.

When the loneliness overtook her, Saya could find herself despondent. Late at night when she looked up at the sky, she would hear herself say, "Jason, you told me to wait, but it seems forever now..."

BEFORE YOU GO

Thank you for reading The Dream Gatherers by Roberto Arcoleo. We hope you enjoyed it. If you did, please leave us a review on Amazon. It only takes a few moments and we would deeply appreciate it.

Roberto is hard at work on the sequel. Would you like to know when it's ready? Do you like deals, exclusives, and early access to new releases? Join our awesome mailing list here: https://www.chandrapress.com/newsletter